S0-BAW-930

Praise for the novels of Ann Chamberlin

The Merlin of St. Gilles' Well

"A rich weaving of fantastic elements with accurate historical detail and imaginative reinterpretation...Expertly tailored historic setting and plausible extrapolation support sound storytelling....Edifies as it entertains."
—*Publishers Weekly*

"Persuasive fantasy elements are seamlessly integrated into a richly detailed historical backdrop: a compelling series opener."
—*Kirkus Reviews*

"Exciting...The clever intertwining of fantasy and history works extremely well as readers will fully relish this novel and foresee that the companion tales will be as great."
—*The Midwest Book Review*

"Chamberlin's lyrical prose evokes the tumult and mystery of her chosen era, and the often retrospective voice she provides for Yann is beguiling and believable....And although by the close of this book the Maid of Orleans is still only an offstage infant, her presence looms over a host of other bright personages any reader will surely come to cherish."
—*Realms of Fantasy*

"Artfully recasts history, weaving the rich color and texture of historical fact with the magic of fantasy, intertwining Joan of Arc's holy destiny with ancient pre-Christian prophecies. The underlying struggle between two disparate religious philosophies serves as a powerful backdrop that intensifies the story's conflict....Launches a compelling series that will delight any history fan who believes in magic."
—*Renaissance* magazine

"Noteworthy for its historical details...this recommended volume is a prequel to the traditional tale and as such will fill a gap in many collections."
—*Voice of Youth Advocates*

"An engrossing mystical epic full of adventure and medieval lore...The author portrays the rough, dark, cold, half-pagan and half-Christian world in writing which is often poetical, and with unforgettable historical accuracy."
—Stephanie Cowell, author of *The Players: A Novel of the Young Shakespeare,* winner of the 1996 American Book Award

"*The Merlin of St. Gilles' Well* transports the reader into a haunted world, shimmering with magic. This impressively researched retelling of the life of Joan of Arc adds a provocative new dimension to her story: Chamberlin allows us to peer through the Christian veil obscuring the life of Joan, and discern beyond the shadow of an ancient, stag-horned face. Written with passion and grace, and steeped in the legends and lore of the day, it brings this era of nobles, knights, and seers to luminous life."
—Donna Gillespie, author of *The Light Bearer*

"A fascinating, perhaps unique, blend of fantasy and historical. Chamberlin's expert touch with historical detail brought home the hard, sad world of the fifteenth century until I wanted to scratch. Paradoxically, she depicts the mindset of late-medieval peasantry so convincingly that the magic seems just as credible. Chamberlin has created a splendid stained-glass window, full of the brilliant colors and bizarre shapes of the dying middle ages, transfixed by a blaze of magic. This is a world as its inhabitants saw it, full of real people and real magic."

—Dave Duncan

Leaving Eden

"Provocative...Fans of Jean Auel, Linda Lay Shuler, and the Gears will enjoy these strong, fascinating, and multifaceted characters as well as the details that enliven the visionary panorama of Chamberlin's fine speculative fiction."

—*Publishers Weekly*

"A gorgeous melding of art and scholarship...Ravishingly poetic."

—*Booklist*

"An incredible prehistoric fiction....The fast-paced story leaves readers enthralled with the characters and Ann Chamberlin's ability to tell an exciting tale....Anyone who takes pleasure from the great biblical love story rewritten based on modern historiography's approach to prehistory will want to peruse Ms. Chamberlin's latest masterpiece."

—Harriet Klausner

"Brilliantly brings a new interpretation to the events [in the Garden of Eden]."

—*The Chieftain* (Pueblo, Colorado)

The Reign of the Favored Women

"Exotic...In addition to capturing and effectively communicating the extraordinary opulence and the devious intrigue of the Turkish royal court, Chamberlin does a marvelous job of delineating a believable female character, working within the constraints of her time and place to achieve astounding goals and ambitions. Lush historical fiction."

—*Booklist*

"The reader is drawn into a world of Machiavellian intrigue where the struggle for power among the women of the seraglio influences the politics of both the East and the West."

—*Library Journal*

"A complex historical tale of two formidable women...Elaborate, lush historical fiction."

—*Publishers Weekly*

By Ann Chamberlin from Tom Doherty Associates

Sofia
The Sultan's Daughter
The Reign of the Favored Women
Tamar
Leaving Eden
The Merlin of St. Gilles' Well

Ann Chamberlin

TOR®

A Tom Doherty Associates Book
New York

The Merlin
of St. Gilles' Well

Book One of the
Joan of Arc Tapestries

ASHEVILLE-BUNCOMBE LIBRARY SYSTEM

This is a work of fiction. All the characters and events
portrayed in this novel are either fictitious or are used fictitiously.

THE MERLIN OF ST. GILLES' WELL

Copyright © 1999 by Ann Chamberlin

All rights reserved, including the right to reproduce
this book, or portions thereof, in any form.

This book is printed on acid-free paper.

Design by Victoria Kuskowski
Family trees by Hadel Studio

A Tor Book
Published by Tom Doherty Associates, LLC
175 Fifth Avenue
New York, NY 10010

www.tor.com

Tor® is a registered trademark of Tom Doherty Associates, LLC.

Library of Congress Cataloging-in-Publication Data

Chamberlin, Ann.
    The Merlin of St. Gilles' well / Ann Chamberlin.
        p.   cm.—(Joan of Arc tapestries : bk. 1)
    "A Tom Doherty Associates book."
    ISBN 0-312-86551-1 (hc)
    ISBN 0-312-87591-6 (pbk)
    1. Joan, of Arc, Saint, 1412–1431—Fiction.   2. Merlin
(Legendary character)—Fiction.   I. Title.   II. Series:
Chamberlin, Ann. Joan of Arc tapestries ; bk. 1.
PS3553.H2499M47   1999
813'.54—dc21   99-22204
                                                                         CIP

First Hardcover Edition: September 1999
First Trade Paperback Edition: November 2000

Printed in the United States of America

0 9 8 7 6 5 4 3 2 1

Again for Natalia,
good editor and best friend,
because it was her idea

Acknowledgments

C'est avec plaisir que je remercie, premièrement en français, tous ceux qui m'ont aidé avec cette œuvre. Mlle. Rachel Hamstead, institutrice de ma jeunesse, m'a permis de découvrir le peuple français et sa langue avec un amour bien sérieux. À Domrémy-la-Pucelle, je me souviens de la propriétaire de l'Hôtel de la Pucelle; à Orléans, le personnel de la maison de Jeanne d'Arc; à Blois, M. Eric Gault; et partout, Mme. Josette Melac et ses filles, Sylvie et Annie.

In English, I have the pleasure to thank Natalia Aponte, Karla Zounek, and all the folks at Tor who pushed this through. Thanks to Virginia Kidd, Jim Allen, and especially Linn Prentis, whose long and detailed commentary helped immensely with the rewrites—and when I needed a shoulder to cry on.

My friends Alexis Bar-Lev, Karen Porcher, and Teddi Kachi were always generous and fascinating with their expertise. The Wasatch Mountain Fiction Writers Friday Morning Group were there from the moment this was merely a little glimmer in need of plotting.

The Marriott, Whitmore, and Holladay librarians never stinted in their assistance.

And of course there's my family. My sons in particular were company on my research trip, drew maps, and bounced ideas. My husband is (sometimes) patient while my mind is elsewhere. My parents introduced me early to France and her people, and my in-laws make it all possible.

Cast of Characters for
The Merlin of St. Gilles' Well

Amaury de Craon—younger brother to Marie, uncle to Gilles

Père Georges de Boszac—tutor to Yann and Gilles

Charles, called the Mad—King of France 1380–1422

Charles the Prince—fifth son of Charles the King

Gilles de Rais—scion of the noble house of Rais

Guillemette La Drapière—Yann's mother, milk mother to Gilles

Guy de Rais—lord of the noble house, father to Gilles

The Hermit—heir to Merlin, keeper of the Well at St. Gilles

Jean de Craon—maternal grandfather to Gilles

Jehannette, Jeanne d'Arc, La Pucelle—called in English Joan of Arc

Marie de Rais, née Craon—wife to Guy and mother to Gilles

Michel de Fontenay, Père Michel—a priest of the Old Religion,
    novice to the Hermit, and tutor to Yann and Gilles

René de La Suze—younger brother to Gilles

Valentine de Visconti—duchess of Orléans

Yann Le Drapier—the storyteller, a boy gifted with epilepsy who
    receives the call of the King Stag

Abbreviated Family Tree of the Valois Kings of France

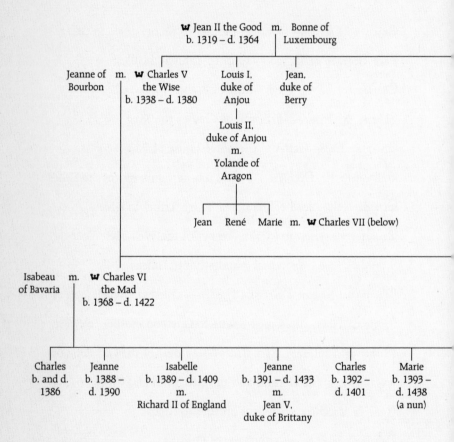

♕ Jean II the Good   m.   Bonne of
b. 1319 – d. 1364   Luxembourg

Jeanne of   m.   ♕ Charles V   Louis I,   Jean,
Bourbon   the Wise   duke of   duke of
       b. 1338 – d. 1380   Anjou   Berry

Louis II,
duke of Anjou
m.
Yolande of
Aragon

Jean   René   Marie   m.   ♕ Charles VII (below)

Isabeau   m.   ♕ Charles VI
of Bavaria   the Mad
       b. 1368 – d. 1422

Charles   Jeanne   Isabelle   Jeanne   Charles   Marie
b. and d.   b. 1388 –   b. 1389 – d. 1409   b. 1391 – d. 1433   b. 1392 –   b. 1393 –
1386   d. 1390   m.   m.   d. 1401   d. 1438
                Richard II of England   Jean V,   (a nun)
                                 duke of Brittany

♕ = King of France

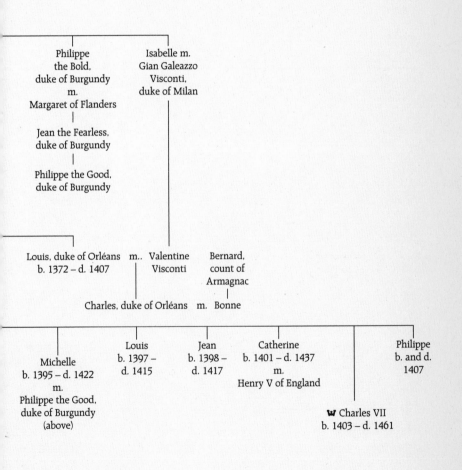

Philippe
the Bold,
duke of Burgundy
m.
Margaret of Flanders

Isabelle m.
Gian Galeazzo
Visconti,
duke of Milan

Jean the Fearless,
duke of Burgundy

Philippe the Good,
duke of Burgundy

Louis, duke of Orléans   m.. Valentine
b. 1372 – d. 1407   Visconti

Bernard,
count of
Armagnac

Charles, duke of Orléans   m. Bonne

Michelle
b. 1395 – d. 1422
m.
Philippe the Good,
duke of Burgundy
(above)

Louis
b. 1397 –
d. 1415

Jean
b. 1398 –
d. 1417

Catherine
b. 1401 – d. 1437
m.
Henry V of England

Philippe
b. and d.
1407

♛ Charles VII
b. 1403 – d. 1461

Abbreviated Family Tree of Gilles de Rais

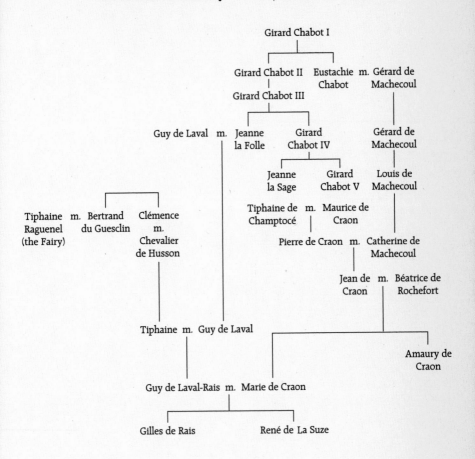

The
Merlin
of St. Gilles' Well

Crimson Tangled with the Call of the Green

Fire girdles the wicker bars of the cage, wind-whipped ribbons of crimson and coquelicot twining in a woman's hair.

And pain like fire twines up my right arm from the fragile, broken framework of my three-year-old hand.

A mangy dog—or perhaps it is a misbegotten wolf—and a couple of cats are tethered within the burning frame.

The smell of burning fur and flesh clogs my lungs.

Pain writhes in my arm like the terrified animals in the cage.

And like their howls of agony, my arm screams to the night, the night thick with smoke and sparks and stars.

That is my first memory of this world, a swirling jumble of fire and heat and pain and choking smoke. For a very long time, I thought it must have been a nightmare, one of my "spells" that so worried my mother. Spells run in the males of her family.

When the fit is on me, I do have a hard time telling dream from reality, the edges of my own being from the vastness of creation. Things other men take as given seem not so straightforward—so black and white, good and evil—to me.

Fire is a friend to men, nestled cozily in the ashes of the hearth on a grey winter's day.

But fire can also be a terror, the wrath of God in the Judgment Day.

The hungry tongue of God lapping at sacrifice.

And what man would not avoid pain if he could?

Or what woman?

Yet even the Christians worship the way their Lord took on the pain of the world.

So pain is divine. Even the pain of a three-year-old boy given to fits.

———•———

I will wear those images to the grave with me in the red, puckered skin and shapeless, frozen twist of my right hand. But in fact, most of the events surrounding my memory of wicker in flames I know because they were told to my childhood ears, over and over. They were the whole explanation of the current circumstances of my life, a Genesis in which others—my mother, in particular—found cause for our present estate.

Although in our case, our state had actually been improved by the events. Improved in most aspects. At least, Mother always thought so.

Of course, as I have said, in fits I have the ability to turn the world on its head and see a rise as a fall.

For all the tale, no one ever spoke to me of anything resembling the swirling flames that were etched so starkly against the black night of my memory.

———•———

The name my parents gave me was Yann in the old Breton tongue. In French, the name is Jean, and as a boy at Blaison, because every second man seemed to be called Jean, they called me Jean Le Drapier—son of the draper—to distinguish me.

But I have taken other names throughout my long life, as you shall see.

Water may be liquid, ice, or mist, as occasion demands. Though I've been witness to fire, the cool and damp, the shape-shifting, has always been more my nature.

It is good for a man to know his nature.

And to live true to it.

My grandfather, as Le Drapier indicates, wove linen for his keep. Likewise did both my parents, until my birth spurred my father to greater pretensions. He began to buy up the products of all the looms in our hometown of Quintin in the duchy of Brittany. He carried them to St. Brieuc, to the merchants and sailing vessels bound for England, France, Spain, the Low Countries, and beyond. Once a year, in summer, he also made a circuit of the inland, buying up whatever produce of the flax fields, the spindles, and the looms was to be had in the markets and small towns there.

His route took him through the Menez lands, called "the Height" in the old tongue, past the monastery of Boquen. Here, the road climbed south, severing the forest of the Hardouinais on the east from the larger forest of Loudéac on the west. It took him, in fact, right past the point where a narrow footpath left the main cart-rutted track in order to visit the shrine of St. Gilles.

Father's mercantile preoccupations never allowed him to make a detour to the Saint. Indeed, the Hermit there sometimes wore skins and had little use for weavery. Still, rumor of the site could not fail to reach my father. It reached my mother, overseeing the shuttles of two maidservants back at home in the big, sunny loft, and I'm certain she hardly needed the word of her man.

That third winter of my life on this earth must have made one or the other or both of my parents think on holy St. Gilles with more than a passing interest. The fits are always worse in winter when I must be confined within walls. Smoke, I think, exaggerates them. In better weather, when I feel a spell coming on, I know a trip into fresh air will turn the possibility of serious injury into what might be considered only a pastoral reverie.

As a child, I didn't know this about myself, about "my gift." I didn't even know that not everyone else in the world had these spaces of restful blackness—or vision, sometimes—that seemed so natural to me.

They were not so strange to my mother, though she was unnerved. "Your uncle Comor swallowed his tongue in a fit," she never tired of telling me—and anyone else who'd listen. "Swallowed his tongue when no one was about and died, blue as a field of flax in bloom."

My father had no such family connections. And he wanted a healthy heir to join him in his business as soon as possible. He never trusted the apprentices and servants with whom he had to content himself until the glorious day that I should come of age. What my father saw in our enclosed rooms that winter of my third year decided the matter: my mother must come with him on the circuit, bringing me to the Saint for healing. For none, it is well known, is better for the falling sickness than St. Gilles, his fountain and his Hermit.

So it was that my mother and I found ourselves on the narrow forest path on that lovely day, almost Midsummer. Ancient oaks reached their dagged-leaf hands, now and then clasping, across the brilliant blue over our heads. On either side hung a darker tapestry, with gnarled trunks. The woods spoke with the cuckoo's lilt, the woodpecker's consonants.

Father had business still at Collinée. Riding, he meant to join us at the shrine by nightfall, but thought we ought not to waste a moment of the healing presence. He had sent us on ahead in the company of a single servant, expecting no harm on such a holy path.

The day was warm, and having made a meal of heavy rye bread smeared with herbed goat cheese and the strong local cider, Mother must have taken a nap. I can see her in my mind's eye, her bark-brown hair compensated for by plump cheeks glowing with the cider as if the apples themselves grew there. Insects hum lazily about her where she lies, spread out on the sward. I see her ample body, amply draped, both coif and chemise, in expanses of crisp, white linen, a sample of my father's wares. That hardly seems a contrite pilgrim's attire, so I must be imagining the scene from other days.

Mother, of course, insisted to her dying day that she never fell asleep, that she was always, always vigilant of me.

"So what did happen next?"

Mother would invariably pause at this point, and any hearer would be obliged to ask the question. I asked it many times myself. She would then narrow her normally bland brown eyes keenly at me. She would sigh deeply and hold up her hands in the gesture of being at a loss for words, a totally uncharacteristic state for my mother.

What did happen next? Mother couldn't say. And without her words to help it, my memory flags.

Yet, in a way, I do know what happened. I may not remember that precise blur of vision followed by blackness. But I've had enough spells since—creeping over me like the hand of God—that the pattern is clear.

Besides, my whole life bears the imprint of those wild moments.

I felt the bubbles in my brain. Black came upon me in rough jerks.

Then, from out of the depths of the forest, curtained with dim shafts of golden light and leaves, green on green, above the chirr of squirrels and the incessant knocking of the woodpecker, I heard a cry.

"Help me, O child of men. Help!"

I felt the air around me panting with the chase, blood pounding in my head until black and bubbles mingled in the edges of my vision.

"Child of men! They're after me. They will kill!"

"I come."

I followed the sound, followed the stiff, thin-legged bounding that sounded like the drum of oak wands on oak. I scrambled up through the thick undergrowth of frond and vine, slipped down again in muddy hollows, but I kept going.

"Help me! I die!"

I know now it was the voice of the Stag I heard. To my childish mind, it seemed a great King who called to me. And when I finally came to him, face-to-face, I saw only the great golden crown of antlers, the proud but haunted limpid brown eyes, as expressive as any human's.

Then I became aware of his enemies. I heard the belling of the hounds, the horses' hooves, the hunter's horn, and the cheerful, triumphal shouts of the company.

I saw the arrow pulled to sight, aiming at my regal friend's breast. I raised a protecting hand—and screamed in pain as everything swirled to black around me.

"We never meant it to happen." More than a few times I heard Madame de Rais pick up the story from my mother at this point. "Had he known there was a child—by the Virgin—my lord and husband never would have shot."

"Had my son stayed by me where he belonged—"

My mother would stop, holding her heart and moaning with memory of the scene she'd come upon not long after. The shaft had transfixed my right hand to the forest floor.

They carried me to the Hermit at the shrine as the closest place where they might find help.

They saw my mother settled with me, the Hermit's skill as he withdrew the bolt. Then, having salved their guilt with a gold coin or two, the lord and lady of the hunt prepared to be off about their noble business. There are lords, my mother well knew, who wouldn't have let an accident to a peasant child stop their pursuit of their quarry for an instant. She was duly grateful for the swift transport their horses had provided and for the coins.

The Hermit, however, was of another mind about the matter. He pulled himself up to his full, ragged grey height and spoke. Never mind which woman repeated his words, my mother or Madame. Both tried for the deep and ominous tones, the guttural Breton accent true life must have held.

"No, monseigneur. You shall not go. You who hunt the deer, know you not that the beasts of this forest are sacred to the Saint? Particularly at this time of year, when the creatures have little ones, it is so."

My lord and lady, being but the guests of the local Menez nobility, and having that day wandered away from the main party of their hosts, had not known this.

"No, you did not know. But the child, he knew. They called to him, the deer. Perhaps it was even the voice of the King Stag himself, and he, a child of three, answered. He saved the King from your rapacity at the risk of his own life. Look! Look at the wound."

Mother would always grow pale at the memory, as if about to faint again. "He held your little hand up to the light—and I could see daylight through it."

"Look! Just such a wound the blessed Saint received in just such a pious act." The old man gestured toward St. Gilles' fountain and its wooden image of the long-robed monk with a protecting arm around the hind, his right hand pierced by the huntsman's arrow.

"Look at the wound," the Hermit said again. "Is it not the very emblem of our Lord's wound, the stigmata? Here am I, a humble servant of the Lord, trying to cure with yarrow and horsetail what may be a particular sign of His favor."

At this point my mother humbly presented the Hermit with the idea that her son was subject to evil spells. Indeed, it was likely the cause of all our mischance. "We had come to pray that you might cure him and instead . . ."

"Cure him?" the holy man snapped. "Evil spells, you say? This is no evil spell that allows the child to hear the forest spirits. This is a sacred gift. I myself have lived in these woods these fifty years, praying for such a sign of favor and, even with severe fasting, have only been granted it once or twice. Now I see that my prayers have been answered, not in my own person, but by being privileged to see it and save it for posterity, in the person of this small boy.

"No, do not seek to 'cure' your son, goodwife, but rejoice with me to see in him the powerful Hand of God, working for the good of the World."

Surely my mother struggled as I have always done to fit such prophetic words to the gross mundanity of life she was used to knowing as her son's. Dirty swaddling was still fresh in her mind, colic and teething. The terror when the blank look would come over me and she remembered her brother's face, "blue as flax bloom."

I have had a whole lifetime of common humanity in which to learn to doubt.

What the Hermit said next was even more disconcerting.

"No, speak not of evil spells in connection with this child, goodwife. Rather, fear those people whose impiety dared to raise arms within the wooded sanctuary. The Saint is known as a friend to wombs the Lord has closed. But certainly he may withdraw such blessings as well. Even if careful steps are taken to avoid it, I know not but that evil is settling even now upon this noble house.

"So." He turned now to the noble couple in their hunting gear. "Be not hasty to ride hence, monseigneur, madame, 'til we determine what penance may be done to appease the Horned One's fearful wrath. As things now stand, I see no heir for this great house. Or perhaps—does my Sight betray me?—it is a great blackness I see descending on the union of this lordly marriage."

Madame's hand flew with instant protection to her belly at these words. More was riding on the fruit of her marriage to Sire Guy de Rais even than the average high stakes ventured on any merger between noble houses. A bride of only four months, she had just begun to suspect she was, indeed, with child.

First Antiphon

A Weft of Dark Woad

Sire Guy de Rais wore his leather hunting jerkin that Midsummer's Day. That was nothing new. Marie de Craon felt he encased his soul away from her in a leather carapace, even when they were in bed naked together.

And now a child's blood stained that hunting jerkin.

So what of the child she carried?

Marie de Rais née Craon considered her marriage as she stood with unease at the edge of the clearing of St. Gilles du Mené that Midsummer's Day. She considered the fruit of that marriage, so necessary, so forced.

She considered her husband of four months as he stood talking to their servants, sending a pair of them back to tell their Menez hosts what had happened. He instructed the men to return with tents and supplies in case the penance for this poaching on holy ground, as it appeared, should take some time.

Marie was shy around this Guy de Rais. They'd been strangers 'til the day they were married. They were still strangers. She would say so until the year they both died. But it had taken her much less time than those four months to realize he was entirely too morbidly pious for her taste, this husband to whom duty had brought her.

Though strangers, they were actually distant kin, Marie de Craon and Guy de Rais. Too distant for the prelates to worry about consanguinity, but their common relationship to old Aunt Jeanne was what had brought them together in the first place. Everyone called old Aunt Jeanne "la Sage," same as they might call a village wisewoman who worked with herbs, delivered babies—and made matches.

Old Jeanne la Sage was a widow, childless. And she would not choose between her Laval kin and the Craons to write up in her will. "Only if the two houses merge will I give the Rais estates and the Rais name to their firstborn son. It is not good to let the blood get too thin."

What blood? Marie had wondered, then and now. Her husband seemed nothing like her.

"Both your houses are descended from Tiphaines," Jeanne la Sage had told her. "You from Tiphaine de Champtocé through Maurice de Craon. And Monseigneur de Laval's mother was a Tiphaine. And his great-aunt as well."

As if that were an explanation. As if the male blood meant nothing to her when all the world knew estates went through the male line.

Tiphaine. A woman's name. And not any woman's name. There was no Ste. Tiphaine to dedicate a daughter to.

Tiphaine meant a fairy woman. Literally.

And the lords of Craon had been pretending their ancestor Maurice was so long ago the taint no longer mattered.

It had mattered to Jeanne la Sage. And she'd made it matter to young Marie.

Tiphaine blood was more visible in her husband. Though not overly short, Guy de Rais was gangly, like all the Lavals. Dark, brooding. Marie could almost smell these things in the sweat the heat of the day and the tension of the situation produced on him. He was, indeed, very like all Bretons, those alien people with their strange ways and the hostility they felt for her barely concealed in their dark eyes under dark brows. In Brittany, everyone was Tiphaine-born. They were all fairy folk, haunting reality as thickly as sprites haunted their tales, hardly Christian and not a scrap civilized.

But if she was descended from a Tiphaine, Marie must be of the old folk, too. Surprisingly, the thought made her warm in a rather pleasant way. She tried to force the thought to be more distasteful.

All her training made her think it ought to be so. When that didn't work, she shifted her thoughts as a whole.

Guy de Rais was nothing like the only other men she knew well, her father and her younger brother Amaury. Amaury at thirteen was hardly more than a boy, but he was already the clear copy of their father, that huge, rotund, fair man whose arms like hams would press "his little girl" to him until the tears came. The tears came now with the memory by the fountain of St. Gilles. They spilled down her cheeks as the spasms of homesickness ran up her belly.

Her belly where the child grew. The child who was also a stranger, though he lived under her very heart. How different would the child be? How different from the red, robust face that was the father she knew and missed and could find no shadow of in this husband of hers on that Midsummer's Day?

Marie might have learned to live with the splintering contrast between the two men to whom she owed duty were it not for one thing. On their wedding night and every night since, Guy de Rais had felt it his husbandly duty to preach to her against her own father.

"Your father Jean de Craon is a cheat, an aggressive, violent, selfish, godless man. Aunt Jeanne la Sage meant the Rais lands for me. Having no other heir, she chose me. She put it in writing so there could be no mistake. Only then that villain who sired you came and twisted her old arthritic arms."

Remembering his frequently repeated words, Marie de Craon-Rais grew weak-kneed and had to sit down on the turf. She sat as far as she could from the bed the others had made for the wounded child, where he shrieked now so pitifully. She wished she could go farther away. Her husband paced. If her legs had been so strong, she would have sent them in one direction instead of only back and forth.

Once again Marie smoothed her hands protectively over her belly. She hadn't told her husband yet. And, until recently, she'd followed the courtly fashion of wearing a small, stuffed cushion over her belly, under the high, thick draperies of her gowns. Every woman should emulate the Fairest of Her Sex, the Virgin in Her Motherhood. Sire de Rais could not know.

One more emblem of the gulf between them.

The child she bore must be a boy and it must be healthy. God did not always give couples more than one chance. If they had no male heir, the Rais lands would revert to the crown.

And Aunt Jeanne's dream of a continuance of the Tiphaine blood must die.

Guy de Rais, for all his looks, had very little fairy in his soul.

If the fairy features were to come from her lord, perhaps Aunt Jeanne meant her to provide the soul. But Marie was a good girl. A good Christian. At least, she had always tried.

Nonetheless, she had seen it.

Well, she'd seen something the instant before the arrow had flown. She'd seen the stag, of course, a thing of proud, heart-stopping beauty, soon to be theirs. She'd seen her husband nock the arrow, raise the bow—

Then there had been something. Something dark—just over her lord's shoulder. Something at the edge of sight, a fairy thing. Something—not in the direction where, a moment later, in the dense undergrowth, they'd heard the child's scream of pain. Something— a shadow.

Marie knew, unfeeling though he was, her husband would never have shot a child on purpose.

And she also knew the sight she kept trying to push from her mind, that sight of the pale, mousy boy pinned to the earth through his twitching right hand—she knew that sight couldn't help but affect the child she carried. The child on whom so much depended.

Much as she tried to deny it, her belly hadn't stopped making echoing little twitches since. She'd already been sick once and would probably be so again very soon.

Her husband saw nothing. Even when she mentioned what she'd seen, he only told her she was distraught. If Guy de Rais looked like his Tiphaine ancestors, Marie knew she must have their soul. And she didn't know if that was good or bad. At the moment, it didn't feel good at all.

The shadow was there again, riding like a halo around the grey standing stones. Of all the good she wished for him, and had hoped to bring by her own obedience, the child Marie carried was bound to this place. Good or evil, there was nothing she could do about it.

The Hermit crossed to them now, wiping blood from his hands on his robe as if he'd done all he could for the wounded child for the moment. Guy de Rais gestured his wife to remember her manners and to stand. When she hesitated—because her weak legs wouldn't let her do otherwise—he reached down and pulled her up beside him.

The Hermit tempered the concern in his face with a gentle smile. The look made Marie's heart pound for no reason she could name. Except that the smile seemed to read right through her. And to love her, unconditionally, passionately. Without a leather shell like her husband's, the sense of love was frightening.

"Do you curse my house with evil, Hermit?" Her husband struggled to be brave but not irreverent and he didn't seem certain where the line between the two might be.

"It is not I who curse," returned the Hermit in his strange accent. "And—and let us say dark rather than evil. Dark may be a good thing, if properly dealt with. The restful black of night, the shadow of sacred trees on a hot summer's day."

Guy de Rais grunted uncomfortably.

"Sire de Rais, I must tell you the child your wife carries—whether for good or evil—belongs to the Saint."

Beside her, Marie felt her husband stunned into silence. Let him be stunned. She liked the feeling of power it gave her.

Finally, Sire de Rais regained the power to move. He took his wife's hand clumsily. "So you are with child?" The gesture seemed to add, "If it is as this holy man says, our prayers have been answered."

But there was also something in the clumsiness that told her his thoughts contained less happy elements. My poor, simple wife, perhaps. Must be told by a stranger and a man what any woman should know on her own.

Or maybe, She did not tell me. She tells me nothing. And a woman with mysteries is dangerous.

I suppose a loving wife would have wanted to tell him herself, Marie thought bitterly, jealously.

But neither lord nor lady addressed the other. What the Hermit had to say took priority. As he spoke, Marie studied the Hermit. How had he known just what words to conjure with?

In his dark, liquid tones, the Hermit had pronounced what Marie already felt. He was a man as dark and unnerving as the place he haunted. A Breton, doubtless. He spoke that strange, inhuman tongue, damp like fog, to comfort the mother of the wounded child. He spoke a passable French, too, of course, to his noble guests, but peat seemed to cling to his accents. He wore black wool, heavily patched and so rough-woven it seemed to be made of rope.

The Hermit's mostly white chin hair had probably never felt a razor. It fell over his trunk to the point where his gaunt frame was unduly exaggerated by a cord belt. Long as it was, the beard was beginning to thin, revealing a wild blue shadow along his jaw beneath. Like the shadow she'd seen in the woods. And saw now, like haze over the great grey stones.

Wrinkles knotted his small, dark eyes into place. They unnerved her, those bright eyes that, like so few she'd ever met before, dared to look directly, almost lewdly at her with no consciousness of station.

Finally, there was his head, bare with his cowl thrown back to his shoulders on this warm day and as he busied himself with the wounded child. At first Marie thought the high brow that gave the man a constant look of childish wonder was only the natural receding of his white hair with age. But on closer inspection she saw that he shaved his head forward from a line running ear to ear directly over the crown of his head. It seemed a sort of tonsure, but so different from the round balding crown assumed by every other holy man she had ever known.

"So, holy Father, what is it you are saying?" Guy de Rais turned again to their host. "When this child—God willing, it is as you say— when it is born, we must bring it here to you to raise in the name of the holy Saint?"

The Hermit rubbed at the startling blue under his beard. "That may indeed be required."

Marie's hand was uncomfortable in her husband's. Even when they were alone, his touch did not comfort. But now she pressed the hand, trying to give him a message. Strangers though they were, he got it. At least, he spoke the words she'd hoped he would to the old man.

"This is a hard thing, holy Father. You must understand that this child, if a boy, must be raised to carry the Rais name or the great lands that go with the name are forfeit to the crown."

"But you do understand, my son, what a serious matter it is to invade the sanctuary of the Saint's land?"

"I do—now. And am very sorry. I've already said it." Guy de Rais was not angry so much as impatient. "I had no idea when I shot that this was sanctuary. But to give up the heir like that—it is a bitter thing, Father."

"Indeed. But let us consider. Perhaps the Saint would be content with lesser signs that the child is his."

"Do you think so, Father?"

"I am not certain. That young lad lying wounded over there—as I've already told you, I suspect were his mind not fogged with pain, he could tell the Saint's will better than I. He heard the voice of the forest's King. In the meantime, we may try for lesser signs. If all goes well with the boy, the Saint will have shown he is content and will not touch your child."

"What other signs are you speaking of, Father?"

"Certainly you must name the child after the Saint to begin with."

"Gilles if it's a boy?" Sire de Rais asked. "Gillette if it's a girl?"

"It will be a boy," the Hermit stated without a doubt.

Marie was pleased to hear the Hermit confirm what she'd already begun to suspect herself. But the other part of his pronouncement did not sit so well with her. She squeezed her husband's hand again.

"Gilles is not a family name," Sire de Rais attempted. "Girard or Guy, perhaps . . ."

Or Jean or Amaury—after my father or my brother, Marie thought to herself.

At the moment, anything seemed preferable to Gilles. St. Gilles, she knew, had lived hundreds of years ago in the far south, near Nîmes. But such knowledge did not help the emotion of her impression that Gilles was a Breton name, a Breton saint, and hardly a Christian one. She was certain there could not be as many places named St. Gilles in any other dukedom in the world as there were in Brittany. This was the sixth she'd visited herself and she knew of three others by hearsay. In fact, an afternoon's easy ride would bring them to another just at the western end of this same forest. St. Gilles of the Old Market that place was called, to distinguish the two.

Gilles was the Saint of woods and wild things. A Saint—could he be called a Saint and not a devil?—of places like this clearing where heavy damp and chill hung on the warmest summer day.

The whimpering of that wounded child, unable to find comfort even in his mother's arms . . . Even on the opposite side of the clearing, the sound was too close. Marie knew she could never hear the name Gilles again but that she would remember that sound and the nausea that still threatened to overwhelm her. And yet, the Hermit was a man who could not be refused.

"I can see that must be true," Marie heard her husband say. "Gilles the child shall be." That was the first time, she thought, they'd ever felt the same thing together at the same time. "What else, Father, do you recommend?"

"A gift to the shrine here, certainly."

Marie tried to keep uncharitable thoughts from her mind about greedy prelates only interested in the next benefice. She would much rather give to the cathedral in Tours, she realized, to add to its rich hangings. But surely no man was more needful than this grizzled old thing in the ragged black robes. She found it easier to feel cynical with her hand in her husband's.

Sire de Rais said, "I vow to build a new stone fountain over the holy spring." He tried to hurry the bargaining along with his tone.

The Hermit nodded but still wasn't satisfied. "An annual gift as well. And perhaps a pilgrimage—with the child when he is born. Every year. At Midsummer. In commemoration. That may ensure his health and happiness."

"Certainly."

Again Marie felt the Hermit's eyes on her—the hunger of no eyes she'd ever felt before.

"And then," the Hermit said, "something for the family of the wounded child."

"Yes, of course."

Marie had to admire the man, for all his strangeness. She didn't think the priests of Tours often considered the wounded family when they set their penances. She admired it, but the request, by its very strangeness, only unnerved her further.

"But what shall this gift for the family be?"

The old man rubbed the beard away from the direction it grew as he considered. This action revealed the skin so that for the first time Marie could see the blue there for what it actually was. A blue stain, not just a shadow. A birthmark? Or—and the mark's even lines argued for this—something set there purposely by the hand of man.

Again she remembered the shadow she'd felt just before her husband let his arrow fly.

Guy de Rais said, "We are your servants, Father."

"Then perhaps we should wait until we know the family better, to know what might be of most service to them. They may lose this, their only child. I am almost certain that, without a miracle from the Saint, he will have little use of that hand for the rest of his life. You, monseigneur, madame, will spend St. John's Day with us here at least, to come to know what might serve them best?"

Guy de Rais repeated, "We are your servants."

Marie's heart thudded with fear at such a relinquishment of their power, their birthright. But it had to be. And with those words, the fate of the child she carried was sealed.

As was the fate of the wounded child as well.

The Lord and the Linen Merchant

My father arrived at the shrine barely a day later, his business in
Collinée completed. He discovered his son and heir struggling for life
on the bare grass by the Saint's fountain. The wound had gone to
fever. A visit to the holy site seemed to have aggravated my case,
not helped it. My father became distracted and the Hermit gave him
a tisane of camomile.

By that time, however, my mother had accustomed herself to
the idea that she might lose me. At least she decided there was
nothing more she could do and resorted to a watchful patience. She
did, after all, have some consolation growing within her.

And Mother's patience always improved when she could fill the
time with chatter. My mother could speak a tolerable French as well
as her native Breton. She'd learned this skill in aid of her husband's
trade and was not willing to let a little awkwardness intimidate her.
She loved to talk, it mattered not to whom and hardly in what language. She did not wait long to reveal her skill to the wife of her
son's attacker.

"*Bonjour*, madame."

Mother managed to catch Madame de Rais on her return from
yet another trip to the woods to empty her stomach that morning.
Mother dipped a bow—but not too deep, geared to exaggerate her
own unsteadiness and thickening waist.

'"*Bonjour.*" Madame was not in a mood for charity—especially
not toward those for whom she felt the most guilt.

Having found her distraction, however, Mother would not be brushed off. "Yes, the mornings, they are the worst. But it passes. You will see. You have felt a quickening, I think?"

Madame nodded blankly.

"Yes, you are almost done with that part. Myself—ah, I have another month of the nausea at least."

"You—you are pregnant, too?"

"*Oui,* madame." Another wobbly curtsy to prove it.

After that, it didn't take the two women long to grow into the tightest friendship. Both went to their graves denying the word. But friendship it was, as near as may ever come between women of such different classes and upbringings, neither of whom ever forgot who the other was.

As the possessor of greater experience, besides the tongue to make up for other deficits, my mother soon had Madame firmly under her wing. Childbirth was something she knew about. Not arrow wounds, about which she knew nothing, could do nothing.

Until that moment Madame had only heard her condition spoken of as either a matter of cursing by the Hermit or a matter of desperate pressure to succeed by her husband. By talking with ease and confidence about their shared state, my mother brought a measure of ease to the young noblewoman. The most common sight at St. Gilles that year was of my mother and Madame sitting side by side in the grass. They bent their heads close together, Madame's elaborate winged and padded headdress so incongruous next to the simpler pleats of my mother's linen.

Ere I was well enough to travel and the pilgrimage concluded, the relationship had bloomed with such vigor that it had to spread. Madame went to her lord and his lordship went to my father.

"Alanik Le Drapier?"

My father bowed. "My lord."

"You are something of a merchant, so I'm told."

"In dry goods, yes, so it please your lordship."

"My young lady could use one with your skills. Someone to oversee the many purchases she must make in refurnishing my ancestral home to her liking. Would you consider the commission—?"

My father didn't need to consider long. The security of a post attached to a noble household vastly outweighed the uncertainty of the life of self-promotion he'd been stumbling after until then.

"My lord, I've long envied those who trade along the Loire. You'll forgive me, but your blessed Blaison sits astride that lovely river?"

"Indeed she does."

"And all this while I have seen no way to extend business there myself—without some sort of noble patronage. Now, as if dropped by the Saint's generous hand into my lap—"

The crinkle of a smile worked at the edge of the lord's usually impassive eyes. "Tell me, Le Drapier. Did your wife know of this ambition of yours?"

"No, monseigneur. Of course not. How could she? Women know nothing of business."

Sire de Rais nodded solemnly. "No, of course not. We've the Saint to thank, of course. Which brings me to my second point."

"My lord?"

"Your wife, Le Drapier."

"My wife, monseigneur?"

"She seems a good breeder."

My father did not express his doubts that his only proof of this lay in me. The formula, "May she please God," seemed to cover all possibilities.

"My wife will need a wet nurse in some months' time, someone with experience. I'm certain they may work out the details between themselves." Sire de Rais glanced pointedly at the pair of them, hand in hand under the trees. "But let me go so far as to suggest that as milk brothers of my sons, your sons will have the opportunity to be raised along with them, enjoying the same education."

Sire de Rais did not have to elaborate. With my hand certainly crippled for life, there was very little I would be fit for in my born station. A bookish education was perhaps the best replacement the nobleman could offer me to replace what he had by accident taken from me. Surely the Saint would then forgive him and remove the curse from his house. Even if I should die.

But I did not die. My father, you see, had not come to the shrine alone.

It was the custom for all the local peasantry to congregate

around the Hermit's haunt at the height of summer. They brought their families, their cattle, a bundle of wood each. Then in the clearing, before the great old stones, they built two pyres. The Hermit himself kindled the need-fire—rubbing oak on oak to release the wood's thundering power into a bundle of dried gorse. He kindled it in the heart of the circled cross on the topmost stone, an even-legged cross having little to do with crucifixion, everything to do with balance in the world. From this pure fire, the pyres were lit as darkness fell on that shortest night of the year, the feast of St. John, my namesake.

As the blazes branded the night sky and swelled the stars from sight, the folk sang and danced and drove their cattle sunwise around and then between the pyres. They carried their ailing the same way, and as the flames died to knee-high, young couples jumped over them hand in hand to prove and strengthen their love. Afterward, each household head carried a pot of live coals back to his own cold hearth, to keep the warming power of Midsummer all year 'til midwinter, when it would be time to turn the year again.

That year my father carried me, moaning, between the flames, my injured hand wrapped in achillea and rags, cradled against my chest. Mother told me he did, and that the fever broke at that instant.

But neither of them said anything about the Vision I remember so clearly from that fever.

Only much later did I learn—from watching the action repeated with older eyes by the same old Hermit—that the cats and dog burning in a wicker cage were not the delirium of my illness but a real thing that happened every year. The folk carefully gathered the ashes of this sacrifice to carry home alongside the live coals of the need-fire. They spread the ashes on their fields once the wheat harvest was done, to put the dark power of that sacrifice into the dark heart of their soil.

Mother and Father did not mention the thing because they'd seen it many times before. I don't know why Madame didn't mention it. Or perhaps she did. Perhaps that was what she spoke about to my mother when she'd lower her voice and I'd only catch the words "evil" and "devil" no matter how I strained.

I'm sure I could not have known until the Hermit himself told me many years later that the lives of cats and dogs were but poor substitutes, for what had been given in the ancient days—the life of a man for the life of all in the life of the soil.

Sometimes such supreme sacrifice was still required. With the Cycle. From the King.

The Hermit gave his blessing to our parents' plan to reunite as soon as my family's affairs could be settled in Quintin. We moved first to the lord's castle at Blaison in Anjou. And not much later Mother and I accompanied Madame de Rais when she returned to her parents' castle at Champtocé, not a day's trip downstream from Blaison, to enjoy the familiar surroundings for her lying in.

So it was, in due time, that the Rais heir was born. No one gave much thought then to the omen: his mother brought to bed in the Black Tower. What mattered the name? The stronghold had protected the family as long as any could remember. The child was a son, healthy and sporting a vigorous mop of wavy black hair. He took his first food, a milky pap, from the tip of his father's sword.

What mattered, too, the wagging tongues of kinsfolk? "Gilles? None of us has ever borne the name Gilles before. Isn't it a strange name? A Breton name? A fairy name."

Jean de Craon, standing godfather, pronounced the name loudly to echo off the winter-chilled walls of the castle chapel and cover the protesting infant wails at the font.

Nobody dwelt much on the fact that my parents lost their own child, a daughter, in a too-early birth not a week before. Mother didn't, not when they set that comely noble child, still wailing, against her ample bosom. My parents had other children soon enough and I never heard the name of my sister—Marietta, named for Madame de Rais—until I was old enough to wonder how my mother had had milk to feed Gilles.

Gilles was the child of that year. Gilles was the only name any of us heard.

A Spiral of Yellow Leaves

I must mention one more thing in connection with the Hermit of St. Gilles before I go on with my tale. While there at the shrine and in my delirium, I first had the Vision.

Although sometimes I think I must have always known it.

The Vision comes so often along with my spells—parts of it separately or the whole of one piece—and is so real that I often think it must have actually happened there in the forest clearing by the great grey rocks. The Hermit, by some drug that he gave me to soothe the pain . . . Maybe it was his way of telling me . . .

But let me only relate it as it occurs, even to this day . . .

The Vision begins with a great, broad view of the land, as if I fly above on the black, darting wings of a martinet. Below I see not the natural, pleasant tangle of woodland, but the tough and single-minded weeds that betray a land stretched, racked, and tortured beyond endurance. Its agony seeps into me, but before I scream in outrage, the black of martinet wings covers everything and sight fails.

Then comes the laughter. At first I hear the laughter outside me, and so natural that it is like the spiral of dry autumn leaves in the wind. Soon, however, it enters me, and I myself am laughing uncontrollably, laughter that goes on so long, I have forgotten the joke. What remains is only the laughter itself—that, and the tears in my eyes and the ache in my sides.

I am this swirling, turning circle of yellow life. And when normal experience tells me I ought to have settled with leaves to the ground,

I continue, on and on, around and around. There seems to be no ground, no up and down, just a continuous, riotous swirl.

Then, suddenly, the circle of laughter is transfixed. Thunk! The jolting memory of a playful little round hand knowing neither up nor down suddenly transfixed to the earth by the bolt of an arrow.

Vision appears from the reverberations of my swirling, laugh-echoing head, brought suddenly, violently to a standstill in this place and time. I see first a lovely young woman, the eldest of three sisters, all equally lovely. Then I see a God come to her in the form of a Stag. I recognize Him. It is the very Stag Whom I saved in the forest. I remember His call, "Help!" But now it is the woman who speaks, who fears, as the shadow of the crowned antlers falls on her.

When I was a child, I didn't understand what happened next. But now I know that as the shadow falls upon her, she conceives. Her people, finding her to be with child and husbandless, lock her in a tower. They wait only for the child to be born before they plan to burn her as a witch for her intercourse with the horned devil.

In due time the child is born—and he frightens away the tower's guards when they see him, for he is covered with thick black hair from head to foot.

The magistrate comes to deal with the matter, flanked by retainers. He smiles, but something in the smile is not true. It glints with gold. I shiver with fever.

The magistrate wears cloth of gold. The staff he carries is studded with gems. Light winks from his richness so brightly I cannot look at him. It seems he has no face, but for that glint. He could, I realize, be anyone. Even someone I know.

Light is good, I tell myself. Isn't it? Did not God Himself declare on the first day, "This is good." But this light—it is unnatural. Its source of metal and gems harbors no soul. It leaves me cold. Then I see why: this light has no shadow. No relief on a summer's day, no blue and quiet rest of winter. It has no smell, either, no sweat or decay of life going through death and returning. The soul is missing. The curve of swirling leaves has hardened out of a ring and fashioned a sword.

I can read the intentions of this being. He means to send both mother and Stag-gotten child to the pyre. He means to pierce the circle of their being by a stake.

But the infant, the little round and furry infant, opens his mouth and demands of the magistrate: "What shall become of us?"

"You shall burn now and go to hell to burn forever."

The magistrate doesn't seem too startled by the precocity of the child. Neither do I. But this is a dream.

"Nay, I say we shall not," says the child. "For I have the Vision to see both what has been and what shall be."

"An evil thing of an evil woman!" the magistrate cries. "Your mother could not name your father. For shame. To the flames!"

"Do you know your own father?"

"But of course. My mother was an honest woman."

"You are certain?" There is an impish little twinkle in the infant's eyes.

"I—" The man falls silent.

"Name him. Or else, with my own Sight, I shall. I promise you, you will not like what you hear. More than one person will hang himself this night for shame. And it will not be my mother."

So the magistrate and his henchmen depart, even as the crowd departed from around the Magdalene in the Christian gospel. And the mother and child are free.

The child grows thus to manhood, in a single swirl of laughing leaves, and instantly I recognize him as the Hermit of St. Gilles, wiry, old, and white-whiskered.

"Who am I?" the Hermit asks. He laughs. He asks a riddle and even before the answer comes, it makes him laugh.

"The son of the Mother," I reply.

"The son of a nun?" asks he, his eyes a-twinkle with merriment above the scruff of beard just as they were in the fat baby pink of the infant's cheeks.

"She didn't look like a nun." But the thought, with its incongruencies, makes my mind swirl on the cyclone of laughing leaves.

"Who am I?" he repeats.

"A war hammer."

"And?"

"The lone blackbird."

"And?"

"The healing grass."

"And?"

"Teacher. Master."

"And?"

"Wizard. Warlock. Robin in the Wood. The Stag."

"And?"

"The prophet who speaks from the tomb."

"Tomb?"

"The tomb into which you climbed of your own will."

How I, a feverish child, can know all this strange catechism, I cannot say. But there is one thing I do not know. "What is your name?" I ask him.

"Ah, child. You would have my name so you may have my power?"

"I want to know your name." And I hold up my hand and it is throbbing and oozing blood again. "By this hand and the Stag it saved, I conjure you. Tell me your name."

The Hermit cannot resist my magic.

He says, "Merlin."

As if it is a name I should know.

That was how the Vision first came to me.

The Yellow Spiral Respun

Years later, when I actually did hear the name Merlin intoned by Père de Boszac in the schoolroom, I raised my hand and answered the question he'd posed.

"Merlin was a prophet. A magician. Born of a nun."

Père de Boszac looked surprised, and a little annoyed, for he had wanted to prove us simpletons again.

"How did you get so smart?" Gilles asked, kicking me under the bench.

"Why, I'm older than you," was my reply.

Truly, I knew the name 'til then only from my Vision. I didn't understand that many folk knew the name. It filled their tales and ballads of King Arthur and his knights, "the material of Brittany" as they called the cycle, from the land of its source. Learning to have to share that part of my secret spell-life with the world was a disappointment.

But learning this sent me to confront the old Hermit the following Midsummer when we went, as Madame and her husband had vowed to do every year.

"No, child," the old man replied. "I am not the great Merlin."

"But you look just like him. From my Vision."

"I am flattered. Tell me of this Vision, my Yann."

So I did, haltingly at first. But then, when the old man didn't at once put me to bed and feed me blackcherry syrup as everyone else had always done, I gained confidence.

When I finished, the Hermit nodded, considering. "I knew, from the moment they brought you to me, deathly white and arrow-pierced, that you had the gift of Sight."

"Like Merlin?"

"Perhaps. Perhaps a little like Merlin. Yours is, in any case, an old, old soul."

That seemed a great responsibility. I didn't believe it. "But you're the one who looks like him."

"I wish I could see what you can See. Certainly, it has been my life's work to try. For I am his heir."

"Merlin's heir? Truly?"

"Master of his Craft. And the keeper of the true prophecies he spoke while in the flesh."

"Tell me. Teach me."

"I will try. A little. Bit by bit. As you grow."

"Can you, like Merlin, really See what has been and what will be?"

"Through his eyes, yes. And through yours."

"Show me."

"You must show me, Yann. I have not your gift."

"I—I can't name what I See."

"Perhaps there is something I can do to help you. To help us both see what lurks in the depths of the future."

The Hermit took his staff and enclosed us both in a circle drawn on the ground. Then he sat and leaned back as if he were going to nap there in the Midsummer sun, folding his hands under the strag-gly ends of his beard. He fixed me with the steel blue of his eyes like fisherman's hooks. In my mind's eye, however, the drawing of the circle went on and on, swirl upon swirl. I had to laugh with it. I felt the Vision returning.

"Listen," the Hermit intoned. "Listen to the singsong of my voice."

I listened and found myself beginning to grow drowsy, swirling on the swirls.

"Listen, and I will give your Vision names."

And then the Vision began again and, under the Master's guiding hand, expanded, dropping through the autumn spiral like the leaves' shadow.

"What do you See?" he asks.

I tell him.

"That is your life. Or lives, rather, for the great wonder of life is the cycle of birth, renewal in death to be born again."

The lesson settles like mother's milk on the mind of a child surrounded day in and day out by Christianity's doctrine of one single life. Of course, the life I'd been handed on Christianity's terms was so impoverished, in such need of salvation.

The Hermit shifts his ancient limbs into even closer concord with the forest sward, encouraged by the rapidity of my learning.

He begins to speak again, "Do you See, my Yann? This is why your leaves of laughter never hit the ground—and why they seem so ancient. When you see leaves hit the ground every year in autumn with your this-world eyes, you must sense that that is but illusion. They fall to the roots of the mother tree, but in the secret dark mold, they feed her again—either her or her rebirth in her children, which to Vision eyes are the same. You cannot see the ongoing swirl of life through mold and root with your this-world eyes. But your Vision has Seen it. Embrace it."

"Yes, Master." My tongue is thick and heavy. "I do. But why, then, do I See no beginning, either? 'In the beginning, God created . . . '?"

"So you have heard from the pulpit."

"God did not create, then?"

"Certainly God—Gods, rather, for who has heard of birth without male and female?—the Gods created. But not in the way you are used to thinking. Praise be to Them, They have made many creations, over and over. The spiral."

"Yes . . . I See it. But the beginning?"

"No, Yann. Think not of beginning. For once you've postulated beginning, you've wrenched apart the circle and hammered it flat on the anvil. In the instant you postulate beginning, you've also created end. And that is the evil greatest to be feared."

"Death? The grave?"

"No, do not fear death at all. Fear the escape from death, rather. The desire to escape the cycle, to remove to a world beyond where death and sorrow no longer come to balance life and joy, to feed them—that is the thing to fear. And to claim that any mortal has the keys to lead folk to such a place—to claim the resources of others' cycling with promises to lead them to it—that is evil."

Thunk! The Hermit feels the force of the impact of the shaft that shatters my Vision. I've no need to cry out, "Help me! I'm pinned." He knows it.

"Ah, that. The spiral of your many lives, Yann. Your spiral has been pierced into this life. Halted."

"Why? I hate it," I cry.

The Hermit moves the Vision on, shielding me, I think, from something very hard.

"What of the magistrate in your Vision?"

I describe the scene, the gold-glinting, false smile, until terror stops my mouth.

"There are many such men, I fear, and not all of them magistrates. There is such a spirit loose upon the world in this age that many people in many walks of life take up the riches of the Earth instead of leaving them with Her. They take them up and place them on their own person to dazzle the eye. In this dazzle, few can see that such people cast no shadow, leave no possibility to start the world swirling again. Light without darkness is death, the end. Beware."

"I'm . . . I'm afraid."

"I will not try to falsely assure you. Fear you are wise to feel. But the fact of the matter is that more and more of the flecks of creation are pinned every cycle. You might have done well to pass through yet another life on the soaring wings of your divine sickness. But the hard fact is that you've been pinned here, to Messire Gilles de Rais and his family, to this forest, to this time and place. To Brittany and France in the first half of the fifteenth century after the Christians began telling time."

"I would rather die," I cry out. "I would return—to be a tree. A soaring eagle. A worm, even, in a dark circle of mold. Anything would I rather be than this that I am."

"The shaft would not have pierced your hand had you not had work to do in this life."

"I do not want it." The laughter is gone, seemingly forever. I am bereft. "I will kill myself. Find another life. Quickly. Not this twisted, crippled life when the world is now set for straight bodies and heads straight as the columns of figures in my father's ledger."

"But you must not, Yann. Don't you see it is not only the spiral of your life at stake here? By removing hopes out of this world and into one beyond, less and less is left for the returning souls with each generation."

"What must I do? I cannot See."

"As long as you remain open, it will come."

"Christianity." My mind struggles for clarity, to find the solid names he's promised and yet seemed not to have given. "Christianity is the evil. The Old Faith the good."

"Alas, Yann, the world is never so easy as that. Good and evil is all a jumble, ever has been. Sometimes to claim good for oneself is the greater evil. Sometimes to work what appears to be bad is what must be done. Throughout your life you will find, as I have done, that a gloss of Christianity holds ancient truths. And sometimes initiates, men who have been marked by the God and ought to know better, still try to skim off the riches of the Earth for their own present advancement. They have forgotten to turn the cycle at all. Then I can only hope to work with whatever vestige of the mark may be left to them. Every day must have a night, every summer a winter. That is the simplest way to see it. And almost all I can tell you."

"Can't you give me some clearer hint as to what I, myself, must do?"

The Hermit settles and shrugs. What he says now cannot have come from my Vision. It comes only from his own years of wisdom. But I know, in the end, I will be left to interpret his words on my own.

"Every time you See the dazzle, you must reveal the shadow. Recreate it if there's none left behind the gold. Every time folk claim life without death, invite them rather to sacrifice. You must curve around the shaft and snap it, even when what it leaves may be as twisted and unsightly to dazzled eyes as the claw with which I've left you."

"People will hate me."

"They will. And worse. They will call you devil. They will hunt you as they hunt the Stag. They will kill you if they can. Is there any comfort to know that you are not the first to whom they've done the same? Nor, I think, will you be the last. A time is coming when half of the world will be called so, will be called witch and demon, and sent to the stake by the other half."

"I would not live through such a burning time."

"Your deeds may help determine how soon that time comes. And how hard. Now," he says, leaning back and straightening. "Now I think it is time to call this Vision to an end."

"Master, no. Pray give me more. I cannot take up this task so alone, so unprepared."

"Very well." He pauses in thought, then says, "Throughout my long years, I have gathered up many prophecies that have, I believe, to do with this time. I pass them to you now, as a guide. I give you first the Vision of Marie d'Avignon, a prophetess, who suddenly appeared at the court of King Charles within the last Cycle of Nine."

"What did she See?"

"Arms. Fields of weapons like corn standing in the head.

" 'And must I take up these arms my own weak self?' she asked.

" 'Not you,' said the voice from heaven, 'but another woman, yet to come.' "

The singsong voice of my master moves me on. "Now the Vision of the Venerable Bede."

"What did he See?" I ask.

"Charles the son of Charles the son of Charles. He rises to take the place of his ancestor Charles called the Great, Charlemagne, in the holy city."

"And he must rise—?"

"With the aid of the arms that stand like corn in the head."

"Finally?"

"Finally. Vision of my own. By which I mean Vision of the Prophet Merlin. A maid shall rise from out of Lorraine."

"Lorraine?" Even as a grown man, I never remembered the name until the Vision said it. I certainly hadn't heard of the place anywhere else before.

"Far to the east. She shall come, when she sees the distress of the Land, Mother of us all. The Maid shall be called."

"By whom?"

"Voices," is all he says. "They will call and she shall rise and come into France and take up the arms that Marie d'Avignon refused."

"Soon?"

"Soon. Within your lifetime. And you, child, must rise to her side."

"How shall I know her that I may help her?"

"When the time comes, she shall be made known to you."

"But her name?"

"La Pucelle. Not only the woman-child who has known no man, but she who has no need of any man. Like my own mother. La Pucelle."

"La Pucelle," I repeat. "The Maid."

And as I say the word, the Vision fades, leaving only the ache from the laughter, the tears in the eyes—and raw red anew in the twisted, useless claw of my right hand.

Candlelight on Loops of Silk

"Oh, why did I indulge myself and join my lord on that ill-fated hunt?"

I often heard Marie de Craon-Rais sorrowing to my mother when I was growing up. They bent their heads together as always, my mother's clean white linen, Madame's latest headdress, something wider, something taller, yet delicately wispy with veils.

Madame and my mother watched young Gilles with wonder and with care as they spoke. Together they watched him, first gurgling, then crawling, then toddling across the floor at their feet. Such a pretty child, that rich tousle of black curls, those dark eyes none could refuse. Seemingly blessed in all ways. Though rather slow to smile, even when he knew the trick.

Certainly it seemed so to a jealous milk brother.

Sometimes my mother would take me aside and speak in our private Breton. "Not only is Messire Gilles younger than you are," she would warn, "he is a young lord. If he wants something, you give it to him, Yann." There was none of the usual talk of "sharing."

And Gilles, as soon as he could want anything, wanted everything. I learned to entertain myself less with toy hoops and pull toys and horsehair-stuffed leather balls than by sitting quietly within the swirl of my thoughts, turning my head to watch one woman's face and then the other, listening carefully.

The forest of St. Gilles refused to leave us, though we had left it.

"Why did I go to that place where normal laws were suspended?" Madame asked. "In the middle of that forest where no pious, sane human should be?"

Mother always knew when it was time to take up her lines in the chorus again. "Because you always loved the sport of hunting as a girl, madame."

"But I am now a Rais, a married woman. I was then."

"You were but newly married," Mother tried for leniency.

"More than a wife, I hoped to be a mother before the year was out."

"And so you were. See the happy product? Oh, see, madame, how your young lord tries to stand. Come, Gilles. Come to nanny."

A little delight in the wonder of the growing child distracted them, but Madame soon returned to the cycle of her concerns. "I was very foolish to try to steal one more day of freedom from my fate, my duty. God will not be cheated."

"You did not cheat God. You did not shoot the arrow. You did not know the woods were holy."

"I knew I had tried to cheat Him out of the obligations He demands of womanhood."

"Those were dire words the Hermit spoke indeed. That a great evil would descend on the union of your lordly marriage because of what had happened to my son. You might well have felt all your hopes in jeopardy, lady."

"No, I knew it before the Hermit spoke. I knew it the minute my husband came to help me dismount."

"She knew the moment the roof of oak leaves had broken over their heads and they'd entered the small, uneven clearing," Mother told me later, when we were alone. "She fights against it. She thinks she must be a good Christian. She thinks she can. But Madame has the fairy blood. And so does her son. A double dose."

"St. Gilles du Mené. A holy name, surely. And my hostess, Madame de Menez, had spoken to me of the place with a certain pride at the holiness it lent to the family lands.

"But when I thought of holy places, until that day I thought of cathedrals. The lovely St. Gatien in Tours, for example. I once attended mass there on Christmas Eve, when the stained glass pushed by a thousand, thousand beeswax candles welcomed me with long paths of jewellike colors on the crisp dusting of snow. Inside, the entire apse had been draped in the most brilliant velvet, damask, silk, all patterned or embroidered. And the candle flames fairly danced on the gold threads in the near loops of fabric."

"A noble girl felt at home in such a place, I suppose. Certainly a girl dressed as Jean de Craon always dressed his Marie."

"I felt welcome in the cathedral," Madame said. "Surely that was the realm of angels."

"Embraced in folds of the same fabrics she herself wore. She felt among kindred spirits—"

"But the forest clearing—Why, there was not even a rough-hewn excuse for a church. A stump of wood carved with the image of the patron Saint and his deer marked the fountain. Otherwise, only three stones—great, grey stones—glowered over us. The stones betrayed no softening sign of human hands, save maybe that cross scratched crookedly into the uppermost one. But that could be just a trick of light and natural fissure in the rock.

"No one can piously believe that mere mortals set that third, flattish stone as a sort of table board across the other two," she continued. "And the Hermit—No place to shelter himself when it rains save in the hollow left under the 'table board.' " Madame shivered at the thought.

"A hound under God's table," my mother liked to suggest.

But Madame would hear of no such thing. "It was not God's table," she always insisted. She lowered her voice at this point, as if God must not hear. "Yes, there is a presence there, a lowering, immovable, grey presence. A heart of raw and untamed power. A heart such as God must have given Pharaoh, left to harden yet further over all the centuries since Moses' time."

And what was there about the grey-bearded Hermit that made
her shiver, and her heart beat faster? The fear was so loud that an
untrained child could read her thoughts. But she never spoke of the
Hermit's effect on her, even to my mother.

"No goodness could come from such a place," she said instead.
"Only evil. The heart of evil. The center of a loathsome witchcraft."

My mother patted the trembling hands and murmured comfort.
But she knew Marie de Craon-Rais protested too much.

"Do you think she ever tells Père de Boszac these things in
confession?" Mother asked me later, rhetorically. "She talks of
being a good Christian, but I think she does not tell him. He
might try to shrive them out of her."

"Wouldn't she want that?" I asked.

"She would not." Mother was very definite, almost scornful
of my naïveté in reading Madame. "Madame—Madame is of
two minds about witchcraft," was all the further explanation
I got—until I got older. "One mind she had before St. Gilles
and the Hermit. The one mind she was christened with at birth
and thought she would die with. And the other has begun,
slowly, to invade her ever since that day."

"Hasn't witchcraft haunted my own family enough?" Madame
grieved. She tried so hard not to look at Gilles when she said it,
whereas I could tell that was the only place she wanted to set her
eyes. My little milk brother was like a spell set on her, on everyone.

Once I had the temerity to pipe in at this juncture, "Yes. I've
often heard my lord your husband call my lord your father a demon,
madame."

For all my care to get the noble forms right, Mother had still
threatened to box my ears at this speech. Madame had stopped her,
laughing dismissively but not a little frantically. As if boxing my ears
would give the rumor more truth than she wanted to credit it with.

Hastily Madame went on, "My own grandfather, Pierre de Craon
of blessed memory, was once a victim of the black art."

And she would tell that tale with passion, over and over.

"One day, when I was hardly out of my swaddling, Duke Jean

of Brittany attacked one of our Craon castles, at Sablé, and took it. As soon as he had word of the event, my grandfather hurried to the place and set siege to retake it. But he knew his own defenses well enough that he had no hope of breaching the walls without help. He appealed to Charles VI, France's King, in the name of the French nation."

"I see no witchcraft there," my mother said gently.

"But it comes. Ah, it comes. My grandfather had never failed his majesty, always provided troops in accordance with his fealty oaths, and fought himself at Charles' side against the English as well as against the Bretons. And his majesty, ignoring the fearful cautions of his cousins Burgundy and Anjou, answered my grandsire's call for aid.

"Duke Jean shook in his boots when he heard of the large body of men-at-arms Charles was bringing. He knew he could not trust to normal flesh and blood power. He turned to witchcraft, in which Brittany has always swum."

My mother's soft Breton voice assured me, "Charles inherited a mental weakness from his mother's side." There was even a suggestion in her voice—though only with the very soul of compassion—that Madame was so closely connected to the French royal house that such an affliction might haunt her family as well.

In any case, the King had advanced as far as Le Mans by early August in the year 1394.

"As the royal party approached the colony of lepers just outside that town," Madame said, "a ragged man of frightful aspect began to run along beside the stirrup at the King's side."

Madame's hands twisted as if the tale were wrung from her and her eyes grew wide. She could not look at her little son at this point, even if he was tugging at her skirt.

"It was at the warlock duke's instigation that the leperous apparition came. 'Go no farther, great King,' the demon said over and over again, chanting. A spell," Madame assured us, "casting a madness on poor King Charles."

"The beggar was only trying to send a warning of betrayal," my mother said. "King Charles has powerful cousins, but false ones."

"The companions of the King finally succeeded in beating the beggar aside," Madame said, "but the harm was done. Not an hour's march farther on, as they came out of a forest and onto a sandy plain, Charles suddenly went utterly and completely mad. Shouting orders to 'Advance! Advance on these traitors!' he laid about him with his sword and had killed five of his retainers—his young pages, no more than children—before he could be restrained."

"And there are some," Mother said, almost wistfully, "who think the madness comes of the King's refusal to do what a King must do."

"What is that?" I'd asked, thinking if I were in his place, I would not be so afraid. Perhaps nobility—even royalty—was not beyond my crippled grasp.

"Never you mind." She quickly remembered herself. "It's naught that need trouble your young thoughts."

"Since that day on the road from Le Mans, not a year has gone by that King Charles has not suffered at least one long and debilitating relapse. It is witchcraft, witchcraft that stalks the land, and who can be safe from it?"

Madame laid her hand tentatively on her young son's head as if she very much feared those curls might spring to flame beneath her touch. She could never trust to his seeming health, his vigor, his obvious will to survive since the Hermit's words had colored his future.

"I do not disagree with you, madame, that the King's malady bears the dark and uncontrollable marks of witchcraft."

Madame thought, perhaps, that in such a world even decrees made by standing stones in wild woods might also be reversed—if only the proper spells were discovered. If madness might only turn to sanity. Or the other way around.

She said, "I have spoken to you, Guillemette, of my own father?"

"Often, madame. We were at Champtocé, you'll recall, when dear Gilles was born. I met Jean Sire de Craon there, and had the pleasure to wait upon him and your lady mother."

"Of course. I forget. Since my husband hates to visit, or to allow me to visit alone, it seems long since I was there."

"I'm sure it must. I, too, miss my family in Brittany." It had been longer since my mother had been to Quintin. But a woman in her station, of course, must have lesser sympathies than her lady.

"My father, you understand, has only recently been able to repair in some way the family's fortunes so ill served by—by all of this."

Mother elaborated to me, "This all culminated in Pierre de Craon's ignominious flight to Spain. The present Sire de Craon, our lady's father, is a very different man from what his father was. Not nearly so rash, for all his sound and fury. He calculates every move, does Jean Sire de Craon."

"For this cause, I could not marry where my heart was."

"This marriage of his only daughter to Guy de Rais was one of Sire de Craon's more astute moves."

"Where my heart was . . ." Madame sighed and looked far away.

"Ah, she was hardly old enough to know she had a heart, poor thing," my mother sighed in chorus. "So I don't think she'd given it elsewhere then. That isn't to say she hasn't now." And Mother looked over her shoulder and made a quick sign against evil.

"And now, by going to those cursed woods of St. Gilles du Mené on that cursed hunt, I, Marie de Craon-Rais—though all unwittingly, I swear by Blessed Mary—I have set all in jeopardy once more. Surely—surely that must be witchcraft of a sort as well."

"A very insidious sort," Mother had to agree.

Turnip-Blue Fog on Damask

Often people ask me, "What do you remember of Gilles de Rais as a child? Were there omens of what he was to become? Did he seem different, difficult, disturbed?"

A monster?

My answer is no. Gilles was my milk brother. Gilles was Gilles, and if that was "odd," I hadn't enough experience of "normal" to say.

And as I have always had a gift for omens, that ought to say something.

What did Gilles become, after all? Evil was prophesied of him— or darkness, rather—but he was as the God made him, even before he was born. And there is no evil not counterbalanced by its good.

Certainly, strange things did happen to us. But I never thought we caused them, Gilles or I. Or brought them on ourselves, unless it was by deeds from previous lives, and for that I can't answer. What was always good and normal to me was that we faced them together.

Well do I remember the great hall at Blaison where Gilles and I spent most of our childhood. I remember the rafters wreathed in a twilight of smoke. Pigeons cooed and rustled their feathers up there.

The tapestries Father provided Madame did little to keep the drafts out. But the guttering torches and the fire beneath the great howling chimney made the tapestries' stitched figures dance, and filled many a winter's night with tales when I was a child, even when there was no storyteller by.

On the east wall, under the gallery, Alexander and his knights conquered the world. Facing them were gentler scenes: Saints Margaret, Catherine, and Barbara in heavenly discourse. And to the south were two panels I could scarcely face even in broad daylight: St. George, not yet triumphant over a very dreadful dragon, and the other, a moral lesson of the Final Judgment. The damned and their Horned Lord were worked with unnerving vividness. Even when I scooted my stool right near the fireplace and kept my back stalwartly toward them, I could feel the heat of their tortures at my back warmer than the real flames in front of me. I could hear their eternal screams.

The constantly shifting play of light and dark sometimes made giant demon shadows of me and a leaping Gilles as well. Gilles was bright, energetic, and heart-stopping in both looks and daring, like a spark shot from the cavernous hearth to one of Madame's few rugs.

I must have been nearly seven, my little lord a three-year-old that autumn night—

That night, among the usual smells of supper about to be served and of wet dogs, there arrived the smell of fog on wool, on brocade, on damask. A party of guests—

In the every-night world of Blaison hall, Gilles and I heard the uncommon sounds of *charet* wheels, horses, men in the yard. We hurried out, wrapless. Late afternoon was already night at that season of the year, and fog dampened down the usual courtyard smells of dung and straw.

Up from the village, subdued by distance, came the peal of bells. They must ring all that night to keep the spirits of the dead at bay. An eerie light filled the yard. Though the fog pressed in a tangible grey—smothering sunset and moonrise from sight—tiny, flickering lights strung every horizontal within woman's reach. My mother had seen to this, choosing the largest turnips and beetroots, hollowing them out over a week, then filling them with tallow and diligently lighting the wicks each night over another week. The translucent vegetable globes danced with a bluish glow, but even in a wind, very few of them blew out.

"Lights for the dead," my mother called them. "So the dearly departed won't lose their way as they visit us at this season with blessing. If they do lose their way, they will haunt the world for the rest of the year. These are the lights of Samonias."

She spoke the name of the old God of the dead with reverence. But the old language, Breton, forces that reverence upon the throat. With the ease of a child who has no idea learning can be a drudgery, I could switch from Breton for her to French for the rest of the world. And though I didn't realize it at the time, I learned most of what I knew about the feast day from my mother and in that tongue. I suppose Gilles knew the shiver of the lights, too, for that didn't even require the little Breton he'd picked up from the breast that suckled him.

I realize now Mother spoke thus not only because the feast demanded Breton of her but also so Madame would not understand. Madame would not have approved, although like anyone else she heard mass on that day and went to the graveyard to leave sweets at the monuments to the family's dead. Madame called that day "*Toussaint*," All Hallows'. As a child, I'd thought *Toussaint* perfectly interchangeable with Samonias.

But of course it is not.

So, ghostlike, the *charets* arrived in the ghost light of All Hallows' Eve. Gilles and I, like most boys, I think, cared little enough for the occupants at first. They were only the whispering furs and damasks of women, anyway.

The horses were new to us, and very fine. No one had a reputation for his stables like monseigneur the duke of Orléans in those days.

Even more thrilling, when they rolled into view through the turnip-blue glow, were the sides of the first of the three *charets*. Mud caked the otherwise airy spoked wheels as they turned up to a height well above my six-year-old head. Between these wheels, the ghost lights glinted on fog-burnished gold.

Then we saw the colors of a most elaborate painting. The light, which caught only the souls of things and not their gross physicality, muted the hues. Even so, they flashed brilliantly.

I was old enough to recognize the letters L and V, but not enough to know that these stood for Louis and Valentine, the duke and duchess of Orléans. The letters were crowned and twined together in the midst of a flowering thorn. A turtledove shared that gilded prison, and a rayed sun shone behind it. I know I couldn't have read the banner with its device "A bon droit!" the duchess' perpetual cry for justice, nor whether I would have understood its pathos had it been read to me. I didn't know, as the rest of the world did, that she'd been exiled from Paris and from court. But the fleurs-de-lis leafed with gold on the rich blue ground could fail to impress no one.

"Pikes," Gilles called them, whispering in an awe that would not let him even point.

And certainly the sparks of precious metal tipping the stylized floral emblem of the royal house of Valois gave the fierce and rigid aspect of weaponry. The sight sent shivers down my spine in that ghost-lit night.

Then the final panel of the vehicle's side creaked slowly into view and I gasped aloud. Surely the night was haunted. A serpent wriggled up the *charet*'s side, its jaws agape to devour a curly-headed infant.

At my side, Gilles made not a sound. But when I looked to him for reassurance (though I was the elder, it was no secret that he was the braver), I saw his black eyes wide, his lips thin and pale with fear.

As if at a signal, we tumbled over one another and over the descending guests in our haste to regain the safety of Blaison hall.

That night Gilles woke screaming from an evil dream.

And the smell of soured feathers said he'd wet the bed we shared.

The Fabric Called Spiderwebs

"She looks like a witch," Gilles decided with all his three-year-old solemnness.

Madame Valentine Visconti de Milan, duchess of Orléans, was a thin woman in her mid-thirties. Through the fox-trimmed openings (which the clergy were pleased to call "the windows of hell") of her sideless overgown, one could see how her silken cotehardie hung from the hooks of her hipbones. Her small breasts had collapsed into her chest.

At the neck, the fox fur was cut low. Only thin, white flesh and no fabric at all softened the startling angles of collarbones and shoulder joints. The tight sleeves of the cotehardie were very long, coming over her hands as far as the knuckles. They exaggerated her half-grown, waiflike aspect. In spite of all the fineness of the fabric from which such extra length was cut, she might have been a girl in her older sister's castoffs.

Premature worry lines spiked the duchess' grey eyes like so many cross strokes around calligraphed letters. She had brown hair, tarnished with grey, brought forward to frame her face with severe, stiff hanks of braid. These exaggerated the thinness, the severity of her features.

A third straight line blocked in her face. This was a wide gold band of simple lines set with few but large jewels she wore pressing across her forehead. The finest white veils—of the fabric known as "spiderwebs," made in Brussels—frosted it. My mother, trained by my father to look for such things, could not keep from exclaiming aloud at the elegance of the cloth.

And Gilles again declared, "She looks like a witch." He had to be hushed by someone with more sense, by a six-year-old. By me.

Gilles didn't say, but I knew he hadn't forgotten the serpent on the side of the duchess' *charet.* I certainly had not. And for the next few days, neither of us went back out to the courtyard where the vehicle rested. Even when the weather cleared, becoming cold and clean, and we could hear the usually irresistible shouts and clangs of men-at-arms practicing—even then, we stayed indoors.

The duchess produced witchlike paraphernalia from the depths of her boxes and cases. These confirmed Gilles in his conclusion.

She had, for example, a set of twelve miniature pitchforks made of silver. She and her ladies used them to eat the apples and pears poached in honey, walnuts, and cinnamon with which Madame de Rais sought to welcome them and take off the chill of their ride. The duchess even encouraged her hostess to try the new utensil for herself. Gilles and I, huddling wide-eyed together at the edge of the firelight, noticed Madame's hesitation. Gilles poked me to confirm his suspicions.

"We are delighted by the honor of your coming," Madame de Rais said, covering her doubts with grace.

"Not at all," the duchess insisted. "I owe much to your family."

"Indeed, madame?"

"Well, although it was probably before such a child as yourself can remember"—the duchess fondly patted her hostess' hand—"it is common knowledge. Therefore, I am not ashamed to speak of the matter, especially as it turned out so well for me in the end. Your father's father, madame, of blessed memory. . . ."

Madame de Rais bowed her thanks for the kind remembrance of old Pierre de Craon, dead in exile and everywhere else defamed.

"Your father's father warned me of a—an indiscretion—on the part of my husband the duke. I was able to confront the offending lady, warn her of my knowledge and—shall I say it? Yes—frighten her so that the next time my lord came to her, she sent him away without the favor of a smile. A woman does not forget such things, especially a woman who has known so few acts of friendship in her life."

After a deep sigh that begged for and gained little murmurs of sympathy, madame la duchesse turned to press her hostess again. "But won't you try the forks, madame?"

Madame de Rais cradled her belly protectively. I doubt either Gilles or I imagined precisely what was passing through her head. It is only after the fact that I must see her thus, great with her second child as she made her guests at home. The swelling had happened imperceptibly to our child's drawn-out view of the world. But we could read worry, no doubt about it, and again Madame's attempt to cover hesitation with grace.

"And how kind of you to come to me at this time, to offer to godmother this child—"

"But it is nothing, madame. A pleasure. And what pleasures are left to an exile such as myself but hopes to influence future generations? To see the little ones of my friends well born, well grown, well matched—there is nothing else."

"Madame la duchesse is most gracious."

And I suppose such words finally relieved Madame's concerns, for her hands left her belly and went for the fork. She ate, and managed to not even poke her gums with the tines.

Besides the forks, the duchess had oranges.

She offered one to Gilles that very first night, tousling his hair— which annoyed if not frightened him—and showing him how to peel it. He gave me the first wedge.

"What a generous child you are raising, madame," the duchess exclaimed, then turned to adult company. She didn't stay to see how that child waited until I showed no signs of shriveling up and dying from my tidbit before he ate the rest.

Of course, once we associated the fragrance with the wonderful, sweet taste, the rest of the oranges became a powerful temptation. In the great wooden bowl, just at eye level in the center of the hall's high table, the golden pyramid stayed stacked. The smell filled the hall so we hated to go there almost as much as we hated the thought of the yard.

Every time we could not avoid the hall, Gilles swallowed hard at the extra juices in his mouth, and dared another sideways glance at the wonderful orange heap.

Then he'd look away and say, "She still looks like a witch."

Skeins of Well-Carded Tow

Valentine Visconti's presence certainly enlivened things at our quiet castle of Blaison. After a late bedtime that very first night, a messenger came for her from Paris. By the time Gilles and I got up, the next morning, all her witch's equipment was being loaded back up into the *charet.*

To Madame's continued expressions of dismay that her guest was to leave her so soon, the duchess replied, "My lord husband had made a gesture of peace to his cousin Burgundy. Burgundy has accepted. In the reign of such amity, my ban of exile will certainly be revoked—"

Gilles and I stood side by side in the doorway—as far as we dared go into the yard. Together we watched the carved wooden case holding the silver forks carried out on the top of a pile of similar chests.

Before Gilles' tight little body burst like a pin-stuck bladder with his growing relief, a second messenger churned the enclosure's mud. If we did not know Orléans' fleurs-de-lis arms before this day, we certainly came to know it afterward, on all his men, coming and going.

"Alas!" the duchess cried.

"What says my lord the duke now?" Madame asked, trying to succor her guest.

"False deceiver! Burgundy refuses to grant me my place at my husband's side."

Later, Gilles and I overheard the messenger tell the servants by the kitchen fire, "My lord the duke of Orléans asked for a few other requests more important than his wife's return to favor first." By that time, all the baggage was making its weary way back inside the keep: the forks there on the kitchen table once more.

Later still, in a hospitable attempt to settle the women over their needlework in the bright solar, Madame de Rais asked her guest, "What news of court? We are so far from Paris here at Blaison, almost among the foreigners in Brittany. We are exiles here—"

Madame stopped in midsentence, blushing with confusion at the look she saw cross her regal guest's face and the anxious tittering of the lady's maids. Too late she realized the pain she must have inflicted on one exiled indeed.

"I mean," she stammered, fumbling stitches and her thimble together, "have you any good word of your brother-in-law, his Most Christion Majesty the King? How is his health, Mother Mary aid him?"

The duchess sighed and stitched with concentration. She paused just long enough to dramatize her grief, her saintly patience, but not so long as to lose her audience.

Then she sighed again and spoke. "Alas, it is the will of heaven to try our King and our country with this malady."

"The"—Madame's voice dropped to whisper the word—"*madness* persists?"

I pricked up my ears. When a grown-up whispered, that was always a good time to listen. So was any mention of the word "madness." People in Château Blaison were usually speaking of me when they said it. "Poor Jean—and his mad fits." My scarred hand didn't burn, as it usually did when I was the subject. Still, another's madness was equally important—for what it might mean for me.

"It comes and goes," the duchess said, "without warning or mercy. When sanity comes, our sovereign looks favorably on Monseigneur le duc, my husband. Sometimes, then, I almost begin to believe it may be possible for me to return to court, for my husband and me to be reunited, for my children to have a father again. At other times, just as rapidly, the demon returns. The demon lets the King look upon my lord Burgundy with innocent favor, never realizing how he is used, how he is led by Burgundy into policies precisely at odds with those he just declared, from those that would most benefit my family—as well as all of France."

"You have seen him when the fit is on him? Is he truly mad?" Madame dropped her voice. "Is he dangerous?"

"When I was allowed to see him, after his first fit, he seemed well. Paler, thinner, perhaps. Blackened around the eyes. Like a man who has wrestled weeks with a long and lingering fever."

"Or with a demon."

Madame gave voice to what the whole room was thinking, for they all crossed themselves. My mother bent to help Gilles make the sign. My milk brother, threading bobbins on the floor, protested, a spool clutched in his hand.

The duchess continued: "But the first time I came to truly believe the tales they told me—and to truly fear and pray for the poor man's soul—was at the ball they have since called the Ball of the Savages. You have heard of this, Madame de Rais?"

Madame de Rais smoothed the deep blue brocade protectively over her swollen belly and said, "I have heard, madame, that at this ball your husband . . ."

"No doubt they have told you lies," the duchess was quick to assume. "All lies." Passion made hot pink blotches high on her thin pinched cheeks though she did not raise her voice.

"No doubt," Madame concurred.

"And no doubt you would like to hear what really happened?"

"I would indeed." Madame leaned forward, draping her hands anxiously over her frame, stitchery forgotten. Then she remembered her needle again, almost as if it had pricked her. "I mean, I would hate to remain in misjudgment of anyone."

"Then I shall tell it to you."

The duchess took three rhythmic, deliberate stitches within her frame, composed her face, and began.

"It was nearly fifteen years ago now, in January, the Tuesday after Candlemas. There was feasting, dancing, a masquerade. What demon possessed those young men?"

"Saints preserve us," Madame exclaimed and everyone crossed herself.

"His Majesty and five companions—the young Hugonin de Gui-say was among them, the count of Joigny, Charles de Poitiers—lively young men, yes, but of the best families. The King and these five companions disguised themselves as hairy savages from Asia. The costumes were ingenious, of fine lawn and flesh-colored, fitting from neck to ankles almost like a second skin."

Madame said, "By my faith, they must have seemed quite na-ked," to another flutter of crossing hands.

"So they did, which more people ought to have taken as mad-ness, not just mere high spirits. Some modesty remained, however, when to these garments, like tufts of shaggy fur, the young lords attached skeins of well-carded tow."

"How did they attach it?" ventured the maid-in-waiting who was taking her turn at the spinning wheel.

"With pitch and beeswax, alas."

"Why alas?"

"In time. I will tell you and you will see. The final savagery of their costume was to lace themselves together so that all six men moved like one great savage beast—or a fuzzy caterpillar—so one could not move without his companions coming, too. In this way, prancing and shrieking and cavorting along, they entered the ball and diverted the rest of the guests exceedingly.

"Now, Monseigneur le duc and I were late to arrive. And when we did, my husband commented to me how curious it was that all the servants holding torches were standing along the walls where there were already sconces. The usual custom was for them to stand in the middle of the company."

"Naturally," said Madame de Rais, "I would instruct my lads to do so. Where their light could be of more use."

"Then my husband saw what had diverted all the rest of the attention as well, the cluster of writhing, dancing, tow-thatched sav-ages.

"As for myself, I had stopped near the threshold to greet Ma-dame la duchesse de Berry. By some divine chance, the King, seeing myself and his aunt there, decided to loose the laces that bound him to his companions and come across the hall to see us. God bless the inspiration! For at the same time my husband, suspecting his brother

to be among the savages, had decided he must pay them the compliment of a closer look. He snatched the torch from the hand of the
nearest servant and took it to the dark center of the room.

"An accident. By God, it was an accident. But certainly, had my
lord taken but a moment to consider, as whoever ordered the torch-
bearers to the walls had done—Just consider a torch, sputtering
sparks, anywhere near that writhing, jumping mass of pitch-soaked
tow—

"Mother Mary pity us." The duchess crossed herself and the
entire room followed suit. "My husband meant no harm, but the
most awful harm was God's will. One spark caught and, laced together as they were, it was only the blinking of an eye before all five
young men were an explosion of shrieking flame, the wax and pitch
melting and clinging to melting skin.

"The air sickened with the smell as of five witches' pyres all set
on one day. And there was no wind or fresh air to ease the assault
of hell to the nose, trapped as we were between paneled and tapestry-
hung walls, blackening with the soot. What could we do? What could
any of us do? No one could do more than I, and that was little enough.
Instantly, I took off my still weather-damp cloak and flung it over
my lord the King lest the flying sparks reach him as well. So I held
him tightly in my arms as he whimpered like a child for fear."

"Did they perish?" asked the maid. "All the five young lords so?"

"All but the young Nantoillet. Farthest from the kindling, he had
time to use his wits, to draw a dagger, to cut the binding laces and
fling himself like a flaming torch into the nearby keg of water where
the servants brought the trenchers to rinse them out between drafts.
He will wear the scars of that night for life, disfiguring a once glori-
ously handsome face.

"But he was the fortunate one. The count of Joigny died there
at the scene. The bastard of Foix as well, crying out, 'Save the King!
Save the King!' He died not realizing the King was not among the
mass of burning flesh around him. Messires de Poitiers and de Guisay
were less fortunate still, dying after two days, in agonies."

Another flutter of hands signing the cross went around the
room, like white moths over a cabbage field.

"Before the fire was extinguished, His Majesty fled the room. I followed after, and it is then that I had my first vision of the King's madness. I followed him to a small salon where he could flee no farther. Because he could not flee, he paced, or ran, rather, very quickly, as if pursued, from one far corner of the salon to the other. He seemed completely convinced he was still making progress.

"Having by now seen the deadly nature of the costume he had on, His Majesty stripped himself of it as he ran, tearing at tow and whole cloth as well. He paced now in only short braies. The room was safe of torches. But it had no fire either and the air was frigid enough so I could see his gasping breaths through the fog of my own. The quick, hard steps of his naked feet slapped back and forth across the cold parquet floor.

"I confess, perhaps I ought to have been more ashamed to be with my brother-in-law, dressed as he was. But truly, I thought he might do himself harm. It seemed very possible, so distracted was he. And I kept hoping he would retake my cloak against the chill. He would not, though his teeth were chattering over the moans of his shivers.

" 'Pray, come, Your Grace,' I begged him again and again.

"But 'They are after me,' he kept saying. 'They will kill me. I will die in flames.'

"I could not convince him that by the favor of God he had escaped that fate.

" 'Pray come,' I said again. 'You must come and show yourself to your queen. No doubt she is mad with grief, thinking you must be among the men in the conflagration.' "

The duchess paused, seeming in want of encouragement. So Madame, ever the diligent hostess, gave it to her. "But he would not?"

"He would not." The duchess pricked at her canvas, as if the scene she described were re-created there. "Over and over he kept saying—"

"What did he say?"

"It was his madness, alas, but he kept saying: 'The queen? I have no queen. I am married to a monster, a monster who would set fire to the very bed I lie on. Keep her away, for the love of God.' Such things as that.

"And then I determined, well, perhaps I should go and fetch help, seeing as I could do nothing alone.

" 'I will go and fetch your clothes. Your valet, men to help you,' I offered.

"But as I turned to go he suddenly leaped out of his pacing and grabbed me by the arm. Then he addressed me with such words as I—"

Again the pause, the passionate spots of pink on her thin cheeks.

"Such words, madame?"

" 'My sister,' he said, over and over, clinging to me in nothing but the barest linen around his loins. 'My sister, you must not leave me. You must never leave me. You are the only soul in the world who has pity on me. The rest of the world would kill me. Only you would have mercy on me, my kind, gentle, beautiful sister.' "

More crosses, accompanied by murmurs of despair. "What is a woman to do?"

"Such is the madness of the King?" Madame asked.

"Such it is. And even after the men came and found us and helped him, raving, away, he called for me."

"The queen?"

"Isabeau he cannot remember. 'Who is this strange woman?' I have heard him ask when she comes weeping to him. 'Give her what she wants but then send her away. She annoys me.' "

"But you, madame?"

"He has never failed to know my name. To beg his attendants to send for me when he will not let them touch him to comb the nits and tangles from his hair, to change his clothes, to wash his own filth from him, to tend the wounds he has inflicted on himself. Even when he denies his own name, calls himself Richard, and tries to rub his own fleur-de-lis from the walls, to throw stones through windows where he sees his arms set in stained glass. Only I, he says, can ease the devils that torment him."

"Alas for Charles. Alas for France," Madame de Rais exclaimed. "But then, my lady, why are you not at your brother's side, if he needs you so?"

"The matter is simple," the duchess said. "I am from Milan, famous for its sorcerers. They say my father the duke has designs on

France. He is supposed to have whispered to me as I left to come to my betrothal, 'When I see you again, daughter, you shall be the queen of France.' " As I live, he wouldn't say such things."

"I am surprised," Madame suggested, "that your husband was not sent into exile with you. He was the one who held the candelabra up to the costumed men, after all."

This did seem a knotty question and the duchess did not answer it to my complete satisfaction. "You know how it is for us women," she said with a sigh. "We often take on the sins of our men. And we are glad to do it, are we not? My lord must remain in Paris, to see to his interests."

Madame was among the ladies who joined their guest in a sigh. They obviously found no difficulty with this explanation. "I am glad to learn that the rumors are totally unfounded," Madame said.

I wondered if the lady of the castle had been tempted to decline the duchess the invitation for her visit at first. Something in her voice said she had, but was now relieved she had not.

"Of course they are. My husband the duke wants to set himself upon the throne? What nonsense is this? Long before his madness, Charles had fathered heirs. A brother does not inherit before sons. What are such fools thinking? That a minority would be less chaos for us here in France than a madness?"

Madame stroked her belly thoughtfully, then shot a glance of concern so intense it was almost anger at Gilles, who had been wiping at a runny nose. "Children can die so easily, madame, God shield them."

I suppose this glance toward us on the floor gave me the thought that I might in fact join in. It had certainly brought my mind to the talk with sharper hearing. "Charles," I repeated so loudly and with such wonder that the women did not continue their stream of speech over it.

I could tell by my mother's eyes she thought I was about to have a fit of my own. Indeed, it seemed so to me as well, for I certainly had a sudden, vivid repetition of the Vision's words about a King named Charles in my head, so clearly I turned quickly here and there, expecting to see—what, I cannot say. The King, perhaps. Vision. Or perhaps the old Hermit of St. Gilles.

"Charles the son of Charles the son of Charles. He rises to take the place of his ancestor Charles called the Great, Charlemagne, in the holy city."

Because the duchess' talk had stopped and all were turned to me, I said, "The name of our King is Charles?"

"Certainly, child." Madame's tone told me she wondered whether she should stop her castle's usual indulgence for children's chatter in deference to her guest. She had a look fearing madness as well.

"Is he the son of Charles?" I asked, ignoring other warning looks.

"Yes, the late King bore the same name."

"And his father?"

"Jean the Good."

I sighed with a child's exaggerated disappointment. "Then he is not the King in the prophecy."

Now Madame certainly would have stopped me, but that the duchess herself asked, "What prophecy is that, child?"

I told them as simply as I could about the Vision and the words the Hermit told me were written in ancient books.

"I am amazed . . ." my mother began.

"So am I," the duchess said. "Such knowledge in one so young."

"I am amazed," my mother repeated, "that he remembered what happened so long ago, when he was younger still."

The duchess shook her head. "Certainly this cannot be the Charles mentioned in the prophecy, son of Charles though he be. His Majesty's malady precludes any greatness."

"God and His Mother may vouchsafe a miracle," Madame offered hopefully.

"Where there is prophecy there might indeed be miracle," Mother added her own hope.

I suppose the duchess had seen too much of the world away from quiet Blaison, for she continued to shake her head sadly, though her tongue was silent.

I had young hopes of my own, hopes for my own generation. Without as yet being able to put it into words, I passionately wished that all the wonders of the world might not be done before I was grown.

"This Charles might have a son," were the words I found to express my hopes. "Has he a son named Charles?"

"Yes, his firstborn was named Charles," the duchess said. "But that boy died very young, God save him, before I ever came and married monseigneur le duc, in fact. Then there was a second Charles, but that boy died in his ninth year. The Dauphin is now his majesty's third son. He is named Louis."

The duchess' words rang with authority, so I fell silent, rejoining Gilles with his bobbins. I knew I should be glad, as my mother's face showed me she was, that I had not demonstrated to the noble guests that Blaison could be the equal of Paris when it came to the curse of madness.

But I couldn't deny the things I had heard in my head, the very closeness to Vision—"Charles the son of Charles the son of Charles." The words echoed so loudly that for some time I couldn't hear any more of the grown-ups' talk, much less any of Gilles' prattle.

"Let not all the great deeds be done before I'm grown," I whispered back to the speakerless words. But in the face of the duchess' certainty, I didn't see how it could be so.

9

Blood Fanned on New-Fallen Snow

Five fleur-de-lis messengers came and went in the course of the first fortnight Valentine Visconti, the duchess of Orléans, was with us. The *charet* was partially loaded three times, then unloaded again.

During this time, Gilles robbed the spinning wheel of its tow and tried to paste it to his clothes with the tallow left over in a turnip lamp. In order to do this, he waited until the *charet* had gone from the yard, carrying the ladies to a nearby chapel for their devotions.

This attempt to play either "the savage" or "the King"—we never were quite certain which it was—had no worse effect than to ruin the heir de Rais' first little black velvet doublet. Still, my father whipped me for letting my charge do such a thing.

The second week of the stay, the oranges were moved to a smaller bowl. A tantalizing heap of them remained, and that week was full of their fragrance, too.

As the third week of the duchess' stay drew to a close, sometime late on St. Cecilia's Eve, Madame de Rais went down to childbed. She was still about it when we awoke the next morning.

"Breech birth," I overheard one of the ladies whisper. "This won't be an easy one."

And most of the women had vanished into Madame's room from which we were firmly excluded. There would be no haunting the women that day, no playing with bobbins between the pools of their skirts and listening to their talk.

There was other diversion. As part of a sudden energy that had come over her in the last day or two, Madame de Rais had ordered a pair of hogs slaughtered. "My women and I will be able to get the sausages made and the hams smoking," she had suggested, "before the child comes. And I would hate to be without good food for my noble guests in the meantime."

So the hogs had been duly kept without food and water in the shed in the yard all that night, which turned out to be the night of Madame's first pains. All night the creatures had complained louder than the woman at the little hunger and thirst they thought was the worst life could hand them.

On rising, the men decided the slaughtering should be done anyway, even without many female hands to help. I think they wanted something to distract them from the women's deep magic happening within walls.

Now, in the three short years of his life, Gilles had found nothing quite so fascinating as a hog butchering.

But the hogs were out in the courtyard.

And so was the duchess of Orléans' child-devouring *charet*.

We were obliged to stay alone in the exquisite orange scent of the hall, an even greater torture since no one had thought to feed us that morning.

Besides all her other strange possessions, Madame the duchess of Orléans also had two lapdogs, yipping balls of white, on which it was difficult to tell head from tail. They were annoying, demanding little beasts the castle's hounds would have devoured in a moment but that the hounds had been banished to the stables and the yard at the duchess' first arrival. The lapdogs were forbidden in the birthing room, too, which seemed long overdue justice to me. The only drawback to this was that it left them in the no-man's-land of the hall—alone with Gilles and me.

Gilles and I played at knighthood, straddling the hall's benches so we could ride at one another, the lapdogs making rather disheartening wolves with their frenzied yaps and little nips into the abused fabric of our hose.

After a while, Gilles grew bored of our game and wandered off. I didn't follow; he went in the direction of the latrine. He was at the age when women still wanted to help him at this business, hold him so he wouldn't tumble down the hole, across the stone face of the castle, and into the moat.

Sometimes when they had their hands full, they would call to me, "Yann, go with Gilles and see that he doesn't fall in."

But my charge had told me often, and in no uncertain terms, that he was old enough to like his privacy, same as any other man. I understood and so, with no women about to tell me otherwise, I let him alone.

After a while, when being a knight lost its appeal with no one to ride against, I began to wonder if perhaps Gilles hadn't fallen down the latrine after all. I thought I'd better go see.

I found him not in the latrine, but in the kitchen. The fire there burned strangely low, and as soon as a single serving maid bustled out, Gilles and I found ourselves most unnaturally alone in that place.

The serving maid had had a great iron-banded basin with her, and it was full of tools, a caping knife, the bone saw. I realize now she must have been heading for the courtyard and the hogs, being one of the unmarried maids, but at the time I'd thought she was bound for the birthing room. I shivered little six-year-old shivers of awe at the power of women and of life, wondering that they would need to cut bone in order to work their magic in Madame's room. Perhaps they would cut little slivers of bone to piece together an infant foot. Just where on Madame's anatomy they might cut it from caused another rain of shivers.

I walked around Gilles, who stood still in the middle of the kitchen. I poked into places that were still strange to me after all the time I'd spent in that room because usually there were women to shoo me away from the spits, from the salting troughs, from the oven, from the knives. I walked around looking at these things, touching them, thinking about women making babies and making things to eat and about how hungry I was.

The squeal of hogs from the courtyard brought me to myself.

"Do you want to go see the hogs?" I asked Gilles.

"No." His voice sounded very small, very thoughtful.

"Are you afraid of the *charet?* Because it's daytime now and we can stay at the other side of the yard and the men will be with us.

They will be frying sweetbreads in a little while, after they've washed them and all."

The thought of browning butter and herbs on the nubbly organs made my mouth water.

I repeated, "Are you afraid of the *charet*, my lord Gilles?"

Still he didn't look at me, the smear of summer freckles just beginning to fade from the bridge of his nose, a tumble of black curls in his eyes. His gaze fixed unwavering before him.

They must have stuck the first hog now. The squeals sawed through the castle ashlar, shifting patches of chill on the spine. Madame de Rais punctuated the beastly cries as well. Sometimes it was difficult to tell which was which.

"Why do they kill hogs?" No hint of pity or cringing packed his voice, no sense that the noises grating on stone were like fingernails on slate to his ears. He was curious, pure and simple.

"Hogs must die so we may live. We eat their flesh, by the will of God. That is the cycle of the world." I think I'd heard my mother say something like that at some time or other.

"These hogs must die so my little brother may live?" I don't know how he knew what the child would be. I was the one supposed to See such things. I hadn't Seen this, though the women had sometimes teasingly asked me. He must have known the sound of his mother's cries. White pinched the corners of his full little mouth.

"A little baby cannot eat pork for many months," I told him.

"Then what must die for my brother to live?" he asked. "So the snake won't eat him."

"What snake?"

"On the *charet*," he said, as if I were a simpleton.

"The snake won't eat him."

Gilles tossed his curls as a precocious child does to show he does not believe the tales with which he is coddled.

"Are you afraid of the *charet*?" I asked sympathetically, for I must admit I still was.

"I will not be." His voice was firm with certainty. Then, "Come, Yann, and touch this."

At that point, I saw what it was that so fascinated him. In their rush to aid Madame the previous night, the maids had washed the duchess' forks but had no time to put them back in their velvet-lined case. The utensils lay now in a double rank on the thick wooden kitchen table, catching the little light as if they were the source.

"Touch what?" I whispered, reacting to the momentousness in his voice.

"Touch a fork."

I looked at him. He did not move his eyes from the forks. I moved my hand toward them.

"Not that hand." He pushed it away, my left hand, the hand I always reached with. "The other hand."

After a moment of my silent doubt, he explained. "That hand is already bad. If the touch of the witch's fork may blast us, it will only blast something already bad."

The idea that my twisted, angry red hand could be useful in some way more than compensated for the hurt his comment on my infirmity might otherwise have caused.

For drama rather than fear, I slowly lifted my crippled hand across the scoured oaken tabletop until it touched a fork. Then I slipped a crooked finger under the silver and picked it up in the best way I could.

Gilles drew in his breath. "Now try the other hand."

I did. I have sensation in my left hand. I could feel the cold metal better, the humps and grooves of the pattern of grapes and vines engraved into the silver on the handle. The fork was heavy, rich. A little magical—yes.

Gilles nodded. "Good," he said, then quickly snatched up a fork of his own, as if it might be a burning brand.

The sight of silver flashing in his hand delighted him. He laughed in triumph, swung his prize here and there like a sword, then shoved it daggerlike into his belt.

"Let's go," he announced, his imperious self once more.

"To see the hogs?"

"Not yet. I'm hungry."

"Perhaps I can find us some bread in here . . ."

"Not bread. No. Something better."

Gilles led the way back into the hall. There, rather than charging each other with the forks, as I had expected, he shoved his father's armchair—brocaded and fringed with the silken tassels—up to the great table. He climbed up and then sat right on the table, his little knobs of knee coming through the worn hose and embracing the curves of the great wooden bowl. There, and with the aid of his newly won tool, he proceeded to gut and then devour every last one of the duchess' oranges.

The skins had shrunk tight and hard during their weeks of display. There were even patches of whitish mold into which his little thumbs stuck, at which I saw him give a start. The smell of mold intensified the sweet fruit fragrance until it nauseated. And, of course, three-year-old hands were not quite up to the challenge.

But he sang a little something under his breath. And nothing deterred him.

I did not join Gilles in his gorging. I simply stood and watched with fascination.

The pulpy mess of hulls he left seemed larger than the golden pyramid with which he'd started. Gilles clambered down. There, the lapdogs greeted him. He stopped to rub each fuzzy white belly, but he didn't stop long. The fork shoved into his belt put a swagger in his step. I followed that swagger out into the yard.

Snow was falling. Fast-flying flakes stung like pinpricks on our faces, warmed and softened by so many days inside. Looking up into that swirl against the darkened sky made me dizzy.

I thought at least Gilles would stop as I did to look around the yard, to test it for safety since the death lamps had gone, burned out, and the turnip hulls tossed to fatten the very hogs who had now come to their time.

But Gilles didn't hesitate a moment. Keeping a safer distance, I followed him directly to the *charet*. Here, climbing on a wood pile and then among the great wheel's spokes, he managed to reach up to the serpent painting. He jabbed the fork into its eyes and teeth until they were nothing but raw and harmless wood, flecks of bright paint and gold leaf mixing with the flakes of snow that drifted in under the overhang.

He repeated the job on the other side of the *charet* where the image was duplicated, all the while chanting the little something under his breath. I couldn't hear the words, but I knew they gave him power, like a spell. And I knew enough about magic not to try to stop him.

When at last he clambered down from the *charet*, Gilles walked straight to the slaughter without a backward glance. We were in time to see the second beast hoisted upside down into the gambrel and stuck. The innards of the first were already tumbling in a great blue-white fall through the rigid black hairs of the carved-open belly, steaming life-heat into the air that swirled with flakes.

"Birds of night, spare the entrails of the child born this night," murmured wall-eyed Pierrot as he tossed a length of intestine into the fire in the age-old gesture. The burning stench made me turn my face away. "We offer you this life instead of a better life."

Then Pierrot fished into the remaining warmth and found the sweetbreads, which he handed to the maid. She began frying them, just as I'd hoped. Another man began to chop up the pink lights for the eager hounds.

"Ho, there, young master." It was difficult to tell which way Pierrot was looking but he winked, which made Gilles assume the look was friendly, at least. Pierrot had moved now to hold the blood bucket under the second snout and had to shout over the dying squeals. "Come to oversee your sausages, have you?"

Pierrot moved back to rescue the juicy kidneys out of their fat pads in the opened belly. Then he deftly tied off the bladder and washed it in water from the cauldron steaming over the outdoor fire where the maid's frying pan had borrowed a corner. Pierrot handed the greyish oval to Gilles, giving him careful instructions about how he must let it dry and then fill it with winter peas.

"It'll make a right nice rattle for your new little brother or sister," Pierrot said with a jerk of his wall eye toward the keep.

"Brother," Gilles said firmly as he accepted the gift as his due with orange-sticky hands, hands coated with a thin layer of white dog hair.

"It will be as God wills." Pierrot grinned.

I knew Gilles would keep the rattle for himself. Holding it like a royal orb, he sat on a stool near the warmth of the boiling cauldron, the lord of all he surveyed. Hogs' blood fanned red on the new-fallen snow at his feet.

Second Antiphon

A Weft of Swaddling Bands

Guillemette La Drapière mopped her brow. She had loosed her own laces and was down to linen, with no thought of display for her husband's wares. Heat may be well for the laboring woman, but it was hard on her attendants.

The air in the master chamber stifled. They were burning their third log and it, like its predecessors, had required four women to drag it in. Every possible source of draft had been stuffed with rags: where draft could enter, so could evil spirits. Heat was known to ease a birth, soften the woman's flesh, hastening the readiness of the child to enter a world he knows may be cold. Just as stoking a fire will quickly brown loaves in the oven.

Looking at Madame de Rais, however, where her attention had been for over forty-eight hours, Guillemette wasn't at all certain she would swear by heat from now on. The laboring woman seemed melted, like a puddle of wax at the base of a candle. A sacrifice at the altar of womanhood.

When they'd first brought in the straw and strewn it before the fire in anticipation of the actual birth, the room had been full of the fresh, clean, grassy smell. There had been all the life-promise of a haymaking. That had vanished now, the straw trodden, its hopeful smell gone, like everything else, to one pool of women's tears and sweat, and the smell of smoke at close quarters.

Right from the start they'd stripped Madame de Rais naked. All things that might hinder—girdles and lacings—they'd put from her.

They had had plenty of time to do up her hair in the mother's style, smooth with ivory combs, without binding braids, though still out of the way.

Guillemette had been to any number of birthings where there'd been no time and it was considered inauspicious to birth with the hair awry. But she was beginning to reconsider that procedure, too. Since those first hopeful hours, there'd been the time—and the pained frenzy—to tumble the sweat-drenched brown to a mop once again.

Madame's plain white linen headdress remained, however, straightened from time to time by a weary attendant. Besides that, she wore only Monseigneur de Rais' old brown velvet doublet, the sleeves removed, to which was pinned the duchess' contribution: an eaglestone. The best of its kind, the best money could buy, this shiny black stone one could encircle with a thumb and fingers. When Madame shook with pains, the stone rattled like a bell. Bits of pebble— or something—had been sealed inside by the Hand of God.

If not by the spell of a sorcerer.

"Yes, it is the best money can buy," the duchess kept saying. Money was, in the end, her final authority.

The duchess was not faring well now, going into this third evening without sleep. She snapped at everyone, even Madame, her voice shrill, larded with self-pity as if she were the one in most pain. Staying up one night had been a lark, a pleasure. It was like the balls and entertainments she missed in Paris. But three nights—and no chance of beauty sleep between—this was an imposition.

Especially when it was plain that no amount of money could remedy the situation.

The rest of the women had given up as well, though in a quieter way. They dozed, muttered a little, and shifted in their heaps on bed and chests when Madame screamed. Then they turned and dozed again.

Guillemette knew it was on her shoulders. Well, she had been the one with too much confidence and now she was punished for it. The duchess had offered to bring a handy woman from Orléans— the woman who had attended all eight births to the duke's house—

and Madame had refused. Guillemette, so confident of herself, had allowed her mistress this confidence as well.

False confidence, she saw now. Now that it was too late. She had been a fool. Fooled by luck.

Guillemette had her tricks like any midwife. That was why the room was so hot. That was why Madame wore Monseigneur's doublet. That was why candles burned before every image of St. Margaret within half a day's ride.

That was why Monseigneur himself had been set to chopping wood, a servant's job, but known to be the best thing a husband, the author of the difficulty, could do to help the process, be he beggar or king. Monseigneur had already wearied at his simple job twice.

Menfolk! Guillemette was too weary to give the word all the scorn it deserved. They thought they knew the meaning of the word labor. Ha! Who ever heard of a woman setting down the ax in the middle of a birth and wandering off for a respite? Not that most didn't call for reprieve at some point during the process. Just a moment, just long enough to catch one's breath, to walk away for a bit, to study the business and consider if it was truly worth continuing. Or perhaps backing up and starting another way. God didn't give women that choice. Probably because too few of them would ever return to the work once released.

Guillemette had learned her tricks just by virtue of being a woman in this weary world. Her own births had been easy, almost too easy, for they had made her grow silently skeptical at the fear with which other women sometimes spoke of "going down." There had been the death of that little girl, Marietta—God rest her—when Yann, her firstborn—God shield him, too—had been just three. But the labors themselves had been fast and easy. Hardly time to call for help and bring in the straw.

Why, the last time it had seemed less bother to take herself out to the byre, just catching one of the serving girls to warn her on the way. Blessed Mother Mary had had the right idea. By the time the maid reappeared, panting, with linen thread and a knife clutched in her sweating hands, little Riog had already been howling lustily, wriggling there, pink and spumey wet on the hay.

Because they'd come easy to her—and given her such pleasure—Guillemette had taken an interest in such things. She'd taken to going out with Old Yvonne here in the neighborhood of Blaison, asking questions of every new mother she'd ever met.

Going with Old Yvonne, they had only lost one babe—two actually. They were twins, months early, no bigger than your spread hand, half the size of a normal babe between them. That had been an aberration, something she never hoped to see again, those little toadlike things jerking, struggling for a life that couldn't be theirs.

Guillemette assumed she had done with such horrors, certainly those that were the product of a dank hovel, and nothing to do with the wealth of the Château Blaison. When Old Yvonne had died, Guillemette, nursemaid to the young lord Gilles de Rais, had confidently offered herself to the women of Blaison. She had experience, she had skill. She had a certain feel for the darker, older powers of women.

Before this deep November evening, she had called what she knew "knowledge" with a certain amount of pride.

Now she realized she had only ever been lucky. The luck had run out. The horror stories were true. Every one of them.

Why did it have to be with Madame? Of all people? Madame, who was like a sister to her, what with their children so of an age and most of the other female company in this place only coarse peasants.

For a long while, Guillemette hadn't been able to figure out what the matter was. This was Madame's second, after all. Young Messire Gilles, for all the ominous prophecies shadowing his advent, had come easily enough, although Madame, being a lady, had had to make a fuss of it. If there were to be any problems, Yvonne had said, they would likely show with the first. There'd been none.

For the longest time these past two laboring days and nights, Guillemette truly had believed in witchcraft, what with all the duchess' talk since the moment of her arrival. That's why she'd set the girls to stuff even the slightest cracks with their rags so assiduously.

Now she was beginning to understand a little more. The last two times she had greased her hands and Madame's privates with new hog grease from the kill and gone up inside, she had felt it. She had felt the neck of the womb, thinned as it should be but opened no more than a finger, with no palpable difference from one venture to the next. Beyond the neck she did not feel the hard roundness of a baby's head, pushing as it ought to. Her first reaction—causing a quick and discomforting withdrawal of the hand—had been "monster." But now she realized that the "lots of little things" she felt did not have to be adder's eggs. They could be little feet. Little knees, perhaps. Little buttocks.

The child was the wrong way around.

For all her experience, Guillemette had never seen this presentation before. Yvonne had told her things to try if this happened, but had never had a chance to demonstrate. Guillemette had led the rest of the women through trials of these processes throughout the afternoon. They'd propped up Madame's hips with cushions. They'd worked at the belly like bread dough, trying to force the bulge around. But the little behind was too tightly engaged and all their shoving and pushing only increased Madame's agonies.

Guillemette was in charge; she had ordered help to be sought. Nobody knew, however, where to send. She'd merely told two riders to set off in opposite directions, to ask at every house until they found some wisewoman. They might keep going until next week.

And next week would be too late. Tomorrow would probably be too late.

Guillemette felt herself alone. Certainly the duchess was more trouble than good. Several times Guillemette had suggested that the noblewoman might like to go rest in another room.

The duchess, like everyone else, was tired enough to be very stubborn. "I must see it through," she said. "I couldn't sleep anyway, hearing her screams down the hall."

The lowliest maid felt the same way. They were all women. It could happen to any of them. They were not like men to put the ax aside. They must see it through.

Guillemette was in charge and alone. And she knew her luck had run out. Her luck and her skill, all at once. As the evening crept into night, she knew she was going to lose one of them. One, certainly. Probably both.

Guillemette's mind kept flinching from the only thing she could imagine left to do. The child could be cut from the woman's belly.

The draper's wife had heard of the process. It was the subject of several popular ballads, if nothing else. But it was dreadful. Witchery, indeed.

And cutting out a child was man's work, not woman's. She would call for the master of the castle, consult with him. He would lay aside his ax. He would decide. She would not be alone or in charge then.

Monseigneur would take the knife and cut through the taut belly flesh to save his child. Either he or one of his men. They would cut her and the insides would come steaming out, as they must have done with the pigs in the yard.

At least then, Guillemette thought, it would no longer be in her own inadequate hands. She got out of her chair and headed slowly for the chamber door. Nobody even raised a head to see her go.

Only Madame. Madame opened one pain-glazed eye from where she lay, half on the straw, half up against one of the great bed's posts. She opened the eye, pleading.

"Guillemette . . ." She no more than sighed.

"I'm here." Guillemette stooped, put up her hand to feel the stumbling pulse at the hot throat slick with sweat.

"Where are you going?"

"Nowhere, madame."

"My husband—?"

"No, no. I had no thought of him."

Madame de Rais could say no more, but her eyes pleaded for the trial to end. Her lips were dry, slightly purple and peeling, like turnips set to roast too long in the fire.

Guillemette reached for a goblet on a nearby stool. She offered the suffering woman wine—"the redder the better," Yvonne had always said. Madame shook her head and a ripple passed through her throat; she was too nauseated.

Guillemette offered plain water and Madame took it, but not much. Not enough to change the ash-white on her lips. Madame's nether parts, too, were looking dangerously dry. No one could birth a baby without moisture.

Guillemette held Madame's hand through a pain so deep that it brought the mouthful of water back up to her lips. Guillemette helped Madame to cleanse her mouth and chin, for Madame herself was too far gone to care.

And then, as if the sharp smell of bile suddenly cleared her head, a thought came to Guillemette. It was one of those thoughts she knew came from a place beyond her, a realm of saints. Or ancient, life-loving Gods.

Perhaps, said the thought, the nausea was good.

Guillemette mused over that. They'd been so busy trying to prevent nausea. But she had often seen laboring mothers lose as much out the top as they would lose out the bottom, and usually near the end of the process. Perhaps—may it please St. Margaret—the end was near.

"Come on," she said, grasping Madame under one limp arm. "Let's walk some more."

No one had had the energy to walk the struggling woman for quite some time. She shook her head, no. Guillemette persisted— mostly because if she did not, she would find herself going after the husband instead. She motioned for the most vigorous of the maids to come and take the other arm and together they hauled Madame, who was too weak to protest, to her feet.

As she got an arm around her patient, Guillemette happened to notice a small white puff of goose down clinging to the lord's brown doublet from the pillow on which Madame had been lying. Another inspiration hit her.

"Come, take this arm I've got," she quickly ordered the next closest maid.

Madame was not walking so much as being carried. Her legs seemed the consistency of the cooled aspic poured off boiled bones. But Guillemette's sudden activity brought the second maid to life and then, with a third, she set herself about opening the seam of the cushion's brocade and extracting a small bowl full of feathers.

If vomiting was a sign labor was nearing its climax, perhaps if more violent vomiting was induced—

The best way Guillemette knew to induce vomiting—lacking any mandrake root, fearing the effect of hemlock on both mother and child—was to make the patient swallow feathers. The mere thought of that many-fingered dryness at the back of the throat was enough to make the healthy gag.

Guillemette was suddenly full of anxious expectation. She let the maids, their mistress between them, make no more than half a circuit of the room. Then she ordered them to bring the mother back by the fire, to stand her over the straw again.

Guillemette shoved a pinch of feathers down her lady's parched throat as a mother bird feeds her helpless chicks. Madame vomited readily, but shortly Guillemette realized that not everything soaking her feet and hem was vomit. The waters had broken in a rush.

Guillemette called for light, for more pork grease, for her stool, and they came, for everyone was suddenly much more lively. Guillemette did her best not to dampen the excitement by commenting on the greenish tint she noticed to the waters on the straw. It might just be a trick of the firelight. Or vomit. Urgently she pulled up her stool and began to rub the warmed pig grease onto her hands.

As she turned to apply the same lubricant to her patient, she had the sudden impression that the reason Madame could not deliver was because all at once she had been enchanted into male form. Cautiously, Guillemette reached out and touched the thin bit of flesh dangling between her patient's thighs. It was a tiny, perfectly formed little foot and lower leg.

Amid the excited murmurs of the clustering women, Guillemette tried to grab the leg and give a little pull. It was like an eel: she couldn't get purchase. She wrapped a corner of her linen shift about the limb and did better, but nothing seemed to give.

"Hold it. Pull gently if you can," she ordered the closest woman.

She herself applied more grease and slipped in up around the tiny limb. She had to call for more light and shoo others away from what there was. Madame was moaning fearfully. Slowly, slipping this way and that and working by feel rather than the light she'd called for, Guillemette reached up into the womb itself, more open now, caught a second little foot and slowly, slowly pulled it free to hang beside the first.

Exclamations nearing triumph passed among the group.

"There. I knew I could not have paid so much for my eaglestone for nothing," the duchess declared.

And Madame even managed half a weak smile when the news was relayed up to her, held still on her useless legs by the maids. The next two pains brought down more: thighs, a little bottom.

"It's a boy!" was the bright news, coming ahead of the usual order of events.

Guillemette could not exult. She had begun to realize that these little parts were easy, too easy. In normal births, once the head was out, everything else slipped free this easily as well. The baby's great head caused the most difficulty. Coming this way saved the most difficult for last. The head could very well remain immovable, the chin snapped back by the force of the contractions, the little neck broken. They would be left with this most bizarre spectacle: a baby boy, perfectly formed, but dangling by the neck like a hanged man, unable to get the most vital nose and mouth out of the choking waters.

As the umbilicus appeared, grey and thickly veined, rising out of the little belly at eye level, this image of possible horror compounded. The cord was pulled very tight. It must be caught around something up above, around the child's neck, perhaps, completing the hanged man image. Surely with such tension, kinks were too likely.

Working quickly, Guillemette looped her finger between the tiny belly and the cord and tried to pull some slack, to keep the air coming for as long as the process ahead might take. She brought down hardly enough to allow her hand to pass through the space. The cord must indeed be stuck. And there was no way she could loosen it.

And was it her imagination? The light? Or were the tiny, visible limbs taking on a deathly blue cast? They weren't moving at all, although once beyond the birth canal the little legs had flexed up into the newborn's natural curl. This caused even more interference with what Guillemette knew she had to do.

She knew a baby's head had to rotate twice in order to make its way past the inner spines of the mother's pelvis. In her mind, Guillemette reversed the rotations, for a head coming out backward. But at least in this case she was not working blind. She could take the little trunk between her hands and turn it side to side so the head would go long and thin where the passage grew long and thin.

Madame's screams and a sudden drop in the little body said that the head was now engaged. Little hands appeared with the drop, perfectly formed with tiny nails and five fingers each. Fortunately the child had held them down and tight against his body. Otherwise, Guillemette hated to think of what dislocation might have happened to them.

Maybe my luck is returning, Guillemette thought, but quickly stifled the notion. She knew now the wages of pride. "God have mercy on us all," she said aloud instead and set the room to a frenzy of suddenly remembered prayers.

Not much more of the cord had come with that drop. And the tiny limbs, perfect as they were, had yet to move. They were definitely blue.

"Take his little weight," Guillemette instructed an assistant as she herself reached up and pressed along Madame's belly on the outside from just under the breast toward the pubis. Her hands left streaks of blood and fluid. The great mound of pregnancy was noticeably diminished.

"I . . . I must push," whispered Madame with sudden wonder. Pushing meant the end was near.

Guillemette knew pushing too soon was dangerous. Who knew what it could bring with that tangle of cord and chin up there? But she met the glaze of hope in Madame's eyes, took a breath, and gave a nod to go ahead.

Two rapid contractions, full of straining and screaming, followed close on one another's heels and then suddenly, there was the baby, whole, in a wad of bloodied linen, in the midst of loud prayers of thanksgiving.

Once the afterbirth had come, the women chose to help bear a collapsed Madame to her bed, leaving Guillemette alone with the child. That warned her, for usually they ignored the mother in the wonder of the baby.

Guillemette knew she must not tie off and cut the cord from placenta until she'd heard the first cry. She hadn't heard it. In fact, she doubted she'd seen the first twitch of movement. Although perfectly formed everywhere else, the little boy's face had suffered. He was badly bruised, his lips so swollen they seemed inhuman. He didn't work them as every other newborn she'd ever seen would do, looking for the breast. Could he even nurse with such ravaged lips? But nursing was beside the point if he didn't breathe.

Surely he looked dead. No wonder the rest of the women preferred to care for the mother, leaving Guillemette La Drapière holding the little body heaped with the still-attached afterbirth by the fire.

Guillemette was not going to give up on this baby yet, not after so many ups and downs of hopes and luck. She began to run through her repertoire of baby-reviving tricks.

She tickled the little feet. She caught him up by his heels and spanked him. She forced a finger in between the toothless gums and cleared out the matter caught there. She did the same with the little nostrils. She didn't like the greenish color of the stuff any more than she'd liked the greenish color of the waters.

She forced a trickle of warmed wine between the tiny lips but no swallowing action followed. The red liquid trickled right back out again.

She took a mouthful of wine between her own lips and sprayed it into the baby's reactionless face.

She dipped him over the head, afterbirth and all, in a warm bath swirled with strong liqueur. She wrapped him in fire-warmed linen. She held the placenta to the fire. She even set it in the coals for a moment, trying to force the blood back up the cord and into the tiny belly. The sickening smell of that procedure made her stop sooner than she wanted to.

Then Guillemette rocked back on her heels in the sodden straw, clutching the lifeless little bundle to her. She'd put a corner of linen over his tightly shut eyes. If he did choose to open them, the glow of the fire after the dark of the womb wouldn't make him change his mind about staying in this world. She raked her free, sticky hand through her hair under her disheveled coif as if she could rake her brains with the same gesture and harrow up anything else Yvonne or any other had ever told her.

"My baby. Can't I see my baby?"

Madame was washed up now, and had a wad of clean but old—old being softer—and fire-warmed linen between her legs. Another large length of linen had been folded into a triangle and placed over her sagging belly. The fold encased warming pepper, cinnamon, cloves, a spicy mixture that would coax the womb to creep back up again into its proper place after its exertions.

Guillemette didn't move.

"Can't I see my baby?" Madame repeated, to silence.

"The baby's dead," one maid finally spoke up.

When one would have thought her all screamed out, Madame burst forth with an even wilder lament.

"Send for the priest," the duchess ordered one of her women in a half whisper. "He is waiting nearby." Then she spoke louder, the edge of impatience to her voice. "I hope, Guillemette, you have not neglected to give the child a midwife's dousing."

Guillemette got to her feet in anger, turned, and stood there before them, clutching the little bundle. The duchess should not have said that thing. Not yet. There was hope. There must be.

In truth, what hope was there? Guillemette had tried everything on earth and heaven . . .

Heaven . . . Suddenly she remembered something, something not from Yvonne, but from her girlhood in Brittany.

"We must not give up," she said, letting her anger at the duchess firm her words. "Not yet. We must pray."

"Holy St. Margaret . . ." someone began, echoing all the lamps they'd set before all the shrines, a repetition of all the past hours' long, vain words.

"No, not St. Margaret," Guillemette said. "St. Anne."

"St. Anne? Our Lord's grandmother?"

The Breton words were vivid in Guillemette's mind as she translated them into the French: "Our Lady of the Bog."

The sacred title didn't sound nearly so dignified in French. She might have tried a different word. Stream, perhaps. Or lake. "Our Lady of the Lake" had a poet's ring to it. But the word was out and the women clung to it.

"Holy St. Anne, Lady of the Bog . . ."

They had all dropped to their knees by now, crossing themselves. Guillemette joined them, though it was difficult, by chance arrangement of the room, not to feel herself a priest there before a fire altar, elevating the flesh and blood of the little baby boy before them.

She prayed with them, but in Breton, the native words she remembered her mother saying that in all the room only she, Guillemette—and St. Anne, she was certain—could understand. They put her in mind of yet another rite.

"Everyone must promise something to the Lady of the Bog in her prayers," Guillemette said. "Everyone must be willing to give up something very dear to her heart in exchange for this one's little life."

Guillemette dropped back into Breton again to make her own promise. She thought of a piece of her husband's finest linen, edged with her own finest broidery.

"Holy St. Anne, Lady of the Bog . . ."

The words conjured a breath of bog cold into the tightly sealed room. Guillemette was only vaguely aware of the murmur of French promises from every soul before her. Even Madame had crossed herself, promising something.

But suddenly Guillemette became aware of the duchess' voice rising above all the others. "Anything!" The sharp, thin woman clutched the silver-set eaglestone in one hand, a string of pearls she had not removed in all the long hours of labor in the other. "Anything, O Lady of the Bog. What is mine is yours. In exchange for the life of this fair boy. Name it, and it is yours."

Guillemette felt a sudden shudder. At first she thought it was her own reaction to the duchess' wild, almost prideful words. Then she realized the source of the jerky movement was the bundle in her arms.

"He moves!" she cried, and found herself instantly surrounded. All the women scrambled up off their knees and crowded to see.

Lifting the corner of the linen, she saw the baby as lifeless as ever. But there was a sudden light in the fog of Guillemette's mind, like will-o'-the-wisps hovering over the bog. *Heart*, this light throbbed in her mind. The baby's heart must be strengthened. How to do this, Guillemette didn't know. "Heart" only released a second light, the thought "left pap" to her mind. So she bent down and took the tiny baby nipple—hardly more than a shadow on the chest, really—between her lips and sucked gently.

There was a second, more definite shudder, a jerk, a protesting toss of the chin, and the baby let out a feeble but audible yell.

The child gained vigor all the while she cut the cord. She left a good three finger's length so as not to hamper the boy's virility in any way. "A girl's should be cut as close as possible," Yvonne had always said. Guillemette tied the flesh off and bandaged it with rose water and linen against the belly.

His color improved while she carefully covered his head so the soul couldn't depart through the soft, pulsing butterfly-shaped soft spot on top. She covered his eyes so the light of the world would not damage the still-weak organs. The signs of life improved yet more while a slice of cooked apple was placed before his tiny anus to encourage the first tarry black matter to pass quickly.

By the time he was tightly swaddled—legs board-straight as they should grow, arms immobilized—and placed by his mother's side, Guillemette could hardly have told him from even the healthiest child she'd ever delivered.

Madame gave him her own breast. Guillemette had offered to wet nurse again, her little Riog being only four or five months at the time and there was no one else in the neighborhood available. In time, she would do so. And, in time, Sire de Rais would want to feed the little mouth pap on the point of his sword. But for this first suckle, Madame thought nothing of performing the function herself.

"He should be called René," Madame said. "René because he was dead, but was reborn to me."

"Thank St. Anne," murmured many in the room, conscious of the vows they had made.

"Thank you, Lady of the Bog," Guillemette said in the Lady's own Breton, but saying it gave her pause. Though generous, this Lady of ancient ways also kept strict accounts. She it was, at least to Guillemette's memory, who'd taken the great old sorcerer Merlin captive and even he could not take back what she claimed for herself.

Just as she thought it, Guillemette saw little Gilles push his way into the room. Is he the Lady's herald, she thought, come to make her claims?

There was nothing ominous about the little lad, however, barefoot and in his smock. Dog hair and—was it?—orange juice covered his hands. Poor mite, no one had thought to wash them before he went to bed. Guillemette looked around for a bowl of water—there must be one left around somewhere—to wash him up. This activity distracted her from the darker, nameless fear that had entered her heart at the little three-year-old's appearance.

Madame cooed at her older son. "Come, love. Come see your new brother."

Gilles lifted his chin a little to look, sniffed, and shrugged. He couldn't find much of interest in the small bundle, sleeping now, even with his mother's encouragement, hoarse with exhaustion, about "What good times you'll have together when he grows a bit," and "I think he has your father's nose. Do you?"

"Nanny." He turned to Guillemette instead and spoke with heightened maturity. "I think you'd better come with me."

The frisson of terror brushed her again but she said, "Yes, of course. I'll come and tuck you in, love."

Gilles rejected the babying with firmness.

"Not me," he said. "It's Yann. The fit. This one's bad."

And as she ran, Guillemette wondered if little René had been reborn by the grace of St. Anne of the Bog—but at the cost of her own firstborn.

Battened with Blackcherry

I came to myself in the great cupboard bed Gilles and I shared. We had a little stair to climb into it. Even after that, the feather ticking was so high and steep, we had to pull or push one another up.

Gilles was not there now to share how the far corner had the face of an old man, how the heavy, turned posts could transform the whole into a battle horse. He must have been spirited away to sleep with the maids during my fit. It would not have mattered if he had been there. The Visions I saw were not our usual fantasies. And they were all the more dreadful because I couldn't share them.

I heard my mother's coos of comfort and relief and the smell of blackcherry syrup filled my nostrils. The taste of it made me gag. This was the drink in which she diluted the leaves of mistletoe, dried and powdered with much difficulty because of the stickiness of the sap. She'd learned this recipe from the old Hermit of St. Gilles.

"No, it will not cure him," he'd said.

"What will it do, then?" she'd asked.

"Ease him."

That sounded good and she'd thanked the old man.

It was only after a moment or so that the Hermit had added, "It will turn his gift to the God."

And she wasn't quite sure what to make of that. I could tell by how she related the saying afterward, with a new inflection each time.

Nonetheless, Mother cut mistletoe whenever she could find it so as always to have a plentiful supply for my equally plentiful spells. She rarely found it growing on oaks. Usually an old apple tree provided the potion. Under such a tree, when the year and the moon were beginning, she would spread her blue cloak before climbing to cut the herb with a golden knife. She sang a song as she went about her work, the refrain of which was in the old tongue: "Hey derry down, down, down derry."

Mother justified her actions to others—others who frowned when she mentioned the source of her recipe—by saying, "Mistletoe was the very wood from which Our Lord's cross was so cruelly made. In those ancient days the plant grew to the size of a tree. But for its conspiracy, mistletoe was condemned to have no life but on other life, like a beggar. Still, some of the saving grace of its contact with the Christ lingers."

This past history was also responsible for its French name *herbe de la croix*, which means "herb of the cross." But that always seemed a French, a Christian, gloss to me, covering a more ancient holiness.

Such was the infusion with which my mother sought to cure my fits, and she never had cause to doubt its power. Nor had she ever had recourse, since the visit to the Hermit of St. Gilles, to cocks' blood or spring water drunk from the skull of a suicide or any of the numerous amulets one could buy to deal with the terrors of my disease.

Well as mistletoe dealt with the convulsions, however, I was certain it also brought on the dreams. I have no recollection of dreams before, almost never a fit without them after she began the therapy. I always became aware of the dreams first with the smell of black-cherry syrup in my nose and its nauseating sweetness coating my mouth. And as long as that smell and that taste lingered, the Visions had more reality to me than anything in this world.

"The baton" were the first two words out of my mouth after the fit that night young René de La Suze was born, died, and was born again. "The knobby staff has been planed."

The duchess of Orléans must have been by, always eager to put her hands to any crisis. Or else she'd been warned of my words at once, for I had not repeated them, delirious, too many times before I heard her sharp demand, "What says the child?"

"It is nothing, Madame la duchesse," Mother replied, hoping for calm and worried that Valentine Visconti might judge these signs of madness in her oldest son too severely. "He has these fits from time to time. He only dreams. It is nothing and will soon pass."

"Dreams, you say? Are they true dreams?"

"I . . . I know not," Mother replied. Her anxiety reverberated in my aching head and increased with both her exhaustion and annoyance at the duchess' interference.

"The baton, smoothed and flattened," I repeated earnestly, begging to be taken seriously.

" 'The baton,' he says." The duchess studied me, frowned at my mother. "Are you certain there is no truth there?"

My mother hinted to Valentine Visconti of the events three and a half years before in the wood of St. Gilles, how I had heard the voice of the deer—and received my crippled hand. "So please—just leave the child in peace."

The duchess nodded, graver still. "Then I must hear this present Vision, what he can remember of it."

I wanted nothing more than gentle hands to reach for me as I sank in the black and bloody Vision. Hands to catch reality and help to tame it. Much as she had always defended me, I'd never been able to win Mother's sympathy to the reality of the things I Saw. I could never make her enter my world. I could never get her to see its importance to everyday concerns. Her crooning, "A dream, love, just a dream," was part of what I screamed against. For what I Saw was never, never "just" a dream.

I turned to the place where the duchess' figure stood out vaguely against candlelight and the Vision. I tried to form words but failed.

"Child, can you hear me?" she asked. "Child, tell your Auntie Valentine what you see."

I worked my tongue through the numbing syrup. I was so anxious to bring someone else into this world, the terror and vividness of which I felt eating me alive.

"I see a porcupine. A silver porcupine."

My mother tittered nervously.

But my words made the duchess grow even graver. "Where do you see this porcupine?"

"A man."

"Yes?"

"A man wears it on a chain around his neck."

Valentine Visconti grew even paler and more pinched. "Where is the man?"

"Far away."

"Can you see him?"

"I see a palace. High walls. Vast gardens. You come upon the palace almost without knowing it. It is not on a hill like other palaces. It is all surrounded by pleasant trees. But lions! Lions crouch at the windows. And the flag of Brittany is washed to blue and white."

"The lad is fanciful," my mother said.

"He is not," the duchess said firmly. "He describes the arms of Bavaria, just as they might appear to a child. The black and white checks of the Breton flag he is more familiar with are blue and white in Bavaria. And the golden, rampant lions. Those are the queen's emblems. She sets them everywhere, over her windows. It must be the Hôtel Barbette that you see, lad, the queen's own palace. She retires there when the King's madness drives her from St. Pôl. Monseigneur—the man with the porcupine—he is there?"

"He sups with the lady."

"With the queen?"

"Yes, the queen." I hadn't given the woman in my Vision that title until the duchess put it in my mouth.

"Thank Our Lady that the King is well enough to sup with his queen," my mother said, looking for the calm again.

"The man who wears the porcupine as his emblem is not Charles VI."

The duchess' lips were thin and white with anger. I didn't understand it then, and thought she must be angry with me. I realize now that she was thinking of the rumors that had put her husband, since her exile, and the queen, since Charles' madness, together too often and too closely.

"The lady had had a baby." I reverted to the title I had given the figure in my mind. "Queen" was not what I had called her, and if the word upset the duchess, it need not be so.

"Yes, I had the news that Her Majesty was safely delivered earlier this month. A son, Philippe."

"Philippe has died," I said. "The woman grieves. The man wearing the porcupine comes to comfort her."

Now I had confirmation that my mother did not disparage my gift of Sight as much as her awkwardness with it sometimes seemed. "Lady," "baby," and "dead" meant only one thing to her, the consuming concerns of her last two days. Since I appeared out of immediate danger, she hurried away to check on the mother and child down the hall.

The duchess, however, thought of other things with those same words. "I had heard of the child's birth, but not of its death." There was no sorrow in her voice. I would hear the rumors later, that her husband had more reason to comfort the queen at this loss than merely as a concerned brother-in-law. And that little Philippe, God accept him, was not the only child deserving the title "Bastard of Orléans."

The duchess did not wait for my mother's return to press my tale forward. She sat on the edge of the bed now, rolling my little body into hers with her weight. She clasped her knobby hands in her lap and did not take her eyes from me.

"So they dine together?" she asked. "Monseigneur and the queen?"

"Yes."

This was bad enough news for the duchess to bear, but she must have sensed there was more. The idea of a man and a woman dining together does not make six-year-olds break out in a fevered sweat, no matter what it does to a married woman.

"And?" she pressed.

"A valet comes in, wearing a livery of blue and gold."

"The King's livery."

"He says he is pleased to report a sudden and miraculous improvement in the King's condition."

Mother had returned to the room by now and said, "God be praised." All must have been well with her other charges because she had attention now for us, the duchess and me. But we were far from Blaison Castle indeed.

I shifted feverishly on the cushions that propped me, but that only made the impression sharper. "The valet is lying."

I described what I saw next, Monseigneur taking his leave of the lady in all haste, his rapid mounting and departure, surrounded by his adjuncts, on foot and bearing torches.

"They turn out the palace gate and into a street."

"The Vieille Rue du Temple," the duchess nodded.

"Here is a butcher's shop. Here, an empty warehouse. The street is dark and deserted. In an upper window, a mother hushes her child. The man rides on, singing a song about a maid like a rose in an enclosed garden."

I was certain I'd given the duchess more than enough to go on, and I think she knew the song better than I, who was hearing it for the first time. But "Describe him," she urged now, as if to avoid the issue.

"About as tall as Sire de Rais. More handsome. He rides hatless tonight. His hair is brown like hickory wood in the torchlight. And the porcupine. He wears the porcupine on a silver chain around his neck."

At last my mother began to understand that there was import in the details. "A porcupine, madame?"

"It is the emblem of the order of knights my husband the duke founded. A porcupine is always quick to bristle its spines in its own defense. And to shoot them like so many arrows, too, when provoked. My husband recently planned to bestow the order on his cousin, the duke of Burgundy, as a token of peace between our houses."

My mother nodded and murmured at the gesture. But my screams interrupted any other reaction. The Vision had wound on to its repeating, inevitable conclusion once more.

There was the smell of blackcherry syrup again. When they did not chatter uncontrollably, my teeth clenched tight against its slime and its too-sweet taste.

The moment the Vision broke, like ice from about my jaw, the story burst from me like a thaw. "There are men. Suddenly. From every side. They have swords. Axes."

"Who are they?"

But I didn't need the duchess' urging now to try to shake the evil from me in words. "They are masked, hooded. I cannot see their faces. The adjuncts drop their torches and flee. Only one man stands to aid his master and he is soon brought down. Oh, he screams like the hogs when they are stuck. He cries out in a strange tongue."

"German? It is my husband's German man," the duchess whispered. "God bless him."

But I didn't wait for her. I hardly even heard her. "Oh, they pull him down from his horse. Oh! 'I am the duke of Orléans,' he tries to tell them.

" 'Good,' say they. 'We have the right man.'

" 'I have money,' says he. 'Riches. Ask what you will, it is yours.'

" 'We crave your blood,' say they, 'and we will take it without the asking.'

" 'Kill him, kill him!' " The assassins' words pushed their way into my mouth like vomit. I felt my eyes wide, aching to blink but they could not.

"My lord husband fights boldly?" asked the duchess.

"But he is no match for six—eight hardy men. His sword hand flashes—here—there. Then it's gone. Ah! Ah! A fountain of blood in its place."

Now it was the dying duke's words that filled my mouth with bile, "Haro, haro! My master!"

Now the assailants: "See, he cries for the devil." And "Then it is well his hand is gone, that hand with which he made the demon's pact."

"It's not true," the duchess exclaimed. "The villains lie!"

"Hand and sword. Cut from him in a blow. He sinks to his knees. Then blows fall to the head."

"Ah, ah!" the duchess and I moaned together.

A round bit of skull pan rolled away, into the gutter, but I was beyond words now to describe it or how the man fell headlong into his own spilled brains.

Then a tall dark man came out of the empty warehouse. I said, "Tall. Dark. He, too, wears a silver porcupine."

"Our cousin Burgundy." The duchess choked. I could smell the bile in her throat.

"He kicks the body over and checks the face. He nods.

" 'You've done well,' he says and gestures the escape.

"They all dash for horses, hidden up the alley. They ride away."

"Where?" asked the duchess in a tight, small voice.

I could only point, straight into the Vision. Blood-matted hair still clung to the white skull pan in the gutter.

I wanted to say no more. I wanted to see no more. My mother knelt, trying to hush my gulping sobs of hysteria. "The baton. The baton, planed."

"Stop!" cried the duchess, her hands over her ears. "The baton is the motto my husband took for himself. And his worst enemy, his cousin the duke of Burgundy—that tall, dark man—always said someday he would plane my lord away to nothing. Oh, my God!

"When was this?" The duchess' voice grew rigid, quiet. "For the love of God, tell me!"

"Madame, madame," my mother begged into my hair. "How can he say? He is a child. Pray, torment him no further."

"When came the Vision upon the child?" the duchess insisted. Then she herself worked the timing out. "It was just . . . We heard the new baby cry in Blaison Castle. His very first cry. And then— there the Vision was."

The duchess' hands were at her mouth, stifling any other word, or what would be less than a word, an animal cry of pain. Her eyes darted like hunted hares, seeking their warrens, from my mother to me and then back again.

"Horrible!" she said. And then, in a low, dark hiss of agony, "By all that is holy, who can say what is worse?"

"Madame, what do you mean?" Mother asked.

"A witch."

"Madame—?" My mother had to back a step or two from the accusing glare in the duchess' eyes.

"A witch who can conjure me to make a vow to a devil. A vow not merely of gold and offerings but of my husband's own life's blood. Vow and change it in an instant for the breath of a petty lordling. This child—it was the will of a righteous God that he should die. And she has thwarted it with black magic. Who is worse, such a woman who stands before a Blaison fire and calls the dead to life?

"Or her son. Her son who sees it all in gory detail?"

Madame the duchess backed out of the room, and by the time I awoke from my drugged sleep, some time after noon, she and all of hers were gone. They rode hard for her Château-Thierry, where messengers straight from Paris, bringing more definite news, would be looking for her.

I would never see her again. She would spend what was left of her short life seeking to bring her husband's murderers to justice, seeking to establish her young son in a shaky dukedom, seeking revenge.

Seeking to find out witchcraft.

Certainly she found good indication of it that afternoon as she saw her things loaded into her *charet*.

"The serpents!" she cried, moving from one side of the convey-ance to the other and then back again in a frenzy of dismay. "The emblems of my family, of the Visconti! Destroyed! Under this roof."

She showed the fork-stabbed and splintered wood and gold leaf to her host. Monseigneur de Rais was apologetic, but more confused than she as to how such a thing could have happened.

"My ancestor took the shield off a Saracen he killed while on Crusade in the Holy Land. We have revered it ever since. It is the emblem of our house's fortunes. The serpent and its fangs are de-stroyed. It is a sign that heathenism has power and will triumph. Rise from this very accursed castle." The duchess continued to rail in a panic, but she didn't let it slow her escape from our walls.

"Madame the duchess was very upset," Monseigneur de Rais mused as he retold the tale to us afterward, rubbing his chin with wonder. By then messengers had confirmed the death of the duke just as I had seen it.

Gilles and I exchanged glances over our simple supper of fresh fried sausages wrapped in buckwheat *galettes*. Until that moment, all our recent terrors had been forgotten with the rapidity of youth and the comfort of good food.

"I will pay for a few masses to be said in the duke of Orléans' name," Monseigneur de Rais decided. Otherwise I don't think he took the fresh widow's wild words—or my Vision—too seriously.

Gilles said nothing, chewing stolidly, grease on his chin, and must have been wondering how long it would be before the duchess realized she was also missing one of her little silver "devil's pitchforks."

But I knew what I had seen. I had seen the assassination in the Vieille Rue du Temple. The assassination that would pitch the house of Orléans against the house of Burgundy in a civil war that overshadowed all my youth. In the end it gave the English reason to cross the channel and pick up the pieces for themselves.

So this was the price of René de La Suze's little life. That night I learned that life could be traded for life in the accounts of the world. And that one had to be careful which life one spoke for. For some lives, such as that of the duke of Orléans, dragged many, many more of both sides down after them with the passing of years.

No doubt the blame must originally lie with Charles the King and his failure to pay life for life, the price of his Kingship in the sacrifice of his own royal blood. Had madness not cursed him for his refusal, Burgundy and Orléans would never have come to such anger over how the regency should go. Or if they had—for they were both hotheaded men—a strong King would have seen that a murderer came to rapid justice.

But I would not see the wider ripples of this great exchequer for many years. All I did see at the time was the coming due of this one debt. And learned that for such a life as the tiny Sire de La Suze's, so dull and lackluster even when it was happening, the good of the entire land was a very high price to pay.

Demons Caught in a Net

That early November snowfall of the year of Grace 1407—after Sire René was born and in which the duchess of Orléans left us—that snowfall was not just an early, freakish storm. It was the beginning of the harshest winter in memory.

Beasts in their stalls froze to death under sheets of ice. Men did so beside their hearths. Many starved, although Madame de Rais saw to it that none in her stewardship did so. Because of the cold, the Parliament in Paris was unable to sit for months; nothing was decided in connection with the assassination of the duke of Orléans until it was too late. The duke of Burgundy had consolidated his power and civil war was in full flower.

Then, when the river ice came to break up, it took bridges along with it as far downstream as Tours, further disrupting trade and news. Earth herself seemed to suffer for the impious acts of that November.

By the time Gilles and I could play outside again with any regularity, his little brother—who had not failed for breath a moment since his birth—was crawling. "*Le petit* René" everyone called him with deep and cooing delight as the blond hair grew in, curly as an angel's. "*Le* René *pestiféré*," Gilles called him, "the pest-ridden René," and worse things—out of earshot of our elders. I confess I, too, joined my milk brother in such sins of childhood. Smallness and cuteness cannot hide the total lack of any vital spark in an individual from younger eyes as it can from older.

Madame de Rais, having the wonder of new smallness to occupy her in "*le petit* René," decided it was high time her older son moved out of his nurses' care and onto the next rung on the ladder of young nobility. Her husband, Sire de Rais, had been hoping for Gilles to take that step for quite some time and had the answer hovering at his elbow.

This was the person of one Père Georges de Boszac whose long, fusty robes and somber manner proclaimed not only his priesthood, but his degree in law from the University of Paris. Père de Boszac stepped in as Messire Gilles' tutor that very Advent.

I was to join in the scholar's lessons, too, of course, as the lord of the castle had sworn before the Saint. That I was three years slow off the mark was as it should be: "You must not show up the young lord, Yann," Mother warned me.

As I have mentioned, I had somehow learned my letters before then—enough to tell L and V on the duchess' *charet.* I suppose I had learned them as a fish breathes water. The prospect of learning to string the ponderous individuals together thrilled me. To give them the wings of reading, to be able to penetrate the closed mystery of books that sat so tantalizingly on the Sire de Rais' dusty library shelves—

And then to write, to put my own mark on the world, that was a secret beyond even desire. It seemed the mystery for which I was born.

I remember sitting on the bench next to Gilles for the first lesson in the high, sunny scriptorium, my back rigid with anticipation. I bit my tongue against the anger I felt at the irreverent way in which the lord's son was rocking the bench and swinging his shorter legs as if they would follow his mind elsewhere.

Père de Boszac had a voice weighted with self-importance. "The first thing young men must learn is—"

I held my breath for the key to all the world.

"Their religion."

I let my breath out. It dropped hard. I suppose he must do this, I thought. I will learn well so we may quickly go on to the other.

But we hadn't passed the "I believe in God the Eternal Father" before we learned Père de Boszac's true passion.

Demons.

"Demons." Père de Boszac's eyes flashed such terror that even Gilles' swinging legs stopped. His voice seemed to caress the word. "Demons are everywhere."

"A boy can swallow them with his breakfast milk. Then they will make their home in the empty spots in his bowels, come out in his stool and urine."

On the bench beside me, Gilles squirmed as breakfast writhed within him.

Père de Boszac had seen demons, black motes dancing before his eyes in a sunbeam.

Women, in their weakness, were great friends of demons. Père de Boszac had seen imps, like so many blackamoors, wriggling and clapping their hands as they rode on the ostentatiously long train of a woman's gown.

"They tumbled about and giggled at their success there like fish caught in a net. They perch themselves in the shadow over a woman's hips when Eve's fallen daughters allowed such lineaments to be seen through wide 'windows of hell' in their sleeves. The fashionable horned headdress is only feigned obedience to St. Paul's dictum to cover their heads. That headdress is neither more nor less than the devil's bonnet. And the bandeaus with which women bind their breasts to unnaturally high and tempting arcs—Satan will turn them to bands of fire in the world to come."

Even nuns were not exempt: "Demons like to ride on beads of rosaries dangling idle when holy women turn their hands to something else.

"Demons tickle a man in his privates at night, burn them with the red-hot pokers of hell."

Demons could be found in any imperfection: when the butter failed to come, in the pus that swelled the maid Paquette's face in a boil.

But they were also in perfection: Père de Boszac had once stopped in a house of pious monks where a brother had a voice of such perfect beauty that anyone who heard it stopped breathing to listen to the wonder of it. Only Père de Boszac had the vision to realize such perfection must be a demon's doing, none of God's.

"I called the evil spirit to come out of that man and, in that instant, the singer fell down dead."

The diagnosis? "Clearly nothing but evil had been animating him for years. He had sold his soul to the devil in an idolatrous love for the gift of his voice.

"What power have simple Christians against such beings which might be in every breath they take?"

At the priest's rhetorical question, I could feel Gilles next to me refusing to take a breath that might be so tainted.

"Not much." Père de Boszac snapped his own reply, and turned from us with a swirl of skirts as from things defiled, choosing to address his remarks out the high, narrow window instead. "I, I thank the Lord, have been blessed with a discerning spirit. And the faith and piety born of long years denying the flesh have given me the power to exorcise. But the average Christian? Born in sin? Of the demon-urged copulation of sinful parents?"

He turned on us now, wild with the pain of his faith, unconscious that his audience had only the vaguest notion of his references. "Average wicked little boys such as yourselves?"

Gilles crossed himself. Belatedly I decided that was the thing to do, too. Père de Boszac cracked his voice with laughter like someone cracking his joints.

"Yes, you may make the sign of the cross, call loudly on God's Name. But the odds are not good." He shook his head, all laughter vanished. "Not good at all."

Gilles' eyes were wide with wonder. He sat, his hands clasped about his knees until I could see white in his knuckles. He was trying to keep from screaming aloud, from swinging his legs to the floor and running, yet he was unable to tear himself away.

Gilles sat this way during our schoolroom days anytime the topic came up—which was frequently. The one exception was the time he brought the duchess' silver fork into the scriptorium. He gouged the fork into the bench between us while Père de Boszac railed. Gilles worked intently, as if at some sort of charm.

That didn't last long. The priest's demon-spotting eyes soon spotted the utensil and confiscated it. I don't think Gilles ever saw his booty again.

That Lent Père de Boszac decided boys who were old enough for lessons were old enough to fast. He demon-threatened us down to nothing but bread and water. We ourselves asked for it, too young even to know what harm such austerity might have on growing bodies. The priest's "Your sinfulness is not capable" made us capable.

And once during those dreadful days of winter's darkness, Père de Boszac brought a block of white, thick cheese to the scriptorium.

"Don't you want some?" he urged. He held it out just at Gilles' nose. Then, withdrawing it, he took a rich, creamy bite himself.

"I may not," Gilles whispered plaintively over the tide of saliva in his mouth. He sounded every three of his brief years.

"Why? Who tells you so?"

"I may not. God will not love me if I do."

"But who is to know? Just the three of us in this room. And we will not tell. We will all share so we are equally culpable. Will we not, Jean?"

I nodded. I, too, couldn't pull my eyes from that brilliant creamy white in the midst of all the darkness.

But the instant we gulped the wonderful food down, letting it coat our teeth and tongues and the insides of our cheeks so luxuriously, Père de Boszac suddenly flared up like liqueur splashed on a fire.

"Wicked, wicked children! Demons possess you!"

"But, Father, you promised—" Gilles whimpered, so confused, so betrayed I thought his eyes must cross and stay there permanently. But I was too afraid for my own hide to worry about him, so much younger and smaller though he was.

"I?" Père de Boszac fumed and sputtered, more explosive liqueur. "I would never do such a thing. I, your God-fearing, demon-commanding tutor who cares only for your depraved souls. No, not I. It was a demon. A demon who could take upon himself my form and speak you fair. Speak you lies. And you are too wicked, with one foot already in hell, to know the difference. A demon. How, oh, how, shall we rid you of this demon?"

Gilles only shook his head in amazement, silent tears streaming down his cheeks. In the end, we were beaten. We begged to be beaten, we ran to cut the willow wands ourselves. Though we screamed for the blows to stop, we pleaded, "Don't stop," whenever breath came again.

A week later, I could still see the marks on Gilles' back, criss-crossing the little beads of his vertebrae. His spine was a rosary, I thought.

But again—heaven forgive me—I could spare so little thought for his own pain, younger though he was. My own back was itching furiously.

And besides, I had been discovered to have more than enough demons of my own to contend with.

This enlightenment came when, at long last, we had our first lesson in quill preparation, a prelude to actual writing, which, of course, wouldn't be on real parchment for a year or more. We would have plenty of practice on slate beforehand. This breach of peda-gogy's *summa*—of the steady, logical build Père de Boszac usually stuck to so fiercely—was urged, I think, by the happy chance of a slaughter of geese in the yard.

We received the expected lecture on the demons that might plague the process: unclean spirits in the water that soaked the feather shafts and made them pliable, demons clinging in the form of mites between the ridged barbules. How the penknife in the hand of a wicked boy might take on a demon of its own and plunge itself into the throat of his partner on the bench.

Finding us finally sufficiently sobered, the priest then handed us our plumes. I reached for mine.

"What?" our preceptor burst forth. "You will pick up the pen with the sinister, the left hand, in my classroom? Over my dead body."

I had, at last, to reveal the right hand I usually took care to conceal, since his wasn't the first bad reaction I'd received in my life.

Père de Boszac's face paled as he diagnosed, "Clearly the work of a demon. Know you not that those who make a compact with the devil vow him their right hand? For this reason the duke of Orléans' assassins took care that his right hand was severed from his body as he died."

"That isn't so," I foolishly began. "They cut the hand—his sword hand off in the battle and—"

"Not so? You would argue with me, who was in Paris when the deed was done?"

He may have been in Paris; I had been in the very alley on that night. The hand had only gone because that was the hand with which the duke had so valiantly tried to defend himself against overwhelming odds. Wisely, I said nothing.

"That such a devilish pact could be made in one so young." The father shook his head and said something else about "Over my dead body" that curious sorts of bubbles in my head kept me from hearing clearly. The thought occurred to me that I would like very well to see that dead body of his when he discovered my other demon as well.

Then he discovered that other demon. I had a fit.

This was a demon that must be exorcised. Madame agreed. Her castle was blessed by the presence of a man who had actually killed a demon-perfect singer. If he couldn't do anything about my disconcerting habit, nobody could.

When I came out of my swirl to the familiar smell of blackcherry syrup, Mother was agreeing as well. Gifted children were fine, a blessing of God and a trial. But normal children were even better. I remembered protesting weakly that I didn't want to be like everyone else—and if I must be, having a twisted hand cured might be a better place to begin.

Nothing for it. The exorcism was already under way while I was too weak to think of more.

I remember lying alone—so very alone—on the bed, a pinfeather scratching the back of my neck. A fire lit the priest's dour figure as if I could see right through him. I remember the holy water on my brow, warm enough to cause a fever. I remember the words, "I abjure you, Satan . . ."

I remember the bones. He stroked my face with bones. I think it was actually the knob of a human long bone. It smelled of the graveyard, not the soup pot. I can't say where he got it, but I think it was meant to frighten whatever it was that possessed me. It did quite well.

I went into another fit.

When I came around, it was to the smell and taste of Mother's

blackcherry syrup once more, but no better cure. Père de Boszac confessed himself defeated by an evil greater than his herculean good.

At Père de Boszac's defeat, Madame despaired of fulfilling her
vow to St. Gilles. The priest seriously urged sending me and my
family away. Madame had the salvation of her own children to think
of, after all.

The only thing that turned her was Père de Boszac himself who,
reading her hesitation, pressed for more drastic measures. He began
to insist that the demon be tortured from me. Failing that, the imp
should be burned to the death and me—the conclusion couldn't be
helped—along with it. Sire de Rais quite approved of the plan but
here Madame came to her senses and stood up to the both of them.

"No child shall be tortured beneath my roof," she said.

And having denied the authority figures in one thing, it became
easier for her to deny them in the next. My mother was Madame's
best companion and her sons' nurse; the draper's family must stay,
I along with them. Père de Boszac need not tutor me if he cared not
to, but the offense against St. Gilles must be on his head, not Madame's.

So we stayed. But I despaired of my great desire—learning to
read and write—for a boy whose very soul was despaired of could
never be allowed in the scriptorium.

Two Black Robes

I wanted all the world to hear my feet pounding across the drawbridge's planks, echoing the pounding of my heart. I wanted them to know of my displeasure. I wanted, perhaps, someone to stop me.

"Go on with you, demon spawn. Run," growled the cruelest member of the watch, and his companions laughed with him.

Pride kept me going after that.

I ran as far as I could before tumbling into a clump of grass under the willows near the River Loire and still smelled the rot. Only when I'd cried eyes and nose full did the stench leave my head.

Then I curled up in the shadows where I was and slept. If the cause of my misery, a dark spell, would not come when I needed it, I must take this other path to oblivion.

Much later, I awoke. The sun had slipped low, under the fringe of willow and, as cruel as the watch, into my face. It dried and puckered the streaks of salt and mucus on my skin. I scrubbed at the discomfort and only cured myself by letting new tears come.

The dry sward was thin between the rocky soil and my buttocks. It slivered into needlelike chaff that worked its way through my hose. And now the mosquitoes were rising off the river as well. I saw the first firefly glow.

Still, I lingered outside. The last rosy light touched the top of the castle's western tower and held my eye. I knew such light from the inside, from the scriptorium, where I had left Gilles to face Père de Boszac alone.

I was not welcome in the world of holy letters. The men-at-arms in the yard had no use for me. I was hardly welcome in Blaison at all.

A dusty blue kingfisher haunted the willows between which the Loire River slipped, a deepening grey. The water was low at this season, and the weather had been uncommonly, dangerously dry, even for August. Broad sandbars rose from the river like the backs of beasts. Still, the sluggish flow of the Loire seemed the most friendly prospect my world afforded.

Swiping at my nose with my sleeve cleaned it enough so I could smell the moat again. If only it would rain and wash moat and river and my head all clean and new. But there hadn't been a cloud in the sky for weeks.

Under such oppression, I couldn't make myself get up and head toward the defensive walls of Blaison again. The castle's gaunt granite gorge rose unmoving in the choking grip of the moat. No, not yet.

But it was getting late. A figure appeared, framed in the high archway that served as a mouth to the castle's drawbridge tongue. Only a moment was necessary to tell me—of course, it was my mother.

She came straight out over the moat, then stooped before a scruffy bush to hide her purpose from the watch on the castle walls. On a rock behind the bush she set a trencher of the evening's potage and a jug of some drink, I couldn't tell which. Next to them, out of the scoops of her skirt, she set a handful of nuts. Then, still bending, she formed signs of blessing over the food in the air with her hands. I was too far to hear, but I knew she mumbled words in the old tongue:

> "O needs of life, lie you there
> So to nourish sprites of air.
> Sprites of earth and sprites of water,
> In return bless son and daughter.
> What I give in its good time,
> Ne'er requite of me or mine."

Presently, Mother stood up. She held her skirt still high before her, showing an expanse of linen beneath on which she wiped her hands while she scanned the land in front of her. I knew she was looking for me.

I dashed at the tears and silenced any welling sobs. My empty stomach longed to believe she'd brought the food for me. But I knew it was not so. Mother had set that food and blessed it "for the fairy folk," just as she did every night. I'd made the blessing with her often enough. Imagining the tiny, luminescent creatures—like fireflies, only more demanding, more prone to fits of temper—who would come and partake, set every crumb beyond my hunger. If any but fairy folk broke the blessing, they would turn to vapor in that moment.

Still, I knew this night the pause afterward was for me, the wiping of hands longer than would be necessary for a bit of potage seeped through the trencher. Wiping until it became a wringing, that was for me. And the anxious scan of every point her eyes could reach.

But she didn't step out farther, she didn't call. I was certain she couldn't see me, sunk behind the bracken as I was and under the willow's shade. And I didn't move. Somehow, I think she sensed, however.

I sensed something of her, an ache for me. I could almost hear her words. "Dear child—"

No. I had to blink away the sight of her. I didn't need one more proof of my unnatural gifts, that I could understand my mother's thoughts at such a distance. I hated my ability—that seemed disability. I turned stolidly back to the river again.

Someday I would escape. I had to escape. With hot tears, I swore it. But at the moment, how could I? I had no place to go but into the lengthening shadows of Blaison. I was only eight years old, after all.

That thought forced me to steal another glance toward the castle. My mother was just beneath the walls, standing with the watch. She was arguing with them. Could I, indeed, hear the words?

"No, please, wait. Let him come home when he's ready."

"We can't leave the bridge down after dark. There's a war going on, haven't you heard? Suppose there's a pack of Burgundians out there right this moment, just waiting for dark. They'd murder the whole castle in their beds."

"Yann!"

That cry I heard with everyday ears. I heard her footsteps running on the bridge. But the guard caught her by the arm.

"We're raising that bridge now, goodwife."

"You going to stay out all night?"

"With the Burgundians?"

"With that demon son of yours?"

"Raise the bridge. Now."

"A boy that age who doesn't know enough to come home before the bridge goes up deserves—"

"Maybe this will scare the devil out of him."

"Yann!"

My mother's shout drowned out the voices of the watch. I scrambled to my feet, answering her anguish.

Then I heard *le petit* René wailing for his nurse. I heard the great crank groaning as the chains crawled over it. I saw the watchman holding my mother back. He looked straight at me. I couldn't meet his glare. The great wooden tongue came up and swallowed my mother whole.

Silence tumbled around me, save for the thudding of my heart. I was too scared now even to whimper and stared around at my surroundings, having to consciously will my head to turn through the stiffness of my fear.

Then my attention riveted. A shadow slipped around the skirt of the moat, different from the rest of the deepening but stationary shadows there. A Burgundian? Was the watch right? Just waiting for night to fall and the bridge to go up? Yet there seemed something not quite human about it. Was it some beast come to encircle me in advance of the sandbank beasts of the Loire?

Or was it, worse, a thing from the spirit world?

A monk's hooded black robes. Discerning that much brought some humanity to the figure. He came to a stop in front of the low board of my mother's fairy food and rubbed his hands in hungry anticipation.

That food is blessed for others, for fairy folk! I formed these stalwart words in my brain. I said nothing aloud, of that I was certain, not even a whisper. And yet, the figure stopped and turned toward me, as if I'd spoken aloud. I flattened to the ground, my heart pounding. The watch, even if they could see what was happening in the shadows at their feet, would never come to my aid.

Instead of the attack I expected instantly, a nightingale warbled, sad and sweet, from the riverward copse just on my left. The call sounded no different from any other nightingale I'd ever heard before. Except, oddly, more like itself. There was such a definite desire to communicate in it, not just with its own kind but with ours, that the sound stood out like whispers in the complete silence of a sanctuary. My ability to sense this seemed above the ordinary. Again, it made me hate and doubt myself, and my will shriveled.

When next I dared to peek over my tussock of grass, I saw that, above the ordinary as the birdsong was, the man in black had sensed the communication, too. He must be very attuned to things around him, beyond his hunger, I thought. He froze, his head cocked to one side, leaning on his staff. It was as if he had taken up the being of the bird with the notes of the song, for he stood as the nightingale does, motionless between hops, listening for hidden insects.

The song came again. The man in black left the food altogether now and glided toward the copse. His movements still spoke of a desire for stealth, but once he reached the cover of the trees, he spoke to what he found there, loud enough for me to hear. The distance between us was now hardly more than a spear throw. And joy expanded his volume.

"Master!"

I could not refuse my curiosity. I had to creep up through the ferns and undergrowth until I could see them both, although it did occur to me that if the first man was terrifying, how much more must his "Master" be.

I found it not so, however. The second man was a good head shorter than the first, and though I couldn't see his face, a good deal older. He wore the same hooded black as the other and carried a similar staff. In this case, however, he had need of the support. His frame was stooped, and a stringy, never-trimmed grey beard lay like a patch of twilight on the breast of his midnight robe.

"Welcome be," the older said with a certain air of propriety. As if he, not the watch on the wall, owned Blaison.

The older voice was frail. The two men spoke Breton, the archaic tongue, though the younger man threw his *r*s forward and curiously flattened his vowels. I was used to having none but my parents understand me when I spoke that language. It seemed an outrage.

I couldn't help myself. I had to crawl closer.

The men embraced and stood, fondly clutching each other's elbows. What words of greeting, pleasure, and surprise the two exchanged I failed to hear for the sound of my own creeping. I didn't think I made much noise—and the men took no notice—but my concentration made me deaf to anything else. Finally I had reached a point behind the trunk of an ash where I could see and hear everything.

To my surprise, I heard nothing. Even ungifted ears as I wished mine to be should have heard something, and I, like it or not, should have been able to sense some meaning. For they were clearly communicating with one another. That much I could tell by their attitudes, bent together with zest. But for all I could understand, a second drawbridge might have been drawn up in front of my face.

The more I studied the two, the stronger my uneasy feeling that I should know the older man. The taller remained a stranger to me, even when he shoved back his hood. He had a high forehead extended by shaving and a beard that brought recompense to the lower part of his face. I began to feel an ease about his presence. But I didn't like that I couldn't hear a thing they were saying to one another.

I'd reared up to my knees, peering intently around the ash trunk in my desire to hear, when, all of a sudden, the younger man spoke aloud.

"But isn't there a boy?" It was as if he dropped the drawbridge down again with one great clang. "Didn't you tell me there was a boy at Blaison?"

"The boy, yes."

The tonsured heads turned as they spoke until they both looked directly at me. I slumped low, burrowing my face between two ash roots. They could not possibly know I was here. They'd given no sign until now, and the shadows were growing darker by the moment. And yet—and yet the way the old man spoke in the old tongue—it was like conjuring.

"Never have I seen such gifts. And the sign of the Stag when first his being was made known to me. The Vision, the Sight. Never such gifts since first I laid eyes on you, my Martinet. And maybe not even then."

"So he brought you here, not I." The jealousy in the younger man's voice was good-natured.

"One visit every Midsummer is not much time to help guide such gifts as this boy has."

Suddenly, I recognized him, that mention of Midsummer. The old greybeard was the Hermit of St. Gilles. I'd failed to remember him at first without the defining surroundings of his forest. But what was he doing here at Blaison?

And who was this boy of whom he spoke? Gilles, certainly. Gilles, who was named for his Saint. Gilles, the young lord of Blaison, Rais, and everything else in between.

"How to get to him, though?" The old man turned away to contemplate the castle as it rose over the treetops, his thoughts as tangled as his beard. "I have yet to discover how I may guide his learning with more care."

"Didn't you tell me his education is bound to that of the young lord, heir to this place?"

"Yes, Gilles is that boy's name. Messire Gilles de Rais."

There, I'd known Gilles would be their interest.

"Perhaps the young lord has gifts as well?"

"He has."

"You don't sound so happy about that, Master."

"His are dark gifts, not easy to tame."

"All the more reason to try."

"Yes, but how? How to get at them? It is as if they were locked away, both of those lads. Beyond my reach.

"Well, never mind." The old man shifted his weight on his staff, changing the subject just as readily with a rake of his knobby fingers through the length of his beard. "The answer may come to me—

now that you are here, perhaps. Let me hear what difficulty ails your land of Lorraine."

"May we sit, Master?"

"Yes, this stump seems to beckon me. And here is a fallen log calling out your name, Michel, as I think."

The younger man helped his elder down but did not yet take a seat himself.

"What are you thinking?" the old man said.

"Can't you read my mind, Master? You always could before."

"You are thinking that since the goodwife has faithfully provided, we must give her cause to increase her faith."

"Exactly. I'll be back in a moment."

The young man moved silently and swiftly as any wild thing, up out of the copse and toward my mother's food. When I saw what he meant to do, I didn't stop to think. I only knew I must keep him from breaking the blessing my mother had set over the spread. For his own good, if not that of the food. The blessing would turn to curse in the wrong hands, magicing those hands to no more than rising mist.

"No! Stop! Do not touch the food."

My fear-blinded run dashed against the black-draped chest (surprisingly firm and strong for a priest's). I flailed with both fists, even though my right, damaged as it was, was of no more use than a feather duster.

The man caught my wrists and laughed. "Son, son, calm."

Like a cock set on, I could not stop myself. Then, his hands moved in some strange action before my face. Wondrously, I felt the deep tones of his voice conjure calm. It reached me from the solid vibrations of his chest as well as through my ears. As I think of it now, he must also have set a glamour over us with his hand signals, over me and my shrill young shouts, for surely the watch would have heard otherwise, even if they could no longer see through the gathering darkness.

"So now, tell me," said that calm and calming voice. "Why must my friend and I not help ourselves to what your mother has so graciously provided?"

"Because she blessed it so none may touch it," I insisted. "She blessed it for the fairy folk."

"And who do you think we are?"

"I do not know you. You are strangers."

"And must therefore be evil?"

I should be the one asking the questions, but somehow this interloper had turned the tables on me. "No. Not—not necessarily," I stammered. "But you must be warned, for any who eat what is fairy-blessed—it cannot go well for them."

"You seek to guard us, then? You seek our safety?"

Still he had the questions. But to my own surprise, I answered, "Yes."

"Well discerned. Very good, my unfledged Yann."

The spell he cast cannot have been very strong, only the reflex of a moment. I could feel its effects wearing off and I spoke sulkily, warily. "How do you know my name is Yann? My old name, my secret name? Most people call me Jean."

"Ah, who else but Yann the Bold should be the great defender of fairy folk in Blaison-sur-Loire?"

The notion had such a ring to it, I quite forgot to attend to the leap of logic it contained. The man stooped to pick up the trencher in one hand, the jug in the other. My heart sprang back at the action—but he suffered no immediate bolt of lightning.

"Something else tells me this is a hungry boy, too. Why don't you pick up the nuts, seeing that I have only two hands and they are full. Your hand makes an excellent third. Come and share this lovely meal with us."

"But—but it is fairy food." I was finding it difficult to remember what that meant.

The man smiled his calming smile. "And who do you think we are, my Master and I?" he asked again.

"I—" I didn't know. They were full grown and robed in black, not at all what I had imagined when my mother said "fairy folk." And yet . . .

"And you, too, Yann?" the stranger said. "Who are you? Who else are we all but fairy folk?"

Suddenly, it made perfect sense to me. I stooped and swept the nuts into my left hand with my right and followed the black robes into the copse.

13

The next time I heard Père de Boszac cite the gospel tale of the loaves and fishes, I remembered the fairy food. For once the younger monk and I got it back to the copse where the Hermit of St. Gilles was waiting, it divided itself into three with great accommodation. The even but small portion the elder handed me made my aching belly snugly, wonderfully full. I could taste the blessing, yes, an extra richness to the gravy, a sweetness to the cider unnatural this close to the time for new pressing. The blessing did no harm. In fact, it seemed to do more good than a dozen common meals taken in Blaison's great hall.

And the nuts I myself had carried? Why, it seemed I was all night setting them on a rock at the Hermit's feet, cracking them with another rock, and eating the rich insides while he and his disciple talked.

They didn't immediately return to talk of Gilles—and of me—as I'd hoped. But soon enough I forgot all about my gifts, good and bad, in fascination of other topics.

"So tell me, my Martinet," said the voice I had always only associated with the flames of Midsummer and pain in my right hand. "Tell me what is the trouble in Lorraine."

"It's hard to say where to begin," the young man said. "And crossing France these last weeks has shown me so many more ills that seem so much more grievous—all that the war and the King's madness have done—the dead, the starving, the dispossessed, the spirit dead within bodies yet alive . . ." He passed his hand before his eyes as if to wipe the memory from them.

"No doubt the ills are all of a piece," the Hermit suggested. "The entire world is, at some junctures, connected: the ill of Lorraine with the ills of all of France."

"Madame Catherine de Bauffremont-Ruppes died this year."

"Ah, she who was such a patroness of the Old Ways."

I heard the shift of bodies and garments in the darkness. The two men seemed to have crossed themselves. At least, that's what I thought they did and, thinking I'd joined them, I thunked my twisted hand at the prescribed spots, forehead, chest, shoulders.

I felt, as it were, a smile come at me from the men. The feeling was full of indulgence, however. I'd made a mistake, but after an exchange of meaning between themselves that read something like, "I told you we must set Château Blaison to rights," they were ready to acquit me.

"She was Goddess to my God, many and many a Midsummer." The sorrow in the younger man's voice seemed to make a blue glow about him.

"Surely I taught you not to see Goddess in a single shape? She is Many."

"Of course you did. It's not easy, nonetheless."

"Such women are found so rarely among the nobility these days," the Hermit said with compassion.

I wasn't at all clear what they were talking about. The struggle was part of what kept my attention, however.

"That's it, exactly," said the man the Hermit called "Martinet." I could not quite call him that; it seemed a pet name for a child. Alternatively, the Hermit called him Michel, so that is what he became to me. Père Michel.

"Catherine's son is set against us," Michel went on.

"Not a God's son, then?"

"Not at all. All the old lord's blood. He's already given Saint Catherine's ashes to her shrine in Maxey, locking them up there against all tradition of passing the fertility around the valley."

"Ah."

"And without the support of a member of the nobility, many of the trancers failed to join the Night Battles this year."

More I didn't understand. The Hermit moved the dark with a nod I could feel as well as see, however. It displaced tiny bits of thick, warm night air at the foot of Blaison Castle. The night spun around the high north star and around us in patterns set out since the world began.

"And that was when I determined I must come to you, Master, to ask your advice, as soon as my Midsummer duties were past at the Bois Chênu."

The Bois Chênu. Now that was something I remembered from my Merlin Vision. But what?

"In such a single-minded land, the ancient prophecy is to be fulfilled?" Michel's tongue hammered as viciously as a blacksmith on those poor vowels. "I must see it fulfilled? Who will be here to receive La Pucelle when she comes?"

More from the prophecy. Now, how did it go?

"Who, pray, is to mother her, let alone teach her as she grows?" Michel, busy with his own questions, had no answers for my own. "Of that, I as a man am incapable. I'd always imagined Catherine would do the mothering, even in her old age. Her age, when she was Goddess, meant little to me. Most of the trancers are men who enjoy the sport, nothing more. Master, I feel myself beyond any hope of the ancient words."

The old Hermit sighed heavily. "I understand your distress, my Martinet. But are there not other, ancient words that say great evil is balanced by great good? Remember, son, the darkest time is just before the dawn. Let us not lose hope for this poor old land. Not yet."

The old Hermit shifted slightly on his stump chair in the dark to listen to the hunting cry of an owl. He seemed to take counsel of the sound. I fully expected a fourth to join our party heralded by this call as the old man had been by a nightingale's song. But none appeared, unless it may be said that the Earth Herself came. Certainly the two men sitting with me seemed constantly to consult these sounds of the breathing Earth and Her creatures in the deep silence of the copse.

And I couldn't help but feel the presence of such things in these men's company more than I'd ever been conscious of them before.

The Loire whispered in the night below us. I smelled the river, the sifted forest litter beneath my haunches. I heard the chirr of night insects and how the men seemed to try to match their breathing to the throb, their words to the spaces between the words of frogs croaked up from the river.

I saw the web of stars appearing between the full-leafed branches overhead, and sometimes a faint glow about the two men who were otherwise invisible. The glow was like the haloes on saints in a chapel, only it changed color as the men expressed anger, grief, concern, love. They seemed to give the black of the night an inner core of warm red, orange, then blue.

The castle of Blaison and all the hurt I felt from it could have been a thousand leagues away.

Michel returned to the only thing he seemed able to think on. "The trancers' negligence has been proved this seedtime and harvest. I fear it will be the same the next time Yule comes around—worse. And the next."

The Hermit agreed, "The connection between our lives and the life of the World around us no longer seems so vital in the eyes of most men."

"It began with Genesis," Michel accused. "That book would have us believe that the God said to Adam, 'Take dominion over all the earth . . .'"

With a single, whispered flap of wings, our owl companion took to the night sky. Hunting, no doubt. But I couldn't escape the impression that he'd left in disgust of Michel's words.

"All you tell me is of deep concern, my son. But one thing concerns me most of all."

"What's that, Master?"

"That you should leave the land of your charge in such a crisis. Surely your leaving is much like that of the Bourlémont son who has gone to the Christian priest. A Master's place is with his land, whatever the difficulties."

The old man spoke with some sharpness toward the end. The haloes—maybe I'd been imagining them?—had dimmed almost to the black of the night.

"No doubt you are right, Master. And yet, I had the impression to come. Here. To Blaison."

A sudden exhaustion seemed to have caught up with the young man, his weary days of travel. The weariness seemed to be more in his mind than in his limbs, and caused by the older man's displeasure chafing against what had been his own hard-won decision.

The Hermit said, "The prophecy. Someone ought to be there to help its fulfillment in any way he can."

Then Michel made an unseen gesture. I heard the owl hoot again, nearby. Whether prompted by black-sleeved hands or by the voice of the hunting owls, the Hermit suddenly shifted his attention to me.

"Yann, do you attend?"

"Yes, sir." That I was thrown off my guard sounded in the croak of my voice.

"I think it is important that you should know of this prophecy, for I feel it will happen in your lifetime."

"Yes, sir."

"And he may be the one who must be there to help the fulfillment, not I," Michel said, as if giving up.

"These words were first given by a great man," the Hermit said, "a Master of Craft and wisdom such as Michel and myself are."

"Only much, much greater," Michel interjected.

"Harken to the words of Merlin . . ."

While the Hermit struggled for effect, I quickly supplied the words for him: " 'There will come a virgin out of Lorraine, out of the Bois Chênu, to save all the land.' "

The aura around both men flickered to golden life with their astonishment. "How came you to know that?" the elder asked.

"You told me, Father. In my Vision."

"But you cannot have been more than three years old. I'm certain I have not spoken of it since that first Midsummer you came to me."

"You haven't, Father. But how could I forget your words, leaping with the Midsummer flames and the searing pain in my hand?"

Michel, suddenly bright, said, "You told me, Master, he had a mind born for magic."

The Hermit nodded. "But what you cannot know, son, is that this Michel lives and is Master in the very valley where stands this Bois Chênu, the ancient oak forest, revered by our ancestors since the world began."

"Is it so?" I had chosen yet another hazelnut, but it lay neglected on my pounding stone.

"I can see the edge of the forest when I stand in my hermitage in Bermont." Michel's voice filled with longing. He caressed the words as he must be caressing the remembered countryside in his mind, like the body of an absent lover. "In the forest flows a sacred spring, grows a most sacred beech tree, and the fairy folk gather there during the great feasts of the year."

"And you left such a place?" I asked in wonder.

Michel sighed. "Truth to tell, much as I love the place, I have begun to wonder how the prophecy is to be fulfilled at all."

The Hermit said, "My dear Martinet. You are young and impatient, else I would wonder at such doubts from you."

"But, Master, pray, where is this Maid to come from?"

The Hermit clicked his tongue with the sound of a disapproving cricket. "Such things happen in ways we never expect."

"I know." Michel sighed again.

"For instance, when you say 'maid' and our young friend here says 'virgin,' you forget. You both have put the word through a mill of French and brought it out again. Remember Master Merlin spoke the old tongue. Put it back into that tongue without translation."

The Vision-word rang like shivers of glass through my mind. The word in the old tongue is holy, so I will not bandy it here. The French La Pucelle is as close as I dare speak to such mysteries.

"La Pucelle," I shouted then triumphantly.

"Very good, Yann. Which means?"

I didn't know, but Michel didn't answer, either.

"Virgin-whore," the old Hermit replied as if conjuring with the word. As if it meant Messiah.

When I put such words in Père de Boszac's theology, the opposites sent the brain spinning like a top. The old Hermit repeated the words like a child who couldn't tire of the magic of his simple toy.

"Virgin-whore. It is a contradiction, a mystery our minds have a hard time encompassing."

Michel added as if reciting lessons, "The office of La Pucelle is found in many rites."

All evening their words had named things I knew. These were things for which I had no words because I'd never been given any before. Or I'd been told, whenever I'd tried to put words of my own to them, that "it was just a dream," or "a demon. I will pray for you." Now I saw these things of private vision not only known, but ritualized—and honored.

Finally I could contain myself no longer. "But . . . but I have had just such Visions."

There was another silence in the copse. But now I could tell by the attention of their black shapes that it was the echoes of my very own voice the men listened for, no bird.

"I always thought as much," the Hermit said at last, exchanging a knowing glance with Michel. To me, he continued: "Yours has been a life crammed with signs since first I knew you."

"I am always afraid," I confessed.

Michel sympathized: "Think, Yann. To your Visions. Does the good in them always win?"

"No. Sometimes I wake up screaming with terror. But that is because I have a demon."

"That is because in grasping for too much good, the people have left too much evil for you to winnow in your Visions, child," the Hermit said. "It is the grasping selfishly for too much good—by men such as your Père de Boszac—that allows the evil left behind to congeal into such a dense shadow as may be called a demon."

Michel added his word. "Do not let the victory of evil terrify you, Yann. It is such fears that have emptied the skies of our flyers at Yuletide. If they had not flinched to go to battle the trancers would have seen that sometimes the angels are declared the victors, but sometimes the devils. Both are good for people."

"I do not understand," I said helplessly.

"It is a thought that takes much meditation, much study of the world around us."

"I do not expect you to grasp the notion all at once," the Hermit said, "or even after years."

"Let us consider manure," Michel suggested.

"Manure is nothing but dross," I said. Then, remembering Père de Boszac, "And crawling with demons."

"But just think what our fields would be without it. Why, at home in Lorraine, farmers vie with one another to see who has the largest heap when the barns are cleaned out in the spring. Much manure means many cows and rich crops in the fields. Perhaps a man who has spent all his life in the sterile world of books has never noticed fields through the seasons. He has never seen the streaks of brilliant green contrasted with the sickly yellow and remembered where he spread the dung thickly and where his supply ran out."

"It is the same with death," the Hermit said, rubbing the joints of one hand with another. "There comes a time of pain, of grief— when death, which all our lives we've fought and feared as the greatest enemy—becomes a longed-for friend. The wise man knows to embrace this friend. He understands that death is but a gateway— like the trial of birth—to something beyond. But this is a mystery of which I should not speak to you at length—not yet."

Michel sighed. "It is certainly something the trance fighters knew: that anything the world calls a curse comes, in time, if embraced, to turn to blessing." He took a breath of thick night air and continued: "Here is an example of which even your priest may approve."

I wondered how much more he knew of Père de Boszac. And how he knew it.

"This example was told by St. Augustine. The wicked son wished his old father to die; the good son wishes him to live. It is God's will that the old man die and rest, soon to be renewed. The good son must learn to call that good, embracing both poles at once in the whole of life. And the wicked son must learn to call his wish— which was, after all, the will of God—he must learn to call it evil."

"My head spins!" I cried.

"That is the very cycling of life you feel," the Hermit explained, nodding when I wanted to grasp out to him for stability. "It is the way things are; it is the way they continue. Otherwise, they drop like deadweight to the ground and stop—forever."

Michel said, "He who wishes only the good for himself and his, and is willing to do anything to get it, he creates, by so fierce a light, just so sharp a shadow behind him. I saw examples of this, time and time again as I crossed France. These great men, wishing all for themselves and having great power to get it, leave nothing but a scorched evil in their wake."

I was quiet, trying to absorb the lesson, without much success. The men, too, felt the import of what had been said. Even if they'd heard it—and discussed it with each other—many times before, they felt the God moving in the night air, though He used Michel's tongue. I felt Him, too.

I had a question. I didn't know quite how to frame it, but with the two men feeling my spirit through the night, my wordlessness hardly mattered.

"Yes, son, I understand," the old Hermit said. "I will try to teach you better about your gift. The holy sickness sometimes they call it. It is a great power."

"My mother gives me blackcherry syrup. Père de Boszac says I have a demon."

"When such a gift isn't understood or honored, it is a frightening thing." The Hermit laid his birdlike hand lightly on my shoulder. "I can teach you. I can teach you to understand, revere, and—yes, in some part—control that divine in you."

"I should love that!" I exclaimed.

"The question is—how?" he mused.

"Right here. This night!"

The Hermit smiled. "It is the work of years, my Yann. I cannot do it in a night."

"I will come home with you."

He nodded. "I have, in fact, spoken to your mother sometimes when she comes at Midsummer."

"You have? She never told me."

"She didn't want to distress you, I'm sure. Burden you with what might not happen."

An angry "Oh—!" was all I could find to say to this child's first discovery that his mother has not always been straightforward with him.

"Your mother has been faithful with the cordial I taught her, Yann, so much is obvious."

"I hate that blackcherry slime." I cried out at one more suggestion of my mother's duplicity.

"It has done you good, and that has been a start. But only in the most passive of ways. Whenever I have asked her to let me keep you in the forest with me—as I kept Michel here when he was young—"

"Oh, could I?"

"So far she has refused."

"You must ask her again. This night," I pleaded.

"I fear I must in some part agree with her."

"No!"

"Your mother is wiser than you give her credit for, Yann. Wiser than she will let herself be."

"What do you mean?" I sulked.

"She is right when she says your life is somehow bound up with the young lord Gilles de Rais. I think it's not wise for you to get one type of training and the young lord none of it, lest you grow so far apart you cannot understand one another."

"But Gilles gets to train in arms while I do not," I protested. Then, with even greater bitterness: "And Père de Boszac says I am too evil to learn to write. They do not really want me here at Blaison."

I went on to tell the two men in a few sentences, chopped short by bile and the threatening cliff of tears, how and why I'd run away that afternoon.

"See?" I concluded. "The bridge is closed against me."

"I think the three of us, working together, could get the watch to open up, don't you?" Michel soothed.

The Hermit added, "Or we could say good night now, if you wanted."

I hesitated. No, that was not what I wanted. These men confused me. They had confirmed that I was the demon Père de Boszac always said I was. But they seemed to accept—even admire—that.

"It is late," Michel said gently.

I shook my head with ferocity and found another nut to crack, just to prove how awake I was.

"We will think on what has been said," the Hermit remarked. "You need not return at once to your stewardship, either, Michel, if it pleases you not. You were inspired to come, so it must be for some purpose. But now we should think of rest. You, my Michel, must have traveled far today and long for sleep."

"It was not the way that exhausted me as much as the things I saw," Michel said. "The land, Master. Forgive my disbelief, but I cannot see how even fulfillment of prophecy can turn things around and bring the holy balance once more."

Loath to have the wonderful night come to so early a conclusion, I piped up, "Yes. I heard the steward say he doubted we in Blaison should have enough hay for the winter what with last winter being so fierce and lingering as it was—the Loire flooding the hay fields late into March. And now, this lack of rain."

Michel sighed fondly in my direction. "I noticed the withering fields as I passed today, the crops shriveled and yellow. It is much the same everywhere."

"The steward said we've been two months without rain," I continued my mimicry of grown-up talk. "It seems so to me, though I've not kept close attention."

"Now see, Michel," the Hermit said. I think he laid his hand on the younger man's shoulder comfortingly in the dark. "Here is a purpose for your trip, if nothing else. You have met the boy, seen his magic. We have partaken of the goodwife's supper. Surely you can think of something we can do to repay the good folk of Blaison here, tonight."

Michel brightened, both voice and surrounding light. "We could raise them a storm. Why not?"

I heard the shifting of garments and limbs. My companions were preparing to get to their feet.

"Raise a storm?" I jumped up before them, quick with my youth. "You mean, make it rain? Here? Now?"

"Yes," both men answered with a mutual chuckle.

I hesitated. "Père de Boszac says such conjurings are witchcraft."

"I must meet this Père de Boszac sometime and speak to him,"

Michel said. "His must be a very twisted sort of soul, to enjoy seeing people suffer so."

I remembered the Lenten cheese and the beatings and had to agree. Good and evil did indeed spin curiously around each other. Then I looked up at the cloudless sky, the stars so clear, I could see their many layers, the nearest close enough to touch.

"But how?" I demanded.

There was a twinkle in the Hermit's voice, in his aura. "Magic," he replied.

I had often heard grown-ups tease children with that same answer. In the Hermit's case, however, it was no tease. "Have we not eaten fairy food?" he asked.

"Come." Michel slipped an arm around my shoulder. "You shall come and see how it is done."

"Help us, too, I have no doubt."

"Certainly there could be no better initiation into the work of a Master of the Craft than this," the Hermit said and led the way.

14

A Heddle of Flowers and Ribbons

Together we walked up out of the copse and toward the castle. Blaison startled me, looming black against the still, moonless sky. I had forgotten all about it. But now I could see the figures of the watch standing out against their fires kept low as possible for a heat already fierce enough without adding flames to it.

We stopped by the moat's murky edge. Michel asked his Master, "Will this do?"

"Certainly," the Hermit replied.

I think the two men must have first set a spell of concealment over their work. They attracted no attention from the walls, even when the Hermit made fire. I'd never seen the trick before. He snapped his fingers and a teardrop of flame appeared at the tip of his pointer. Then, by directing his point toward a hollow in a nearby rock, he set the flame to illuminate their work, which it did as merrily as if provided with wick and oil. I can perform the trick myself now, of course, and know it one of the simplest feats to which a novice can turn his budding Craft. At the time, however, I was full of wonder.

The men shifted their attention to the water. I stood behind and watched, hardly daring to blink or breathe.

Their work did not take long. They passed the burden of incantation back and forth between them, then raised their staffs together and struck the water three times. The surface seemed to have grown as hard as glass. But then, at another word, they plunged the staffs in deep and made simultaneous stirrings in a sunwise manner.

I could see it by the orange light of the supernatural flame. Tiny particles stirred up off the water's face, slowly spinning, rising. Again, I knew Père de Boszac would see demons there, but none of us did that night. Soon the vaporous cloud had reached the level of my head, then the men's, then the treetops, soon the height of the castle walls, still slowly churning to the command of the magicians' wands.

When the tiny cloud reached the sky and the lowest level of stars, the old Hermit nodded that it was enough and the stirring stopped. Overhead, however, the heavy, wet cloud continued to roil and thicken and grow. The patch of stars blotted from view started as no bigger than my hand, then both hands.

"We should be seeking shelter," said the Hermit as he bent to extinguish his magic flame. "This storm won't wait long now."

Even as he spoke, a sharp wind rustled up through the tinder-dry grass at our feet. The flame guttered so it was difficult to say whether the wind or the Hermit finally plunged us back into darkness.

A deeper darkness it was, too, with more of the stars blacking out at every minute. Michel took my arm and said, "Come, lad. Let's get you into the castle. And they'll take a pair of strangers in, too, I hope, on a stormy night."

But I stood rooted to the spot, staring still at the point in the turgid water where the storm had arisen.

"I see . . ." I stammered. "I see . . ."

"Come along, Yann."

He took my arm more firmly, but the Hermit took his and stopped him.

"Wait, Michel." The old man's voice dropped to a whisper, weighted by much awe for one whose eyes had seen as much as his. "The boy Sees something. The Sight. It's come upon him."

Michel squatted to my level now, trying to look where I looked. "Yann, tell us. Tell us what you see."

"A cart . . . a horse . . . flowers . . . ribbons."

"A festival?" the Hermit prompted.

"They celebrate weddings thus in Lorraine," Michel offered.

Michel grew more definite still when I saw "A cradle, wreathed and decked with scraps of silk."

"A cradle always has pride of place in the final cart of the bride's procession to her new home," he explained quickly, quietly so as not to interrupt.

"A man named Jacquot. The woman . . . Za . . . Zabir . . . no . . . I cannot say it."

"Zabillet. It must be. That is how Lorrainers familiarize Isabelle."

"A good name for a woman," the Hermit commented. "Full of magic."

"The boy wouldn't make it up. And how could he know Lorrainers otherwise?"

The Hermit must have made a sign for peace, for attention, though I was too transfixed to notice. "Is this something familiar to you, Michel?"

Michel kept prodding me instead. "Is he a square man? Not tall, but strong? Red complexion? A stranger to Lorraine?"

I may have nodded to one of his questions at least.

"Yes, Jacquot d'Arc they call him. He fled the fighting in Champagne, married a local girl named Zabillet Romée—small, dark—in the usual fashion and set up farming. That wedding—what the child sees—occurred more than a year ago. I can't think why he should find it so important."

I don't think I said anything. Michel simply knew his thoughts confirmed. "Zabillet was with child when I left the valley."

"She is delivered," I reported. "A son. They've named him Jacquemin."

"Well, that will please old Jacquot d'Arc."

"How so?" the Hermit asked. "You speak as if it were more than any other man's wish for an heir."

"Jacquot was greatly troubled by dreams when first he was married, and then when his wife was with child. He came to me for interpretation."

"What were the dreams?"

"He dreamed he had a daughter who ran off with the soldiers to war. Well, that must be very distressing to any respectable man, to think his daughter destined to become a camp follower."

"So what was your interpretation?"

"Frankly, at the time I suspected he was haunted by specters from the war in Champagne. He would never speak of it directly, but I understood he lost a great number of his family there—perhaps even an earlier wife and children—and such things are hard for any man to live through. Still, the dream affected him so deeply.

" 'I will drown her,' he kept saying. 'At birth, like an unwanted kitten. I will drown any daughter of mine who fulfills that dream. And if I haven't the strength, Father, you must swear to me you'll do the job for me.' "

"Did you promise him?"

"I told him this was something on which he ought to wait and see. And just look, he has had a son and need not have feared for a moment."

"Jacquot may himself be an older man, but his wife is young, I think. The couple may hope for other children."

"Of course."

"They may yet have a daughter or two, there within the shade of the Bois Chênu."

"Of course, Master."

The sorcerers' flow of words passed over me like the rising wind against my cheeks. I heard them, but hardly thought of them. I was an epileptic at the edge of a fit. I was a child with a new toy.

Michel continued: "I can only think how much easier old Jacquot d'Arc must be resting to have a son in that cradle tonight."

"It must mean more than that," the Hermit insisted. "Surely the Sight would not have come so strongly to this child simply to assure you that a poor farmer you once counseled has not this night become father to a whore."

I spoke now, far away, the voice not my own, the Vision closing. "The virgin-whore." I echoed the word off the old man's tongue. But it meant more than that. "La Pucelle."

Then I sank to the earth in a fit.

Knots Tied on the Wrong Side

When I came to my senses, Michel had me in his arms and we were heading through strong gusts of wind toward the now-opened castle gate. What magic had brought the bridge down, I couldn't guess. Probably the wonder of the storm was enough, to the watch up by their whipping fires.

The Hermit was speaking rapidly, helping himself along on two staffs by the younger man's side. "But just think what the boy might have been able to tell us had his Sight been properly trained. No, I am convinced, my Martinet, that it was for this purpose you left Lorraine and came to Blaison. He seems to have the power to tell you of any event near the Bois Chênu that might need your attention even while you remain here. He will warn you in time for you to return and attend to it. Surely it was for this you came, Michel. I am not free to leave my post, but you—you could stay here and become the lad's tutor. Certainly it can be done. Certainly it *should* be done."

Michel did not speak. He only nodded, his black beard tickling my limp arm. The first drops of blood-warm rain were blowing into his face with the steep force of castle walls behind them. They seemed to have stolen his breath.

And so the two magicians worked up a story and a glamour that were so strong, they even got past Père de Boszac's demon scrutiny that evening. I heard the Paris scholar chatting happily with the new arrivals while my mother, dashing away tears of relief, bundled me off to bed and more blackcherry syrup.

"You are well met, brothers," I heard Père de Boszac say. "Dominicans? Yes. I have always had the highest regard for your St. Dominic and the order he founded to combat heresy. Well are you nicknamed the 'hounds of God.' Tonight you've proved bloodhounds, indeed, returning the lost sheep. And how charitable of you to offer to take our poor, sick Jean under your care, Père Michel. He is a great concern to all of us."

Michel never did disabuse Père de Boszac, but found a respected place at his side as the castle's second tutor, Père Michel de Fontenay. Père de Boszac let him have complete control of me, the common, sickly child, and not too infrequently that of Gilles as well. The demon hunter had interests in his life other than children.

To me, Michel shrugged off any deception. "It was that Dominic they've sanctified who first appropriated our traditional robes and tonsure. He used them to deceive. Faithful people thought they were coming to us, to Masters of the Craft, only to find themselves betrayed into the hands of the most vicious heresy hunters, hounds indeed. If they may be mistaken for us for their deadly purposes, why should we not turn the tables and be taken for them—when it suits us?"

———————

After my first deep sleep, such as comes on the heels of my spells, I awoke. I suppose it was at the height of the storm. There was lightning and crashes of thunder.

One of the maids set to watch me was crying nearby. "There is the devil in this storm, surely," she wept.

Others were praying and only one said, though still not without wonder, "What a blessing it will be for the hay."

I wasn't afraid, but a little confused that over the maidservants and the storm itself I could hear the authors of the night's weather talking lowly together. They had been welcomed to sleep down in the hall with the swains, away from the family and the maids. There was no way I could have heard them with my natural ears from the bed where I lay next to Gilles (who managed to sleep through everything). So I counted it up to just one more of the night's wonders.

The Hermit spoke first: "I haven't seen you, Michel, since the Sacrifice."

"Yes." Michel seemed to feel the weight of his word.

"We were all grateful when news came as to what you'd done. The Land was grateful."

"Master, having shed royal blood yourself, you must know the priest does nothing. It is the God who makes the choice, who makes the offering. It is the Sacrifice himself. And the God in him."

"Yes, and we thank the King's son. But for such a powerful, terrible thing, a God often needs encouragement. And He needs the priest to make Him divine."

"In the case of the duke of Burgundy, very little was needed. He knew it was time—and understood."

"His blood has made our lives."

"Would every Sacrifice were so easy."

Again, I heard the shift of bodies and garments in the darkness. Again, I thought the two men had crossed themselves. I know now, of course, they were not crossing. It was a very similar sign, but the sign before being stolen and only slightly altered, like robes and tonsure, for the uses of a different power. A power that pulled away from the Earth instead of toward Her.

The two men formed the sign of the Horned One. And instead of remembering Christ, this gesture remembered a more recent Sacrifice, yet an older one, a long deep cycle of Sacrifice after Sacrifice. And the gesture remembered the blood of the God now coursing through their own veins, through everything around them, and giving them, with every heartbeat, the blessing of life.

After a moment Michel said quietly, "Yet I wonder: Where the next shall come from? King Charles is as mad as ever, refusing to heed the call."

"We're not yet halfway through the nine years of the Cycle. Trust. The God will provide Himself."

"So we all hope. His ways are wondrous. All the more wondrous when I see no Sacrifice today half as willing as Philippe of Burgundy was at this time last Cycle, and I must confess I never thought he'd come. I thought I would be burned at the stake myself as the Sacrifice. Until the last moment, I never thought he'd come."

"The God will provide," the Hermit assured.

Because I could not fathom what they meant, I quickly went back to sleep.

But my dreams were full of an aching cry for "Sacrifice."

The Magic Net

The cold, grey air was like the cold, grey porridge of the Advent fast. My limbs moved heavily, sluggishly as I followed Michel and a bouncing, skipping Gilles up to the ramparts of Tours. My brain felt stupid and depressed. I didn't want to watch any somber procession.

"A Craftsman can always learn something from acts of faith," my Master had said.

But did a Craftmaster never take a holiday?

"I wish we'd never come," I complained, stopping to pant on every stair.

"To Tours?" Michel asked. "Or just to the wall?"

The notion of coming to court this Christmastide to offer a show of fealty to our King had had a grand sound to it during the flurry of packing back in little Blaison. For Madame especially, the holiday represented a glamorous recess a mere three days' easy ride away from home even in indifferent weather. Her husband agreed and had decided his eldest son, too, might profit by a court appearance.

That Tours was a land of exile for poor, mad Charles VI had hardly chronicled itself upon our rustic point of view. But something of the like entered my chronicle now.

"Both," I replied. "Both Tours and this silly wall."

"Holidays are made for learning the Craft." Michel encouraged me, then turned to the grey stone of his climb again, the hem of his black robe for me to follow.

"I've learned something already," Gilles bragged as my head finally raised out of the stair shaft and took the slap of brisk air. "Tours is impregnable!" He loved the big soldier's word.

So saying, Gilles pulled himself up onto the lowest crenel of the battlement. He squirmed across the expanse of stone and then swung himself upright to sit, enraptured by the sights that spread out below him, both legs dangling over the edge in *nihilo*. I knew the position; he took it everywhere he could, as if in love with emptiness. The sight of him thus made my head swim. I could not even consider trying to join him in looking at the view. I wanted to scream at him to come down as others always did—for my own comfort if not for his own.

Père Michel was the only person I knew who could watch Gilles de Rais with apparent equanimity. Our tutor actually seemed to encourage his charge's daredevilry, as if saying, "Yes, child, go. Try. These are the things for which you were born, to break the bounds of fear and caution that hold ordinary mortals."

Michel told me he stretched a magic net under every stunt Gilles undertook. It was a difficult spell, one I hadn't begun to master on my own. Surely a man must have such a skill to remain so calm in the face of his charge's constant and wanton flirtation with death.

But then I had to be jealous that Père Michel spread no similar net for me. When I fell, I got hurt. The Master, like all the others, called to me constantly to "Be careful, watch out." He never pushed me to my limits, except, perhaps, the limits of my mind. Or, as it often seemed, the limits of my boredom.

Physically, I remained the cripple. My hand was still clumsy and twisted. I continued to have spells, and woke from them exhausted, head throbbing, bruised where I fell.

It wasn't fair. *I* was older. *I* was the one rejected by Père de Boszac. *I* was the child most advanced in the Craft. In fact, Michel always spoke carefully of his powers when Gilles was around, using euphemisms, not answering questions directly.

"The newly completed wall is remarkable, yes." Michel seemed to be ignoring me in exclusive favor of the little lordling. Everybody always did. "Do you see, Messire Gilles, how the two halves of the town, once separately walled, have been joined? This is the work begun just after the defeat of Jean the Good by the English Black

Prince at Poitiers. Its completion is hardly older than yourself."

Michel stood next to Gilles on the safe side of the wall, gesturing wide over the prospect, casting his safety net with the same gesture.

"This is not Craft," I complained, quite forgetting that Michel did not like me to say the name of our power too carelessly.

"Crafty-wafty," Gilles mimicked. He had not been kept so much in the dark that he didn't know how to abuse when it would rile.

"Everything is Craft," Michel told me quietly, patiently, but not apologetically. "And remember. Gilles' share of the Craft is that of a warrior, not the same as yours."

This did not make me any more gracious.

Fortunately, Gilles had grown bored with our talk and skipped off for a circuit of the next tower's crenellation. Michel let up his vigilance—but only for a moment. Soon enough, Gilles had found a fascinating gap in the wooden catwalk that ran behind the battlements. A beam overhead provided the means to swing from one side of the eighty-foot drop to the other—back again. And back again. Michel quietly, patiently spread another net.

I pulled my cloak tighter around me and thought I might have stayed in the warm hall if this lesson was just for Gilles. Blood always had a hard time getting to my crippled hand.

And then suddenly, blood was bursting at every vein. My limbs dithered in a panic. They dithered even when I realized the horrific noise was the toll of the great bell of St. Martin's rising up from the heap of delicate white tracery so very nearly at our feet and to the left.

The noise startled Gilles, too, almost to flight. He lost the momentum of his swing to the overwhelming swing of the clapper and clung to his beam by one slipping hand.

Michel had to stretch his body into the force of his spell to save his pupil. He snatched Gilles by the fur of his collar from midair and brought him in with a toss, sharp yet so playful that the young lord never realized how close to death he had come. He only squealed with delight and begged Michel, "Again! Toss me again!"

Our tutor did so. Between tosses, his voice somewhat concealed by Gilles' crowing and demands for more, Michel spared sideways looks and words for me.

"Time was when our people feared the ring of bells," he told me. "And our enemies gloated that we lost our power within reach of their sound. To this day, in many places, the bells ring all night long at our holiest seasons—Samonias, Noël, Midsummer—because certain Christians hope they can knock the Night Flyers from the sky by the noise. Or wake the trancers."

"Can they?" I certainly felt knocked from my equilibrium.

"They can." He tossed Gilles. "They have." He tossed him again. "You can feel it." Gilles' black curls flew up like ravens' wings and he laughed a hoarse caw. "Bells generally mean settlement." Toss. "A city." Toss. "And nothing is more anathema to our power than the power present in a city."

After another toss, Michel paused, laughing and tickling Gilles while he caught his breath. Then he said, "A man working in the Craft today should never let church bells startle him, be they never so near or sudden. He must learn to pace his work around them. He should have a sense of the air so that he can feel the intake as the bell swings back for the first strike.

"You knew what we came up here for," he concluded. "You knew that bell ringing was likely to accompany any procession. You knew this was not the little parish church of Blaison. You ought not to have been taken by surprise."

I kicked at the new wall as if I might knock it down.

Yes, I should have been prepared. As prepared for St. Martin's clamor as I was for St. Venant who answered him, then St. Denis, the high, clear chime of Notre Dame l'Ecrignole, the tinnier sound of Holy Cross, all trying to match the ominous throb of their great mistress, the basilica's iron heart.

Then, almost petulantly as if left behind, the deep bass of the double towers of St. Gatien Cathedral was drawn in to catch up the other end of sound. St. Jacques out on his island, St. Pierre of the Corpses and St. Jean of the Wounds out in the distant fields, and even the abbey bells of Marmoutier up and across the river, these church towers ringed space with the ultimate echoes.

In the heart of this ring of sound, Michel finally swung Gilles up to the wall where he seemed content to walk back and forth.

"Look!" Gilles cried from his vantage point. "Look! The procession begins."

With such temptation I at last found the nerve to creep closer to the edge so I could see, too. Yes, the bells had shaken a great black surge of people out of the château keep, residence of the counts of Anjou since time immemorial and now of the Valois of all of France. This was the massive but irregular stone rectangle far on our right.

"Will we get to see him?" Gilles hopped from stone to stone in his excitement. "Will we get to see King Charles?"

"The procession is for His Majesty," Michel began.

"I know that," Gilles interrupted, hopping. "It's 'cause King Charles is mad as a buck." My milk brother quoted some grown-up's proverb with little understanding himself. "Will we see him run wild in the streets?" Gilles himself ran wild on the throbbing city wall.

"We may not see him for precisely that reason," Michel deliberated. "Such is his illness that they may think it best to keep him in confinement on such a public occasion for the dignity of majesty."

"Locked up in his own deepest, darkest dungeon," Gilles thrilled. "But he must come in contact with the holy relics of the saint or he will not be cured. And I don't think the saint—a heap of bones in a box—is likely to come walking to him, even if he is the King."

So far, all the procession offered us were the preliminary ranks of local dignitaries. First came the archbishop bearing a great gold and bejeweled cross. White-invested prelates flanked him and choirboys swinging their censers in time to the continuing pulse of bells formed an outer bank. Then, with slow and measured steps, came eight times eight canons of the saint's basilica. Then followed nine by eight ranks all in black, robes almost identical to what our Master wore: the monks of St. Martin's own house, Marmoutier.

Infrequently my bell-numbed ears caught the rising, somber tones of the *Te Deum*. Such chanted words were a better-known comfort for these one hundred and seventy throats than common speech.

Then followed the strangers, the pilgrims of many lands. They were a much less disciplined company than the first three groups so it was impossible to try to count them with any accuracy. They took up more than twice the space of the regiments that had preceded them. Their tail end was not even all visible beyond the castle walls by the time the first of them had gyrated and crawled and shouted and clanked their way into the Grand Rue.

Here were those come to Tours not of their own free will but as an alternative to the gallows. Murderers wore the weapons of their crimes forged into collars of shame about their necks. Adulterers and thieves of church property faced the December-chilled street cobbles barefooted, with little else on but their hair shirts—and the massive chains the prelates in their home parishes had had them locked in to. Such men and women were condemned to wander the world until the emblems of their sins dropped from their bodies of God's own will. I knew such chains cut into the flesh and putrefied the wounds. Other pilgrims were covered in ash they could not wash from them—along with dirt or vermin—until the same sign of Grace was shown. I was glad of our vantage point in the open air with only the wood smoke of so many chimneys to clog our lungs.

Centered in the throng but given wide berth were the lepers with their rattles and bells, some on crutches or little carts, some carried by their fellows. The blind, the lame, the spastic, the deformed, all followed, hoping for a cure. Mixed in with them were those for whom pilgrimage was a choice. Two or three dragged great wooden crosses over their shoulders in emulation of Our Lord. They might have found the peregrination an escape from responsibilities, a holiday. An excuse to beg. Or cut purse strings.

"This is God's view of the procession," I murmured.

And Michel, the author of our view, did not contradict.

Teetering on the wall, Gilles threw off the tutor's hand, spread his arms as if to embrace all he saw, and shouted, "All the people in the world are in Tours today."

"They are not," I said with an older boy's wisdom—or with God's.

"Are so." Gilles turned on me with such suddenness that only Michel's nearby hand kept him from losing his balance.

Michel spoke to make peace. "You remember, Gilles, what Père de Boszac told you about visiting St. Martin on this day?"

"The Holy Father in Rome says any visitor on the thirteenth day of December gets one hundred years and one day indulgence from purgatory," Gilles spouted.

"Then I wonder Père de Boszac did not care to come and shave off some of his evil deeds with us." I did not miss the priest at all. I grumbled to have his name mentioned when leaving him behind was the only good thing about coming to Tours.

"Père de Boszac has no evil deeds." Gilles allowed himself to be drawn into our usual battle over whose priest was better—for we did tend to lay claim to them, each to the one whose view of the world liked us best. "He can sense demons and avoid them. Demons like you, Jean Le Drapier."

"I'm no demon," seemed the response of a little boy with a crippled hand.

While I scoured my brain for something better, Gilles won the argument by withdrawing to another subject.

"I do hope there is benefit even staying so far from the relics today," Gilles sighed with a seriousness I might have found comical in one so young—if I'd not been so vexed. "Père Michel, you promised it would be so."

"For one with your young sins, Messire Gilles, I think this is close enough."

"For my part, I cannot tell demons until it's too late," Gilles confessed, suddenly standing quite still on his treacherous perch. "Only one hundred years and a day? December thirteenth comes too rarely. I know I commit more sins in a year than that."

Michel's high-shaven brow clouded with concern deeper than I'd ever seen when he looked in my direction. We boys fought over our priests while the priests fought over us.

"Perhaps what you imagine as sins are not so, Messire Gilles," Michel suggested. "Perhaps they are only the shadows that give depth to your life."

"But Père de Boszac says—"

"And has he never quoted to you the tale of the Magdalene? That he who is without sin should cast the first stone?"

"No," said Gilles.

So Michel told him, rifling yet another holy book for his lessons. When he was done, I sought my fair share of the attention by asking, "December thirteenth is the commemoration of the day when St. Martin's remains were returned to their rightful place here in Tours?"

"That's right," Michel said, letting his younger charge balance off along the wall, casting the net spell again.

"When the trees all along the route burst into bloom, the birds sang, and candles ignited themselves for joy when his bones passed?"

"That's what they say. And weather that causes flowering out of season is always called a St. Martin's summer to this day."

"I don't see any flowers now. The trees over the cloister wall bloom only with clouds of incense. And look, all those people have had their candles blown out, not relit."

Michel nodded. "The angle where that street meets the Grand Rue must create a sharp breeze."

We watched the canons scramble with as much dignity as they could to relight one another's tapers.

"Will the flowers bloom once the procession reaches the relics, in the basilica itself?" I asked.

"What do you think, you with the Sight?"

"I—I don't know." I didn't want such a miracle to happen: it would give too much support to Père de Boszac's preaching. But I knew that my desire against it was so strong, it must color my vision.

"Well, let us watch and see what does happen," Michel counseled instead.

17

Sackcloth Beneath the Flying Stag Banner

---·•·---

The archbishop's censers were fogging the half-timbered walls of the finer houses clustered about St. Saturnin now. That was when, back to the left, we caught our first glimpse of the nobility in their proper echelons. From least up to greatest, they'd begun to exit the château.

"There she is. I see my mama," Gilles declared.

"Where?" I demanded.

"In that blue. She was wearing her blue today. 'The closest I have to sackcloth,' she said."

I had to admit the color was right for Madame. It was, however, a very popular shade among the ladies that year and the gentleman walking close enough to be that particular lady's lord looked nothing at all like Sire de Rais. Certainly that handsome wine color was not the austere hair shirt Monseigneur had said he must wear for the solemnities.

"I am so glad my lord father and lady mother decided we should spend the Christmas holiday in Tours," Gilles said.

Michel agreed. "It is always good to present yourself to your liege lord, especially when the King is as hard-pressed as he is now."

"There are so many others here doing the same thing," I complained. "I cannot see how you will be noticed among so many other lords and ladies."

"I will be noticed," Gilles insisted.

I had to admit, he probably would be. The scarlet of his doublet brought out the bloom in his plump, windblown cheeks. And at the

edges, his linen, still brilliantly white, exaggerated the almost otherworldly pallor of his clear skin. Madame always took care that he
was dressed most becomingly, but especially here in Tours. The odd
thing about Gilles was, he didn't seem to mind as any other boy
would. Indeed, he seemed to thrive on such fussing.

"But not by the King," I insisted. "The King notices no one. The
King is mad."

"And do you know why he is mad, Yann?" Michel asked sternly.

Of course I did. But I hated to have to recite the obvious lesson.
"Because he refused to do a King's duty."

"And?"

"And die for his people."

"When?"

"When the Grand Cycle of Sacrifice was due."

Michel didn't even bother to look to see if Gilles might overhear
the word; the Cycle was something he made certain both of us understood, no matter who might find it wickedness. Michel nodded.
"Good. I thought you might have forgotten."

I kicked again at the wall of Tours, as if in boredom.

"Then is it possible that you have forgotten the death of the
duke of Orléans?"

I shook my head.

"I did not think that possible, since you actually saw him cut
down there in Paris' Vieille Rue du Temple."

Did he remind me as punishment? I closed my eyes as if only
against the briskness of the wind. But still I could not push from my
mind the vision of the white brain pan rolling in the gutter. I said
nothing.

"Why is that murder not avenged yet?" Gilles took advantage of
my silence to press his own education. "If it were my blood to avenge,
I swear I would not have left it so long. It happened the night *le petit*
René was born. My pest of a brother is already walking and nobody
does a thing. Don't they know who committed the crime? But Yann
saw the man—in his dream. Don't they believe Yann?"

"The duke of Burgundy has confessed openly to the deed. People
know."

"So why don't they act?"

"Burgundy said he did it for the good of the state."

"What does that mean?"

"I suppose he means the good of Burgundy. He certainly can't mean the good of France. Even less can he mean the land in the way we—our—our wisdom—understands it."

"During this last fighting season," Michel went on, "friends of the Orléans cause were quite incapable of meeting Burgundy's twenty thousand in open battle. But the friends of slain Orléans do have one *cheval de bataille*, one thing on their side. That is possession of the royal person of Charles VI. Do you know who leads the friends of Orléans?"

"The constable of France, Count d'Armagnac," Gilles piped.

"Correct again. A man who more and more lends his name to the whole cause on behalf of the duchess Valentine. On the night of this most recent All Souls', the Armagnacs struck their coup. They dressed His befuddled Majesty in Celestine robes and led him from his barred and padded cell in Hôtel Saint-Pôl. They led him through the neighboring monastery and down to the Seine. A boat with muffled oarlocks carried him beyond the city walls to the abbey of Saint-Victor. From there, military escort brought the whole party, by easy stages, at last to Tours."

"It's true. For the traitors in Burgundy have allied themselves very closely with the heathen English."

" 'Heathen' is not a curse word, Gilles," I protested.

"Is so." He countered me with the reflex of *responsa* in a mass.

"Sometimes the worst thing you can call a person is 'very Christian.' " I could tell Michel was growing tense as I touched on things he'd often warned me I must not share too freely with others. But I couldn't resist calling Gilles on the common knowledge he spouted so blithely.

"Blasphemous heathen," Gilles said. "Père de Boszac always said so and it's true."

The only good thing about Gilles' anger was that it brought him so close to the edge of the wall that he toppled inward to my level.

"Christians kill people whose hearts are different than theirs," I said. "Heathens do not do so."

"They only wickedly sacrifice their own faithful. No wonder Christianity triumphs."

"But a heathen also knows when to hold his tongue."

These were Michel's words, spoken so sharply I felt I'd been slapped, though this tutor never raised his hands to us no matter what the provocation. Then, looking back at Gilles, I realized only I had heard the threat at all.

Aloud, Michel deftly turned our attention back to the nobles appearing in ever-ascending rank. "You see, it is no more than a court-in-exile to which we have made pilgrimage this Christmas season, Messire Gilles."

"They do seem—they seem—small—not much—" Gilles hunted for the word.

"They lack glamour," I said, and was rewarded by a smile from Michel. Finally, I had covered my meaning by using a word that has magic connotations as well as the mundane. Men of the Craft always speak this language of two levels.

In the miniature streets below, a rank of very young people had passed out of the shadows of the château and into our view. Herded by tutors of their own, these were very noble lords and ladies indeed to be where we were not allowed. Princes perhaps.

"Yes," Michel said, as if reading my thoughts and pointing. "That is Jean, the second son of King Charles."

The little prince didn't seem very powerful, although he was trusted to walk unsupervised.

"He has two years on you, Yann," Michel said. "Prince Jean is ten. Can you sense his royal blood?"

I could not, but I said nothing.

"Ah, and now this—" Michel said as a figure only slightly larger than Prince Jean and dressed in the royal azure appeared. "This is the oldest prince, the Dauphin Louis, duc de Guyenne, a year older than his brother."

"He will be King when his father dies." Gilles, too, was impressed.

"If it is God's will," Michel replied.

I looked sharply at our Master. Did he See something others did not? Should I See something as well? I looked back at the young man's stately march but found my mind blank, telling me nothing one way or the other.

"Ah, look! It is! It is the King!"

Gilles' excitement was such that Michel had to concentrate full-time on his net spell. Except for the conscienceless bells, everything else seemed to fall silent, too, with awe. It was as if we were all holding our breath, willing the thin, frail figure not to crumple before us—or to run stark raving mad.

A banner portraying a flying stag preceded the monarch. The powerful, royal emblem so evocative of my time in St. Gilles gave a lie to the figure who followed it. The King walked on unsteady legs under the rich blue canopy strewn with gold fleurs-de-lis, circled by a thick and tensely vigilant guard of pikers. Charles himself wore only grey sackcloth.

The instant he turned into the Grand Rue, most people fell into the rigidity of awe. One or two pushed forward, however, trying to reach the royal personage. The pikers fiercely shoved these brave souls back.

"They are people afflicted by scrofula, the King's evil," Michel bent to whisper in my ear. "That is an illness for which St. Martin offers no cure. Only the King. They hope that by touching His Majesty, just the hem of his sackcloth, they may be cured. But a King who cannot cure himself, how can he hope to cure others?"

Indeed the King flinched from those who pressed around him. Their outstretched hands and cries for mercy sent him scurrying, first to one side, then to the other. The pikers had to step in and shove the sick away.

There was one final item in the procession. Surrounded by several dozen prelates, held aloft on a gilt pole, was a single scrap of greyish cloth. This was blessed Martin's cloak, the very garment the Saint had divided with a freezing beggar while a soldier in the Roman army and so set his foot on the path to sanctity. No one would think to give this other half to any common charity these days, no matter how naked the body. St. Martin's cloak had been revered by French Kings since the Merovingians, carried into battle, granting them victory. True, its power had been somewhat eclipsed in recent years by the banner, the Oriflamme, dipped in the blood of St. Denis. But the

Oriflamme was with Monseigneur St. Denis, in Paris, in Burgundian hands. St. Martin's cloak was remembered, therefore, and supplicated once more with all the guilt of forgotten duty.

"The change of air has done His Majesty good, they say," Gilles commented. His Majesty's canopy had removed the royal sight from our view.

"He frightened me," I admitted, my first ability to fit words to all I'd felt.

"Scaredy-cat," Gilles said. "I was not afraid."

For that I had to strike him. Even with him precarious on the wall, I knew I'd get the worst of it. But I had to do it, anyway. Gilles fell on me, with the full height of the wall added to his solid weight.

After what seemed like an age, Michel finally separated us with patient firmness. As I staggered back, heaving with sobs and nursing a scratched face, I was certain I'd get the worst of the scolding. I'd struck first, after all. I was older. And I'd known full well how dangerous Gilles' position was. At home in Blaison, Père de Bloszac would already be whittling his switch.

But "Remember to take your counsel from Yann," the tutor told Gilles in my behalf. "Always remember he has a sense of such things beyond the ordinary and that is his calling, to counsel the power of your arm. The arm of any lord who holds the second estate. What are the three estates of men, Messire Gilles?"

Gilles, hardly panting from our scuffle, recited the answer grudgingly: "Laborer, noble, druid."

Michel nodded. "There are those who work the magic of work: farmers, laborers, millers." Much of what he said we had heard him recite, over and over. But he made us hear it again. "There are those who work the magic of battle: the nobility. This is your estate, Gilles. The greatest of these is the King. But he is not the greatest of all, only the greatest of his estate. And what, Gilles, is the first estate?"

I held my breath. Would he say it? Would Gilles actually confess?

"The first place of estate belongs to the druid who is also called the Master, the priest." Gilles scrambled up on the wall again as he spoke, defying any estate to beat him at his.

"Very good," Michel said.

Did the Master spread a net again as he slipped his hands casually into the sleeves of his black robe? How else could he speak so calmly, so warmly, like an embrace of safety around the heart-stopping rashness of the second estate.

"There may be petty Craftsmen, Gilles, Yann, just as there are petty Kings. But no King can be great unless he is well counseled by a Master, unless he turns the actions of his arm to the counsel of the trees and the birds, which only a Seer can see. There can be no greater honor for a noble after his death than to say, 'He was well counseled.' And how he fulfills the constraints of his station in this life determines what station he may attain in the next.

"I must agree with Yann in this case and urge you, Messire Gilles, always to heed him. A mere matter of weeks cannot erase the haggard gauntness of insanity from the royal face. The King is not cured, nor will he be, until he takes counsel of the Craft as you must learn to do. Until he submits as his oath to the land requires."

"Then they are right when they say he's been bewitched."

"In a way, yes, they are right."

Gilles turned his back and crossed his arms over his chest in a petulant attitude, strung there on the wall like a bird between heaven and earth. "I wish you witches would mind your own business."

Well, he knew so much. Knew to call us witches. But did he say it as Michel might do? Or as Père de Boszac had taught him?

"This is our business," Michel said quietly.

Gilles said nothing. He turned his back and stretched his wings as if to fly.

"None of the trees around the basilica are coming out green, either," I complained, turning back to watch the procession's progress.

"Which is just how it should be," Michel replied.

"Why do we come to Tours if we don't get to see a St. Martin summer?"

"And if all the apple and pear trees were to bloom today, what should become of them in a week or so, when the hard freeze sets in again?"

I considered, and did not like the answer I came up with. "The frost would blast the tender fruit to the heart. And no bees would fly to them in the first place."

"Exactly." Michel nodded so that the beard pillowing his chin buckled wisely. "It would mean no apples or pears next year, anywhere along St. Martin's path. The trees would take a year to recover from time out of season, maybe more."

"Then Martin is no saint."

"He is a Christian saint," Michel corrected, "famous during his life for broad exhibitions that pitted his power against that of many Craftmasters."

"He had a magic?"

"He did. A Christian magic."

"What's wrong with that?"

"Like many Christians he thought that putting a sheen of unalleviated goodness on the world is the sign of true power. It wins converts, yes, for who would not enjoy the bloom of spring when his limbs suffer winter's chill? In the end, however, breaking the cycle of seasons, upsetting the Earth's taut balance, is never the best magic."

"And I wish we had never come here to Tours!"

The seething frustration in me had finally burst forth. Perhaps, I thought, if I spoke suddenly enough, it would startle Gilles and send him tumbling off the wall. It did not.

"Are you homesick, Yann?" Gilles tried for sympathy, but I saw more of a smirk.

"It's—it's St. Stephen's Day," I stammered.

"Not for weeks yet. Not 'til the day after Christmas."

"But I wanted to go a-wrening." I burst, unhappy tears starting in the corners of my eyes. "Père Michel, you promised this year I could go a-wrening and now, here, we won't."

At my words, Gilles remembered himself on this subject. "Yes, Father, you promised. Say we can still go a-wrening, here in Tours."

"Tours," Michel sighed, as if renewing a spell that had begun to fade but was still needed. "Tours is such a grand town, it may have forgotten the tradition."

I'd never gone a-wrening before, being considered too young or too crippled every other St. Stephen's Day of my life. Certainly a small village like Blaison always kept the rite, and I had looked forward to it this year at last. Michel had promised to plead the case that even a boy so young as Gilles or as crippled as I should be allowed to undertake the motions of the hunt.

Now he had to admit, "Lords and ladies will take no part in such activities."

And, "There may not be many birds left in this neighborhood. The safety of these massive fortifications are what attracted the King's partisans to Tours. But they have left little habitat for the wren, you may be sure."

"The wall is of stone, not wood," I protested, kicking at it yet again.

Michel turned his back directly against the procession now, against the insistence of the bells and the crowded city. He faced south where the sun nearing its lowest point in the year seemed to drown in a watery bank of grey cloud. These were the closest forests, along the southern ridges.

"Naturally. But masons need scaffolding and rollers to place under their stones as they haul them up from the river. And they need huts to live in and wood to warm themselves and to cook their food."

The forests did seem very far away indeed. "I see."

Michel paused for a moment, pausing as he often did, as if debating in his mind whether what he was about to tell me was something I was old enough to digest or not.

This matter of St. Stephen's Day, still nearly a fortnight away, did not seem such a great concern to Gilles, in spite of his earlier urging. Well, the young lord's son would have plenty of consolation among the nobles and their keeping of the feast. I would only wait on tables. So Gilles had balanced off, arms outstretched, to investigate the rest of the wall or to see better how the head of the procession, reaching St. Martin's now, was faring. Michel kept his eye and his spell on him, but he spoke to me.

"If Gilles were near, I would not speak." He cleared his throat and took on teaching tones like the drape of long, dark robes over his voice. Or feathered his voice like the plumage of the martinet.

"The wren is a measure of the health of a region. Such a tiny bird, it is the first to feel the effects if men encroach too much upon the wild. The hunting of the wren in olden times let men know where they stood in the balance. At this time of year, now, during the hardest, darkest days, if there was no wren to be found, or none that let itself be caught, men would know they had encroached too far. Another sacrifice would be required of them, to make room for the bird."

What sacrifice? I wanted to ask. But I didn't. I always grew uneasy when Michel brought up the word "sacrifice." There was something in his emphasis . . .

He'd often spoken of sacrifice before. "Sometimes a measure of flour baked into a cake. Sometimes blood: a cock, a goat. Sometimes more."

What "more" I hadn't yet had the courage to ask and he hadn't told me. That was something, I sensed, even he thought beyond my youth.

And suddenly he seemed to regret what he'd told me this time. "It is best not to break the mystery, the ritual, by speaking so baldly of such things." To the uninitiated. To me. "People are more likely to forget things if there is no mystery."

"How can that be so?" I asked. "I think their minds would crave understanding."

"This, too, is a mystery. Nevertheless, it is true. The more logical a thing is, the easier men find to logic it away. Because logic can always be changed to suit the necessities of the moment, the ambitions of a certain man in a certain place and time. Mystery is not so susceptible. With mystery, men remember all the details. Because they are not certain which are important and which not.

"Just listen, in future years, as the time for hunting the wren comes around again," he continued. "You will find every man discovers a reason to suit his taste. The different reasons defy logic— but so tradition sticks. When reason has outmaneuvered the mystery, as with the wall building here at Tours, then the tradition is in danger."

What Michel said was so. Even Père de Boszac at home in Blaison could give two good reasons to continue the practice and so found no demons in it. "Boys throw stones at the wren on St. Stephen's Day," he pronounced, "to remember the first martyr, likewise stoned to death on this day."

Another time, when his logic had forgotten the first emblem, he had said, "The wren was sacred to the men of this land in heathen times, a goddess to their benighted brains. Therefore it is good to stone and kill the wren, as we chase and kill all evil from our lives."

"And the man is not altogether wrong in that last saying," Michel expounded to me now on the wall. "We of the Craft do treat the wren as a Goddess. We always have. True fairy folk have the power to turn themselves into this bird. And is she not called 'the Mother of Heaven's little hen'? Have I not taught you to take auguries from her, as a messenger from the Gods?"

At this point, he made me recite some of what I'd learned like a catechism: " 'If the little bright-headed one call to you from the north, dear to you is he that is coming. If it come from the northeast, pious folk are on the way. If it call from the south side of you, provided it be not between you and the sun, it is the slaying of a man dear to you.' "

When I finished the recitation, Michel nodded, approving. "I will teach you more in time, omens for every other corner of the horizon. And out in the fields, in the villages, away from town, you will still hear stories that the wren is a Goddess and should not be hunted or harassed any other day of the year. She is a Goddess who sometimes demands men in sacrifice. But this one day a year, when she takes on the form of a tiny bird, she puts herself under the power of men. Like any Goddess, she lets herself be sacrificed for the good of her children."

"So we should go on St. Stephen's," I insisted, "whatever the strange folk here in the city have allowed themselves to forget. We should not let the day go unmarked, even if the wrens are gone."

Michel looked across the great expanse of cultivated land and flood plain we should have to cover before we could even begin to hunt for a bird. He looked at the vigorous little figure of Gilles un-slowed by any height or cold or vigorous activity. Then he looked back at me.

"Very well, we shall try."

He welcomed the thankful hug of my arms. And I welcomed the realization that while he taught Gilles what the second estate must know by letting him walk unflinchingly along the parapet, he did not ignore the lessons of the first estate, either.

And yet, in the closeness of the embrace, Michel's veiled thoughts became mine.

What if She will not sacrifice Herself this year? What sort of sacrifice might She demand?

Then my heart skipped a beat or two in panic as I heard Michel's do under the thick wool of his habit.

Will this perverse Bird perhaps demand human sacrifice this year?

18

The Boy in Green

So after days of Noël light, warmth, and overeating, on St. Stephen's Day outside Tours, I stumbled across the wren-colored earth. The whole world might have been a wren on that St. Stephen's Day. The same colors feathered the land, lifeless, leafless brown beaded with patches of snow. The snow was a week old, more, and lay in the shadows as if it had done so since the world was created. The sky seemed the same, white barred with the brownish grey of a storm that hung but seemed too lethargic to fall.

The only way to pick the wren out of such a world would be by the darting vitality of its little life brought to these same colors. And we, leadened as we were, were supposed to catch the thing?

I knew that Michel, were he close enough to talk to, would call my attention to the manner in which the Old Ways invited us to embrace the contrasts of life. When our bodies were dozing with warmth and lethargy, we should bestir them out for a vigorous day in the cold. I would have liked a chance to argue the point with him. But my mind was too slow to prevail in such an argument against the Master's knowledge. Any day, but particularly today.

And I was the one who had insisted on this excursion, after all.

Père Michel had gathered six boys to go along with us. The three oldest—young men, actually—were the sons of a friend of his, another Craftmaster who worked in the royal household, playing the harp for one of the princes. There was a younger boy, also from the household, not much older than Gilles although taller and awkwardly lanky, wearing a stained green coat. And the final pair of lads we'd passed when we were already on the road. They'd thought hunting wrens would be a fine lark.

Michel hitched up his long black skirts once we left the road the better to clamber with us. His bare shins must have itched with the cold, but he was laughing and talking and bellowing snatches of song through the smoke-frosted black of his beard.

"Ah, I feel like a boy again!" he exclaimed more than once.

I felt no such thing. I felt old and crippled.

The other boys were armed. They had nets and twine, stakes and scraps from the Christmas roast for traps. They had sling shots. The oldest boy had a bow with arrows headed with lumps of lead to stun the bird.

Even Gilles had his dagger, his young lord's emerald-handled dagger. Of course, a dagger was no good against a tiny bird you couldn't get within ten paces of, so Michel fashioned his youngest charge a sling from a forked branch. The wood he chose was green, with plenty of spring to it—and a bit of bark for the pocket in which the stone rested before slinging.

"He who kills the bird is named King for the day," Michel shouted the challenge.

"Then there's no chance for us," laughed one of the older boys. "Monsieur Le Vert will be King."

That was how they referred to that young boy in the grimy green surcoat, Monsieur Green. I could tell it was a teasing name and the honor that went along with it was rich with mockery. The boy seemed not to mind. He shrugged himself more firmly into the re-markable garment. I could see it was elegant satin but snug for him, leaving his bony wrists exposed between it and his red and puffy chilblains. Heavy woolen hose revealed his knees as knobby and decidedly knocked. The coat, I surmised, had been the castoff of some great lord's son, and they teased him for it.

But why should they tease that boy that he would be King more than any of the rest of us? They might as well tease me, with my twisted, useless hand and ignoble birth.

Still, I would show them. Creatures of the forest had spoken to me in time past. I could understand the Stag, the very King of the Forest. I *would* catch that bird.

As if he could read my thoughts, Michel came and put an arm around my shoulders. "Some have other gifts, my Yann. The gift of Seer is to look beyond the single point of the dead wren. The Seer remembers the rest of the year when the wren is sacred. The Seer sees patterns in the single event sent backward in time. And forward. He sees the spiral swing round and round and up and out from the singular. Use your Seer's eyes today, Yann."

But Michel cut me no branched stick for a slingshot. There was no use arming a boy with only one good hand. The Master merely ran his fingers slowly down the leather strap that crossed my chest as we walked. Then he patted the small earthenware pot that dangled from my hip. The weight seemed a hindrance, and I considered tossing it aside. If I must be crippled in my hand, why should I be burdened across my shoulder as well?

And yet, greater than the unguent the pot contained and its carefully measured ingredients was the weight of the spells Michel had taught me to infuse into the stuff. It was four months now, almost as soon as he'd arrived in Blaison, at the first full moon, that the black-bearded priest had taken me by night to strip the bark off young holly shoots.

We'd chanted. We'd steeped the bark in clean water, then boiled it, chanting, 'til it separated in layers as if by magic. We'd carefully skimmed off the top layer of bark and taken the middle, green portion, setting it aside to ferment. We'd chanted over it every night 'til the moon waxed again. We'd pounded, washed, fermented while moon and chants cycled on themselves again and finally we'd mixed in just enough goose fat, taken from the goose with the crooked wing feathers, to make it the proper consistency.

I felt the weight of the potion's magic more than itself. I could not toss it. Certainly not while Père Michel looked on. He had armed me, after all, as best he could.

Michel's naked legs worked on past me, up the wooded hill. They seemed comical, more hairy than ever as the cold made each dark filament rise on its own. He sang, deep-throated, "Roitelet, Roitelet!" He used the French name for our quarry that means, literally, "kinglet."

> *"Roitelet, Roitelet, where's your nest?*
> *'Tis in the bush that I love best.*
> *'Tis in the bush, the holly tree,*
> *Where all the boys do follow me."*

I wanted to shoot forward myself as the other boys shot their practice stones, hither and yon. But in spite of such desire, the words of Michel's song curled my thoughts in on themselves. It was almost more than my patience could hold, to have them do so.

"Nest?" The wren had no nest in the winter season. But she had had, in summer, when we'd striped the holly bark. "The bush that I love best . . . the holly tree." There was holly again. Holly that even now served in great looping garlands to adorn the palace's Christmas hall. No, I refused to say I loved it best. The memory of stabbed and prickled hands scraping among its low-growing branches was too keen.

Michel sang more, to the same tune but words in the old tongue now:

> *"Drui-en, drui-en, the King of all birds,*
> *St. Stephen's Day was caught in the furze."*

Drui-en, the old name slurred now into "the wren." Drui-en, druid's bird. No small brown ball of feathers, this. No petty kinglet. The druid's very bird. And what was a druid? Master, in the old tongue, lord of the oak forest, Keeper of the Craft, Seer, Prophet, Bard.

"There are three stations of men," I could almost hear Michel's explanation beneath the words of his song.

Then he drifted back into French again:

> *"Although he was little his honor was great,*
> *Jump up, my lads, and give us a treat."*

He knew very well what he was doing, spinning my mind with his words in two languages while the single language the other boys understood spurred them like arrow shot. He knew his bellowing voice, and the jubilant shouts and laughter it encouraged in the younger members of the party, must frighten off every wren within earshot.

"A Master sees patterns," he told me.

There were ravens, dark clouds of them, settling to graze on the stubbled fields like so many self-satisfied clerics. They croaked cheekily back at our merriment.

"If the raven speak with a small voice—" I tried to recite that omen lesson of the Craft to myself now. "If its cry is 'err, err,' sickness will fall."

But no sooner had I thought I could, indeed, detect that odd sound described as "err, err" than I heard a louder "grob, grob," which meant horses would be stolen. Or maybe it was "grack, grack," which meant warriors hard-pressed. And then a long call, which meant nothing of warriors, but had to do with women. Since the word of the world couldn't mean everything at once, in must mean nothing at all.

I saw no pattern beyond the spinning.

The oldest boy used his blunted arrows and brought down two rooks. It would have been hard to miss, their ranks being so thick. The dead birds' companions seemed to take little notice of their loss. They settled again after a few nervous circles and squawks as if nothing had happened.

Michel possessed less equanimity at nature ravaged. He told the young man that if he shot anything else but what we'd come for that day, he would curse him. The boy took the threat seriously and hardly raised his bow afterward.

We had to walk over a league and cross the River Cher before we were beyond the mark of the masons' axes. Then, when the shadow of Bréchenay Forest began to touch us, it grew colder, darker, greyer. Michel had spent much of the summer trying to teach me the differences between species of trees, but I still couldn't tell ash from alder, lime from plane in the faceless winter forest. They all had ivy twining up their trunks like garters 'round the best turned-out legs in court.

After the ravens, once the shrubbery grew dense and high about us, there were knots of robins, their tiny heads shrugged into their winter-dulled breasts, or scolding each other over hawthorn berries.

There was a V of honking late geese overhead: "I knew immediately there would be a flitting, and no blessing after that," said the omen recitation I'd memorized. I wondered what a "flitting" was.

And a single eagle "by whose midday wheel I know it would not be long until I heard evil news."

Was everything an ill omen? It certainly began to feel that way to me. I looked for things without omen, at least none that I'd been taught as yet: a covey of quail chirping off through the brush and the heavy whir of their wings. Squirrels busily burying nuts.

Then, low in a bush, there was a plop of snow knocked loose, melting, hitting the ground. And then, in precisely the same place: "There." All at once Michel scarcely breathed. "The wren."

The bundle of brown-and-white bird bounced before us, low through the bare boughs of shrubbery like the ball that got away.

Everyone instantly realized with a blush how rowdy we'd been. And that if such a quick darting of restless energy were to ever be caught, how exactly opposite we must be. Michel could not have told us better had he scolded us to silence all the way from town. He had waited for Nature Herself first to exhaust, then teach us Her humility.

That initial sighting—after a bounce this way, then that—soon dissolved into the silent brown-and-white world.

Without a word, almost without gesture, we knew we must split up if even one of us was to have luck. The oldest went off westward to try his bow alone with no more company than the threat of Michel's curse.

His two younger brothers went farther north, their net between them. The common lads squatted where they were to set a trap.

And Gilles, who was, after all, very young, had to stick with Michel. I might have stayed with them. In spite of his youth, Gilles was never a crybaby, nor was he raucous. Even tired, he moved, froze, crouched, watched like a cat. "Although he was little his honor was great," said the words of the song. Well, catlike, Gilles just might catch the bird. Michel's experience couldn't hurt, either. I would do well to stick with them.

But there was that one final member of our party, Monsieur Le Vert. He was in need of a nursemaid, too, I thought, and ought to stay with Michel. For some reason, however, he latched on to me. It wasn't fair. It was like the weight of an earthenware jar on my other shoulder.

But Michel, holding Gilles' hand and gesturing up into the forest canopy as he explained some wisdom, nodded quietly over his shoulder at me. This was what my tutor wanted me to do. I sighed, hoping that sound would keep the moisture in the corners of my eyes from falling. With all but one tear, the effort was successful.

I wandered off a bit in front, hoping the boy in green might take a hint and stay behind with the safety of the adult. But he did not. For some reason beyond all augury, he stuck to me—well, like lime. My mind was spiraling again.

We walked on together, the boy in green and I. The day progressed, though there was no way to tell that save by the steps we took, one after the other, marking the snow like minutes. We took so many steps that presently I realized we had made a complete circuit and come back to where many, many prints in the brown-white ground sprayed off in all directions. The two brothers were squabbling over whose fault the failure of their trap was.

"Be off!" they yelled at us, seeming relieved to have somebody new to yell at beside each other. "This is our place."

We trudged off in old footprints.

Now I'd been with Monsieur Le Vert long enough that I felt I ought to say something to him. Especially in light of the fact that he didn't squabble and kept gazing at me as if he expected wonders. It might not catch us a wren, but I couldn't help but be flattered. Since the older boys were still bickering close at our backs, it didn't matter at the moment how much we talked.

"Green was a good color to wear on such a hunt, Monsieur Le Vert," I told him. "Scuffed green like that blends well, even in winter. And green is what fairy folk wear, fairy folk who must move soundlessly through the forests."

The boy's eyes brightened on either side of an unfortunately ponderous nose. A smile didn't help the nose, either, but it told me, Yes, I was right to go with this boy.

He'd known I at least would understand.

"Your brown is even better," he remarked. "I would almost think you were the wren's brother."

New flattery, with words now, seemed to sharpen my brain. Or, rather, sent it spiraling. On that thought, I set our course perhaps twenty yards inside our first circuit, like the tracks of a game of fox and geese. A spiral would have a center, would it not?

"We've been this way before," the boy in green commented. My remark about his coat seemed to have loosed his tongue, which was not a good thing.

I gave no reply.

Still the wren eluded us, though we began to see her often enough. Or maybe it was more than one we saw. We never got close enough and probably didn't know enough about wren to tell. But we were learning.

Flutters and chirrups—or rather tiny, feathered threat—lured us on. The wren never held still for more than a breath. We saw her eat seeds, beetles. She hopped effortlessly from low branch to low branch over distances five times her tiny size. And quick bursts of feather fans were enough to carry her thrice again as far. When excited, she shot up her stumpy tail. Like a cooper's oft-hammered thumb, I thought, which he cocks in the midst of a ribald joke for emphasis. Was the bird just trifling with us?

"What's in your jar?" Monsieur Le Vert asked the next time I stopped to let us catch our breath. I judged we were on our third, even tighter circuit.

I wanted to snap at him to be quiet, but he did whisper, standing on tiptoe on his knock-kneed legs to get close to my ear.

"A potion," I replied, using as few words as I could.

"I knew it."

"Bird lime."

"Made from?"

"Holly bark." I blew on my hands, gone patchy, white and red with cold.

"And magic."

His grey-brown eyes were sober. I had no need to explain. He knew. And showed more reverence than I.

"So why don't you use it?" he asked, but only after he'd given me plenty of time to say something to that same effect if I'd wanted to.

I looked at him. Blue chilled the corners of his mouth. That green coat really was too small for him. And of a summery fabric, if I wasn't mistaken, for all its once-fineness. He had a good warm cloak to wrap around it. His boots were fine, too, I noticed. Good leather and fur-lined. Nevertheless, he was cold. No one could avoid it on such a day. But a lesser child would have been crying.

I sensed determination between his pale brown brows to match the straight, lanky, undistinguished hair. If I'd told him, no, we must march another ten hours, that would have set equally well with him.

This boy will be King.

The thought came suddenly into my mind.

King of St. Stephen's Day, of course, I amended the words at once. Who would not? Any other kingship was beyond the imaginings of this grim, silent wood.

"Very well," I said aloud.

I swung the thong over my head and prized loose the bit of soft leather Michel had tied about the pot's mouth.

I knew what the stuff would look like. And smell like: rotted, of living things past their prime. I held it down so the other boy could see and smell. He wrinkled his nose, but reached one finger, visibly throbbing with cold, toward the greasy white-green.

"No, don't touch," I said, pulling the jar away.

"Will it harm me?"

"It's only very, very sticky," I assured him.

"Ah, I see. You spread it on . . . on a branch or a limb and the bird gets stuck fast."

I nodded, bending to pick up a stick to stir and spread the potion. I mashed one end of my tool between two rocks to make a better brush.

"Oh, no," I exclaimed then, wrens forgotten.

"What is it?"

"I can hardly get the stick in, let alone stir it. The cold has made it too thick."

"Then we must warm it." That was obvious, but I must admit it didn't occur to me as a possibility until he said it. "Do you know a spell?"

I didn't, but I wouldn't let him know that. I made up some verse. And I didn't neglect more mundane blowing on the pot, rubbing it, and taking turns with the boy in green shoving it down our surcoats and jerkins. We walked briskly around in our spiral until we no longer shrieked when the solid clay was laid against our naked skin. Soon enough we got it supple again.

I've used that spell ever since.

"Which tree?" Monsieur Le Vert asked hopefully.

I looked around. We hadn't noticed any wrens since I'd uncovered the pot and I didn't see any now. But I knew it must be the tree at the center of our spiral. One more circuit should let me judge.

"There," I said.

Of course. An oak, flanked by two hollies. I wouldn't want it to be one of the prickly hollies.

I replaced the leather lightly over the mouth of the jar with my stick inside. Then I tossed the thong back over my neck and swung myself up onto the lowest branch.

How did I know this was an oak without the dagged, telltale leaves of summer? Of course—the gnarled branches, so good for handholds. The yellow, tumorlike galls. A little way off was a sycamore, tasseled with woolly balls, there a linden with sprays around its crown, all that was left now of its cat-tongue seeds. The maple's ends were knotted with embryo blossom like women's stitchery done in wine-colored silk. The past season's growth on the bushy wild plums held the color of the next season's tart fruit.

All at once, the wood around me was whispering. Past, present, future, speaking to me in a single breath.

The oak limbs lured me higher.

"The King," I heard the spiraling world say. And then, very clearly, "The boy in green is to be King."

My right hand failed me. I slipped and fell.

The oak's sturdy arms reached out and held me fast in such an embrace that his bark only scraped one elbow. But the jar of lime bounced against the trunk and tumbled to the ground.

"I've got it," the boy below me cried, the boy all the wood declared must be King.

"Good," I managed to gasp.

I saw that only a chip had been knocked off the rim. Besides what had oozed out over my useless hand and kept it clinging to the tree, all the potion was intact. I saw Monsieur Le Vert poke at the mess with his own stick. I saw the hood of his cloak thrown back a man's height below me. The straight brown hair sprayed out of the single crown at the top of his head.

A crown. The King.

The forest swirled. I clung to the trunk for all I was worth. Blackness arose. I understood why the same word is used for an enchantment as well as for my fits. This spell did not last long. Nonetheless, I certainly should have fallen to my death but for the strong arms of the oak, his stern but loving whisper, "The King! The King!"

I came to. I took several deep breaths of clear, cold air that laid a fog on the grey bark into which I pressed my face. Then, slowly, weakly, I began to climb down. By the time I reached the ground, the poor, scarred skin of my crippled hand seemed to have become part of the tree, coated with bits of bark and debris.

Monsieur Le Vert was just backing out from under one of the holly trees on his hands and knees. In one hand he clutched the little pot, as empty as it could ever get of such greenish stickiness. The heel of that hand, all of the other, and both knobby knees had been treated by "the bush that I love best" no kinder than it had ever treated me. I saw him rub at scratches, pull out thorns, brush at beads of blood. But he was grinning broadly.

"You limed the holly?" I tried to sound stern.

The boy bubbled with his own success. "Yes. I hope it was all right. I mean, does a wren lay eggs?"

"Of course a wren lays eggs." My snap was only weak, like a miscracked whip.

"But all this time we've been watching him, I've thought he must be the mouse's brother."

"First you said he was my brother for the clothes I wear, now the mouse's. Am I also the mouse's kin?"

The boy was too full of his own excitement to mind me. "Well, she's always so low to the ground, this bird we're following. Never higher than my head, as if heights frightened her. Like a mouse. She never perches high for a view like the rook or eagle. She must be down where her prey is, beetles, grubs. And, like a mouse, she keeps to the brown-and-white cover, too. I do not think a great, open, naked trunk like that tree you climbed would attract her. The holly, still with all her leaves and bushing low to the ground, that would be better. So I have limed all the branches on both these trees. Besides, the holly. That's what the song said."

Of course. That's what the song said.

I tried not to let him read too much in my face as I cursed my stupidity.

"I know you climbed this tree for something. To hear a message, did you not? An augury." He said it like a word he had only recently learned, but of which he was proud—and quite in awe. "Well, did you get one? What did it say? We will catch the wren, will we not?"

I stammered on the first word, but finally got it out: "We will."

"Then we ought to slip away so the lime may work. I think there is a bird—at least one—here in the bushes to the right. If we walk toward them and hide there, she must fly elsewhere, mustn't she? Perhaps she'll work her way back to the holly, soon or late."

It happened just as he envisioned and almost before my reeling brain could encompass it. There were a few familiar, taunting bounces of brown and then—a high-pitched scream of tiny terror. The frenzied fluttering on a branch of lime, with downy feathers, made the entrapment worse.

By the time I had scrambled close enough to see, only one wing was arched for a flight it could never again attain. The stub of a tail beckoned for quarter as may a man with a maimed arm on the field of battle.

Monsieur Le Vert was before me, on his hands and knees again, completely oblivious of the pincushion of holly litter. Oblivious, too, of the limed branches that set his featureless head with a coronet, green rowels and antlers both at once.

He put the sacrifice out of its misery with a speed I shall never know, two whole, firm boy hands stealing the life with a single press. Seeing no way to remove the tiny body undamaged from the slime, he used his dagger to cut the entire branch out at the trunk.

Then we were shouting and jumping for joy. Michel came up quickly in response, almost as if he had been hovering nearby. Gilles jogged and hallooed pickaback behind him. Michel's beard stretched over a wide grin, but his eyes met mine keenly.

"Who did it?" he asked.

The boy beside me was jumping and waving his trophy. At the tutor's words, he settled a bit and looked at me. I knew he was willing to share the glory. I was the elder, the counselor, the maker of sticky potions, the druid. In fact, he would say nothing if I claimed it all. No one else would know.

But Michel's eyes told me. *He* would know.

"He did," I spoke quickly, before I lost the will. "Monsieur Le Vert."

I caught a look—of pride, of gratitude—from Michel before my attention was distracted elsewhere.

The other boys were not far behind in Gilles' and Michel's wake as group echoed to group through the forest.

"The wren?"

"It's caught?"

"Who's done it?"

"Monsieur Le Vert."

"No!"

"I can't believe it."

"The little prince?"

And then came the concession from the eldest, solemnly shouldering his useless bow and quiver. "Well done, Your Highness." A deep and courtly bow. "Noël. The King."

The others followed suit. Then all helped to spread the bird to best effect among the limbs and cut festive branches of their own as trophies. The two oldest boys hoisted the young King to their shoulders. I could see him almost rigid with cold and exhaustion, but with their strong legs beneath him, he rallied and held the trophy high. Everyone else followed, shouting "Noël, Noël!" between verses of the song:

> *"As I went out upon the mall,*
> *I met the wren upon the wall.*
> *Offered my cudgel and gave her a fall*
> *And brought her here to show you all."*

"Master," I murmured up to Michel under cover of yet another chorus.

We trailed behind and I was letting my holly branch drag across the road's ruts striped with mixed mud and snow. I was the youngest now with no one to carry me and I was exhausted in mind and spirit perhaps even more than in body.

Michel had let down the skirt of his robe to lend more distinction to our triumphal procession. Against his back, Gilles' head pressed, asleep. I was always struck by how pretty the young scion of Rais looked in his sleep. One might almost say angelic, with the tumble of dark curls over the soft bruised-blue look to his heavy, closed eyelids. The scarlet of his doublet—that must have driven all game away—now added dignity to our march and again brought out the bloom in his plump cheeks.

Gilles asleep . . . when that thing which animated his waking face also dozed. That thing—well, what else can I say? That thing others might not see at all, but anyone who knew him knew it demanded eyes in the back of one's head.

"Master." I found more strength for breath now.

"Yes, Yann?"

"He will be King."

"Who's that?"

"Monsieur Le Vert." I waved my branch rather vaguely in the right direction.

I noticed a sudden caution in Michel's voice. Caution that he lead me to nothing before its time? "Yes, he did well. He is the King of the Wren today. 'Although he be little, his honor is great,' as the song says."

"I thought that line was talking about the wren."

Michel shrugged without commitment.

"But I didn't mean today," I pursued. "I mean later. And not just King of the tiny wren. King of . . . King of . . ." I struggled for a word big enough. "King of all the Land."

"You do not know who that boy is, do you, Yann?"

I shook my head. "They only called him Monsieur Le Vert."

"He was among the royal children and their tutors in the procession we watched from the walls of Tours. His name is Charles." A sudden cold ran up my spine as my tutor said it. "Charles the son of Charles, King of France. He is the youngest of the royal princes."

"He will be King." The awe in my own voice terrified me. Although I didn't know the fact any more strongly now than I had before, only now did its true magnitude strike me. "He is Charles the son of Charles the son of Charles, like in the prophecy."

Michel gave a hiss that I shouldn't speak loud enough for others to hear. I tried to obey with my next words.

"Master, did you know that? Did you know he was Charles the son of Charles? The other boys didn't treat him much like a prince."

"Their father has been the prince's tutor for a very long time. They have been raised almost as brothers. Since Charles is not the Dauphin now, many at court ignore him. The forms of majesty don't cling to him."

"But did you know he was the prophecy?"

"Of course I knew he was Charles the son of Charles. As for the prophecy—? Well, every infant son the royal couple named Charles gave me hope. But two little Charleses died in their cradles before this one. I almost feared to hope again. So, no, Yann, not really. I haven't the Sight as you do. No amount of training or wishing it so can give me what is given to you. But I do have the wisdom to see a pattern and to—to imagine. Yes, Yann. Let us say that I imagined it would be so. I imagined that in our lifetime what the Land has wept for for so long . . .

"Now your Sight has helped me to see clearly and confirmed what I only imagined. I thank you, Yann." He concluded with real feeling, and that feeling kept us walking side by side in silence for a while.

Then Michel turned to me with pursed lips. If he'd had a hand free to gesture with, I think he would have used it to pat those lips in a sign for silence. "Yann, it would be wise if you told no one else about what you have Seen. Not yet. Not for a long while yet, perhaps."

He was so earnest that I could only reply, "Yes, Master."

"Charles is yet young. His father is not a very old man, either, only just forty. But he is mad, dispossessed first of his faculties and now of his capital, exiled here to Tours. There are many players on the field, and powerful men. There are those opposed to both the King and his progeny. There are so many debts still unsettled. Besides, Charles has two older brothers before him—not named Charles—in line to his father's throne."

"You mean, if I speak, it may be counted treason?"

"Worse than that, Yann. Prophecies are, in the end, only words. There are always contingencies. The wrong words in the wrong ears may be very dangerous for your new little friend."

"You mean somebody might try to kill him?"

Michel would not commit to the storyteller's trills I tried to infuse in the discussion. "It may mean that there is no Charles the son of Charles to fulfill the prophecy. It may mean that things go very ill not only for the prince, but for all our Motherland."

I nodded with the weight of such possibilities. The brilliance of my vision had blinded me to them. "I will not speak," I swore.

The boys ahead of us had found second wind and were singing now as we approached the great new walls of Tours. The noise awakened Gilles, who had to scramble down off Michel's back to march in on his own.

Then the noise turned heads and brought them out of casements. Young ladies laughed and waved their kerchiefs. Children fell in behind us. And the older folk of Tours who remembered, and pilgrims from places where the custom had never been forgotten, taught the rest.

"The wren, the wren!" they cried and joined the songs. "Noël, Noël!"

They offered small coins, which one of our lads collected in his cap. Every coin claimed a feather plucked from the sacrifice. It wasn't long before these tokens found place of pride in belts, purses, and hatbands. Often bannered by brighter or longer plumes, still no feather was worn more proudly. Among sailors on the Loire, it is well known that no man can drown who has about him a feather of the St. Stephen's wren. Those who stay on land know the stemming of many other tragedies that might otherwise overwhelm them.

By the time we had made the circuit of Châteauneuf and retired at last to the triumphant prince's apartments, the poor little sacrifice was no longer recognizable. Indeed, she hardly existed anymore. But what was left we cut from the branch, gutted, and solemnly roasted over holly wood. Each of the hunters swallowed a morsel, then drowned the taste quickly in too many sweetmeats and in swigs of wine that our gleanings from the populace allowed us to buy.

"To the prince," we toasted. "Nay, to the King."

And none said it with more fervor than I.

19

A Heavy Drape of Feminine Power

After St. Stephen's Day, Gilles, Michel, and I spent a great deal of time with young Prince Charles. There I met Master Gwencalon, the father of our three hunting companions. Master Gwencalon was blind, his eyes milky with cataract.

He had been music tutor to Charles ever since the prince had been but a year old, hired to play the harp "when the royal child be ill-disposed." There were some who feared that Charles, even at such a tender age, had inherited his father's unstable mind. He did have a penchant for melancholia, some fretfulness. Who might not, with such a father? But madness, I never saw.

Of course, so skilled was Master Gwencalon at his art that all madness might have been strummed and sung away. Bard, Michel instructed me, was a rank of the Craft reckoned nearly as high as that of the greatest Seer.

"I am glad," my instructor said when we were alone, "that the young man on whom so much depends should have such a holy Master always in his entourage. Of course, there must be many other influences on a prince of a Christian land: priests, Dominicans, university men. It cannot be helped. Charles has his own chapel, chaplain, vestments, a portable altar, and is considered very pious. Still, I do not think we could hope for a better influence with him for our cause than Master Gwencalon."

Surely we had to credit Master Gwencalon for Charles' attachment to fairy green. The Bard had given that coat to the prince as appropriate Craftsman's wear for May Day. And Charles loved the coat so well, he wore it day and night until it was too small, grimed, and full of holes. When he grew bigger and finally had to give the coat away, still the livery he ordered for his suite would be of the fairy green. Such attachment boded well for our cause.

As did his attachment to the only toy he'd brought to Tours with him out of Melun.

"There wasn't time to pack anything else," he explained as he showed it to me with pride. "We left in such haste. I carried it with me so"—and he encircled it with his young arms, hugging it close—"all the way to Tours."

It was, of all things, a gold-leafed cauldron.

"Not your hobby horse?" Gilles asked with concern as he named all the things he had been loath to leave behind in Blaison, when we came just for the holiday visit, that he certainly would never go into exile without. "Your wooden sword? Your shield? Your helmet? I have a real pony, too. Do you?"

Charles did, of course, back in Melun, but cared for the cauldron more.

Rolling a wooden ball around inside the cauldron made a fine noise. And we had contests to see who could toss the most balls in from the greatest distance. Gilles hadn't the grace to let the prince win even some of the time.

But I think its exterior gave the cauldron the most worth. Some Master in some ancient day had incised it with powerful symbols: creeping vines, snakes, birds flanking the Horned God. Charles didn't know the meaning—though he made up some fanciful tale to match the pictures so as not to appear ignorant—and Michel wouldn't tell more, no matter how hard I begged.

"In time. When you are older," was all he'd say. I had to be content with that.

After St. Stephen's Day, the Earth circles to the Feast of the Holy Name of Jesus, and after that, Epiphany. We did not remain in Tours very much longer after the Epiphany that followed hard on the heels of that revealing wren hunt. That January, the bridge of Tours, which had been destroyed by the ice of the previous winter, was destroyed yet again. Had we not left court when we did, we should never have returned home until late spring.

In the greater world, Valentine Visconti died of grief. King Charles regained his sanity in Tours only to wonder what he was doing there. When he heard the reason, he was incensed that such enmity should exist among families, the royal family most of all. If the dead duke of Orléans had been his brother, the living duke of Burgundy was no less than his cousin. His cousin he promptly forgave in a lavish public ceremony and declared that any who sought further vengeance for what had happened in the Vieille Rue du Temple could be no true subjects of his.

So Charles was welcomed back into Paris, where he was immediately incarcerated again, either for a return of the madness or simply because at such close quarters he could observe just what sort of fearless man his cousin was. Fearless even of God, folk said— and that cousin, who controlled Paris, was no fool. Such treachery might bring on madness indeed.

"How," the world asked, "are we to get on if sanity returns when our King raves, but when he is lucid, he does truly mad deeds?"

Burgundy now had the King and Paris. But the Armagnac-Orléans alliance still had the hearts of many if not most of France's lords, including that of Sire de Rais.

———————— •–•—— ————————

No matter how the world outside ran, we returned to our quiet corner at Blaison. Three full years passed for us, years that were uneventful save for the wisdom and Craft I gained by daily instruction from Père Michel. Everything had the power of that wren hunt on St. Stephen's Day, or so it seems when I look back. Each lesson shines bright now and hard as gems, though fogged in mystery as it occurred.

I learned the Four Powers of the Craftmaster: to know, to dare, to will, and to be silent. I learned that there are three great events in the life of humans: love, death, and resurrection in the body of a new being. Love may not be fulfilled save by living many lives with the beloved. This may not be fulfilled save by resurrection. For both, death is a necessity and a blessing. And by magic are all three brought to fruit.

So I learned magic. I learned to cast with my power hand, my left because the right was already given to the God. I learned to surround myself and others with the white light for protection, the shadow for curse. I learned to look at the blue at the bottom of the burning wick: not to picture any desire in so much detail so as to limit it to the dimensions of my own imagination. I learned that though my conscious mind could never believe in the spells I cast, my unconscious, rising to the surface, was where the magic would occur.

But I should remember the fourth of the Powers, to be silent, and not speak overmuch of such things. Sorcerers who talk about their Craftsmanship, or even look at it too closely, will never achieve real magic.

So it happened that the dark days of winter rolled around once again, and we at Blaison remembered the Epiphany that year of Grace 1412. The crumbs of the rich Three Kings' Cake—spice- and sweet-wine-soaked raisins, currants, and bits of candied orange peel—lay on the great silver platter in the center of the table.

Gilles had won the prize again, the dried broad bean baked into the cake that gave its finder good luck all year. He always won. I suspected he cheated. Either Cook hinted to him as the cake was cut; or all the rest, in some grand conspiracy to flatter the lord's young heir, quickly switched plates with him if ever they found the bean in their own piece.

Or, I was even content to believe, that was simply the way the world worked. Some were born lords and lucky. Others, like myself, were not. It was simple.

However the matter, that Epiphany, sated by the food and fire, I was content to have it so. I was content to have a crippled hand and the falling sickness. I was content to be the son of a draper and a baby's nurse below the salt in a great lord's house.

Then I began to notice that I was not the only one to be bathed by what seemed to be an unnatural glow. Monseigneur and Madame were chatting and smiling together, they who usually had no more than icy reserve toward one another. Gilles and his brother were quietly playing, taking turns and having no quarrel over the rules. Père de Boszac and Michel were enjoying an exchange where both seemed to have nothing but the highest regard for the other's views and powers of deduction. Even my colicky baby sister dozed with contentment against my mother's breast.

It was as if the peace always promised at Christmastide had finally come true. I felt if I went out to the byre, the animals would be content enough to speak to me without my having to resort to the force-spell Michel had taught me. However, I was too sure it would be so to bother getting up and investigating.

Even Christmas that year had not avoided drunken brawls among the men, a maid with her eye blackened by her jealous lover, Michel and Père de Boszac cursing each other soundly. And Madame fleeing the festivities in silent tears she would not give her husband the satisfaction of seeing. But now, at Epiphany, all the world had settled beneath a glowing cover of festival well-being and I could not be bothered to wonder why this should be so.

Then, across the board, I saw Michel look up suddenly, as surprised as I was to find himself content with the moral of one of Père de Boszac's demon stories. He looked around as I had done, wondering, until his eye met mine. Then he excused himself from the priest—still with the utmost civility—and came around to stand by my elbow.

"Something," he said quietly, "something has happened."

I nodded, stupefied with unconcern.

The old bronze soup tureen sat on the table before me. All but empty, the maids had not removed it. They were basking in the communal bliss, idling on the benches with the men, and their mistress was too content to shrew them.

Michel reached over and picked up the tureen by its swinging handle. "Come, Yann," he said.

I knew what he wanted me to do. Why must we delve into this? I wanted to ask. Can't we just enjoy it?

But I was too content even to argue. I arose and followed Michel out of the cozy comfort of the hall.

I knew what must be done. I took the tureen and went down to the yard. I emptied the last of the soup out on the dung heap. The great contentment had settled here as well, just as I'd suspected. Old cockerel had left the heap to roost under the stable eaves with his ladies and had let the capons in, too, without the first show of spurs.

Hounds and the new litter of kittens had all curled up together in the warmest corner. They were even letting the mice in to scamper through the straw. No creature actually talked to me, but their actions were eloquent enough. I would have been content to stand there and watch all night, oblivious of the cold creeping up my legs.

But I felt the pull of the only present urgency, Michel's curiosity, vibrating like a discord through the torpid air toward me. So I scoured the tureen out with the clean sand kept by the doorway. Then I filled it, not with well water, but with water channeled into a stone cistern from rainfall on the roof.

Everyone knew such heaven water was reserved only for my mother's remedies—and for Michel's magic. The barrel sat backed into the kitchen wall so it was warmer than most spots in the yard. Nonetheless, no one had been into the reservoir for a while and the crust of ice had had time to grow thick. I replaced the notched wooden lid on the cistern carefully so no vermin would fall in.

Now I had to return to Michel's tiny chamber without a word to anyone. Other times we had divined, I'd found this the hardest part of all.

"Where're you off to, lad?"

"Run and get me my thimble, will you? It's up in the solar."

"Come and watch the fighting in the lists with me."

But that night, everyone's content was such that they would not disturb it to spare me more than a glance, quite content that all was well with the world.

Michel had a fire going in his small brazier—he had no hearth in his cell—but it hadn't had time to warm the air yet. Our breath stood out like new-carded tow before our faces.

I put aside the penknife, the medal of St. Gilles and his Stag I always wore as an amulet at my mother's behest. I undid the points of my hose, the lacings that bound leggings halfway up my thighs in the other direction. I bared my legs to the room's chill. I undid my belt, the thong at the neck of my jerkin. I took off my jerkin as well. Then I turned, arms out before my Master so he could be certain: I stood in my linen without a cramping knot on me, nor a scrap of metal to interfere.

Michel nodded, making an effort to be satisfied when the rest of the world found it only too easy to be so. He set the tureen down on the floor so the light of the brazier could fall upon it. He spread a full black ram's fleece beside it for me to kneel upon so I should not grow too cold.

He tossed aromatic herbs into his fire, chamomile and wood betony to clear the head. He unsheathed his white dagger, gave the water in the tureen a stir while he murmured words in the ancient tongue. And then he stepped back and left me to do what only I could do.

He stayed with me, though. When he'd first taught me to use the water as a tool to focus my gift, I would often go blank, then wake with no memory, neither of what I'd Seen, nor of what I'd said under the impression of my Sight. As I learned more skill, I learned to control the pressure, centered between my eyes, that always begged for oblivion. I learned to retain the Visions, to fill out the words Michel heard me say with ever greater remembered detail. Still, he stayed with me, just in case.

I knelt. My knees sank gratefully into the fleece. My limbs grew heavy, stupid with the cold. But it was as if my whole being had also found such a resting place. I slipped beyond care into the fleecy contentment of the world in that soft darkness.

Michel had to prod me back to task, rubbing one thought against the next, trying to find any nap there. "What do you see?"

"Nothing." The word sat heavily on my tongue.

"Look, Yann. Peer deeply."

"Nothing," I repeated after a languid pause. "The entire world is at peace."

"Look farther."

"Out in the yard, the cockerel . . . The ill-tempered bull in the meadow has forgotten his griefs."

"A heavy drape of feminine power," Michel mused.

The first detail I'd named in my dreamy ramble had, of course, been seen with my physical eyes. But having said it, the others followed, sliding easily over the surface of the water.

"In the forest, the owl blinks carelessly down at the hare."

"Farther, Yann."

"The wolf dozes with his nose on his paws and thinks nothing of the deer who trip idly down to the river to drink."

That was the remarkable thing. Even after the dagger's stirring, even when I jarred the vessel slightly getting to my knees, the surface remained perfectly still. Usually dancing flame must catch some imperfection. This time, it caught none. The water in the tureen remained as smooth as if I'd never cracked the ice in the barrel. It was smoother than the smoothest glass I'd ever seen, bubbleless, fleckless, crackless. Like air caught under a barely visible film.

"Yann, farther," Michel urged.

"It is the same as far as I can see."

"Across France."

"Across all of France it is the same. Smooth. Peace. The King's mind does not haunt him and he rests like a child. Armagnac and Burgundian. They stick their boots—boots muddied from chasing each other all over the land—they stick them up to the same fire and exchange toasts with one another."

"Farther."

The wonder of it was washing all urgency from him. In a moment, his tongue would be as heavy as mine.

"Lorraine?" He pushed his torpor and mine.

The moment he said it, something like an acorn in size and shape bubbled slowly up from the bottom of the tureen.

"The Bois Chênu," I said.

"What of the Bois Chênu?" Urgency crept back into his voice like a mouse on watch for the cat.

"Nothing," I said. "In the mountains, the men allow their neighbors down into the wine caves to give one another a pull of the best barrels, men they normally feud with, men they would otherwise only grunt at in the lane. They climb down into the caves let into the limestone Vosges. The men prop their elbows up on the vats in the moist air so good for wine. They cradle the draw as if they may divine by it. And it is as if all fermentation has stopped, even in such good air. No must foams. All has stopped in this peace."

"What has happened?" Michel's voice echoed at me as if from one of those wine caves in the Vosges.

"In the village of Domrémy, the men and women sit around their Epiphany tables, same as we do here. They sing the ancient song about the sweet fragrance at the Christ Child's birth with meaning it's never held before:

> *"Quelle est cette odeur agréable,*
> *Bergers, qui ravit tous nos sens?*

> *"What is this agreeable odor,*
> *Shepherds, that ravishes our senses?*

"Because the fragrance is with them, now, pervading everything. It is not the cloying sweetness of incense, but the fresh fragrance of cut hay and apple blossom and it lures them all to peace they've never known."

And then I saw.

"Zabillet, goodwife of Jacquot d'Arc, has come to her time."

The image swirled just above the water, like mist at dawn.

"She is delivered. The child is covered in a milky white veil."

"Ah, the sign. The caul. Born a Godsend for the Night Battles. Does the midwife know how to deal with such a thing?"

"Yes. She quickly breaks the membrane so the child may breathe. But she sets it aside carefully, a safeguard for the child to keep throughout life."

"A boy or a girl, Yann?"

The sex appeared like pink folded petals in the water. "A daughter."

"Ah—at last. After three sons." Then he remembered a complication. "Jacquot? He doesn't want to—?"

"No, he will not drown her. The peace weighs too heavily on him tonight."

"But in the morning? When this passes?"

"I think not. He has three strong sons now. The death fields of Champagne are somewhat forgotten in those strong, happy lives. He knows how his wife has longed for a girl. If he comes to remember his dreams for his daughter, he has those sons to help him counteract it. 'Watch for your sister,' he will say. 'If she shows any interest in the soldiers, you will drown her. I may not have the strength, but good sons like you, you can do it for me. I need not fear my dreams now.' "

Michel nodded pensively.

"I see the midwife washing her now," I continued. "On the child's left neck, she discovers a wine-colored birthmark, shaped like the kick of a goat's hoof."

"Initiate from birth. A miracle! Does the midwife realize it for what it is? Yet another sign?"

"Yes. She tells the mother she should rejoice, not grieve that her daughter's beauty is so marked."

"Ah."

"The midwife rubs honey and salt over the infant. To dry and comfort the baby's members."

"Tell me, who is this sage woman who attends?"

I described the brown face, like walnuts, the kind, farseeing eyes, things from a birthing chamber no other man in the peace-weighted world could see.

"It is Jehanne the wife of Tiercelin the clerk. That is very good. Hers is an ancient faith and wisdom. She has seen the fairy folk with her own eyes and may teach her charge likewise to see. Very good."

Michel was pacing now, his steps cramped by the narrowness of his room. He'd shaken the numbing peace entirely, his head seething with what must be done.

But I continued to stare into the water, mindless of the heavy cold seeping into my limbs.

"I must leave, Yann." Michel was thinking aloud. "I must leave you at once. It will be hard. I like it not. But you are almost grown. And able now to grow in the Craft on your own. Have I not perfect witness of that here, tonight? Yes, you are older, you and Gilles. You, strong enough to help your milk brother when he falters. And the Master of St. Gilles is not so very far away, ready to help you. I must go. Yes, I must. Tomorrow. Is it possible? I should be there, there where the shadow of Bois Chênu dries imprinted with honey and salt on that newborn skin. Am I, perhaps, already too late?"

His words had no effect on me. In the morning I would grieve. I would beg him not to go, not to leave us to Père de Boszac alone. To take me with him or I should die.

But that night, I only knelt and watched, impervious to cold, to cramping muscles. Impervious to all but the glimmer, newborn in the heart of a bronze vessel of rainwater. That tiny, amorphous thing, more amorphous still because she was a girl, her shape closed, inside, immature, potential. All that she might do . . .

"La Pucelle."

Michel thought aloud: "Surely they won't call her that. Not yet. Not in her family. What will they call her, Yann?"

"Jehannette. Little Joan. Jehanne d'Arc."

Third Antiphon

A Weft of Chain Mail

"Here they come!" hollered Gilles de Rais. "I see them!"

Marie de Rais heard the shrieks of her firstborn son echo down the stairwell outside the solar door. The stairwell played havoc with the raucous sounds of his downward plunge until she had the sick feeling he might be falling.

Falling to his death down this very Black Tower of Champtocé where he had been born.

Marie's stomach settled a little as she saw a bit of russet larded heavily with white linen flash past the open doorway. At least young Jean Le Drapier, crippled as he was, was doing his best to keep up with her son, where nobody else could. She sent the Saint of the Wood a prayer of thanks for that, at least.

"So the boy must have seen your father and brother returning," Marie's mother, Madame Béatrice née de Rochefort, said. "At last."

Marie suppressed her fears for her son, turning in concern to her mother instead. "Shall we go down to greet them, *maman?*"

"But, of course. And they'll be wanting their supper."

Madame Béatrice gestured her maids to her elbows. She moved nowhere without both her cane and a maid on either hand these days. It pained Marie to see just how much her mother's strength had deteriorated since last she'd been able to visit. She hated not being where duty told her she ought to be. But then, she was also secretly, wickedly thankful. The pain of the sight would be too much day in and day out.

The prick of duty in her side, Marie moved to take the place of one of the maids. But her mother said, "No, no, we'll manage. You go on ahead, child. I know you'll want to see them as soon as possible."

Except for the Black Tower, the seven towers of Champtocé Castle were built of a reddish-brown stone, banded here and there with whiter ashlar. Before she had time to appreciate more of home than that, Marie had to back aside under the gateway's arches to let the horsemen pound over the very long wooden bridge.

Her Gilles was the first rider she recognized, hoisted up into his uncle's saddle. For surely that was her brother Amaury's fair hair she caught a glimpse of behind Gilles, the light to her son's shadow. The sight of those two faces, triumphant under the bold red and gold geometries of the arms of the ancient noble house, made her heart leap with relief, with pride, with joy.

What quickness her body had produced in Gilles, what strength, what perfect beauty—thank the Virgin. Thank the Saint of the Wood.

And yet, by the Virgin, it panged her to see her son growing so fast. Growing into a man's world. That strength and beauty, pressing away from her. The pangs were almost as sharp as birthing him had been.

And there, there was her father, Jean Sire de Craon, his chest like some great gun in its armor. She turned, never minding the dust, to follow quickly after the last flick of horse's tail. Only the sudden and silent arrival of her husband at her elbow reminded her that she wasn't a girl anymore, that she could not run, shrieking for joy to her father's arms. That she could never really come home.

The lord of Champtocé let his voice boom like cannonade off the walls of his home as he got help to heave his full armored weight out of the saddle.

"Well, that was a fine piece of work if I say so myself. A fine piece of work down at Ingrandes. And my reward? The sight of my daughter, her man, and my eldest grandson here to greet me on my return."

"You know, Father, we would never fail to stop by on our way home from our Midsummer pilgrimage to St. Gilles."

Marie attempted a double buss in the direction of Sire de Croan's face. His old-style helm and its attached curtain of mail *aventail* formed a tight oval of silver through which only a portion of his face appeared, crinkling with good humor.

"At your service, sir," her husband said, more subdued in his greeting while he got his hand crushed in his father-in-law's great plate-studded gauntlet.

This was the first time in years Guy de Rais had condescended to come on the Midsummer pilgrimage. His hand had shot the arrow that had been the start of all of this, yet, "This is a matter for you and our son Gilles," he usually said. It was this greeting with his father-in-law Marie suspected he sought most to avoid.

Her father practiced similar avoidance but hid it by taking great, stiff-legged strides across his yard. Marie loved the squeaks and groans of her father's movement in armor, always the music of her childhood that told her he was home. But the old warrior's eyes were seeking his grandson, still among the horses, instead of his son-in-law.

He said, "You're doing all right with that one, Rais."

Sire de Rais followed his host into the armory. "I hope so, sir. With God's favor."

"Why, man, you speak as if you did not believe your own words." Sire de Craon guffawed.

"Gilles is—" Sire de Rais looked back with a sigh. "He is sometimes a trial. Although, I do think these trips to the Saint are helpful."

Sire de Craon removed his gauntlets and tossed them to a squire. At last he could reach up for his helm. Without it on, his voice lost its disembodied echo. But it still boomed. His face ran with grimy sweat. He mopped at it with the towel another squire hastened to offer him.

Sire de Craon was fleshy and very red under the thinning white hair. And without the peak of metal, he was revealed as not a very tall man, though broad-chested enough. Deep red creases from the weight of his headgear ran across scalp, face, and neck, vying with the natural furrows of his years, years spent mostly out-of-doors. At almost sixty, however, the lord seemed as hale as a man half his age and would wear his full armor in spite of this heat, to prove himself so still.

Craon looked back at the subject of their conversation. He could not help but be proud at what he saw. "Well, boys will be boys." He guffawed again.

The sense of Rais' answer—"One would hope for a *Christian* boy"—was lost on the older man.

"Come, Gilles—" Marie reached a hand toward her son as he entered at Amaury's side. Suddenly, she wanted to protect him from this world of men.

But she could see Gilles had eyes only for his uncle, her brother, Amaury. She, too, could not resist the attraction. Other women would see to the table.

Sire de Craon's heir and only son was younger than Marie, nineteen on that hot summer's day. She was used to thinking of him as a child, but in the intervening years since her marriage, he had become a man.

He was not a tall man, either, no taller than his father, although the lack of bulk made him seem so and gave him more grace. Whereas the father seemed to have let his head be molded to his casque, Marie never did see her brother in the helmet he handed over to the armorer now. He did not even cut his hair to suit, but wore it long, about his shoulders, where it teased the eye with golden highlights riding on the rims of the curls.

Graceful limbs and that long, maidenly hair gave the young man an almost feminine aspect that the squires by no means dispelled as they cracked the very masculine shell of armor away from him. He was nonetheless well muscled in the most masculine places as long hours at training must do. And his face was that of a young Greek god, finely chiseled, delicate even when it thrust to a male chin and cheekbones. Across that chin, for every frequent attempt at a close shave, a thick and surprisingly dark beard was sprinkled, like pepper and herbs on white fish suntanned in butter. His dark brown eyes were Gilles' exactly.

"We'll joust a bit together after dinner," Amaury promised Gilles in the low tone of a co-conspirator.

"Such a lad." Sire de Craon tousled his son's long hair as Amaury bent to step out of his greaves. "Cannot keep from the sound of battle."

Sire de Craon turned to instruct the armorer, which was just as well. He missed the look on his son's face, a look of impatience with an old man who cannot guess half the pains of the younger.

"See that you dry and grease every part well," Sire de Craon said, and the armorer took the instruction with no sign that he thought it obvious. My lord's cuirass had tufts of reed caught in the hinges.

Sire de Rais said, "You saw some action down at Ingrandes, did you, sir? Madame your wife told us you had to charge off early this morning after receiving news that couldn't wait."

"Indeed we did." Craon's voice boomed as his squire heaved the breastplate up and off before his face. "But I'll let Amaury tell it. He played the bravest part."

Everyone looked in the young man's direction. Amaury smiled, a little shyly, Marie thought, and shrugged. Instead of answering, he snatched the chance of attention to make his own invitation. "Brother-in-law, I asked you last year and I ask again now. Won't you leave Gilles with me this year? Last year you said he was too young to page. Now I ask if he can't squire me."

Gilles and his uncle turned those identical dark eyes, keen with identical hope, toward Sire de Rais. Marie saw her husband stiffen with distaste across from her. What could distress her lord so? Unless it was the near idolatry in Gilles' hands as he worked to unfasten the buckle under Amaury's right arm.

Sire de Rais likewise refused to answer the offer he was given. "Bothered by brigands, are you? At Ingrandes?"

Amaury decided to show the most grace and conceded first. "Not brigands, sir. Only a few boatloads of recalcitrant merchants."

"Merchants?" Rais exploded. "You must go in full panoply to deal with merchants?"

"If they will not pay the tolls, I shall treat merchants no different than I would a pack of godless Saracens," Craon declared.

"What you charge in tolls, sir, is robbery." Rais spoke between clenched teeth. "Fifty percent on all goods, even more on salt."

"Are you afraid for your fair share when they get farther upstream, Rais?" Craon grinned. "You can always take half again, half and half forever."

"I worry how such merchants are to come to their destination with any profit at all."

"I never demand more than forty on the hundredweight."

"That is outrageous."

Her father was still grinning. Could it be he enjoyed the exchange? Perhaps as well as any good tussle in the lists. He'd stripped down to his surcoat now. Of simple muslin, stained and worn, the tow padding tufting out in the spots with the most stress. Her mother was unable to keep up with the mending, nor to urge her maids to do so for her. Her father's recent dunk in the Loire—after merchants, so it seemed—enlivened years of sweat and filth in the garment. It released the man's smells with the sudden vigor of prisoners set free of the oubliette.

He said, "It is one of the benefits due to the lord of Ingrandes. Amaury knows, don't you, lad? When I die—"

"May God grant you many years, Father."

Craon charged over his son's piety like no more than a shock of grass. "He'll be lord after me and continue the practice. Fill my shoes, won't you, lad?"

"I shall try, sir."

Craon ignored his son's note of doubt and addressed his son-in-law. "You know what the great standing stone at Ingrandes means, do you not, sir?"

"Pagan idolatry," Sire de Rais said.

"Not a whit of it. It marks the site where the duchy of Brittany abuts on Anjou. Such a border surely allows—demands—more than your usual toll."

"The toll ought to go to the lords of the two countries, then, not to you."

"I'd like to see mad Charles come and claim his share. Or Brittany's duke. I'd like to see them try." Craon laughed out loud.

Fourth Antiphon

The Tapestries' Weft

———•———

"God can refuse nothing to the men of our house."

Jean de Craon made no attempt to moderate the boom in his voice for the echoing confines of his great hall as he, laughing, drew the moral from his last tale.

"But if He did," he went on, winking at his daughter so she, too, had to laugh in the old way she'd almost forgotten. "If He did, we could always turn to the devil."

Sire de Rais squirmed uncomfortably and stole a glance down the table, past his wife, at their son, hoping Gilles was not listening. Gilles was, in fact, still intent on Amaury.

"Amaury is fated to be the next of this worthy line," Craon said. "And I have seen many proofs of his prowess, how God blesses his arm anytime there's a weapon in it."

At Marie's other elbow, Amaury smiled patiently at their father. She decided to turn the subject.

"You haven't yet given my brother one thing he needs to be a great knight, Father. You haven't married him off."

Amaury lowered his eyes and laughed at her teasing, so quietly she couldn't hear him, only see the gentle spread of his lips.

She continued, "*Maman* tells me the match with the Rohan girl has fallen through as well. Amaury is nineteen and—"

Sire de Craon interrupted her. "Nineteen is plenty young yet. A man with all the gifts of your brother, Marie, can afford to be choosy."

"You did not like the girl, brother?" Marie turned and studied

Amaury's beautiful, almost angelic hair, the firm set of his jaw, and the spicy flecks of beard growing there.

Amaury squirmed with obvious discomfort and spoke quietly. "I *could* not like her, Marie."

She met her husband's eyes pointedly for a moment before bending her head to tease her little brother, grown so big, so beautiful—so troubled. "What has *like* to do with marriage, Amaury?"

"I could not," Amaury whispered in reply, almost in terror.

"There's time, there's time," Craon boomed. "Amaury has all the time in the world to marry."

Having eaten his fill, Gilles reached across the ruins of loaves and fowl for his uncle's hand. "Come, let's joust. Uncle, you promised."

"Your permission, Father?" Amaury shoved back his chair.

"Oh, sit still a minute," Craon refused. "Sit and talk with the rest of us. The once-in-an-age we have guests, you can oblige us, Amaury."

Disappointment registered in the violence with which Gilles and Amaury reclaimed their seats. Marie could only be grateful for the sign her brother gave her son. It taught patience her otherwise dangerously volatile firstborn did not possess at all.

"A new tapestry, my lord father?"

If she could do nothing for the disappointment of her brother and her son, Marie could still salve the tension that stood raw between her husband and her father.

"Do you like it, my dear?"

"Very much."

"Madame, you surprise me." Marie knew the low hint of scorn in her husband's voice and knew she must tread carefully if he entered the conversation on such a tone.

"I . . . I like the colors. I confess I haven't had a chance to examine it closely."

"Well, I have," Guy de Rais said with increasing coldness. "All this morning while you were up visiting with your lady mother, leaving me down here with nothing better to do."

"My lord, I am sorry . . ." Marie began, but her father drove right over her.

"What, Rais? You do not care for the subject?"

"Not at all." Her husband was adamant.

"Yet I was certain you would. It represents the life story of your own ancestor, after all."

"Bertrand Du Guesclin."

"*L'Épée du Roi*, the Sword of the King, famous for his battles against England's Black Prince."

"That is so."

"Why, in royal circles, Du Guesclin has grown into the very type of chivalric knighthood, even ousting the lords of Arthur's Round Table on occasion."

Guy de Rais said: "I cannot like the portrayal of my ancestor training under a sorcerer in the forest of Brocéliande."

But that scene reminded Marie so much of the Hermit of St. Gilles, as close a match as anyone could capture in parallels of tightly beaten weft. It unnerved her, even, how fast her heart set to beating at the sight. Her husband could only condemn how much she missed the forest, how much she missed the Hermit. How long it took her to settle into real life again, to even feel it had any reality after the pilgrimage every year.

And yet she knew full well the old man himself, like the black-robed, grey-bearded man worked in the wool of the tapestry, was an image, a symbol of all sorcerers, back to Merlin and even beyond. The tapestry showed him with arms raised and streaming wide sleeves in a conjuring gesture, the forest behind him alive with the wind-carried veils of fairy folk.

Marie quickly bent forward to meet her husband's eyes squarely over the burnt crumbs she'd picked off a good pasty. He must not guess a half of the things that part of the tapestry made her think of. Just so had she looked him calmly, straight in the eyes all the while at St. Gilles and thereby kept him from guessing what the pilgrimage, year after year, had brought her to see. To hope. To long for.

But the handsome young serving man bent across her view at that point to refill her husband's flagon, and Marie hastily looked away.

Guy de Rais, freed of her eyes, his tongue whetted on wine, began his commentary on the third corner of the tapestry sequence. "And can this be appropriate to show young men and ask them to emulate? Du Guesclin in women's dress, the rough white hemp of a peasant, and carrying a bundle of faggots?"

"That dress is Du Guesclin's disguise as he sneaks his way in to take the castle of Fougeray from the English," Marie's father said. "Why should young men not see examples of any ruse that may succeed against the enemy?"

"And how do you, sir, justify that spinning, dreaming, upward-looking lady in the fourth scene?" Guy de Rais asked.

"Tiphaine Raguenel, his lawfully wedded wife," Sire de Craon replied in all innocence.

Marie liked this domestic scene best, with Du Guesclin sitting on the ground at his wife's feet. Threads dyed in black walnut twigs or comfrey mordented with iron indicated the Moorish complexion for which the hero had been notorious. Uneven stitches in the face were taken on purpose: the family of this man knew perfectly well how his mother had screamed at his ugly, twisted, and blocklike features when he was born. Growing up had never done anything to improve them, even if it had won them more acceptance in a man's battle-scarred face.

"Tiphaine, the witch," Guy de Rais exclaimed.

Tiphaine the fairy woman, Marie thought. Tiphaine who could read the heavens and tell the future from them. But did Marie like that scene so much because such respect in domesticity was something she would likely never enjoy?

Du Guesclin had a line worked in crimson yarn on one thigh in that scene. Many men at the Midsummer pilgrimage had worn the same thing, an emblem of some sort of oath, she imagined. She liked how it drew attention to well-hosed thighs and she couldn't help but wonder how the young serving man might look in one. She might even make the suggestion to him, perhaps give him a ribbon from her baggage to try out.

"But it is the center scene that disturbs me most of all," her husband went on. "Men, dancing, crowned in oak leaves and flowers—just like they were only last week at St. Gilles around the Midsummer fires."

Sire de Craon said, "Hangings such as these, on the same theme, are in demand in all the best houses. In fact, I have it on excellent authority that the merchant carrying this piece to its new owners hoped to get seven hundred francs for it. And I, my good Sire de

Rais, hoped you'd write me out of at least that much of the fifteen hundred I owe you still in dowry if I were to have it taken off its brass hooks this very moment and handed over to you."

Marie's husband fell silent, confused and disarmed by her father's generosity. No one could refuse to grasp hands as open as Sire de Craon's.

"Seven hundred francs, Father?" she asked. "Can it be so much?"

"Of course it is so. The craftsmanship is excellent, the subject very popular. They cannot weave enough of them. The merchant himself told me when I took it from him. It got dragged through the water in the tussle a bit—hence the water damage along that one side."

Marie saw the grin on her father's face fill with the thrill of pursuit and victory. She had to smile in response.

Craon continued, "I had the maids spread it and try to get the mud out, of course, but as you see—"

The sudden fierce growl of her husband's chair legs across the flagstones interrupted the recital. Sire de Rais was on his feet, his fists shoved hard against the linen of the tablecloth so that it dragged up and threatened to spill his flagon.

"By the Saints, you stole it!"

"I wouldn't exactly say that," Craon grinned. "Not exactly."

"You stole it."

"I took it as toll, my proper due as lord of this land."

"You stole it."

Marie looked away. Her husband's loss of all words but those, in varying degrees of shock and horror, was too shameful. They'd been through this subject already.

"I only took one. The best, yes, but I left the fellow four others to peddle when he got where he was going. Once I'd claimed my very small share, I sent him happily on his way."

"Happy you hadn't cut his throat, no doubt. And you dare to hang your shame here in the center of your hall for all to see, you greedy, violent . . ."

"Greedy? Sir, I beg you." Craon continued to be highly amused. "When I took only one of five? And I do not mean to keep the hanging for myself, after all. I never did. I thought of you at once, the moment I saw it. It is your ancestor, after all, much as the rest of us in Brittany like to claim him. I meant to give it to you from the first. After all—"

And he cast a glance down the table toward his grandson.

"After all, when a man's daughter has a son going on nine, it's about time the dowry was paid off, isn't it?"

"You remain in my debt, Craon. Heavily, wickedly in my debt."

"Oh, Rais, by Christ's blood. You sound like God Almighty. 'Wicked'? . . . 'Debt'?" Craon shook his white head in amusement.

"I will not take your filthy lucre for my wife lest she prove like-wise loose of morals."

With these words, Guy de Rais snapped his attention to Marie. She felt her womb clamp down on itself at the implied accusation, that nothing she had done in the past nine years had been anywhere near good enough. Nothing she could ever do would ever help, either. She was, forever and always, her father's daughter.

And it didn't help that at that moment, the young serving man set a bowl of cherries down between her father's place and her own. The harder she tried to ignore the servant's presence, the more fascinating she found the brief glimpse she got of fabric caught up to his codpiece, at just about eye level. Not until that presence had gone could she clear her head and return it to the matter at hand.

Marie felt her father's shoulders shrug beside her and that gesture was oddly comforting.

"So, take it or leave it," he was saying. "Just don't get on a high horse against me, Rais. Where else do you think I got the fifteen hundred francs I already paid you for this girl of mine? Just because gold coins don't get water-damaged. You're going to give me all those coins back? No, I didn't think so. Coins are so able to rub off the evil that gains them. That's why men such as yourself like them well. Oh, come on, Rais, sit down. Relax. Don't take the tapestry if it doesn't suit your decor. But sit down, for God's sake, and have some cherries."

Craon shoved the bowl—the beautiful, glossy red fruit in the glossy chased silver—carelessly down the table. And at an odd angle, on the vessel's other side, Marie saw the pinched white face of Jean Le Drapier.

20

Under the Sway of These Hangings

The buxom redhead's round hips jostled me for space on the narrow bench. I tried to ignore her, letting my mind wander back to the more comfortable days I'd just left behind at St. Gilles. Such diversion wasn't difficult. For weeks, even months after the pilgrimage, I always held the ability to hear the Master's voice quite close to me, explaining the world's many mysteries.

He'd already told me about the one tapestry, the one the noble folk at the high table were having such disagreement over. It was during the woodland festivities portrayed in the center of the hanging that the Hermit of St. Gilles had initiated Charles VI. "I myself marked him with the permanent blue woad on the curve of his thigh," his voice told me.

For a moment, my forest-darkened eyes thought they could see the mark on the King standing to the left of the central image. Through the gold and blue stitching of his ceremonial robes, a darker blue patch, shaped like a goat's hoofprint, stood out between one golden lily and the next. I knew then that I would be able to sense the mark on living people with as much ease—or more.

In a way, Sire de Rais was right. The King's madness did date from that event. For from that moment Charles understood: he was bound by the highest calling of his blood royal as well as enjoying its luxuries. He understood that his blood might be called for to reinvigorate the Land at the next Cycle. And, of course, at the next Cycle, he'd declined, for fear.

At this moment in my reverie, I suddenly found my head pulled sharply back to rest on the gap of freckled flesh beneath the redhead's throat. No more than a lip's breadth from mine, her red mouth rasped at me, "Did your mama ever teach you how to kiss, lover?"

I didn't know what to say. I was, in fact, scared quite beyond all speech. Not the least of my worries was what others must think. Those at the high table must look down on us from their dais like the audience on actors in a play. What must Sire de Craon say? Would he grow violent, as he did so easily, that I was being too forward with his serving woman? What about Sire de Rais?

The redhead had been chopping onions. Eating them, too, and more than just the ones in the overcooked pasties left for us at the bottom table after the nobility had taken their choice. The smell of onions teared my eyes. My heart was pumping so quickly that black-red began to invade the edges of my vision.

I kept wit about myself enough, however, to think of working a spell before I was overcome by one of my own. The only one I could think of at the moment was the one against wild beasts in the wood. The Hermit, when he'd taught it to me, had been quite sure I'd never actually need it, friend to the King Stag and all his subjects as I was.

The words and hand gesture worked quite well against the redhead. In any case, she let me go with a raucous laugh after no more than flicking my lips with the tip of her tongue. Her action, unnerving as it was, did have the effect of releasing my attention for the room's other tapestry. I stared at it unseeing for a while, more interested in showing my bench partner my back than in anything I might see.

Presently, however, when my composure had had time to settle like layered leaves in an autumn wood, I began to make the figures out of the old, faded yarns. The Hermit's voice, buzzing like late-season wasps in my head, told me I studied the woolen story of King Comor of Brittany, yet another ancestor of the house, though a much more ancient one. This tapestry was much older than the first, as well. The brighter colors protected from light and dust under a curled corner gave a hint of what it must once have been.

"King Comor married three times," the voice in my head began, much as a minstrel might have done. "And each wife he put to death most cruelly as soon as he got her with child."

My "Why?" was a child's "Why?" forgetting that such ancient stories needed no rhyme or reason. Why was the sky blue? It simply was, that's all, and a person must learn to live with it.

"But his fourth bride," my Master continued the tale uninterrupted, "was the protégée of St. Gildas and her name was—"

I knew the answer.

The figure of another woman of the same name on the tapestry directly across the hall had made Sire de Rais so uneasy. I whispered the fairy name aloud.

"Tiphaine."

The solid flesh of a pair of raised red eyebrows came between me and the vision on the wall. My benchmate halted the veal bone she was gnawing on halfway to her greasy lips and looked at me quizzically.

"Call me what you will, sweetheart," she said. "I'll be your little fairy woman, if you wish."

I clamped my own lips firmly together, determined to listen but not speak aloud again as my part of the dialogue running through my brain.

"And when the heathen King chopped off her head, the holy man replaced it. He turned the blade on Comor, who was consumed in the fires of hell. And then St. Gildas retired to confess his newly veiled little nun the rest of her days."

So the hanging showed. But the impression of such words on my old Master's tongue set my head spinning with the old whirl. "Heathen" was a virtue to him, as beloved as the heath itself, tapestried with head-high gorse, carpeted with bilberry and heather. And "nun," not so honored. Good chased evil and evil good until my head was in the familiar spin and I began to see the world as the Hermit saw it—the world behind the world the Christians saw.

Tiphaine—"fairy woman" of course. And Gildas?

"The Christianized form of the deity who animates the Isle of Houat, the hundreds of other small islands surrounding the Gulf of Morbihan," the Hermit's voice explained. "Let the cathedral of

Vannes boast that they have contained his relics in a small, golden box. His power still rolls in the tides faster than a man can run and sets the wave-stallions leaping high upon the patient shore.

"Christianity is a veil over what once was," the Hermit had explained to me this trip to St. Gilles. "Over what once was, what will be, and what, in fact, never leaves us, the God-moved World all around. In the days of our ancestors, of Merlin, Gildas, Gilles, the reality was easy for the faithful to see. Craft came easily. Now, in order to become a Master, a man born with the din of church bells in his ears—and who is not so born these days?—such a man must learn to grow deaf to them in order to hear the voice of the God underneath. His eyes must learn to strip away the veil of every image. He must train his heart not to fear what a trembling Christian shuns, but to embrace it, lest unwittingly, by his fear, he loose upon the world an even greater dread. Such is the path to Craft. To magic in harmony with the Powers That Be."

So now, as the remains of roast veal and goose pasties was cleared from the trestle tables in the great hall of Champtocé, I practiced stripping the layers from the tale told by the tapestry. We were given cherries now, and below the salt, these were the overripe ones, those bruised or fringed with mold, those pierced by little white worms. My benchmate made a great deal of gleaning out the nicest ones. When I wouldn't let her feed them to me "like a little bird," she ate them herself, with great relish, and collected the pits, counting them out.

"But you're not a soldier," she said. "Are you a lawyer?"

She kept eating them, insisting she would find the man in her verse who must be me, and that was where she would stop, when the verse told her whom she would marry.

"So who is the man on the left in this picture?" the voice in my head drew me back again from tinkers and tailors.

"St. Gildas, haloed in gold thread. He's just replaced his proté-gée's head, although a thin line of red silk still marks the joint. The Saint is signing it, his two fingers raised in the sign of the Stag. Tiphaine, on her knees, has continued to pray throughout the whole ordeal, her hands pitched over the obvious fertility of her belly. Happily, not a thread of red has stained the rich green of her gown."

"Green, my Yann?" The Hermit's voice urged me to see beyond. "Fairy green."

"And St. Gildas?"

"The Man in Black, though Christian eyes would see in him only a monk."

Then "Ah," my exclamation came aloud as the realization hit me. "These woolen folk, too, protect the Old Faith. Tiphaine, in her swelling green, looks nothing so much as like the very fertile Mother Earth Herself. King Comor, in great evil, has been wounding that Earth, the greatest of all divinity. And the God of the Isle of Houat has come at the last and interfered."

Feeling very proud of my growing powers of Seeing through the veil, I let my eyes wander to the tapestry's background. Here Tiphaine's three predecessors, collapsing time, were represented in colors which, ill-lit as the hall was even by daylight, made them difficult to make out. Nonetheless, I could see that theirs was a style heavily influenced by the time of the Black Death, as if the weaver had felt the very pest breathing over her shoulders as she worked. The king's dead queens were brown mounds of denuded earth, little more than fresh graves. A grinning death's-head surmounted each of them from which dangled looped braids of hair strung with broken strings of pearls to indicate what once had been.

"Consider the folk living in the hall today," the voice said, "under the sway of these hangings."

So I did. The Death was not such an ancient memory. Sire de Craon himself must have been born just after the time, in days when a woman might feel her labor pains were all in vain, to bring forth flesh so weak and perishable.

"Do the dead queens represent fertility King Comor wantonly destroyed through ignoring the Old Ways? Was, then, the Black Death caused by similar ignorance?"

I received no answer just then to these questions from the pulse of gold that rimmed my mind, brought like a skein of gold threads from the Midsummer shrine. Certainly Sire de Craon could give me no answer to these riddles himself. I must ask the Hermit face-to-face when next I saw him.

"There is the enigma of King Comor," the voice of the Hermit instructed me again. "He stands in the center of the great stretch of fabric."

"Yes."

My eye had been drawn again and again to his face. To his beard, more precisely. In good part, it was worked with the same black threads as St. Gildas' habit. But among them was also a very startling blue, the same skein that might have worked the sky above the scene or the bluebells dotting the grass below.

"Blue is a rare color in tapestry." The voice seemed to ramble, to be thinking elsewhere and only keeping words in his mouth to be sociable. "Hard to come by, I understand. The dyers can only use elderberries." Listing things is an easy way to keep the mouth full while the mind wanders. "Or a weak elecampane . . ."

"Or woad!"

The word burst from me, quite startling my poor benchmate this time. She looked at me askance and decided perhaps she'd had cherries enough when she stopped at "rich man"—which clearly wasn't me. I hardly took time to apologize to her, so eager was I to dash off after the thought.

For the moment I thought "woad," I understood, as a Craftmaster's brew suddenly comes to its power by the addition of one final herb. Woad was the warrior's plant in ancient times, the fermented leaves good as a paste on wounds. Or as a war paint before the action, anyplace one thought he might be wounded, to make the effect less grave.

And it was possible to make the blue marks permanent by pricking the paste in under the skin. This was accomplished during initiation into the Craft. As I had already been reminded by looking at the figure of Charles VI in the hanging opposite.

"Among the few who choose to take their ancient beliefs so far these days," the Hermit had often told me, "most take the sign under an arm or on a buttock. In such places, it is less likely to be noticed as they go their ways in a Christian world."

"But how was it in the days of King Comor?" I asked, almost certain of the answer before it came to me.

"Then it was common to put the mark upon one's face, on one's chin, a permanent blue beard. A mark of pride for all to see."

The maker of the tapestry must have known this, too, for the beard was wild. Blue grew not just on cheeks and chin as in normal men, but on the forehead, between the brows and across the bridge of the nose, everywhere under the antlerlike crown the King wore. This was no beard, then, but a mark of ancient faith, a solemn swearing the King had undergone when he'd married each of his brides in turn, swearing to love, honor, and protect.

And his brides were not women, but the Land.

This was the cause of the old King's nickname, Bluebeard. The name with which nurses liked to threaten their unruly children and credited with many more sins—and more immediate ones—than the tapestry portrayed.

Of course, such strange marks on the kingly face gave him a terrifying aspect. With the horns of his crown, most Christians would surely see Satan in that face. And there, there at his feet were the madder and Saint-John's-wort flames of hell, coming to claim their own. But stripping away the Christianity, I could now see an older meaning to the tale.

"Comor was an initiate, wasn't he, Master? Initiate as Charles our present King is, sworn to care for his Mother the Earth and all her creatures. And he was crowned as the Stag, honored to play the part of the God among us mortals as only few are chosen. Chosen to actually marry the Mother and quicken Her womb."

The story continued to rush upon my brain. "But for some reason, King Comor forgot his sacred oaths. He abused the power of kingship, leaving the land barren, death's-headed heaps. And he would not fulfill the most sacred of obligations laid upon those who take up the crown. He refused to give up his life when the Cycle of Earth's Sacrifice came to claim it. Comor forgot the true calling of a God."

"Like Charles?" came the echo of the Hermit's voice.

But I wasn't ready for present parallels yet. "Perhaps his first three wives were priestesses," I thought, "giving themselves to fulfill the supreme renewing act. And he turned on them, feeding the Earth their blood instead of his own royal gore. That would be something, wouldn't it?"

"Yes," the Hermit answered, "but not the offering the Earth demanded."

"Then came Tiphaine. Was she a high priestess? Perhaps Goddess herself?"

"Perhaps."

"And he refused her as well."

"The Craft gives power enough even to restore life—when it is a matter of claiming what it must have."

"So the touch of the Man in Black revived Tiphaine."

"And?" my mentor urged.

"And, seeing the miracle, Comor remembered the blue touch of the God on his face, remembered his oath and what was required in exchange for the gift of Kingship over the Land."

"So it was. The holy altar's flames had lapped up their due. The Earth, in due season, bore Her fruit once more. And ever after, the world must be grateful to all three figures immortalized on Champtocé's wall."

This was the obvious interpretation; there could be no other. And the whole notion of the needful sacrifice had been reinforced by my recent stay with the Hermit of St. Gilles, by the horrifying shrieks of the dogs and cats caught once more in the wicker-supported flames.

But the minor sacrifice of every year was not what most concerned the Master. Cats and dogs were easy enough to come by, and nobody worried if they understood their fate. In fact, their whimpers before, their shrieks after, would tend to the belief that they did not understand. But that was not a question in the Master's mind. Something greater concerned him. For this was the Year.

The Cycle of Solemn Sacrifice had turned again.

"And I do not know who will step forward to lay down his life this year." The Master's plaint came back to me, solid as the thump of his fist upon my back. "None has stepped forward these nine years since the death of the old duke of Burgundy. And to make *him* willing was a challenge. Charles is mad. Jean of Brittany, the dukes of Berry, Orléans, the new duke of Burgundy—all of these men with the Blood to shed are too concerned with worldly things. None of them are initiates. The demands of their petty lives overwhelm them, blind them. A Man in Black mentions 'sacrifice' and they laugh. Even 'the Lord Jesus' they mock. 'That has nothing to do with me, with governing and Kingship in this day and age.' "

In spite of the attention this Vision demanded, I found myself being drawn back into reality. Up at the high table, Gilles and his uncle Amaury had asked once again if they might not be excused to the lists. More because they resented the interruption than anything else, the grown-ups again denied them.

The look on my milk brother's face as he stewed over this reminded me. He had been present during at least some of the discussions the Hermit and I had had on the sacred subjects at the shrine.

"I'll go cut their throats for them," Gilles had offered. "These royal dukes who won't pay the price of their station."

And I had asked, "Could you not kill them by secret magic?"

The Hermit had smiled gently and shaken his white head. "You children do not yet fully understand Sacrifice. The bloodletting of a thousand thousand men in battle has not the equal of a single life, offered freely at the full. Every nine years, or the spiral is broken. But where such a life is to come from this year, I cannot begin to see."

The Hermit had set me to gaze in water, but I had given him no clearer picture.

Now here was the year past Midsummer. The year for Sacrifice ended with the year for growth—just as winter began. There remained but four months—no more—to find the willing royal victim.

And somehow, the power of such need gathered like the smells of well-seasoned food here in the great hall of Champtocé-sur-Loire.

21

Linen Churned in River Mud

My head cleared; the Vision left me. I hoped the scowls sent my way from the high table were meant for the redhead and not for me. I thought so; the scowls were mostly from Sire de Rais. This was Sire de Rais' means of punctuating his stern lecture of innuendo toward his errant father-in-law, since Mesdames de Craon, de Rais, and young Gilles could also hear.

But the redhead had come up with a new diversion that demanded my full attention. She'd tied a bit of ribbon 'round her neck and it was my task to undo it.

"I will only marry the man who manages to untie this knot," she declared.

When I told her I didn't want to marry her, she said I must make the attempt or I would have to become her groom anyway.

It was a tricky knot. I'd never seen its like before, and in the slippery silk, with my bad hand, the task went badly. The redhead giggled at first, and won the jests of our neighbors as well. My struggles put me in indelicate positions that must have seemed scandalous from the perspective of the high table. More than once, I tried to call off. She would not let me until I began to make the ribbon tighter and tighter every time I touched it.

"Help! Ah! Oh! Help! I'm choking! Get it off! The boy is trying to choke me."

The woman's pleas took on a particularly frantic quality in the gap of silence that had suddenly opened in the sounds of Champtocé hall. For the great doors to the bailey had just been flung open and the ragged forms of ten or twelve men stood dusted by the golden motes of light they let in. At the high table, even Sire de Rais, his fists still planted in anger on the table, fell quiet to appraise the newcomers.

"Get it off!"

But suddenly the game with the ribbon seemed the least of my mortifications and even the redhead dropped her voice, knowing her troubles only play. Among the shadowed figures I recognized my father. My father, along with six or seven others, in chains.

I ran to him at once. Ignoring the redhead was easy enough. I suppose someone else released and won her that day. I had no trouble ignoring even the lancers and their weapons ringing my captive parent.

He was too weak for much of a greeting. Muddy and exhausted, the men had been force-marched the full league up from the Loire in the heat of the day, all sporting wounds untended and baked black by the sun. What good was embracing now, in any case? My father knew himself a man who could hug a son no longer. Hardly more than an animal, his fate rested now in the hands of the lords, the high table of nobles whose tempers were running high. Father set his hand gently on my shoulder and turned me to face that table, to watch and listen.

Sire de Rais shoved himself from the table with such violence that his flagon toppled. His face, like the cloth, was white with rage, stained wine-red on the cheekbones.

"My vassals!"

"What? Are they yours indeed, son-in-law?" Craon did not seem as surprised as his words might indicate.

"They are, but what matter whose they are?"

Craon had his own complaint to make. "Ignace," he barked to one of the newly arrived men, "why ever didn't you take them straight to the dungeon? This is not the place for captives, disturbing ladies at their meal."

My father jostled me a little because he was jostled by one of the lancers who meant to shove him back out the door. But there was too much discord among the lords for the lower folk to come to any firm decision about what to do and where to go next.

Sire de Rais said, "How dare you, sir, do such things to other men's vassals? To any Christian man?"

"When they do not pay, such things may happen."

"Pay your exorbitant tolls, you highway robber? I should hope no man of mine would ever stoop so low as to do such a thing."

"Plenty of other lords are nowhere near their merchantmen when they happen by the great old stone of Ingrandes."

My father slumped exhausted to the floor, hardly listening. I slumped with him, holding his hand where I could reach it between fetter links.

"You will release them, sir, this moment," Sire de Rais said. He'd jumped off the dais now and confronted his father-in-law face-to-face across the table.

"But, of course, son-in-law. I shall not even ask the customary ransom in this case."

"You would demand ransom? From me?" Sire de Rais touched his chest tenderly, as if feeling a deep, perhaps life-threatening wound.

The lord of the castle shrugged. "I don't care who pays as long as someone does."

"You shall not—" Sire de Rais struggled for words, for control. "You shall not get a sou from me."

"No, I shall not." Craon chuckled out loud. "I still owe you dowry, after all."

With greater flourish and less speed than one might have expected, Craon wordlessly gave a sign to the men who stood around my father and his fellow captives. Fetters began to fall with slow creaks, as if of disappointment.

"And—and you shall restore every finger's width of cloth to them," Sire de Rais insisted.

"Now, I'm not certain I can do that," Craon said placidly, leaning back in his great armchair and drumming one hand's fingers against the other. "I'm afraid much of it sank to the bottom. Linen, after horses' hooves have churned it in river mud, hasn't much of its former value. And salt, once it hits the water—"

"You shall, Craon, or neither I nor your daughter nor your grandsons will ever set foot in this house again."

There were women's cries of protest, but these were ignored. Craon laughed out loud, as if he'd never heard so good a joke.

But it was no joke. Sire de Craon refused to pay and Sire de Rais called his bluff.

"Wife, go get your things. We will not spend another moment under this roof. Son, leave that table at once."

Gilles reached a hand for Amaury, "But we wanted to joust—"

"Gilles, this instant." Sire de Rais' voice had never sounded so still, so terrifying.

Gilles looked to Amaury. Amaury patted the boy's hand and jerked his own head, telling his nephew he ought to obey. Gilles did—obeyed Amaury, not his father—and scampered out of the hall after his mother, looking back toward his uncle all the way.

———•———

At the time I was too grateful to our lord of Rais for my father's release to consider the repercussions. Nor did I take his comment as anything but a compliment.

"Did you see, my lady?" he said as we rode out of the shadow of Champtocé's Black Tower and down the honeysuckle-clogged *boire*. "Did you see how this lad went at once to his father and the other captives with no thought for his own safety with all the lancers around?"

I basked in the lord's words even when they ended with sentiments I cared for less: "It is just as Père de Boszac says. The boy should be trained for the priesthood. A ministering order, perhaps."

Madame would not be drawn into such pleasant speculation. Once the château was out of sight, she pulled the shutters of her *charet* against the man who'd dragged her from her family. She must have suspected that, true to her lord's word, no matter how she might weep, neither she nor Sire de Rais would ever set foot in that keep again.

The same was not true of Gilles, however, nor of his little brother René. And this might not have made much difference.

Except that I had the strangest feeling it was the sight of his son's hand in Amaury's that had upset the lord of Rais infinitely more than my ill-used father and his colleagues.

And by that evening I also knew Gilles' life had much more to do with the tapestries hung in Champtocé than those in Blaison toward which we rather ignobly hastened.

That year of grace 1413, the guild of merchants and mariners plying the Loire appealed to Paris against Monseigneur Jean de Craon. Charles VI gave him a warning which he obeyed—as long as the King remained lucid.

That wasn't, of course, very long at all. For King Charles was soon lured back to the dance of the Horned One, the orgy swirling in his mind.

The Poppy-Red Fields of Crécy

*"Upon the poppy-red fields of Crécy
The flowers of France rode out
And found death."*

Master Gwencalon's voice trembling over the solid, somber chords of his harp had power to bring the whole scene to mind: the shimmer of heat waves just above the parched August ground almost eighty years ago. Hot sun blinding off the white-hot forge of knights' armor. The standards limp in the breathless air. The quick hiss then—before one had time to think—the thunk of deadly Welsh and Cornish arrows.

So deep was the power of the Master's music that I was startled—and somewhat annoyed—every time my mind was called back from the field of Crécy to the present and great hall at Angers castle. I suppose the series of tapestries besieging this hall helped the old bard's music: they portrayed scenes from the Apocalypse. With Master Gwencalon to animate them, horsemen of doom and souls in torment had no difficulty turning into the fifteen hundred French knights who fell on that day so long ago.

I had help feeling the parched heat of Crécy, too, though it was now the end of October, 1413. A fire had been set in the great fireplace, the great table set close enough to keep the nobility comfortable. The rest of the company down on the trestle tables and benches may have felt the drafts driven by a wild autumn storm in spite of fire, in spite of tapestries. I had suffered such placement often enough myself.

But my station tonight was with the lords, running back and forth in front of the long white drapery that hid their legs, seeing that my two young lords had all the one-part-to-five of water and wine they needed. The stress of the situation added to my heat. I kept my twisted hand covered with the serving napkin, but I feared that at any moment it would fail me, here, exposed on the dais, in view of all the company.

I would not be free to sit and whet my tongue and fill my belly until the lords had risen. Such was my duty, and I doubted by then there would be any of that Valencia quince jelly glistening in its salver-like armor under heavy sun. No, nor none of the confection of breast of fowl mixed with sugar, milk, and rice flour the lady of the castle praised so highly, a dish of her Aragonese homeland. I think I personally helped *le petit* René to more than half of the charger of this *manjar blanco*. Every time I moved the spoon, it tantalized my nose with the scents of almond, ginger, and rose water.

Gilles preferred the pine paste and thrushes stuffed with rice. Rice was a delicacy I had never tasted myself. Nor was I likely to sample it tonight, I decided as I watched my milk brother press the last white kernels left on the plate onto a wet finger he quickly returned to his mouth. Rice looked as licelike as anything, but that didn't keep me from craving it. I'd be left with the braised fennel, perhaps, or the medlars baked in honey. "Good for the digestion," I'd be told.

No wonder the power of the Master's song, the heat, and the hunger drew me off again and again to the field of battle.

The lord of the castle also seemed removed from the present world. But I didn't see him at Crécy. Louis II was the King of Jerusalem, Sicily, Naples and Aragon, count of Provence, and the duke of Anjou, titles that seemed too heavy for his sloping shoulders. He was lately returned from yet another expedition into Italy to try to claim the lands that went with the Naples and Sicily part of his inherited title, lands that no member of the family had stood in since his grandfather's time.

Jerusalem was an even more archaic fantasy. Indeed, I had the impression, looking at those shoulders from the unguarded angle granted only to serving lads, that Louis II had retreated from most of his claims. Only those connected to this rock jutting up at the confluence of the Mayenne, the Sarthe, and the Loir Rivers remained to him.

Louis II duke of Anjou had set himself at table well buffered from other disappointment by his favorite sort of people: doctors from the university. Lost in the wilderness of their dialectic, I doubt it was to Crécy the music had carried them.

Louis' queen, countess, and duchess was made of altogether different stuff. Madame Yolande had positioned herself quite close to me, which was, by no mere chance, closer to the world's present political battles. The object of her interest was on the other side of her so mostly I saw a bulky padded headdress with the *bourrelet* arranged in the shape of a spreading heart. Even from the rear, it gave her the warm, exotic air of the Aragon where she'd grown up.

To have beaten a retreat to this exposed rock on a cold, northern October night must be intolerable to her. And she was doing everything she could—her intellectual husband be damned—to amend the fortunes of the family in the persons of her three young children. This was the cause of that evening's feasting, the cause of children to be seen on the dais—where they threatened embarrassment at any moment—instead of being fed with their nurses in the kitchen.

More recently than they had been in Sicily, both her husband's family and her own had been connected to the royal house of France. As was so often the fate with the families of lesser sons, they had been unable to marry their way back up soon enough, consanguinity being what it was. Over the generations, power had seemed to crumble beneath them like the softest chalk. Now that consanguinity was no longer an issue, her family's standing was not at a level to tempt the highest princes.

And yet, through her own ceaseless efforts, Madame Yolande had this night in some part succeeded. No thanks to the Sicily-less King of Sicily, I read in the looks she tossed her scholar-buffered husband from time to time.

And she, Yolande of Aragon, had done so. Here was her son, young Louis, entertaining a son of the King of France at their own table. True, young, awkward Prince Charles was only a fifth son—elevated up to third now what with the fragility of royal infants—but she was back in the royal family at least.

And there was that third young man at table, Gilles de Rais, technically a vassal of Anjou but destined in time to become very, very rich indeed. The three boys were all of an age, seemed to get on famously, and would form companionships at her table that adulthood would not wither.

I found it easy to read in her face with its dark Spanish eyes just how well Yolande of Aragon congratulated herself on having talked Queen Isabeau into handing over her youngest son to be raised by her here in Anjou.

Yolande of Aragon now had charge of the young prince with whom I'd hunted the wren, my own Monsieur Le Vert, Charles the son of Charles the son of Charles.

We were come to see him, to renew the acquaintance. And to solidify the acquaintance with the young prince of Naples and Sicily who would someday claim liege lord rights over every estate Gilles stood to inherit in Anjou. *Le petit* René had come along as well, Blaison being quite close to Angers. There was also a Sicilian prince René's own age with whom to form ties, a second little René, Louis' younger brother, born the same year as Gilles' pesty sibling.

The final child that night upon the dais over whom Yolande of Aragon watched with a mother hen's care was the actual cause of all this sudden conviviality—though none of the boys would confess it. This was the princess of Sicily, Naples, and so on (the titles more ridiculous on her than on her stoop-shouldered father), four-year-old Marie. It was her betrothal to ten-year-old Charles that had been Queen Yolande's great coup, giving her cause to celebrate—and totally ignore the power of the Bard that night.

As far as I could see, Charles had no natural affection for the little demoiselle to whom he was now tied. Had he had any, Gilles and Louis would have quickly seen that he suppressed it.

"We'll have no girls here." "No babies." "Go off to your nurse," was the boys' continuous chorus. I joined the chorus myself. Marie had a most annoying way of clinging to Charles' arm as she did even now at table, delighting the watching court but making her mother just a little anxious, and infuriating the prince completely. They had told her he was to be hers and she took them at their word with a child's imitation of adult flirtations, their innocence making them just that much more annoying—and embarrassing.

"Never mind her, Charles," young Louis assured the prince whenever he was reminded by his manners not to take it all as a joke.

"It's easy for you to say," Charles would complain. "She's your sister. She's not mine. She leaves you alone."

"You're new to her. In time, she'll leave you alone, too. Just stay here long enough and it will happen. Don't I know? Mine wasn't just a betrothal. I was actually married. In time, everybody got tired of Catherine of Burgundy and sent her back to her father and so here I am as happy as ever before."

It wasn't a necessary part of the boys' banter to understand that little Catherine had been sent back to her father, the marriage too youthful to be consummated, as a condition of the alliance with Charles. Yolande had placed her bets now for the Armagnacs in the civil strife that tore at France, irredeemably turning her back against Burgundy. Such an insult could find no repair.

And it was a long shot. The masterful way in which the duke of Burgundy had put down the tradesmen's riots in Paris that summer had made him a very powerful man indeed. Rejecting Catherine of Burgundy and taking on Prince Charles was a very long shot. Queen Yolande couldn't help but exude nervousness from under her heart-shaped headdress. But if such wild odds should pay off . . .

Like the long shot of the English bowmen at Crécy.

So it surprised me when my attention was pulled from the spell worked by the old Bard to realize that the Queen of Sicily was not under that same spell at all. Quite the contrary.

"This minstrel has been with Prince Charles for quite some time."

Queen Yolande turned her attention from the children—Marie sprawling all over her betrothed in a way that would shame a full-grown married woman and Charles barely restrained from hitting her—to Sire de Rais seated at her other hand. I bristled at once when she gave Master Gwencalon the common name "minstrel" that went with jugglers and jesters, not the "Bard" that gave true honor to the man's powers. Within me, the force of the spell crumbled and I resented it.

"Since his infancy, lady, I've heard it said," replied Gilles' father.

"What can his mother the Queen have been thinking?"

"I don't know, madame."

"Well, he's outgrown such nonsense now, surely." Her native Spanish gave a decided hiss to her speech.

"I . . . I suppose so . . ." Sire de Rais stammered in his confusion.

"I will send the man away. Give the prince more suitable tutors."

Sire de Rais took enough time to register all the implications of this plan before he said, "Perhaps I could take the Master as tutor into my own household."

"Would you?" Madame Yolande turned to him with bright gratitude.

"We've had but one tutor since Père Michel de Fontenay returned to his homeland, and now that René is old enough to leave his mother's skirts, a second hand must come in useful. I have heard good things about this Bard." I recalled it was Michel himself who had said these good things, with an accompanying magic symbol of glamour over the lord of Rais' eyes. "And he is one who was tutor to a prince."

Then, as if schooling himself not to hope for too much, milord added, "Of course, it is a step down for the man himself."

"Old blind men who give themselves airs ought not to expect more." Queen Yolande had not had any such glamour placed on her eyes.

"Certainly, yes. You may give him the offer to ease the sting of your blow, madame, when you must give it. If you must." Sire de Rais had doubt in his voice.

"Of course I must."

"I fear the prince is very attached to the man. More than to all his other tutors combined."

"Well, he is a prince and must learn, therefore, that servants are expendable. Yes, I shall present your offer—and the facts—to that man this very night. As soon as he has finished this interminable and glum song of his."

Yolande of Aragon turned to her pine paste with a settled, satisfied air. At her back, the storm shot a blast down the chimney that spattered my face not only with heat but with bellowed sparks. My hands full of wine ewer and serving tray, I could only rub my sleeve against my face to put the stinging out.

Charles was too occupied fending off little Marie, who was shifting her bodice down lower—and it could shift much lower over a featureless chest—to have overheard his *belle-mère*. While wondering if I should tell him about this threat to his household, or what I should tell him—or if I should warn Master Gwencalon—I was much relieved as well as surprised to see that, at the other end of the hall, the storm had blown in a new and comforting arrival. When he tossed back his black cowl and shook it of the rain, I saw at once that it was none other than the Hermit.

The Hermit would never have left St. Gilles without reason. He must have foreseen this crisis and come in time to prevent the prince whom I'd Seen crowned as King from losing this influential and dear confidant. Much as I would have liked Master Gwencalon as my tutor—any counterweight to Père de Boszac's demons—there was too much at risk here with the blood royal than to consider my own desires. I was proud at my growth in the Craft that let me say this: to lose Master Gwencalon would go so against our hopes for this Charles the son of Charles the son of Charles.

While I desperately tried to attract his attention, the Hermit was shown a place among other beggars and handed what scraps had trickled down to that end of the hall. Gilles must have seen the arrival, too, if he hadn't overheard his hostess' words to his father. In any case, he read my distraction, for he gave my shin a kick and ordered me after more wine.

"Excellent idea," I hissed at him. Favoring that leg, I hobbled off the dais with enough sarcasm in my walk to let him know he could have thought of a better way to help me clear my head and find an excuse to go talk to the man.

I did manage to catch the Hermit's eye while I waited for the butler to refill my ewer in portions of his brew suitable for children. Master Gwencalon was the first object of the Hermit's interest, but until the Bard's song was finished, it pleased me that the old man should seek out my eyes instead.

I waved, he waved back. Then I tried to sign more of the urgent news I had for Master Gwencalon in the secret hand signals of the

Craft, signals that the Church had outlawed. But I would never be very proficient at that with my twisted hand, lacking several knuckles altogether. Some signs can be made on any straight edge—nose or leg or dagger hilt, even. But still it was like writing when you couldn't form half the letters of the alphabet.

The Hermit returned a sign, urging peace. I could gesture no more in any case, for the butler thrust the tray and ewer back into my hands.

Even as I recrossed the room, Gwencalon finished his song to a smattering of applause. I realized those of us who'd come under the spell were enthusiastic but few. The old, blind Master may have sensed this, too. Nonetheless, he settled the harp and touched a few strings, reaching for chords that would accompany a song in a lighter mood than he'd first been inspired to, a mood that would better suit the company.

Yolande of Aragon gestured for him to step down, however. And when his white eyes failed to see her, she spoke, "That will do, Master Harper. Thank you," with enough volume and sarcasm that she must have assumed him deaf as well as blind.

Master Gwencalon sat in some confusion, for his youngest son, taken by surprise, moved slowly to come and help him off his stool and back into the crowd's anonymity. The Hermit was at his elbow almost as soon. The Bard breathed a sigh of relief and joy, then, to hear his old friend's voice bent down to the grey sideburns of his beard, sweeping away the confusion.

Yolande of Aragon gestured a young, foppish troubadour up in the old Bard's place. A Spaniard from her mother's famous court, the young man spoke with a decided and affected lisp that did not vanish when he sang. Rose-colored ribbons decked the neck of his lute as if the instrument were some shameless tart.

But even such a man could not escape the spell Master Gwencalon had cast. The song he chose to sing was romance, all right, but it was the romance of Lancelot and Guinevere. The tale, for those who have ears to hear, commemorates a Sacrifice of ancient times. Or rather, what happens to an entire kingdom when, for individual love, the saving Sacrifice in the proper year is "rescued" from the flame.

On the dais, the children had grown restless. Children always know when true power—not just the retelling of that power—has gone. Charles, Gilles, even *le petit* René, had sat, if not in rapt attention, at least patiently when a Master wove the charm that brought their brave ancestors to life, all fifteen hundred of the nobility, to die before the guile and faithless English unchivalry once more. Now they began to squirm and squabble and fight, and Charles even took up his pudding spoon to beat off Marie.

"Very well, children," Yolande of Aragon sighed. "You may go."

I met that mad tumble off the dais as I was trying to make my way up. Ewer, wine, tray, napkin, all tumbled from my hands, down across my fine new tunic and the linen of which my father was so proud.

Charles bolted fastest of all, out of Marie's possessive, plump little hands, and I doubted I would see him again that night. Certainly his little fiancée would not.

"Wait, boys. Wait, my lord prince. Wait, stupid boys." Marie yammered a rising lament as she tried to keep up on her short, skirted legs.

But when she'd lost them all, even the two Renés, her anger spilled over into tears and her nurses had to come and fetch her and carry her from the hall.

Mordred's treachery as played upon a pink-ribboned lute was lost in all of this. And Yolande of Aragon, in exasperation at the sight of me in my ruined clothes when she'd been particularly assured I would cause no trouble, sighed and waved me off with the rest of them. I gave the high table a quick bow, at the same time picking up the ewer and making a vague swipe at the spill with the napkin before leaving the rest for others and fleeing the scene altogether.

I did not go after the young noblemen, however. I sought the Hermit and Master Gwencalon and joined them in the farthest corner of the hall. They'd retired here with as much privacy as they could have hoped for even if they'd chosen to walk out in the yard. Two old men with their heads bent together in such a storm would have instantly aroused suspicion.

They may have set a vanishing spell over themselves, too, one it took even me a moment to see through. Joy overwhelmed me when I finally did. I felt we were in good hands now, four hands so strong in the Craft. But Master Gwencalon's spell must have still lingered about his person, for what joy I did feel seemed bound up with a sorrowful ballad as well, like a prisoner in chains at the end of the tragedy. The closer I got to the two men, the stronger I felt the words he'd repeated so often in the song's chorus:

"Met death at Crécy . . .
Rode out and found death at Crécy."

So strong was the impression that I'd hardly greeted the two with due respect before I had to interrupt whatever else was in the air between them and ask: "Is death like that, Master Gwencalon? Is it something you can meet on the road like an old friend? Or find in a field like an abandoned treasure?"

"I wish I could tell you, boy," the Bard rolled his blind, white eyes in my direction.

"I cannot say, either, Yann," replied the Hermit. "But I will soon know."

"Hush, Master," Master Gwencalon said. "Say not so in the boy's hearing."

"Don't you know, Gwencalon, that this is a lad with rare gifts?" The Hermit fixed me with the blue flint of his eyes.

"No matter what his gifts, why must you bother him with what will not come to pass?"

I could tell the argument that had consumed them before I arrived was picking up again. But I had no clue as to what it might be.

"It will come to pass," the Hermit insisted. "It must come to pass, for the good of the world. Tonight is the night. The Year of Sacrifice ends tonight and there is no better offer. So I have come to you, Gwencalon. Tonight you must sacrifice me to turn the world and become High Master in my place."

Then I knew the matter, and the words dropped like lead to the bottom of my soul.

23

Snipping Off a Thread

"This Jean Le Drapier is an excellent influence on my Gilles," said Sire de Rais. "I think the Drapier boy may have in him the makings of a priest. It seems he has some vocation and I may take credit myself for seeing that he got the necessary education for such a godly calling."

Yolande of Aragon looked at me hard, twisting her thin mouth with consideration. Charles, Gilles, and I had interrupted the lady of the castle as she was leading her guest from Blaison on a tour of the famous tapestries. They'd thought of nothing better to do while waiting for her husband to come to a conclusion with his university men and for the servants to finish cleaning up.

Queen Yolande nodded slowly, still not convinced, at her liege-man and guest, the lord of Rais. I suppose songs of my virtue were a little hard to believe, such piety so soon after the rowdiness of dinner.

For my part, I concentrated all my energy on the glamour, the veil of Christian piety I was learning to cast over myself in order to do what I knew was my true calling. Sire de Rais I was used to fooling. But his hostess, as I'd already discovered, saw the world with less self-delusion.

The wax candles in the sconce guttered as she narrowed her eyes, at all of us, but at me in particular. The sixth angel blew his trumpet with pink-cheeked authority from the tapestry of the Apocalypse hanging on the wall behind her.

Then, I felt a surge of power through me as if ratcheted up another cog. Was the Hermit giving me a hand? From another room?

"Very well," she said. "I can see no harm in it. A night's vigil in the castle chapel in the company of the Hermit of St. Gilles? It seems a pious activity. Good preparation for knighthood, yes."

The power of my glamour swelled with her belief.

"Yes, yes, very well. You may join your friends, Charles. But will you tell your tutor the Bard I have something to discuss with him when you see him, child?"

At my side, Monsieur Le Vert nodded. "Yes, madame."

"I'll speak to that old man in the morning. I only ask, children, that you try and see if you can't find my Louis and have him go with you. A little chapel wouldn't hurt him, either."

"Yes, madame. We will certainly try. Thank you, madame."

Prince Charles and I let Gilles speak for us. Although he hadn't the Craft to throw a glamour, there was no denying his skill with a lie. We had, of course, not the slightest intention of trying to find Louis of Anjou. The old man had particularly warned us against him, a child who had had no tutor but those of the priestly or troubadour ilk, no introduction to the mysteries at all. We must try to avoid and even evade him if necessary, tonight, the last night of the Year of the Sacrifice.

Then we all three made our most courtly bows before the Queen of Sicily and Gilles' father and scampered from the room. I let the glamour go gratefully, like letting breath go when it's held too long.

———•———

Louis 99 King of Jerusalem and Sicily had just dedicated the castle chapel east of the royal lodging. Holy to Ste. Geneviève, it was called simply the Grande Chapelle. It smelled of fresh-carved and -waxed wood.

The Eve of All Souls' was come, the time that is no time, halfway between midnight and dawn. The end of the year. For this reason, the seven of us carried turnip ghost lights instead of tapers, and they gleamed on all the new gold and silver appointments. Only Charles carried no lamp. His arms encircled the great golden cauldron instead; he'd brought it to Angers just as he had brought it years ago to Tours.

The impression of newness changed the moment the Hermit led us around behind the altar and opened the locked door to the crypt with a bit of hammered wire and a spell. Suddenly, everything was very, very old, as old as the earth itself, and the new Grande Chapelle but a thin new varnish overlaid. The downward-twisting steps were hewn from living rock, worn uneven because the hands that had done the work must have been dead and dust for hundreds, possibly thousands of years.

Our lights picked out the carving that animated either side: mostly curls and flourishes of stone vegetation in a very wild and archaic style. Every now and again, however, a face seemed to pop from the chiseled bushes with seed pods for his eyes, a laughing oak leaf for a tongue, tendrils of vine for hair and beard.

Farther below sprouted veritable monsters—devouring dragons, demon gods, birds of prey—into which the flicker of our lamps breathed life and movement. A wild-eyed Goddess, no doubt the guardian of this place, this natural cave, held open her grossly exaggerated private parts as if to swallow all us mortal men whole. The womb from which we'd come and to which we must all return.

Every footfall, every crunch or cough, echoed as if the earth pressing in around us were eager for the soft sound of our presence and so made the noise boom. There was no condemnation in the mimicry. An interest, more like, earnest and caring. But none of us made any more sound than we could possibly help.

The smell of death and decay assaulted the nostrils, growing stronger with every step. The chill etched my limbs. It was stronger than natural for such a cold, damp place.

And yet, I had to remember what the Craft teaches about stone: stone has life, too. A different sort of life, more wonderful in that it is more constant. A stone standing erect in an open field has forever that divine vitality that visits a man only occasionally. And a womb of stone does not dry up and wither with age but, with the introduction of the right magic, can always bear.

At last the stair ran out and we reached the small chamber that undercut the fortress rock of Angers. We fanned out in a half circle facing the room's centerpiece, a huge, uncut dolman forming a sort of altar that came chest high to a twelve-year-old boy. In a niche over this altar lay the wooden casket that held the relics of Ste. Geneviève.

My Craft-touched eyes could peer through the veil enough to doubt this identification. The remains of the pious nun of a thousand years ago would not have left the city of Paris of which she was patron. The holy—and decidedly female, I sensed—remains in this casket must be—

Well, who could say who or what the years of reverence had given sanctity here? Geneviève was the only clue. That and the very feel of the place, where the soul seemed to walk on thin ice over a black and bottomless firmament. Geneviève. "White lady of the wave" in the old tongue. A Goddess, undoubtedly.

A low ridge presented itself all around the cavern. Streaks of soot radiating above declared others had used it for the same purpose many times before us. We set our turnip globes there where they continued to flicker, giving an odd half-light to each figure. Faces were difficult to see around the circle, just a haunted eye or cheek, a chin that seemed carved from the same stone in which we stood. But against the purple glow, I noticed the auras' rims more clearly than ever. They were all a unified sort of warm, steady golden luster. In fact, they mimicked very closely the color that radiated off the curves of Charles' cauldron.

Filling in the opposite half of our circle were the graves of others, those the priests of Angers had considered holy enough to join the Saint over the years. In this crypt, the dead reflected the living like a mirror.

At my side, I heard Charles strangle his breath almost to whimpers. The sound rose up in lifeless echoes from the belly of his cauldron. I reached for his nearest hand. He shifted all his burden to the other side and took my hand in his. It was as cold as death.

The Hermit took the Bard by the elbow and led him to the empty spot before the altar. The two old men stood facing us there at the very fulcrum between the worlds, between life and death at the between time that was no time.

The Hermit's hand lingered lovingly on his companion's arm. "Are you certain, my friend?"

"I am certain. You are not. In such matters, doubt must step aside." The Bard's voice was strong and musical, even while his harp was still slung on his back. "You doubt because I am blind that the Sacrifice will be as perfect as it ought. In the old days, no man could be King if he lacked but a single eye. As for the offering . . . But when the King is mad, the world is mad, and we must make do."

"Gwencalon, I will . . ."

"No. In times such as these, to offer a maimed Sacrifice is one thing. But to leave the world with a maimed Master . . . It's not to be considered. Surely, Master, you could not care to trust your death to these vacant eyes of mine."

"Very well. We will consider it no longer. Time is short."

The Hermit gestured Gwencalon's three sons out of the circle to come and make their farewells.

"You will greet our mother for us, won't you?" said the eldest. This young man's eyes streamed tears but he managed more control than his smaller brothers. He rested his own hands on their shaking shoulders. "As soon as you see her and our little sisters on the other side, you will remember us to them."

The Bard nodded but said nothing. His tongue had swung into death already.

"Assure them we are coming, too, and we never forget them. Or you, Papa."

"Papa, good-bye."

"Good-bye, Papa."

The choked words of the youngest let the old man find that one's head and face, which he reached out to touch and bless with the gentleness of touching strings. The Bard swept the harp's strap then over his own head and placed it over this son's shoulder.

"No—Papa—" The boy wiggled under the weight, but his father set calming hands upon both son and harp, and they were still.

Then the Hermit stepped forward again and the boys moved back into the remaining comfort of one another's arms.

Together the two old men stripped off their black robes, the Hermit to his officiating white and the crown of autumn's leaves upon his head, the Bard down to nothing but a loincloth and a similar crown. Master Gwencalon's sagging flesh shrank before our eyes in the cold and leaping light. It seemed weaker now than newborn's flesh and closer to the other world.

"Charles, King's son."

My attention had been so focused on the flesh at the edge of the world that I had forgotten the priest in his white until his voice called attention to himself again. It was a conjurer's diversion. The Hermit of St. Gilles held a great knife now, poised aloft.

Charles' hand trembled in mine; it had gone colder still. I tried to let go. He would not. I could hear his difficulty in swallowing over the lump in his throat.

I gave him a little nudge and he went. The Hermit relieved the prince of the cauldron and set it aside on the altar. Master Gwencalon smiled encouragement and kindness as he heard his young pupil approach. There was love, too, in the hands that ran over the little form in the place of eyesight, love identical to what he'd shown his own sons.

"You do right, King's son," the old Bard murmured. "Remember? Remember the fairy green on the first of May? Remember me in that springtime, every time you see it come."

"I . . . I shall," Charles gulped.

"Good. Now I must ask a little something in return—"

Without the Hermit reaching for it, Charles stretched out the flesh of his own right arm from which the white royal linen had been pulled back. The Hermit was so quick and skillful that the young prince hardly had time to gasp in the surprise that precedes pain before his blood was pumping into a matching wound in the Bard's right arm. The Hermit spoke sealing words in the ancient tongue over the link.

The Hermit sent the young prince stumbling back to me. I helped him wrap his arm in a bit of clean linen I'd brought for the purpose while the Hermit addressed the final words to our sacrifice and hope. He called him "King's son," now as he'd a duty to and prayed to him like a God, asking Him to turn the world for us, please, with the gush of His blood.

Then Gwencalon turned to face the altar, exposing a poor back of knobby vertebrae and starting ribs like a carcass already half picked. The Hermit raised the knife, but did not move until he had given a meaningful look to me.

"In ancient times, prophets could read the future from the death of a Nine-year Solemn Sacrifice," the Hermit had told me as we'd discussed this moment before ever setting out for the crypt. "The secrets are mostly vanished, I'm afraid. Yet watch closely, Yann. One with your keen Sight might be able to repair some of what has been lost."

His look reminded me. I did as I'd been told. I watched closely. He plunged, just as he ought, just above the diaphragm and up. But I saw nothing in the Bard's deifying jerks and gurgles, as His life's blood streamed over altar, into Prince Charles' golden cauldron, and in runnels onto the weakened earth. I saw only death.

Afterward, Charles, Gilles, and I were dismissed. The Hermit and the dead man's sons would see to the rest. They would see to the gathering of enough renewing blood in the cauldron to send to all the fields that might ask, to work spells for those who might come with griefs so deep and unassailable that only blood of the Nine-year Solemn Sacrifice could avail.

And they would lay their father's body in among the others in the crypt, reverently easing the older bones aside to make room for His. They would arrange things so this Sacrifice might not be recognized by any misunderstanding priest, yet clearly known to those who cared. Future years of worship and communion with other holy things would magnify the dear worth of what we'd given up that day.

———•———

Above ground, once more amid the new smells of the Grande Chapelle, I saw how sterile was its statuary, how flat and dimensioned with but a single rule. It sought to portray all good, eschewed all evil. In seeking to capture only life, it seemed dead indeed.

I saw Gilles looking about us with interest, too. Did his thoughts parallel mine? I couldn't tell, only that his eyes seemed very wide and moist, the pupils dark and very dilated. I remembered the note in the "Ah!" he had expressed as the blade went in, almost as if it had gone into his own diaphragm.

I had been concentrating so hard on the old man's death, I had given the life around me little thought until now. Now, when it suddenly occurred to me that it might be not the twitchings of death that were important to observe for prophecy, but the twitchings of life. Now, I thought this. Now that it was too late.

Seeking, again too late, to make up for what I'd lost, I studied Charles more closely now as well. Charles, who stuck tight to my side, carefully nursing his bandaged arm.

I recalled how the Hermit had approached him with what must be done.

"Master Gwencalon must be given royal blood, so even though he was not born with it, it may be shed, as is proper to the Sacrifice. Yours, Charles, is the most royal blood in Angers, and certainly the only we may beg for without fear of betrayal."

Charles had asked, "So I must die myself someday? Some Cycle of the Nine?"

"Perhaps it may be so. It is the burden—and the great gift—of your Blood. The same Blood that pulsed in Clovis, the first of your line to carry your same name, Charles Martel, and then the greatest Charles, Charlemagne. And consider the wisdom of the Craft: bloodshed, when offered willingly, is not the taking of life but the giving of it. Blood is not death, but life."

"But not now." Begging for assurance in his ten-year-old's voice.

"Too much is prophesied for you, Charles the son of Charles the son of Charles, for you to perish. Yet. And yet, the time may come, yes."

"There are prophecies of me?"

The Hermit had considered a moment. Then he'd sworn the prince's breathlessness to utter secrecy and told him. "You will be King. It has been prophesied. And Yann has seen it."

"But my father? My older brothers—?"

"We cannot read so much yet, Your Highness. All we can say is, this Cycle is not your time. Through whom is the anointed blood to pass to the next generation if not through you, for example?"

The thought of little four-year-old Marie could hardly have been avoided at that moment, but Charles must have suppressed it. He neither laughed nor showed distaste, only sobriety at what he was being told.

"But must the death be Master Gwencalon?" Charles' eyes

glistened, but he did not let the tears fall. Gwencalon's harp had been his best comfort since infancy.

"You know what Yann has told you, Your Highness. Your *belle-mère* will send the good Bard away tomorrow in any case. It is his will, his final desire to take on this honor. He is a free Sacrifice, as the laws of the Craft demand. The only hindrance is, to make the Sacrifice more worthy, we have need of your anointed Blood this night. You will do this, won't you, for the sake of your beloved tutor?"

After that, Charles had agreed, and taken oath.

But I could see now, in the little form that walked so mutely at my side through the deserted chapel, this oath and the night had cost him more than a pulse or two of royal Blood.

He knew now. He knew something of his future. The Craft teaches that a man must embrace his fate. Charles had embraced it just as he had embraced the golden cauldron. But Craft also teaches that it is never good to know too much of what will be. The cauldron would be returned to the prince's safekeeping when its holy job was done. But the placid innocence of his childhood would never return.

I had to stop in my tracks for a moment under the weight of awe. Real time had returned to us like the sticky smell of fresh varnish. Still I could see that with some twinge of Sight, Charles the son of Charles the son of Charles had recognized his own future in Gwencalon's death struggles.

And accepted that they might one day be his own.

My heart swelled in the presence of such bravery, such faith. And what it must mean for the fate of the Land.

The Loom of Initiation

The following spring saw King Charles VI in better health than he'd been for years. I knew it was thanks to the Blood shed—by another—that All Hallows' Eve.

When sick, the King had been a puppet jiggling in the young duke of Burgundy's hands. Well, now King Charles took up the sacred Oriflamme banner, turned on the puppet-player, and chased him eastward from Paris across the land. Prince Charles' older brother, the Dauphin Louis, duke of Guyenne, took his place at his father's side as commander of three thousand men-at-arms and fifteen hundred bowmen. Arthur of Brittany, count of Richemont, marshaled the troops.

By Lammastide, however, the King's madness was back. Sacrifice by another had only so much effect. The seventeen-year-old Dauphin was unable to hold on to the advantage his father's health had given him. He had to sue for peace with both Burgundy and the English, and by the next All Saints' the puppet-player had control of all the strings again.

The next summer was my fifteenth. I decided this was an age when I should be initiated in the ancient mysteries. I chose the hands of the aging Hermit of St. Gilles at which to accept them, and the highest arc of the sun as the best season. I had known this would be the way of my life for many years and I could put off taking full responsibility no longer.

Shortly after Easter, the Hermit came for me and, at the last moment, Gilles had his way and was allowed to come, too. I was of two minds about this. I was jealous of the sacred that was mine. At the same time, I knew the sacred was for sharing and I couldn't help but be glad of more youthful, carefree company: Gilles, who feared nothing.

I see now that the entire trip was a ride on the cusp between childhood and the adult state. It was meant to be, and Gilles' presence was a good thing, to underline my transition from his state to that of an initiate in the Craft.

For over two months, we three traveled together throughout the Land from Dol-de-Bretagne (near the famous Mont-Saint-Michel where we bought small trumpets to call the Gods, as pilgrims have always done) to Finistère to Morbihan. This was the *Tro Breizh*, the visit to the seven Saints, the ancient circuit of greeting and acquaintance to all the ancient, sacred land of Armorica or, as present tongues would have it, Brittany.

Brittany, the treasure chest of sacred secrets on the sunset side of France.

Day by day it became clear to me why such a long journey is part of the initiation. Christian pilgrimage shares the straightness of that superimposed faith, whether the goal be no farther than Tours or as far as Rome or even Jerusalem. We worked our way in the holy, ancient spiral instead and, at first, with my mind burdened by "goal" and "end," I was impatient with the way we went. Like Gilles, I would often pester our guide by asking, "Are we there yet?" "How long 'til we get there?" until I began to realize there was, in fact, no "there" to get to.

"Placing a goal in life is to finalize it with death." This was as close as the Hermit ever came to an explanation. "Every day we travel, stop, sleep, then rise to travel again. Each day is like a life and the Master knows that today is but one day in an endless cycle of lives."

I came to feel the truth of it for myself over the weeks.

Of course I learned countless other things as well. I learned the land as I'd never hoped to learn an insentient thing. I learned, in fact, that she is not insentient at all.

I speak of Brittany, of course, and not of France.

Brittany lunges out into the Atlantic horns first, like a spry young heifer. Mountains running down her east-west spine hackle with black forest. She seems less a part of the plodding herd of France than she does of the firmament into which she leaps. That is, of course, what makes her holy, like all in-between things: the moments of birth, initiation, and death. Crypts where the living meet the dead in a place of air and earth. The congress of men and women.

There is always a streak of terror in such places. We felt it often enough on our journey. For example, once a run across a heathery meadow brought us suddenly to the edge of a cliff, one step from thin air and a death plunge to the pounding sea below. We stood panting on the edge, wheeling our arms like wings for balance, our hearts sailing out of our bodies and into the void without us.

Or, another time, our plying shoulders sent a little skiff skimming over a smooth bay, only to draw up short as we scraped against a hidden sandbar. Or the tide suddenly sank below us, leaving nothing between us and the vicious rocks.

Such encounters are the meeting of the earthly and the divine. The panting, the rush of breath that follow the sublime fear of God.

Amid the giddy, leafed knots of the Forest of Brocéliande we discovered the Fountain of Barenton, boiling with bubbles though it never gets hot. Nearby is the tomb of the great Merlin, overlooked by an ancient holly. We slept there in the company of the cats that guard the place and left offerings of flag iris and tender *muguet* between the stones leaning with age.

To say we had no goal is not to say our journey had no path. Veins of power ran through the countryside in that spring's full and vibrant beauty. These were ancient veins, as old as the Earth Herself. The ancient ones had felt them, too, probably more keenly than we did, and had set up great stones to mark the way. Cromlech, menhir, dolman. As we went along, I began to be able to tell when we were coming upon one of the markers. The feelings intensified, became a sap-throbbing, bee-buzzing sensation that often made me think I was about to suffer a spell. I would sit down, hold my reeling head, gasp for breath.

Life and time returned from the place between, however. The constraints of goal and end resumed. We had to be in the forest of the Mené at the shrine of St. Gilles in order to accomplish the final, most serious, most dangerous phases of the initiation.

And we had to accomplish this before Midsummer and the return of our parents.

———•———

Part of our quest over the face of the land was to gather certain magical herbs in the times and places that their powers were at their peak. Roots, dried leaves, fruits had made the trek with us in a swelling sack and now, under the Hermit's watchful eye, we spread them out on the level stretch of stone beside the woodland spring of St. Gilles du Mené.

"Now, Gilles," said the Hermit, "you should take yourself off. What follows is only for initiates."

"But I'm going to be initiated with Yann, too," my milk brother insisted.

"A boy is usually older than your eleven."

"But I came all this way with you. I'm ready. The arms master back at home says I can already fight like a man."

The Hermit considered, and I knew his thoughts. He had never had a coven with which to work, as Masters had always had in olden days. In times of weak faith like these, perhaps the initiation rules might be bent with justification. However, "I'm not certain the drugs in a smaller body won't . . ." he worried aloud.

"Please, Master. It's my heart's desire." A note of childish urgency underlined the grown-up words.

In the end, the Master acquiesced, saying he would "Trust to the spirit of the plant."

I think my own attitude had something to do with his acquiescence. I was glad to have a companion to this serious trial. All our months together, my stomach had turned sick with apprehension every time I thought of the unknown I must face. It helped that I would not have to face it alone, and also, now that I was the elder, I knew I couldn't shy in Gilles presence or I would be shamed. Gilles, as usual, was afraid of nothing.

I must not speak too closely of these rites. One ought not to do so; they are sacred and, in times like these, too much that is sacred has been opened to the scrutiny and scorn of the faithless and ignorant, stripped of all mystery. But one or two things I must hint at, if only to give comprehension to what must follow.

First, we molted "like bird chicks." Our childhood clothes were burned. Eventually, days from now, we would be given new men's clothes. But not yet.

We washed in the sacred spring. Then, still birth-naked, we made the ointments. One ointment consisted in large part of woad and wood ash, which we set aside. The second was boar grease with the most careful infusion of belladonna.

"Belladonna, incautiously used, can kill," the Master said.

He looked at Gilles, crouching forward eagerly on his young, naked knees. The Master looked at the pinch of grey dried leaves and berries in Gilles' fingers held eagerly over the wooden bowl of grease.

"Consider the power of the herb," the Master said. "Feel it. Weigh it carefully against the weight of yourself."

Gilles looked at the powder in his fingers. He put a little bit back on the stone. The Master nodded and Gilles tossed it into his pot.

Poplar leaves went in as well, water parsnip and sweet flag. The mixture smelled quite raw.

When all was prepared, we slathered the belladonna on to our naked skin. We sat sipping the waters of the well for a while and then—from far away, it seemed, although I hadn't noticed any change in perception until that moment—the Hermit began to talk to us. How much was talk, how much dream? I found it impossible to tell. And how much really happened on the wild flight of drug?

Slowly at first, the Hermit began to talk us through the dissolution of our old, childhood bodies. It started with the press of a stone knife on my chest. Then, the first cut, the sharp sting of air on open flesh. The blade slipped quickly, surely between skin and muscle. I stretched out beneath the awe-full press of sky, flayed.

Blood-smell blossomed in the back of each nostril. It filled my mouth. Every thew and sinew, then every organ was laid bare. Flies buzzed to the feast. Bone was hacked from bone, marrow pressed until its white beaded with blood. Then all was placed in the Great Mother's cauldron to cook.

At the height of our dissolution, the cuts were made and, when the blood flowed freely, the woad and wood ash paste was rubbed in. My indelible proof of devotion to the Mother is in the usual place, on my left shoulder, where I cannot see without twisting.

Throughout all this fearsome, painful process, I was much too concerned with my own sensations to consider what hands did this to me. And I certainly had no place in the splinters of my self to consider Gilles. But as the cauldron began to simmer and stir, agitating a new sense of life and rebirth, a glance with eyes yet flayed revealed the worst of nightmares. Blood was dripping down my milk brother's chin, covering the linen-white of his boy's smooth chest with stark gore.

With a swirl of my head around the cauldron and back, I saw it was no vision but reality. On some wild pulse of illusion, Gilles had taken the knife into his own hand and scored his chin—not in illusion but in the flesh. His chin wore three long, bloody cuts quite to the bone. His own hand smeared in the woad paste as well.

"Gilles—" The Hermit's own voice broke into the hum of his chanting. Then it stopped. The old man realized he was already too late.

"Why should I hide what I am? I am the Mother's slave," shouted Gilles over the hoarse, slurred speech the ointment gave him. "Didn't my ancestor King Comor wear the blue marks proudly on his chin for all to see? Do not you, Master, under your grey beard? Why should I hide it under my shirt? Why should I not be another Bluebeard?"

What could our Master do at that point but agree with him and bind the markings with clean leaves just as he did with mine?

After that, we received the personal prophecies for our manhood. Mine held little surprise since I had always been able to See for myself better than the Hermit could. There were words of "helping to save the Land" and "Merlin to Charles the son of Charles the son of Charles."

With a twinge of jealousy, I noticed that the words addressed to Gilles seemed to have more poetry: "You are prepared from this day forth for the supreme moment when in zest, fearlessness, and pride you shall meet death for the Mother of us all."

If only I'd had the courage to cut my face perhaps my prophecy might have been equal. But dismembered and simmering, I knew more clearly than in real life that this was the innate difference between me and Gilles de Rais.

After that, the Hermit led us blindfolded to the heart of the stone table.

"In former days," the Master had once explained, "before treasure hunters came and dug away the mound of earth that once covered these stones, before, when there was but a narrow opening through the sod to that cell, then the image must have been more complete. The initiates spent these days in the dark so very like a womb. But they were also then among the bones of the ancient dead. Then, how the Mother works her magic, taking the dead to Her Womb in order to build new life, could not be missed at all."

Excavated as the stones were now, here we must wait three days without food or water until the hacked and massacred flesh of our childhoods should be regenerated into the flesh of men.

"What sort of taking holy orders is this? The children secreted away, out of sight. Where is the bishop who has charge of this? There is none? I thought not."

The all-too-familiar voice raised shrilly over every other sound of the gathering Midsummer crowds. The babble of happy voices, the shouts of children, the whinny of horses, the bray of donkeys, and the chink of harness and trappings suddenly parted like drapery from before our shadowy cavern.

"Oh, God," Gilles said, craning as best he could out around the most forward megalith.

A gleam of sweat etched the lines of his birth-naked limbs. Some of it came from the still, close air of the day under the stones, some from the latest application of unguent. But mostly now, the excess moisture came from the sheer nerves that man's high-pitched voice would always give us. We never knew where to jump to avoid his demons under the best circumstances and now, drug-slowed and naked, the reflex of jumping had been effectively removed from the possibilities.

"Ought not the children's proud families be allowed to see the ceremony, as is usual in any initiation, even to minor orders?" said the voice.

"It *is* Père de Boszac," groaned Gilles.

But the Hermit, by some magic, kept him from us—for the moment.

Fifth Antiphon

The Merry Weft of Midsummer

Marie slipped out of the saddle and into her brother Amaury's strong, waiting arms. She smiled him her thanks as he went to join her husband in seeing that the squires handled the mounts properly. Then she smiled more quietly at the sunlight-sifted forest, dense on either side.

How strange this place was, she thought. By all rights, she should face it with dread and humility, like purgatory. She came here every year as penance, after all, in remembrance of that day so long ago—exactly twelve years it was now—that had begun so dreadfully, with the child's screams on the forest floor beneath her horse's hooves.

And then had come the Hermit's dreadful prophecy concerning the child she'd only just begun to suspect she was carrying. At the time, a shy, new bride, she had wondered how anything could be right again after that.

That child he had made her think she might never raise was now her strong, beautiful Gilles. God forgive her for thinking it, but she couldn't help herself. René was a dishclout to Gilles' red cut velvet.

Now she realized that she loved the sacred forest. Everything right with her life stemmed from St. Gilles du Mené.

This year, she would ask—more forcefully—for one last thing to add perfection to all the rest. She would ask for a daughter.

Oh, truly, she was ungrateful. Hadn't the shrine given her enough already?

Every year, as early as Easter, her heart began to throw off winter's gloom with the thought that, yes, Midsummer was coming. Then, every year after her return, she seemed to glide effortlessly along through all the disappointments of July, August, even into September by clutching the memory of the pilgrimage close to her.

"Your mood follows the light of the year."

As if she read Marie's thoughts, Guillemette La Drapière caught up with her and matched step for step along the forest track, soft with moldering litter. Even the nobility were required to walk this last half league or so to the holy site. Guillemette must have noticed the lightness this duty set in Marie's steps.

"You are sensitive to light, my lady, that is all, and happy during the seasons when sun is most with you."

"But what gave me this sensitivity, eh, Guillemette? I am sure I did not have it any summer before I met you."

"You were just a new bride then," Guillemette said.

"Only just learning that within doors is the stifle of my lord husband, yes."

"Tush," Guillemette half scolded, half hushed. Sire de Rais was on the same path, certainly not too far behind them.

Marie slipped her arm companionably into the maidservant's. The maidservant who was, in fact, her dearest friend.

"It's all a part, it's all a part," she said.

And it was. Here, before St. Gilles, no distinctions observed out in the world had any virtue. She trod the same path with the common Midsummer throngs.

And what the crass world saw fit to bind as man and wife was blissfully loosened here.

When she'd first met Guillemette all those twelve years ago, her face an agony of grief for her little son, Marie never would have guessed they'd find any common ground. She never would have believed the woman could ever forgive her. Or that she could ever forgive herself. Certainly never her husband. Or forgive Guillemette for having a son who wandered.

But now, here, she did. She forgave it all.

"I am pleased my husband decided to come after all," she told Guillemette.

Guillemette looked at her, astounded. "You are?"

"And that my brother Amaury, when he learned that Gilles was here, decided to join us, too. Everyone. Everyone can be here, where they cannot help but love each other. Even old Père de Boszac. What do you suppose inspired him to come?"

"He had his doubts about the old Hermit having charge of Messire Gilles for so long."

"Surely not."

"Then it is my son that concerns him," Guillemette said, "odd as that sounds."

"Why should that be odd? Boszac is Jean's tutor as well as Gilles' and René's."

"It is odd," Guillemette explained with a touch of impatience, "because he never liked my Yann. To my face, Père de Boszac said, 'A priest? Who would have thought it of such a demon-possessed child?' "

"The idea has since grown on him."

"Yes. Now that my Yann is taking this first step toward a religious life, he wants to take all the credit for himself."

"I suppose he might."

"I am more surprised by your Jean," she said to Guillemette.

"How so?"

"In his attitude to Père de Boszac. What I mean to say is, I thought Jean disliked the priest so much that he had no wish but to be the exact opposite all his life."

"My Yann would never be evil."

"No. No matter how many times that tutor says, 'The priesthood. That is just what such a hell-bound creature as that Jean needs for his eternal salvation.' "

Guillemette had to chuckle, even if she feared the priest himself might be within earshot behind them on the path. And she added the rest of the quote, in a perfect mimicry of the man's stilted air. " 'A healthy and continuous infusion of the holy.' "

"Your Jean is always a good, pious influence on my Gilles. No doubt being Père de Boszac's opposite doesn't necessarily mean evil at all."

Marie gave Guillemette's arm a squeeze. Yes, female companions were best, no matter what their station. Guillemette was all that comforted her for the fact that she had no daughter. And Guillemette's girls were like daughters to her. Still, she could not shake the grief that her René was already eight years old. Her husband had come to her bed no more than twice in all those years.

"A man goes to his wife to make an heir," he always told her. "We have two. More is lustfulness."

He had his two boys. But she herself longed for a little girl.

And there was another thing. She felt it connected, though how she couldn't quite tell. Being here within the magic chant of forest birdsong reminded her. When first she'd come to St. Gilles du Mené, Marie had been afraid of the demand her aunt Jeanne had placed on her, to carry on the family's fairy blood. Now it was her own dearest wish. And having a daughter seemed the best means to that end.

Surely these were things above and beyond the usual blessings of the place that made her heart so light. She would soon rejoin her favorite son—riding on the verge of manhood now.

And she might have hope for a daughter.

A daughter she would name Tiphaine.

———•———

Night fell, that year's shortest. The sacrificial beasts burned in their wicker cage, as was the custom. Marie found she did not have to run away into the woods to escape their death screams this year as she had on other years. She hardly even had to cover her ears and simply stepped upwind to be free of the dreadful, acrid smoke. Somehow, this year, she understood it all a little better.

She understood it well enough to look for Père de Boszac when the flames had gone up. Surely he must protest that he saw demons there. If he did, he found the demonstration a suitable warning of the fires of hell. Either that, or a heavy spell weighted him. She found the idea of a spell easy enough to believe when she looked through the shower of sparks and saw the Hermit of the place looking at her. He nodded a grave welcome. Later, as the bonfire blazed, he stepped closer to her and put that greeting into words.

"The new curbing your husband gave our fountain continues to serve us well," he said.

"Yes, I noticed. When I first came, while it was still light. It looks very nice."

"Your son is doing well, too, madame. Your son named for the Saint."

"I long to see my Gilles," she said.

"Soon," was all the answer he gave her.

She knelt and kissed the old man's hand—and found it surprisingly sweet to her lips.

The last cow passed through the dying embers, the last man jumped with his sweetheart. Marie's husband was unwilling to jump with her, but sat to one side with Père de Boszac, not exactly condemning, but not participating, either. Amaury refused the advances of several attractive girls and jumped alone.

"Go on," Guillemette nudged her.

"What is the matter with the Craon house?" Marie asked. "Is it the fairy blood that makes both of us have to jump alone?"

Guillemette found the idea amusing. "Go on," she insisted. "For a daughter." And she passed Marie the skin of cider yet again—for courage.

The drink burned going down her throat. But after it, Marie reset the wreath of flowers carefully on her head, heaved up her silk skirts, and jumped alone, too. She felt it, the coals warming her privates, her womb radiating its own power back into the earth.

The fire died, the folk anxiously gathered up the embers to bless their own hearths throughout the year, ashes to vitalize their fields. With the fire gone, Marie could see every star, the Milky Way spun across the heavens like the finest tow. The weather was so fair this year that Sire de Rais had had the servants erect no tent. Contented, perhaps a little drunk on peasant's cider, she laid down on the gentle sward at Guillemette's side.

And she would have slept like a baby. By rights, she ought to have. But very shortly, through half a dream, she felt Guillemette rise and stealthfully move away, leaving that half of her body cool and exposed. Through the dream, she remembered that Guillemette was always gone at the pilgrimage when she woke, late, the next morning. She went away—somewhere—without telling.

Suddenly, Marie was wide awake. "Guillemette—?" she whispered.

She felt the other woman beside her in an instant. Guillemette begged her for silence, but with no more than an earnest press of the hand.

Marie shifted her hand in her grasp. It needed no words. That was enough to send the message, "Where are you going? May I not go, too?"

Marie felt rather than saw her friend's consideration in the dark. Then another, double squeeze told her, "Yes. Come."

Hand in hand, they left the sleeping company. No moon lit the way, only stars, but Guillemette would have known the way blindfolded. Indeed, the path seemed illuminated by a sort of glowing pull of energy that Marie felt she could have followed, too, even without her friend to guide her.

They went through a close tangle of woods for a ways, then down a slope, up another, down again until they were out of sight and sound of the sleepers they'd left behind them. Here, suddenly, the great table of ancient stones blackened out half the sky's stars.

"Gilles." Marie couldn't stifle her whisper. "My Gilles is here."

She didn't know how she knew it, but she did. And even so, she had no idea where the sharp presence of her son might be, if not enclosed by enchantment within the very stones themselves.

"My Yann, too," Guillemette hissed back. She squeezed Marie's hand, but that was all.

Around the other side of the dolman, where the clearing opened up, Marie and her friend found, not their boys, but—in stark contrast to what she'd felt—a group of women gathered. She didn't take long to wonder at this, because her mind soon came to understand that wicker cage, fire, dancing, none of the ceremony before this point was more key to the turning of Midsummer than this secret convocation. More than that, it had a cozy charm she could not escape.

One of the women had a flute, another a drum, a third a harp. Marie listened to the instrumentalists play a few tentative notes, then phrases, trying, tuning. Then a high voice joined them.

It was a bawdy song at first: the singer declared she had worn out twenty lovers in a night. "And where am I to find the twenty-first?"

Marie found herself joining the others on the chorus. "Though I know nothing of lovers," she reminded herself. "Almost nothing—of love."

There followed other songs, all disparaging menfolk and praising women. They described men as strong as oxen—and about as sensitive, numb to the simplest emotion—but infinitely complaining of physical pain. It occurred to Marie that her Gilles might be close enough to hear all this. She wondered if she should censor herself, even if she could not censor the others. Could it be good for a boy to hear his sex disparaged so? His sex, that would soon have to take manhood's command?

But it was as if a little chink had been made in the dike stemming her emotions. She felt herself flooded, unable to stand, to do anything but swim with the tide that was not so much a spell put on her helpless self by others but herself come to itself. This was something in her blood, surely. In her woman's blood. Or in her fairy blood, perhaps. There was more truth here this night than she'd heard from a pulpit—well, since she could remember. Truth she'd never dared to share with another soul before.

Then the rhythm of the drum shifted, the flute took a rest, and the harp plunked out a simple, slow, deliberate melody. Another woman began to sing alone. Marie could tell this one made up the words as she went along, a personal plaint against the specific men in her own life.

When that tale had finished, another woman followed the example set by the first. Then another. This one did not have much of a voice. She did not even have much wit, but the tune was such that one after the other could hardly help but stumble into clever rhyme. And if she failed, there were half a dozen voices ready to offer her their suggestions for conclusion.

Those tongue-tied in daily life found themselves freed on this night and in these surroundings, their faces obscured, among strangers whose acquaintance seemed magically to be of eternity. Marie would have wanted to say that the night was under an enchantment. Except that it felt nothing so much as if the evil spell of everyday life that kept woman from woman were finally, joyfully broken. That everyday spell which kept a woman trapped within a magic sphere of glass created by her husband's station, by the hocus-pocus of his demands.

The camaraderie gave each woman's words the power, the mystique of prophecy. The old, worn complaints against father and brother, local noble or lusty neighbor that Marie had heard since childhood in any women's quarters took on a luster brighter than noonday.

There was such a rightness to this, such a feeling of cycle. Then Marie understood something more. Her Gilles had first come to her, from her, an infant in the exclusive company of women in Champtocé's Black Tower. Now he would come to her, a man, in the same exclusive company of women.

But first Guillemette by her side had to sing. Guillemette complained of the business that kept her husband away from home so much, at the beck and call of inconstant nobles and—Marie had never known she suspected—other women.

"When he returns, we are strangers," Guillemette sang in a solid voice. Though still as unmusical as ever, it didn't matter. "As if we spoke different tongues."

The women were passing a skin of drink among them—not the burning cider, this time, but a smooth, sweet wine. They pressed it into her hands. Marie took another squirt, let it coat her palate. Then she realized all attention had turned to her. This night was not like the rest of life, when a noblewoman could enjoy the labor of others and call it her own. She had to share the burden, equal with equals. What they had given her, she must return—with interest, perhaps, to make up for the rest of the year when things worked by the sorcerer's way of take with no return.

"I cannot—" she began, realizing only after the fact that she had begun on cue with the drummer, but had dropped her part.

"You can," said others.

They, too, could hardly help but speak in rhythm. They pressed more wine on her. She rubbed it over her lips and then down her throat with her tongue. Then the burn up her nose seemed to enter her brain and she thought of something. She waited on the round of drum again, then began:

> *"A noble's wife has not a happy lot.*
> *A noble's wife has not a happy lot.*
> *A noble's lovely wife*
> *Trades estates for a life*
> *And must own to have honor when she has it not."*

The circle laughed with pleasure and congratulated her. But they were not satisfied. They wanted more. She lifted the wineskin, a baby's wriggling weight, from her lap and took a swig. She let one round of the drumming pass her, waited on the next, then sang:

> *"When no more than a child, I was married-o*
> *When no more than a child, I was married-o*
> *When no more than a child*
> *To a man who's never smiled*
> *And the desert no less than his soul is arid-o."*

More. She saw how the repetition helped one to compose and she gained confidence.

> *"Once we said 'I do,' there was nothing more to say.*
> *Once I find his shoes, he has nothing more to say.*
> *He is silent as the tomb*
> *And—"*

She dropped the rhythm.

"Doom," one woman suggested.

"Gloom," said another.

Everyone laughed with pleasure at the anticipation, at the game.

"And he will not fill my womb." There, she got it out, and, scurrying, managed to keep up.

"And I'm sure that my suff'ring must all sins outweigh.

"He should be on crusade, this lord and master-o,
He should be on crusade, this lord and master-o
He should be on crusade
Where he cannot me upbraid,
Making of our bed such rank disaster-o."

The rhyme of "master" with "disaster" delighted the company. They shrieked with laughter and clapped their hands. The drummer pounded her response and the flutist trilled. Many repeated the couplet, storing it away to work into their own next piece. Marie had stopped worrying that Gilles might hear them. It crossed her mind that her husband and Père de Boszac might, as far away as they were. But she, as the company, was too delighted to care. She went on.

"I've a mother and a father he will not let me see,
I've a mother and a father he will not let me see.
I've a mother and a father,
I'm their only daughter,
And his Christ'anity eats up all his charity.

"A woman wants a daughter like a father wants a son-o,
A woman wants a daughter like a father wants a son-o.
A woman wants a girl,
But this man is such a churl
He's stopped coming to my bed so I can't get one-o.

"If a woman tempts a man, she's like Eve-y-o
If a woman's not a nun, she's like Eve-y-o
If you ask me now 'quid nunc?'
Well, I'm living like a monk,
And a noble's wife can never hope to leave-y-o."

The women around her were on their feet now, dancing with the thrill of her words, the release of their day-to-day restraints. She joined them, for she knew that the words were not all their own, but had come from the magic of the drum, the company, the night.

> *"This lord and master-o*
> *Is such disaster-o."*

Shrieking, laughing, singing, hugging, the women celebrated a triumph. Marie could barely see more than shadows in the night, but she could tell the women around her had begun to shed their clothes. They shed their clothes to aid in the wild abandon of the dance, to turn themselves into—into something quite different than the mundane women as which they'd come. Nymphs was the word that came to Marie's mind.

Goddesses.

Marie was hardly conscious that she herself was down to her shift. She'd come with no headdress, she knew, and now the precious silk of her overdress was gone. But she didn't care. She felt the otherness, the divinity that she hardly dared take into herself. And yet, there it was already, without the asking. Filling her from the belly outward. The belly, warmed by the sacred fire, now spread to every limb, until she was all the heavy, beating center of her creativity.

And then, it seemed to Marie that the moon had risen. Yet she knew it had not, for it had set while the fire still blazed. And the direction she felt it rise was behind her, the direction of the great stones, a direction—unless she was so helplessly turned around—that she had set in her mind as north.

Slowly, she let the dance turn her 'round until she faced the spot where she felt the power of moonrise. Her heart stopped in her throat. It was not moon, bright and shining, but the exact opposite. Something black, that sucked all light to itself. It rested just on the brink of the topmost stone, watching, waiting. And from its empty roundness rose—like from the moon in her phases—a pair of great curved horns.

Sixth Antiphon

A Weft of Goat Hair

———•———

"Marie." She thought she heard the shadow call her name.

Other women had noticed, too. "Ah, the Horned One!" they cried. "The God. Hail! Welcome, Master."

"Welcome be, my children." The voice came with deep echoes, as if from a hollow tube.

The figure stood as he spoke and Marie saw his form more clearly. Never in her life had she been so certain that she saw a devil, never in the shadows on an uneasy night, never, even, in the lifeless representations churchmen offered her as moral lessons of the Day of Judgment.

This might even be the king of demons, this form like a man, yet shaggy about the shoulders like a beast. The head was that of a beast, a tail swished around his legs. And at the end of those legs, on the surface of the stone, she heard the skittering of sharp little hooves.

He was a devil, no doubt. But Marie found herself totally unafraid. She felt herself relieved somehow. Joyful, she might almost say. Joy, certainly, she caught from those around her. She was vaguely conscious that there were not only women in the clearing any longer. White-robed men had joined them as if arisen like mist from the ground. The only light now seemed to come from their garments.

Up on the stone, the fiend turned this way and that to greet his flock. As he did, he threw a sort of cape back around his shoulders and the huge shaft of his member stood out, black as pitch, against the spangled stars. Again Marie caught her breath, and when it came again, it was in quick little gasps. The thing rose higher on his belly than his navel must be. She was certain she would have difficulty encompassing it with one hand. And she could see the quiver of its life, its aching rigidity, as its point pulsed from star to star against the sky.

Marie sank to her knees. She couldn't help herself. She would rather have run, but she could not. She might have appealed to those around her for aid, but they, too, were sunk to earth, worshiping the idol before them.

Then, "Marie." She imagined she heard her own name in the pound of blood in her ears. The hollow echo of the beast's unearthly voice. In all her awe, her sheer terror, it seemed the devil returned the worship—and called, with a God's longing, to her. "Marie."

From far away, it seemed, Guillemette spoke to her. "Ah, he's chosen you. Madame, this is honor indeed. Madame—Marie, it's you he calls. Your prayers will be answered."

She couldn't find the strength to run from there. But somehow, her feet moved by themselves toward the deep blackness of the stones. The dark lord upon them reached down a hand toward her. She found, by stepping on a low boulder, she could just touch, fingertip to fingertip. His hand felt slick, old, as it caught hers in a grasp she couldn't hope to escape.

Marie was barely aware that the men and women behind her had begun to come together in twos and writhing threes. She had attention now only for what passed between her and the God—and of that her perception was so keen it hurt. She supposed her feet found hold upon the rock, but truly it seemed that at the touch of the Horned One's hand, she took wings and flew up to join him on the perch of rock.

The moment she was there, he began to sniff at her all over, as a dog does to his prey. And yet, at the same time, it was a greeting, as one dog does to another, even an old friend. She found the idea simply glorious, that somehow her scent could be attractive—yes, beloved, even, without its everyday addition of violet essence and pomander. Greeting? The gestures partook more of the essence of worship.

Indeed, "Goddess. My Goddess," spoke the hollow voice, more than just a few times.

Now the creature lowered the horns of his head and, with his lips, began to nuzzle at her breasts like a horse seeking chunks of sweet carrot. She felt her nipples grow hard, tip up like standing stones, under the linen of her shift. He nuzzled, then began to lick and gnaw. Hard little animal teeth scored from the base of each areola outward, just hard enough to make her want more. She felt the seams at her neck give way and the magic night stared unashamed down at her naked flesh.

As the garment dropped to the stone with a whisper, Marie found she had to follow it. The shaggy arms caught her and eased her down with the utmost tenderness. The Horned One then produced a wooden bowl of some sort of unguent.

It burned a little as he slathered it on her, all over, with quick, caressing pressure. "With this unguent, I worship you," were his words as he did so. "With my body, I worship yours."

She smelled hartshorn and gall, and they seemed sweet, contrary to all nature.

By the time he slipped his hand between her legs to mix his unguent with that she herself was producing, she had found liturgy of her own. "Please . . . please . . ." she prayed, and the Horned One, like any true God, understood her need and answered it just at the moment when she thought she must die if she didn't get it.

The object of her worship no longer stood teasing outside, but entered her, ravished her, as mystics declared happened to them with the very spirit of God. Marie found two little niches in the rock to brace herself against the assault, and then felt, as St. Hildegard had said, "I am a feather on the Breath of God."

The ecstasy she had never known transported her, tossed her as a great man tosses a child in the air, until she feels herself flying. Then he caught her again and tossed her again. And again and again. This way, that. She knelt on all fours like a goat and he mounted her like the buck, teasing her with his horns, while the man in him milked at the pendulums of her breasts until she bleated aloud. He folded her together like an upright fleur-de-lis and settled into her like a bee.

Then he laid her on her back and tossed her that way, that way again, and like a little girl, she squealed with delight and the half fear, half wonder of flying, free of all attachment to the earth.

And yet the whole earth was there. Marie felt it, rocks and wind, grain fields and rushing streams, pounding at the gates of her being. She opened for them, opened again, and could always open more.

She smelled feverfew. She tasted it. There must be great quantities growing about the rocks, being crushed by the other couples, although she hadn't been aware of its distinctive earthiness before.

"Feverfew is an aid to conception," Guillemette was fond of telling her. And she had diligently eaten it. But nothing she could concoct herself, she knew, could help if her husband would not sleep with her.

What was happening now had nothing to do with conception, unless it was the world she was conceiving. This creature with her was no man, in any case. Never had the lord of Rais come anywhere near giving her such divine, such demonic pleasure. No, she would not think of Guy de Rais. Why should she, when this man she was with was no man, but a God? And the conception—immaculate.

At length, even the God seemed to be faltering. His heavy breathing was matching hers. The back of her calves were cramping. And yet, she wanted still more. One more. She, a Goddess, must have her desire. Fearlessly, she approached him, pushed him down across the stone before her. Her frenzy seemed to skin the Horned One alive. She tore aside the shaggy, goat-hair cap he wore, the helmet of horns. She tore aside the extravagant member, recognizing it as the leather stuffed with straw that it was, even slick with her own fluids.

Just as she found the hard living flesh below, she recognized the face beneath the shaggy hair that wouldn't be torn free. Her God was a God indeed, she thought as the hot seed burst across her steaming field.

She fell across the grizzled beard while her soul soared one last time.

God indeed Whose spirit could so transform the wizened old Hermit of St. Gilles.

Why? she wondered from the high point of her arc. Why can I never do anything of this vein without the intrusion of Guy de Rais' voice?

Her husband's voice. And that of Père de Boszac—rude and screaming. Blasphemy.

25

The Curse Is Tightly Braided

That was another thing I learned at initiation, for the rhythm of the time was not the short, quick burst of manhood, but the long, continuous crescendo of feminine ecstacy. In fact, the juices do not stop flowing for her when a woman conceives. They have only just begun, to peak again when the child is born, followed by all the little tugs at breast and womb as the child suckles and grows.

Our coming forth as men was simply another peak in the lifelong orgasm of women.

It is for the women just as it is for Mother Earth, who bursts and blooms so obviously with the spring, but is no less exuberant for summer's growth and fall's rich harvest. Even winter's rest is luxuriating for her.

And that is why She deserves our honor.

And why we worship women in Her stead, Her presence in every female form.

Midsummer's night swirled around the stone womb where Gilles and I lay closely nurtured. In the dark, the women arched their backs and spread their legs, misty as new-plowed ground before sunrise on the day of sowing. Their combined groans were those of rocks pressing together deep in the heart of the earth. I'd always wondered, when I'd heard them, if they were the groans of pain or of desire. In women, too, the opposite curves of this spiral are so very close together.

The visions Gilles and I had could be nothing to what the women enjoyed. They can take the magic herb directly into themselves and yet not die. That night I certainly believed, as with all I have heard, that the women flew and saw the world with Goddess'-eye view.

With envy, yet no hope of similar attainment, I dipped into my own bowl of ointment and reapplied. It hardly had time to make my skin glow before I felt its renewed effect. With all that passed before my eyes and all that panting, groaning in the night around me, my manhood had swollen until it ached with the force of blood pounding through it.

I knew to my very core that I was a man now, that no power on earth could keep me from being so. Or keep me from bursting out of the womb where I'd been cowering like a child. Keep me from taking a man's place in the worship.

They had reserved her for me.

I remembered hearing her sing to the wild drum of a father who intended her to marry before Michelmas and against her will. I'd seen her other Midsummer pilgrimages and been too shy to speak to her. I knew only too well how wrinkles furrowed young girls' brows when they saw my hand.

I tried now to think of a name for her and Pieronne came to mind, but I wasn't sure. It didn't matter. She was Goddess.

And I was a God, bursting full grown from the Mother's womb.

It was a little difficult to tell in the transport of divine passion. But I think it was her initiation, too. I might have asked in the gasping afterward. Or at least made sure of her name. Or considered more closely how I was to keep her holy once I had lost my grasp on the divine in the awkwardness of first times. 'Til cock crow was the usual goal.

But I never got the chance.

Those who say the holy rites are the haunts of demons should have been there that night. Surely, all hell broke loose.

It began with the long, thin wail of a child. Gilles.

Gilles must have had a very different experience of the honor the Horned One had shown his mother that night, inviting her to make with him the center of the holy rites up on the roof of the stones. Michel had taught him the proper understanding, even as our tutor had taught me. And the Hermit, too, over two full, long months of wandering.

But Père de Boszac had his claim, too. A much stronger hold on this lord's son than any of us had suspected.

I'm certain Gilles' youth is to blame as well. The Hermit had had his doubts about making this attempt, had he not? Who is to say what effect the drug may have on those who apply it too raw? Like barley corn taken from the fire while still hard enough to crack a tooth.

In any case, something forced him untimely out of the Earth's matrix. And it was hardly manhood.

Judging by the few coherent words that studded the otherwise bestial tissue of his cries, Gilles was hallucinating. I heard, *"Maman, maman,"* the wail of the smallest of children, not of a man. And then, "The beast! The beast!"

Gilles stood birth-naked and slick with sweat in the starlight. His wail was the sound no mother can ignore. Unless she is at that moment a Goddess. With all of the world to attend to.

But his father heard. And Père de Boszac. And his uncle Amaury. They came running, torches high. They took one glance at what was happening in the clearing around the stones. And on top of the stones.

The noblemen drew their swords. And, like Lancelot of old, rescued Guinevere.

I scrambled to my feet, taking my partner by the hand. Quickly, I led her to the cover of the closest trees. I went back and helped a few more women, finding scraps of clothing for them to share among themselves. Then I helped some men, fleeing, wounded, but with the wounds of honor, full on their naked fronts. All were weeping— either that or cursing.

Some had begun to vomit as divinity brought too quickly to earth wrenched at their insides in an effort to get out. Too deep a breath and the smell gagged in my own throat. I, also, had to kneel at the edge of the forest and empty an already-empty stomach.

That cleared my head. One of the rescued women, I saw with relief, was my mother.

"You're all right, Mama?"

Hers was one of the tongues given to curses, and in this manner she soon convinced me I could leave her in charge of all I'd managed to salvage. I left her and walked with a man's determination back to where a man should be when a battle was raging. But the screams and curses, the sounds of metal on stone—and on stone after the sickening silence of its brief journey through flesh—were over. The enemy was gone, dragging off their booty.

Only the echoes were left in my head.

Shadows mounded the clearing unevenly. Some of them moaned and stirred, but I could tell these sounds were from the opposite side of the circle of life than the moans and stirrings that had filled the same space earlier.

I picked my way carefully to the stones and reached for them; they of anything seemed safe, secure, eternal.

I brought my hand away in haste. The sticky wetness that caught only silver from the first grey of dawn was still too dark to be water. For one heart-stopping moment, the sensation convinced me the stones themselves had been struck a mortal blow. Then sounds from the upper rock made me realize a different source for this sign of mortality.

I scrambled up the rock face and found but a single body. Madame was gone. Whether one of the dead in the field was her, I didn't know. That thought made my heart lurch, but this body was all I could deal with at the moment. This was the body of the Hermit.

How bad his wounds were, I couldn't tell. The blood spilling down the rock might have belonged to his consort, spread there on her descent. The wounds were bad enough, at any rate, for the hairs of his vestments to be sticking to him in his own blood. And one of the horns of his crown had been hammered through the flesh of his leg when he took a fall. I removed both as carefully as I could and stanched the new flow of blood with the fine linen of Madame's shift. Then I helped him off the shrine.

A wind had come up suddenly, blowing across the clearing like the departing souls of the dead. It tossed the full-leaved trees at the clearing's edge as if it would tear itself enough brush to build a lean-to. The air seemed lighter, but it might have just been the energy of the stacking clouds. A storm was gathering over what had been a perfect Midsummer's Eve. Nature would not let such impiety go unpunished. And perhaps the Hermit had had something to do with raising this sign of righteous ire.

I helped the old man, suddenly frail as a child, under the shelter of the rocks. As I did, I stepped on something that at first made my stomach turn. Then I realized it was just an empty, flaccid wineskin. I took it and went the hidden, forested way to the well for water.

That was my first water in three days, and I felt somewhat more hopeful after I'd taken my share. This was the woodland spring of St. Gilles, after all. Never mind the lord of Rais' stonework around its rim. The stonecutters themselves had been simple, pious men. The water maintained its name for healing. But could even St. Gilles heal such wounds as the Master had sustained?

In spite of the improvement the water brought to my physical state, something still seemed not quite right as I ran back to my Master with the skin sloshing full against my naked hips. Crossing the field of the dead and the dying, I realized what the matter was. Every shadowed hump had an aura, a soddened, purplish light.

Just outside the Earth Womb, I stopped and carefully set the waterskin down against the upstanding stone. I hadn't found stopper or tie and I didn't want it to spill. Then I began to sit down so I wouldn't get harmed myself in a fall. I don't remember actually getting to the ground before blackness came and the spell was full on me.

I awoke flat on my back to the first merciless pounding of hailstones, the flash and explosion of thunder, very close. I could heave myself no farther than my hands and knees, and those threatened to give under me with every movement. But somehow I managed to drag myself and the waterskin under the stones to cover.

"With the living once more, are you, my Yann?"

The Hermit's voice was weak, rasping with pain, but good-humored. Nonetheless I jumped when I heard his words rising out of dead blackness.

"Master." My own voice sounded hoarser than his. I helped him to drink. "Master, you're alive."

Not far outside the dolman, I found a discarded initiate's robe that I scurried to fetch and began to tear. I meant to wash his wounds as the bursts of lightning revealed them to me, starting with that vicious gash across the face still leaking blood enough to glisten.

"Nay, keep that rag to cover yourself, my friend." He'd never called me "friend." Always before it had been only "child."

"I will worry about that later, Master. First, I will see you comfortable."

His voice seemed dangerously weak now, as if he meant to warn me he was dying. "You must go and find your friends."

"No one who has done such deeds can be a friend of mine."

"No, Yann.".

"I will never see them again, but stay here with you."

"The time will come—and soon, too, I've no doubt—when you will come to fill my place here. But it is not yet. Not quite yet."

"You are my only friend, Master."

His voice found a sudden force I no longer dared to contradict as he firmly pushed the cloth away from his wound and said, "Gilles needs you more in this instant than I do."

"Gilles?" I rocked back on my heels, confused.

"You must go to him, Yann."

"Is Gilles hurt, too?"

"He is confused, disoriented. Hurt in his soul rather than his body."

"How can I help him?"

"You must. There is no one else. Besides, if you're too long away after what has happened on a night like this, the Sire de Rais may have difficulty accepting you back into his home. His eyes have been opened somewhat this night, and his heart closed."

I looked out through the gap in the stones to what the world offered outside the safety of the Mother. I had to close my eyes against the sights the watery grey revealed. "I wish Sire de Rais to hell."

"That much is clear. But quietly, Yann. You must return to Blaison. For Gilles' sake."

"What on earth can I do for Gilles?"

"I'm not quite certain. But I do know, without your steadying hand, he . . ."

The Hermit swallowed thickly and I gave him more water. He continued, "I fear these events may unhinge him. The drug was too strong. He was too young. He was not ready to be ripped from the Mother's belly half formed. More time, and he might have done better. Wherever the greatest blame lies, he needs you. You may be his only friend as this dreadful night comes to an end and there is a great work yet in this world for him to do. I have seen its shadow. And so, my Yann, have you."

At last, the Hermit convinced me. Loath as I was to obey, he was my Master, and he gave me no choice. The Sight gave me no choice, either.

I wound part of the torn, damp initiate's robe around my loins, draped the rest sadly over my shoulders. Then I looked up to the roof over our heads, as if for succor. The hail was deafening there, grinding like a shower of gravel.

"Farewell, Yann. Blessed be. Goddess go with you."

"Farewell—" I meant to tease out a string of nice phrases as he had done, but I'd gone no further than this when fabric failed me.

"Yes, this is best," the Hermit said, lying back, his long white beard and streaks of his own blood the only coverings on his naked chest. "What you prophesied in your fit—Gilles will need you."

I had gotten to my feet, stooping beneath the low stone. Now I crouched back down at the old man's side. "I prophesied this time?"

"Indeed you did, howling over the wind and thunder across the field of these dead like the very spirit of this storm itself."

"What did I say?"

"You do not remember?"

"No."

"It must have been a deep and truth-finding trance indeed."

"What did I say?"

"Gilles will need you. You foresaw the extinction of his house in the next generation."

"Oh, God." I buried my face in my hands, as if that could keep me from seeing what I'd already seen.

"And more."

"More?"

"You cursed the hands that did these deeds this night. None of those responsible, you said, would live to see Samonias—the Day of All Souls in the fall."

Three Blue Streaks

Gilles swept the helmet off his head and tossed it to the armorer as he strode from the practice yard. The expressionless face of steel-plated death vanished, but now revealed equally expressionless features set into flesh. The crease the headgear left across his sweat-grimed forehead was more declamatory than eyes or mouth. He rubbed at it with his kerchief, hoping to erase even that sign of mortality.

But the three blue streaks on his chin he could not rub away, try as he might. And they were more eloquent than a tree full of starlings.

He'd been like this since Midsummer's Eve: blue-bearded, but distant and quiet as well. Prodding him was like striking the barrel of a cannon: it revealed a hollowness within. A hollowness which I sensed was packed with black powder and very sharp-edged rocks.

Gilles was trying desperately to fill that void with something, I could tell. He filled it with action; he filled it in the practice yard and in the lists. He was there in the morning: the dull thud of his sword against the post woke me. He went from trainer to trainer all through the day. When he wore one man out, he moved on to the next.

"My son does very well," Sire de Rais said with broad pride to those trainers escaped to the sidelines.

"Yes, milord," the trainers agreed.

But their glances out into the sawdust where yet another colleague was growing winded were not without unease. They could tell in meeting him, thrust to parry, just how the gun was loaded—to a hair's balance—even if the father could not.

And now Gilles was quitting at last, having listed this past half hour to torchlight. The horse—his third of the day—had grown winded and dangerously frothed before its rider had. Now Gilles tossed the reins impatiently to his groom. I think he would have beaten exhaustion from the beast if previous experience hadn't taught him that it was impossible to gain any other effect than the opposite of what he wished for by such action.

This was the man brought forth by that Midsummer's Eve. Any woman will tell you birth is a time fraught with danger. No matter how many children they've had, a woman always counts fingers and toes. Abortions, stillbirths, these happen all too frequently, at any time to anyone.

And the birth of monsters. These are serious omens.

Black smoke smears from the torches filled the still-hot air of the summer's night with yet more heat, and the stifle of pitch over-laid the smell of hot horses and dung. Gilles noticed none of it. He didn't notice me. I had to step directly in front of him to stop his progress. Even so, I think his muscles would have feinted instinctively around me in some sort of swordsman's parry had I not caught his sleeve with my good hand and held him there.

Only then did he acknowledge me by saying my name. It came out more like a grunt.

"Come with me, Gilles," I urged quietly.

His eyes darted around the surrounding darkness like those of a hunted creature. But he saw no one else to fight, so where else was there to go?

"The full moon is about to rise. Come with me. Come raise it with me."

My tones prickled my back a little. They were too close to those of a wheedling lover.

Gilles didn't notice. He looked blankly eastward. At least he remembered other directions besides "toward the target."

"Has it been so long since Midsummer?" he asked. "The moon was waxing then . . . I remember . . ."

He remembered other things, so much was clear. Too clear. But this was the second full moon since then. That he had forgotten. Forgotten in a heap of listing posts turned to kindling and splintered lances. His mind had been shut off from the ways of the Mother ever since.

"Come," I coaxed.

He shrugged, and after one final look around the lists that offered him nothing else to conquer, only weary men and hunger-cranky boys scurrying to clean up yet another day's destruction, he sighed and agreed indifferently. He turned greater care on the unbuckling of his armor. He was wearing the complement of a grown man these days, forcing his young limbs to grow to the weight: "And someday I shall be a knight—like Uncle Amaury."

Gilles sluiced his face in water from the armorer's barrel, let it run into his hair. He scrubbed his fingers viciously to the scalp, careless that he splattered me with water. The drops I felt carried blood heat and seemed unhealthily stagnant.

After that, he came with me over the drawbridge, down the slope, to the forest, and into the clearing where we'd come so often with Michel, sometimes even with the Hermit. The memories tugged at me. I doubted I'd ever see either man again. The Hermit, indeed, was probably dead, and I made the sign of the Horned One for him in the dark.

I'd brought everything myself, knowing Gilles would have no mind for such details. I stripped and drew the circle around us. Gilles followed, like some great gun dragged across the countryside to fulfill other wills than its own. For iron and black powder have no will.

I kindled fire, divided it among the cardinal points, chanting, gesturing to each in the forms that are as ancient as the toss of tree limbs in the wind and the babble of brooks in their beds.

The clearing looked eastward to a low hill, meadowed so the silver light that announced the approaching moon lay spread before us like taut skin. I circled, drawing Gilles with me, and the moon rose, big-bellied like a woman nearing her time. The rich beauty of the sight made my breath come faster, though I tried to keep the chant as it should go, steady and slow. My mouth dried and my eyes stung with moisture in the corners.

In the otherworldly shimmer of light, everything seemed to

thrum to the pulse of Her silent power. Beside me, Gilles gave a great sigh ending in a sob. I knew he was healing in the great arc of Her silvery arms and that I must not break the spell. It would take time, but this night was a beginning.

Waiting was no hardship. I opened myself to thoughts that might come only when one sought not to think at all.

It must have been nearing midnight. Keeping our faces to the moon now required craning, and so sometimes I rested, leaning forward and simply feeling the silver bath on my naked shoulders and spine. I rested and sent my well-being on moonbeams in the direction of the young man beside me, like butterflies, like chirring night insects.

And then, I saw her.

At first, it seemed that she was the Goddess Herself given form there among the trees on the warm, still evening. The tenor of my thoughts, so sensitive to Her presence, found nothing strange in the apparition. And it did seem, at first, that a shaft of light shot between trees and liquefied the ground on which she walked. I instantly warmed with love for her, urged by hot memories of the last time I'd met a Goddess, in the grass by the stones of St. Gilles at Midsummer.

And then I saw that the garment she wore was the white serge of the nearby Carthusian convent of St. Anthelm, flowing with wide sleeves and the white veil of the young postulant. The convent was not far, close enough for Père de Boszac to serve as their spiritual adviser.

St. Anthelm's was a stringent order, not allowing even widows to offer themselves to God, but only virgins. For one of their sisters to be up at this time of night was perhaps not unusual. They were known for their nights when midnight mass crowded sleep to a mere three hours. But what such a woman might be doing out of her walls at any time of day, let alone in the woods at this hour—when we were drawing down the moon—seemed stark madness.

The nun carried something in her arms, something small and wrapped in white serge like herself. It wiggled, like kittens in a sack. She did not carry it like kittens, however, rather with much more tenderness.

And surely no Goddess ever walked with such heavy, earth-bound feet before.

Gilles and I watched her make her solemn way past us, unseeing, through the trees until she came and stood before the moat of Blaison Castle. There she knelt and began a series of long and agonized prayers, as if, like some sort of strange siege machine, she'd come to subdue our fortress. I wondered what our guards would think to see her. But I doubted they would: nun though she was, my first sense of her had been of Goddess, and I knew whatever business enlivened her mind, it had been set there by a divine hand that would reveal itself only when ready.

At length, with a cry like the weird White Ladies of Norman legend, she put the bundle from her, laying it on the scummy waters of the moat.

Without ceremony, Gilles burst the bounds of our circle. He snatched up some article of clothing and struggled into it as he ran toward the scene. Over his shoulder he called, "Run for help, Yann! Get help."

I was not slow to obey. I had seen what he had seen, a tiny pink limb wriggling its way out of the bundle. Baby toes. And one hearty wail as it hit the water.

The nun had vanished like moonbeams behind a cloud long before my feet pounded hollowly over the drawbridge, long before I heard Gilles floundering in the moat.

I had the guard about me in a moment and sent them off. My cries wakened others, too. I thought nothing of it at the time, but Père de Boszac was one of those to whom I sputtered my hardly coherent tale: "Sister of St. Anthelm," and "baby in the moat."

But I did notice how the priest's face grew pale, his eyes drooped with horror. "I told them—" he croaked. "I told them under no circumstances to—"

Every other face I addressed registered similar reactions and I would have thought no more of it—but that I was glad to see the priest level with the rest of mortals. He could not scowl at every mishap as the failing of lesser, demon-benighted creatures.

When I got back out to the moat, guardsmen had waded in up to the points of their hose and were poling the thick, slimy mud with their spear butts. In all, they recovered the remains of three new-borns. Two of the mites had been in the water so long that they were little more than a handful of soft bones, worms slipping from empty eye sockets and scraps of mud-grey serge. Nonetheless, they still had clearly once been tiny morsels of humanity.

"The sisters," I heard muttered among the soldiers—and they stole furtive glances back at the castle, at the castle chapel and its chaplin as if the precise truth could be told through layers of stone. "The sisters may not talk much, but they will lay the fruit of their sins at the door of the demon who led them to temptation. As if they would take Blaison by storm. And what defense have we poor men-at-arms against assaults like these, eh?"

When I came out to him, Gilles was still holding the newest bundle in his arms trying to revive it when all others had given it up. He raised his eyes, but not to the men standing clumsily around him. Gilles had eyes only for me, great, dark eyes, fathomlessly filled with pain.

"Be at peace, my young lord," I urged him. "The child is with God."

"With God?" He laughed scornfully, almost wildly. "You really think the demon priest would have baptized his own bastard?"

I, too, stole a glance in the direction of the chapel. Such a baptism did seem very unlikely. I looked back, leaned forward, and saw a sweet, fair curl twisted with green moss lying across the crook in my milk brother's arm. I had to look away. But Gilles remained un-flinching.

"There was nothing you could have done, Gilles."

I wanted to hold him as he was holding the child. It would have done more good for the world. But I couldn't push myself to the deed, and for my failure, I saw the moon-healing that had distilled upon him earlier vaporizing like dew before the rising sun. In a sim-ilar manner, Gilles must have watched the life expire from the infant.

"Here, Messire, give that to me. I'll take care of it."

When Gilles at first paid him no heed, the guard presently bent over and worked the little figure out of the young lord's arms. The moment he lost contact with that death, Gilles broke and ran.

"Let him go," the man told me. "Poor lad, he's had a shock. A good cry will help it out."

I took the man at his word, although the face I'd seen on my milk brother seemed to have not a single tear behind it.

When, somewhat later, I followed the guards back inside, our heavy, sleepward steps were drawn aside by sounds coming from the chapel. Though we had studiously tried to ignore that part of the keep, it pressed on our minds. Now it was discharging crack after crack so like the sounds of the jousting yard that we had to go and see.

"Gilles." My first thought had such force it burst from me aloud.

And when I pushed open the heavy studded door with the guard at my heels the name came again. "Ah, Gilles."

At this hour, Père de Boszac's domain was lit only by the blood-red that announced the presence of his sacrificed God. In that eerie light it seemed as if Gilles were indeed running at a straw man again. But the soldier's quick actions soon helped me to see the new horror come in the midst of the other, still fresh.

Not long after I'd run into the keep with my tale of nuns and babies, Père de Boszac had retreated to this place. He'd tied one end of a rope around his own neck and tossed the other over a ceiling beam. Between heaven and earth, he'd hung himself. Coming to this place for solace, Gilles had found that sight instead. Then my milk brother had taken a willow wand, perhaps still warm from his own backside, and set to applying it to the dangling figure with years of retribution.

The figure tossed and twisted before the blows like the straw man in the lists until the men forcibly yanked Gilles from his task and pinned his arms behind him. Though when they cut him down they found the body still warm rather than cool like straw, they could no more revive the priest than they could his tiny son.

I stood, clinging to a red-running pillar for support. What a narrow faith was this. Priests of the Old Faith welcomed the birth of their children—or rather the God's children, as they were called, blessed with great powers. Père de Boszac had lived a life hedged all 'round by demons. by women and their demons, I remembered, and the clinks of the chains of hell in nun's rosaries. Now I saw that nothing created the demon of hypocrisy faster than the sharp rejection of so many things as unreleaved evil.

But I also saw that, unlike the baby's case, I might have stopped this dissipation—if I'd dared. I begged the Moon's forgiveness that I had not.

"You know, Yann, don't you?"

Gilles stopped a moment before me on the arm of the guard who was trying to help him away from the sight and off to bed. Only the outer planes of the soft, boyish curves of his face caught the bloodred glow. He seemed unnaturally old, quite a death's-head himself. A death's-head with three dark blue-black streaks running down its chin.

He spoke in a mixture of reproach, horror, and awe. "You know what all this is."

I shook my head helplessly. "The Hand of the Goddess. I saw it move here tonight."

He shook his head firmly, splattering ill-smelling moat water. "You cursed them all, Yann. At Midsummer's. You cursed them."

"In Her Name and by Her power."

"Before Samonias they will all be dead. And we are already almost to Lammastide."

27

English Wool on the Shuttles

"The Sire de Craon is not welcome at Blaison, nor anywhere beneath the cross of Rais."

Gilles' father stood beneath that cross—black on gold—on the battlements of that castle. Archers flanked him, their bowstrings pulled back to their ears, their shafts trained on the small cluster of men-at-arms below.

"No!" Gilles jostled his way past the taut weapons with total disregard for his own safety, his eyes riveted on the helmetless tumble of blond curls so far below. "It's Amaury! It's Amaury, not Grand-father."

I caught my milk brother's arm and stopped him. I could not have stopped him had he truly wanted to spring at the nearest bow-man. He was that much stronger than me now. I had to resort to magic. I quickly made the signs of a calming spell, but those did take time, especially since I had to do with only one hand what any other Master could do with two. And it seemed I had to use them on my milk brother so frequently these days, since the death of the infant and Père de Boszac, that he was growing inured to my powers. I was doing my best to strengthen the spell to meet this challenge, but I was far from perfecting it.

So Gilles must have come to the realization himself that to jar archers in this pose would send the arrows flying wildly. And they were aimed all too closely on that sun-spun patch of blond.

My milk brother stood rigid, breathing heavily from our run to this place and unable to catch more even breath for the tension he felt. His knuckles started white from his hands where they grasped the edge of the wall and his eyes never moved from Amaury's face.

The man below was such a splendid specimen of young knight-hood, it seemed impossible that any fortress could hold out against him for long. Sire de Rais was a dark shadow to the brother-in-law he was challenging. I could share Gilles' attention—some of it, any-way.

"Sir, I understand the animosity you hold against my father." Amaury de Craon's voice rose sharp and clear through the September air as if he expended no effort to shout. The great horse beneath him stood proudly still on his shaggy feet while the others around tripped here and there in undisciplined contrast. "But did you and I not fight side by side against the demons this Midsummer's Eve? Doesn't that count for something?"

My heart twinged at the word. Amaury's evocation gave Sire de Rais excuse to signal his bowmen back to ease. It must be true. I had been unclear in my memory as to Amaury's actions that night and hoped against hope that he had not raised an impious hand. Now his admission and Sire de Rais' reaction could leave me in no doubt. My curse could not be withdrawn for anyone. And Samonias was now hardly one month away.

Still, Amaury's death was not destined for that moment, much as he had tempted it by appearing helmetless beneath his brother-in-law's walls. Rais' archers slipped their arrows back into their belts and a deep groaning began within the bastion's bowels: portcullis raised and drawbridge lowered.

"Welcome to Blaison Castle then, Amaury de Craon," Sire de Rais said.

Gilles pushed past the bowmen once again to race below so as to be the one to offer the welcoming cup to his beloved uncle.

"My lord the duke of Brittany is mustering all his liegemen to march against the English," Amaury explained at more comfortable range when Sire de Rais had welcomed him to his apartment. "He hopes to place twelve thousand under King Charles. God willing, my men and I mean to make up part of that number. We march to meet Duke Jean at Rouen within the week."

"I must confess, you do surprise me, sir," Sire de Rais said.

Gilles took the refurbished tray of wine from my hand at the door and moved silently to offer his father and his guests more. This brought him close enough to Amaury so they could touch, even surreptitiously as goblet went from hand to hand; I knew this was Gilles' purpose. And had Amaury's purpose been merely to flush the road from his throat, I doubt he would have waited quite so long before replying to Sire de Rais' suggestion.

"What surprises you, sir? I hope you do not suggest it is out of my character to answer my lord's call to arms."

"No!" Gilles burst with indignation and I had to move quickly to restabilize the tray in his hands. I flashed the beginnings of yet another calming spell in his direction but I think, in Amaury's presence, he managed to calm himself.

"Not at all," Sire de Rais assured his guest, waving him to a seat and taking one himself across a chart-littered table.

"Or do you think the occasion not desperate enough? The English usurper's son, Henry of Lancaster, had the audacity to land on French soil at the Vigil of the Assumption of the Blessed Virgin, little more than a month ago."

"That's well enough known."

"Within that month, he has engaged the vital port of Harfleur."

"Harfleur has fallen?"

"She either has or soon will do so."

Sire de Rais settled back in his chair, comfortable. "You have received no clear words?"

"No. Only that Monseigneur de Gaucourt, commander of the town, was suing for truce until St. Bruno's Day, hoping for relief. I doubt very much hot-tempered Henry will give him much time."

"He cannot afford to, I suppose."

"Indeed. The marshes around Harfleur are taking their toll on the English. Half his landing force is now down with dysentery."

"So perhaps we may leave God to protect France in His own way. With the putrid airs of a marshland."

Such a God sounded much more like divinity I should worship than Sire de Rais had any right to after Midsummer's Eve. I was certain his hope would have no effect. I knew it from the feeling of this room of his, a shrine of sorts. But a shrine so lacking in the sense of presence that I usually associated with that word "divine" as to be the antithesis. It was so muffled from nature as to not admit any natural light. Even now, at midday, candelabra had to be burning as if in the depths of night. I knew I could trust nothing of what Sire de Rais thought of either the strengths or the purposes of a God of marshlands.

"The defenders are hardly without sickness themselves," Amaury enforced my feelings. "And I fear they may have to wait 'til doomsday for relief. King Charles and the young Dauphin dare not move from Paris, for they fear the moment they do, Burgundy will move to retake the capital in their absence."

"Hasn't Burgundy sworn to fight the English?"

"He has," Amaury agreed. "But his allegiance can only be called mixed. If he earns England's disfavor, what are his Flemish weavers to put on their shuttles in place of English wool? Everyone knows Burgundy is not to be trusted. Why, he's openly confessed to the murder of the old duke of Orléans."

"Sin not yet avenged or given penance for."

I had to turn from the conversation, for I still could not hear talk of that night Messire René was born without flashes of horrible vision. By the time I returned my attention to the room, Amaury had shoved himself to his feet by the armrests of his chair and begun to pace. His spurs chinked on the stone floor with every step, as if trying to claw their way through to something that might give inspiration on such a situation. But he was a Christian and couldn't hope to see clearly in a battle between other Christians. Not that my Sight wasn't somewhat hindered by the thick walls of this room as well.

"It is clear what Henry means to do once Harfleur falls," Amaury continued. "Indeed, he may already be about it. He means to march across Normandy—those lands he claims from William the Conqueror of ancient days—who is, in fact, no direct ancestor of his. He will strike through Picardy then and make for Calais, that toehold England has long held and where he has more and fresher garrisons."

"Brother-in-law, I doubt none of this," Sire de Rais assured him. "Nor do I doubt that with Burgundy and the Armagnacs shattering the allegiance of Frenchmen in a thousand pieces, Henry may very well succeed. What I do doubt—and find it very hard to credit that you do not do likewise—is Brittany's part in all of this. Most important of all, I doubt Brittany's faith."

"Why should my lord Duke Jean not answer France's need?"

"Because Duke Jean is liegeman to the King of England as well, that's why."

Amaury stopped his pacing at the tone of exasperation in Sire de Rais' voice. I read in his face that he knew what his brother-in-law said was true. Amaury hated to be caught in any dishonesty, even when the man being fooled was himself.

"Duke Jean's lands in Richemont in England are not to be sniffed at." Sire de Rais studied his wine to hide an ungracious triumph in his eye. "And everyone knows English ships are always welcome in Breton ports. More so than are French ships, I daresay. At least, there are many more of them. I wouldn't be at all surprised to learn that Breton ships took part in ferrying the English over to Harfleur in the first place. Burgundy's Flemish and Dutch ships certainly did."

"You question my honesty and good faith, sir?" Amaury's spurs ground with a noise that set the teeth on edge. That was the only expression of just how much self-control it took for him not to seem to move at all.

"Never, Monsieur Amaury, never," Sire de Rais said with an open smile. "I only fear that in your youth you lack caution. You may sign on to causes when more sober men—wiser men—hesitate. We here"—and he took a sip of wine to give himself a philosopher's air—"wait and test the wind."

"Sir, it is such 'sobriety' as you would call it that keeps the French army frozen in Paris while Henry does as he pleases with our Channel coast. Harfleur sits at the very mouth of the Seine. Paris is now effectively cut off from any ocean trade—"

"And you will ride for Brittany who has, perhaps, more to gain if all trade is diverted down the Loire and through his port of Nantes? Past your father's stronghold at Ingrandes," he added meaningfully. "How much will you wager, Amaury de Craon, that Duke Jean, through this excuse and that, never manages to meet up with whatever forces eventually find themselves face-to-face with Henry of Lancaster?"

Amaury recrossed the room and flung himself back in his chair, defeated. I could feel Gilles' whole being yearning toward his young, impassioned uncle on this route. Desperately, my spirit fought through the stone surrounding us, stone defaced and tamed beyond recognition, to something without, in the Gods' world, that I could offer him as strength.

"You are right, sir," Amaury said in a monotone.

"I may be right, but it gives me no pleasure," Sire de Rais assured his brother-in-law.

"My father didn't want me to come. I fooled myself into thinking it was because he is old and timid."

"Timidity is hardly a vice with which I credit Jean de Craon. I wish it were."

"I see now too plainly he is against my coming because of his own interests at Ingrandes. A pox on him!" Amaury pounded the arm of his chair. He'd taken off his gauntlets, but clutched them still in his hand and a metal plate spiking the boiled leather plowed up a groove of new raw wood.

In spite of the force in his hand, I knew the young man's curse had not the force behind it to worm a finger's breadth into the mortar around us. I had made a curse of my own, under the great stones at St. Gilles, and knew when there was power and when there was not.

"So you came without the old man's permission." Sire de Rais spoke gently to this young knight he'd almost not let under his roof. More soothing than I think I'd ever heard him before.

"I did. And only so many men as would follow me over him, as you see."

"As I see," Sire de Rais agreed.

"And of course he wanted me married first."

"Of course. And with an heir."

"Yes. And with an heir."

"So what do you intend to do?"

The fire sprang to life in Amaury again, as if he'd damned both father and heir with a single word in his mind and so attained a sudden freedom. Even his curls seemed to gain new brilliance.

"I intend to meet at Rouen with any Bretons there may be. Arthur de Richemont, Duke Jean's brother, I know will not fail to present himself. And neither shall Amaury de Craon, with any man who'll follow him."

"Amaury!" Gilles croaked hoarsely.

The adults ignored him. Sire de Rais got to his feet and came around the table. He took his brother-in-law firmly by the hand.

"Were I but five years younger," he said. "Were—things"—what things he hesitated to say—"more peaceable here, Amaury de Craon, I would join you in a moment."

"Father!"

Gilles gave another croak. But this one was heard and answered by Amaury who turned in his chair and fixed eyes bright with joy on his young nephew.

Then he turned back to his host. "You don't know how pleased I am to hear you say that, sir. It makes the real purpose of my call much easier to ask. May I, sir, beg your son in your place. The page I have had ere now is the son of a man who follows my father and so I have lost him. Could Gilles, I beg, come with me in his place— and yours—to serve as my page?"

Sire de Rais paused only to clap his left hand on Amaury's shoulder before answering, "Yes, I suppose it is time my son began to take his place in the world. I cannot pretend he is a child I can protect much any longer. Since the—unfortunate—death of his tutor last month, I have been torn between searching for another tutor or just such an arrangement as you propose for his future education. And now I see that Heaven has made the decision for me."

Gilles could no longer contain himself. He sprang from my side and into his uncle's arms.

"What, what?" Sire de Rais laughed, but with sternness and no mirth. "Is this blubbering and hugging how a young man old enough to page ought to react? Do you need a mother, not a knight, to follow?"

"No, sir," Gilles said, springing to attention at once and dashing angrily at a stray tear.

"That's my lad."

Amaury laughed and, tossing both his gauntlets aside, roughly tousled Gilles' hair. Then he let his fingers slide down to examine the blue streaks on the boy's chin, healed over now and no less faint than they'd ever be. Amaury raised one eyebrow and that corner of his mouth, bemused at the scrapes children must get themselves into that may ruin the beauty and innocence we love in them forever. And yet the love never faded from his eyes.

Their interchange was too intimate to watch for long. I looked away, trying to think, like everyone else did, that the road to knighthood was a sort of initiation. It might stand for the botched one of Midsummer. But still there was my curse. None could escape it. It hung now over the lord's chamber like smoke from a chimney that will not draw, thick and choking, and my mind could find no outlet to refresh itself. Amaury was slated for death; must not his page follow him there?

"But that reminds me." Amaury disciplined himself to break off his rejoicing with his young nephew. I don't think his feel for the curse was the cause, however. "I must ask you, sir, one more favor before we go."

"Certainly you will stay the night," Sire de Rais said by way of answer. "Longer, perhaps. I'm not certain we can have this boy ready to go overnight."

"But I could, Father—" Gilles began, then stifled himself lest his good luck fade.

Sire de Rais smiled. "As long as you remain my guest, Amaury de Craon, anything within my power to give is yours."

Amaury bowed his thanks. "Then I beg your permission to visit your wife during this time." He laughed a little, nervously. "A man without a wife hopes his sister will give him the token he may carry when he goes into battle."

Sire de Rais was suddenly sober, a raw nerve touched. "As I said, Amaury de Craon, anything within my power. I will send to your sister and see if she will receive you. I may even order her." His voice dragged to a halt.

"Is Marie not well, sir? God forbid."

"Let us rather say she is . . . she is difficult. Ever since Midsummer."

"I see." Amaury glanced off in the direction he imagined either his sister to be—or to have been, two and a half months ago, on Midsummer's Eve.

"She never even leaves her room. She never sees me or even the pest René," Gilles blurted out. I think he hoped to convince his uncle time with his sister would only be wasted.

"I see," Amaury repeated.

"But I will send to her," Sire de Rais promised.

"Yes. Certainly Marie will not refuse you, sir, her liege lord."

"I think rather she may not refuse her brother," Sire de Rais grumbled. She had, indeed, consistently refused him.

Amaury spoke brightly, hoping for diversion with another topic. "And in the meantime, Gilles, I think you will come with me. Show me my room. Help me out of this damnably hot breastplate and into something more pleasing for the ladies."

"Of course, Amaury." Gilles reached for his uncle's hand, but hard glances from both men instantly changed his demeanor. "Follow me, if it please, my lord," he said with a perfect page's bow.

And then it hit me. It had been trying to reach me in this place, but the sterile walls, the unnatural light, the presence of Sire de Rais and Amaury de Craon had made it difficult. But once the first inkling of the out-of-doors managed to reach me, it came in a flood all at once and I Saw.

I Saw a field new-plowed, not as it was now but as it would be perhaps a month hence, and glistening, smoking after a night-long rain. I Saw a wood pinching in the French pennants so they had no room to maneuver. I Saw the sky grow suddenly dark, as if rain clouds were returning. But there was the hum before the thunk of a thousand, thousand English arrows. My ears rang with the cries of the wounded, the dying. My nose filled with the smell of straw on mud and the dying about to become part of that smell. Blood pushed red-black before my eyes.

"No, my lord, he must not!" I gasped.

"What ails the lad?" I heard Amaury say as I slumped to the ground.

"He has a devil," were Sire de Rais' words, the first I heard when I came to again, though I suppose others just like them had been spoken while I saw nothing but blood on the battlefield.

"Young man, are you all right?" Amaury's face peered into mine with concern, but hard as I blinked, I couldn't help but see the death's-head behind his youth and handsomeness.

"You should not go," I gasped, clutching at someone's hand. It might have been Amaury's. "Gilles should not go."

"It is the devil that speaks in him," Sire de Rais said. "Pay him no mind."

"But what did you see, Jean?" That was Gilles' voice.

I could only find one word. "Agincourt." But I didn't know what it meant, except as a blanket for all the horrors I Saw.

28

Keeping Threads Untangled

They brought me to my room and, in time, time full of blackness and vision, Mother brought her blackcherry syrup there. She held her bottle straight upside down and didn't fill the tip of the little wooden spoon. She'd been neglecting her motherhood of me and failed to make more.

"But perhaps you've outgrown this," she said, setting the empty bottle aside carelessly. "Perhaps you don't need my syrup anymore. From now on, your spells are your own, to do with as you must."

The thought of being on my own with this black magic frightened me. I didn't like to grow up, when it meant leaving the safety of her skirts. But I squeezed her hand. I knew she was right.

It had been long since I'd seen her. Neither she nor Madame nor any more of the maids than were necessary to serve appeared at any meal. That had been the way of things at Blaison since Midsummer's Eve, since Madame had sworn she never wanted to see her lord again.

Since my lord had declared his lady "despicable," "a whore," and "beyond redemption." And beaten her so she'd worn the veils of a nun all the way home from the shrine of St. Gilles to hide the bruises.

The arrival of Amaury de Craon and his men as guests had not flushed out any more of the women.

"Are you better?" Mother asked me now.

"I think so." She helped me to prop up against the pillows.

"Can you walk?"

"I think so," I said again. "But I'd rather rest. You know how it is with me after a spell."

Then I caught the intensity of her gaze on me.

"Very well. I'll try. Where am I to walk to?"

"Madame's room."

"Madame? I see."

She helped me to my feet.

It was that season of the year when the nights are chill but fires have not yet been set in the grates. Insects creep into every nook and cranny for the warmth. A walk through kitchen or cellar means a walk through a haze of fruit flies. The flag flooring scurries with earwigs and centipedes.

Insects even found their way to Madame's chamber. My mother's usual vigilance against wool moths, spiders, bed bugs, and lice failed in this season, certainly against larger, less insidious prey. A great moth swung away, then back, ever back again, as if attached by the thread of its own death throes to a flame sputtering low in a pool of tallow. A wasp sleepy with cold snored dangerously near a pile of folded linen where it would very likely bring to grief the next maid to make the beds.

The chirrs, buzzes, and pings of this insect life overshadowed the sounds of humans in this place. Mother sent all the maids from the room, easy enough to do when they had the novelty of handsome male guests to keep them in the hall.

I realized the silence that so impressed had less to do with a lack of life than with its massing. Magic brewing. The homey magic of flies and moths. But magic all the same.

I looked sharply at my mother. Who else could be the author of this sort of enchantment save she? But what was her magic? Just the little, domestic spells that kept threads untangled on the loom, milk from souring in hot weather, apples crisp in their winter barrels. They were the spells for infant colic, to ease the eruption of milk teeth, for the dark, moon-owned mysteries of women's cycles. I hadn't considered them much before, any more than I thought about the salt in my soup.

But suddenly, there was too much of that sort of salt. Had I been at table, it would have sent me groping for the wine flagon and the water to dilute it. I could smell the thick concentration of women's magic suspended in that room like incense, gathering, waiting.

Waiting for me.

What can she want? What can it want from me, this dark women's magic? I had too much else to worry about. On the morrow, Gilles, who had so much else to accomplish in this life, would leave to page a man condemned to death both by the Vision I still felt at the edge of my Sight as well as by his own actions on Midsummer's Eve. My voice of warning was heard only as the voice of a devil when I sought to turn the tide. If Gilles did not live to accomplish what he must in order to bring about the advent of La Pucelle, perhaps she could not rise at all and the Land—and all her children—must perish with him.

My mother's bland, linen-framed face told me nothing.

"What is it?" I said with impatience.

"Madame." Her voice was hushed, as if the magic caught in the room were the greatest of all—death.

I looked where she gestured at last, among the hangings and drapes of the bed where Madame lay. I still couldn't see her face; it was swathed with a cool linen compress. I could see that the hair of her brow, always plucked so fashionably high, had been allowed to grow back to a dark stubble.

"What ails her?" I asked.

Mother hissed me to silence. I had tried to modulate my voice to her example and it still wasn't enough.

"Is she ill?"

My mother's eyes narrowed. I could tell she had brought me here hoping initiation had made a man of me. Now she had her doubts.

I lowered my head with the proper reverence due women's power from a true man. Mother decided that in such straits she could not be choosy.

"Not ill." She spoke Breton, very low. "With child."

"The Mother is with her." I gave the old congratulatory phrase.

My mother forced her breath into a considering hum. Certainly she didn't mean to blaspheme.

"You remember Midsummer?" she asked.

"Of course."

"Sire de Rais hasn't been with his lady since."

"I understood it was she who would not see him."

Mother's impatience rose. "Sire de Rais hadn't been with his lady—that way—for three years before at least. The child is the God's."

"The Mother is with her indeed."

I knew no greater blessing than a child conceived by the God on the holy night. Père de Boszac had died because he couldn't accept the force of such divinity. Grain grew a hand's breadth right before the eyes in any field such a child passed, so I'd heard. I'd never seen it myself. The last child I'd heard of so conceived had died an old woman before I was born. That's how rare and blessed an event such a conception was in times like ours.

Or perhaps that was an indication of how few honored such an event anymore.

Mother let out her breath in exasperation and then tried to regain patience. "But think, Yann. Just think what our lord is going to say when he finds out."

"He doesn't know?" With a sinking heart, I realized my words were just beginning to sketch the outline of what was amiss here.

"How should he know?" my mother snapped. "She retired to this room when first we returned from St. Gilles and would not admit him in her just fury for what he'd done. As soon as she discovered her condition, she tried to make overtures, thinking to make him believe himself the father. But you heard the song she sang that night around the standing stones: he fancies himself a saint of celibacy. Besides that he now considers her a vile piece of less-than humanity that is beneath himself to touch. Good only to be consigned to the flames of hell."

"He will kill me."

The choked sob rose from beneath the compresses. Madame could not have understood our Breton speech, but its content could not have been a mystery. I started at this first indication that Madame was indeed alive. But, I thought, as her words so clearly indicated, if we did not do something, she was unlikely to stay that way for long.

"As long as he doesn't know, things may yet be well," I said hopefully. "And you haven't told him."

"Of course not." My mother's tone was sharp with shards of failing patience. "Though how much longer she hopes to keep it a secret, I don't know."

"Perhaps—" I groped for adulthood. "Perhaps she should go away. Until the child is born."

"And that is what we planned to do." The exasperation in my mother's voice did not grant me adulthood yet, not by a long shot. "But where shall she go? To her mother is the obvious choice, but that my lord has forbidden. He has forbidden her any contact with her family at all."

"Except with Monseigneur Amaury," I said quickly. "Amaury is in great favor this evening."

Ideas were forming rapidly in my mind. Amaury could—could be prevailed upon to do—something—anything—instead of riding straight toward Agincourt.

"Ah, Amaury!" A cry from the bed dashed my thoughts to confusion once more.

"Yes." My mother's voice dripped with an unexplained sarcasm. "Yes, Monseigneur Amaury's in excellent favor."

"She could go on pilgrimage," I offered brightly. "For her sins."
Mother grunted.

"Although I don't suppose she should travel too far in her condition, so that is what she should *say*—that she is going on pilgrimage, but only with the most trusted companions. She should really stay with some friends until the child is born, then give the child into fosterage. You, Mother, might not be able to nurse this one. But you can't deny there'd be plenty of women—in Brittany, certainly—who would be delighted to undertake the task, even for no price— once they are told the child is a God's son, conceived at the Midsummer fire."

"Yes, yes, we were planning something like that," my mother said, without enough impatience to stop me from continuing further in the same vein.

"But what friend should it be? Angers with Madame the Queen Yolande, perhaps. Except that it is too close. My lord is bound to visit sometime within the next six, seven months. Even if Gilles is off being a page and not able to befriend young Prince Charles and Anjou's heir Louis, there are the two little Renés . . ."

I let my voice trail off, seeing my mother's pinched face.

"I will help you any way I can." I dwindled my words down to that. "Only tell me how."

"It's too late. It is eternally too late," came weakly from the depths of the bed. "Amaury knows."

"My lord Amaury knows," my mother repeated in case I hadn't picked the words out of the mumble. "Just now, he came to see her. He saw in his sister what I doubt the Sire de Rais would see for another two or three months. He guessed all. He was there at Midsummer, as you know."

Mother leaned forward hoping, I think, that her words to me would not carry to the bed. "It was his sword that splattered the God's warm blood all over my lady."

"He called me a whore," Madame cried. "His own sister. And I let him come to see me. I, who loved him as my only brother."

Mother elaborated on the grief that came in such chipped fragments from the heap of pillows and coverlets. "He said he would not carry the token of such a woman into battle were the Saints themselves to come down and tell him to do so. And then he stormed out."

"He can't have told my lord de Rais yet." I offered that hope.

"So much is clear," my mother agreed, "or I think we should have heard of it by now."

"It is only a matter of time," wailed the compresses in the bed.

My mind felt suddenly inspired. "So what must happen is the discovery of some sin in Amaury so great that his silence may be counted on. Something that will keep him from tossing the first stone, in Christian parlance. Then, madame, he may not only beg for your token. He may even be induced to be your escort wherever you choose to go—above and beyond his desire to fight the English."

"What sin will you discover?" Madame asked helplessly. "Amaury not only looks like an angel, with all those blond curls. He *is* an angel."

"No man is so holy, madame." But I confess I couldn't force much brightness into my tone. Surely a sister knew her brother.

"My parents never had a moment's trouble with him since the day he was born. I was the one who gave grief. When I refused at first to marry my lord de Rais." The wistfulness in her tone hinted that had she truly had virtue, she would have continued to refuse to the present day.

My mother said, "You have not been close to your brother since he became a man, madame. Men may have vices not evident in the boy."

"Amaury's an angel," Madame insisted.

"He has defied his father enough to set out for the campaign against the English," I mused.

"Enough to ingratiate himself to our pious lord of Rais, which may be virtue," Mother countered.

"Still," I insisted, "the law—not of the Christian world, I know, but of the world of the Gods—is a balance. Too much good must create a shadow."

Mother looked at me before she spoke again, and there was pride growing in those bark-brown eyes. I was proving not so slow and immature as she'd feared at first.

"They may be vices that are not really vices," my mother comforted her lady, "like your getting of this child, madame. Vices not in the eyes of the God, but only in the eyes of pious priests and lords who have other goals in mind. Goals much more shortsighted than the fruitful union of heaven and earth. You and I need not count them at all."

"Or—" I quickly spoke what had just come to my mind, spurred by my mother's words. "Or such vices—or the appearance of such vices—may be created. In any man. By a glamour. By one who has enough knowledge of the Craft."

"And you would do that, Yann, would you not?" Mother said. "For our lady's sake?"

"For the sake of the God's child, certainly I will try."

"Because if you will not, Madame has declared I must use my women's magic to rid her of this daughter she has wished for for so long."

Now I understood the amassing magic I felt in the little humming creatures in the room. "It is a daughter? Certainly? Your magic has told you so?"

"My Tiphaine," Madame said.

Mother nodded. "The God knows how to reward His faithful."

Feeling flooded me with this confirmation more than the promise of a son ever could. They were feelings of tenderness and protection I find difficult to explain. Except that I knew in this moment that should I ever march off to war—an impossibility, surely, but imaginings must have their own force—here was a young lady whose token I might sue for. My lord's daughter, Gilles' sister. And the daughter of the God. I blinked as that emotion stung the corners of my eyes.

"And if you do not help us, Yann"—my mother knew just when and how to strike—"this maid shall never be born."

"Very well," I said. "By your leave, madame, I shall go and consider what my poor power may do with this. I pray you, look cheerful. Such grief cannot be good for the daughter you carry."

But the main goal of magic that floated back to the top of my mind as I closed the chamber door behind me was once again connected with the carnage I'd seen of a place called Agincourt. And keeping Gilles de Rais safe from it.

29

The Threads Sundered

The candles at the power points of my circle sat in the golden puddles of their lives' remnants. And then, one by one, they drowned in them. The power was called, concentrated, sent. Nothing was left in the hollow darkness where I sat. Yet still I sat in the chilling cold, facing the keep into which I'd forced the spell. I am tired, I thought, still exhausted from the bout with the falling sickness I have not yet had time to sleep off.

But I knew it was more than that. I was afraid to stir. Afraid to move and face what I myself had brought into the world.

From time to time I was certain I could see the heavy walls of the keep differentiated from the night by more than just their heavy stone in contrast to the sky made light and airy with stars. A glow of pulsing power limned the keep from time to time, as if low lightning beat in some clouds behind. Only it was in the keep, not behind.

I imagined this lightning streaking through the sleeping, silent halls, here and there about the twisting stairs and, slipping between sill and door, into the shadowed chambers. Like some beast prowling after prey, sensing blood heat. And moving fast.

I willed my heart to stillness so as not to be found out. But the more I strove for silence, the louder my rib cage battered with the bait trapped within.

And then I heard the scream. Gilles. Lightning fangs had found the jugular. And I could remain passive no longer.

Following screams and shouts and a horrible blasphemy, I came panting up to the landing outside the room Amaury de Craon had been given for the night. There I stopped, fearful, as if the warped oak slats of the door were themselves the shaggy fur of some nightmare monster, animated by the force I'd conjured. Although I was certainly responsible for the form it took now, I was not such a fool as to think I could master it. The growls and snarls behind that door seemed the display of this monster.

I didn't dare approach it. I put my back to the wall just beyond the small puddle of light cast by a torch burned down almost to a bare rim of red coals. There I stood, still but for the panting which, rather than subsiding with my inactivity, grew.

The monster gave a great roar, shuddered, then splintered the old oak off its hinges. Two men rolled through the jagged wood and into the patchy light of the landing: Amaury and his host, the Sire de Rais.

Amaury had the upper hand when they came through the door. Although almost naked, he had all the advantages of youth. Indeed, Sire de Rais must quickly have been defeated if not killed outright, stranger to the lists and training years as he was these five or ten years. His search for piety had made less a man of him.

But that same search put the force of righteous indignation behind his blows. And Amaury, though defending himself reflexively, seemed almost to wish he could not. An obvious sense of having offended not only his host and chivalry, but the deepest constraints of nature shackled his every blow. This constraint caught each fist just at the skin of his opponent, held it back from ever inflicting any real damage. Amaury's blows might have been inflicted by a two-year-old. His elder might have laughed at them—were the rage that drove Sire de Rais not so all-consuming.

Both men are condemned to die, I thought, sickening. Must tonight be the night? And this the place?

I doubt anything Sire de Rais said in his anger, his struggle, echoed more coherently on that landing than the blackest of curses. However, part of the magic I had called up made the blows of the two men as eloquent as words—at least to me.

Sire de Rais' blows spoke: "By all that is holy, what do you do? To my son. My firstborn? My heir? I entrusted you to make a man of him. And what do you do but make a woman of him while you are yet under my own roof? By God, the spawn of Craon is the very spawn of the devil, father, daughter, son, all. You fooled me into thinking you were different than that highway robber, your father. I hoped that when he died and you inherited, I might have a fellow Christian as a neighbor and a kinsman. Your actions against the heathen on St. John's Eve, fighting at my side . . . I hoped.

"But you betrayed me. Betrayed! In the worst possible way. In the deepest, most unspeakable sin. Within my very door. With my own son. The sin for which God fired down brimstone in ancient times. Upon the cities of the plain. Sodom and Gomorrah. This sin is the cause of earthquakes. Famines. Plagues. Fire and brimstone. Unspeakable heathendom. Unspeakable."

Amaury defended himself physically, but his blows had little answering speech. They seemed the hardly verbal cries of a broken child.

It wasn't until Sire de Rais' blows said, "By God, you are a monster. An aberration of nature," that Amaury's at last came in a little burst of anger.

"I am not."

A blow to Sire de Rais' gut curled him to a ball that rolled helplessly to the rim of the landing.

"I am not an aberration."

In two leaps, Amaury loomed over his opponent again, kicking him, his bare feet booted in the heavy leather of self-justification.

"This *is* my nature, as pure as anything ever created."

He stooped down and dragged Sire de Rais up to his own height, a man's height again. The torchlight gave a reddish cast to the ripple of sweat that ran from Amaury's shoulders, under the blond tumble of his curls, and down, around arm and elbow, to his wrists. These were muscles harrowed into great, smooth mounds by much swinging of heavy swords. And all those years of effort and hope—and struggling with pride and with denial—surged down through those muscles to those hands as they closed around the lord of Rais' throat.

And then I was aware of Gilles, blue streaks trembled on his young chin. He'd probably been there since the beginning, but the action kept the attention diverted from the pale little figure, naked under a rough blanket, that stood in the splinters of the door. Perhaps he'd even tried to speak before, but these were the first words I heard.

"Father, please, don't."

His father was the one closest to death, but it was his violence Gilles spoke against.

"Amaury did nothing," Gilles insisted. "Nothing I didn't ask him to. Don't hurt him, Father. I love him."

At these words, Amaury's hands slowly relaxed. He released his adversary, and the older man slumped against the landing stones, coughing and sputtering. Amaury turned his back on his host and caressed Gilles across the space that separated them with a look of such agony that ripples of its pain hurt my stomach, too.

"We go."

Amaury spoke to his gathered, huddled subordinates, but did not break his gaze from Gilles. The men scurried to their tasks and Rais' men mostly let them go, although brief skirmishes in the process would leave a man dead on either side before the night was out.

Another change in Amaury's tone indicated that he was speaking to his host now. But still his eyes did not release Gilles. "Devil's spawn you called us. Aye, perhaps 'tis so. I've often thought almost the same myself."

He turned suddenly to fix a look on Sire de Rais that sent him slipping back against the flags from which he'd been struggling to rise and regain his dignity.

"But I'd think twice before casting such stones if I were you, lord of Rais. I'd consider who may have fathered the next scion of your house. Yes, consider what child it is my sister carries under her belt this night—and who it was put horns upon your head."

He turned and the sight of Gilles softened him once more.

"Gilles," he said. Then "Gilles," again, a cry of agony. "Adieu."

There was nothing else to say to the young boy's face, crumpled with tears.

One of Amaury's men jostled Gilles aside as he came out of the room carrying a jumble of clothes that he shoved into his lord's bare arms. The color of Amaury's jaw was perfectly rancid. After one last gaze, Amaury tore himself away.

I tried to send magic after him, white magic this time, like a silver blade that might slice through the black woolly threads that clouded his brain.

"Nature's God is not like the Christian's." I closed my eyes to send him the words silently. "If such is your nature, then nature's God made you that way and will not perversely condemn you for what She Herself has done. Indeed, if you are more like Her, no doubt She loves you more."

But I doubt the faintest barb of my magic reached him. For one thing, I was too oppressed by what I'd witnessed and knew to be my own handiwork—necessary, but no less wearing in its horror for all of that. Besides, I'd sensed the dark around Amaury as he'd passed; it was too thickly knotted. Not just my night's magic, but years of spells cast by others, many others who would have claimed they eschewed all enchantments as the devil's work if you'd asked them. The young lord of Craon probably cast some of the spells himself.

And he was moving too quickly. Every step he took into the night—and soon, the gallop of his wildly spurred horse—made the distance between us all that more unbridgeable.

And—finally—hadn't I foreseen much, too much, connected with a new-sown field called Agincourt? I knew the darkness would follow Amaury all the leagues until that place. He was destined to fall, one among nearly fifteen hundred lords of France, on St. Crispin's Day.

Indeed, I almost saw him look up at the hum as a cloud of English arrows darkened the sun. He would pick out one, remove his helmet as if in greeting.

And step purposefully into its path.

The World Spins

The devil's spawn.

Whether or not one took Amaury's words literally, the child she carried that year as summer turned to fall proved the death of Madame. "A women's complaint" was all the cause that entered the main hall. Most of the folk suspected some such thing, connected with Madame de Rais' refusal to put in any appearance since her return from St. Gilles at Midsummer.

"She was wearing a veil to hide blackened eyes and a swollen lip," only a few bothered to remember.

"But this 'women's complaint,' common as it is, was not what folk usually mean by the term."

My mother spoke wringing her hands, having to tell someone and trusting me because of the magic. Trusting also that I'd carry the tale no further, particularly not to Gilles and René, the sons Madame left behind.

"My lord came in that morning. Learned it was true, what the young lord Amaury had said. He knew the child wasn't his. There's only one other it could belong to. My lord took up the flat of his sheathed sword, that weapon he hadn't touched for years, and beat his lady wife until a clot of blood burst from her nether parts. Satisfied, he left. She was dead ere evensong, for all my magic."

They sealed Madame in the family vault. I walked away from the ceremony under the burden of my mother's words, longing to be alone. Was my curse the cause of this death as well? Madame had

had nothing to do with disrupting the Midsummer rites. Indeed, she had been chosen to represent the Goddess at that time, and played her part so well her womb had quickened. But certainly she had died, certainly because of that night. And her child, the God's child within her, the new little Tiphaine, had died as well, brutally, at impious hands.

I could see no justice in it, sense no holy way, particularly not within sound of the intonations of the burying priest. He was the man from a neighboring village, since Père de Boszac had not yet been replaced.

Samonias was a week off, no more. The year was clearly, almost visibly turning, shifting under a blow of dried leaves and empty, turned soil like a sleeper arranging pillows and coverlets, just before the deep, even breathing comes. There had been rain overnight. I still had to wipe my face from time to time of the effects of a drizzle, the shedding of barren twigs. Or of tears.

The lowing of cattle pursued me into the forest. The smell of earth's sodden death was so like that of women at their moon time, and to the same purpose. The smell moved toward me through the grey tree trunks like incense through the granite piers of a cathedral.

The smell drugged my brain so it was some time before I noticed the figure standing there on a rise, watching me. Or perhaps my notice was an effect of the figure himself, so attuned to his surroundings that if the wood was a cathedral, he was a statue, carved from the same stone as the plinth in which he stood.

A figure in black. Well, Blaison swarmed with them, friars who came at word of a noblewoman's death like flies to a carcass. They gave her passing sanctity—and hoped for handouts from noblefolk too grief-stricken to have sense.

The Man in Black. Even as I stopped, cleared my head, and felt I should know him—for the intense gaze with which he fixed me, if for nothing else—I did not. Then I saw through the angry scar, still fresh and red, twisting his face. The way his body slumped on his stick with a heaviness was totally strange to me. And yet—

"Master!" I cried, running to him, the weight of Madame's vault spun off me like granite turned suddenly to wisps of fog. "You're alive!"

"Easy! Easy!" The Hermit of St. Gilles tried to laugh, but the ability was weak. "I'm not so steady on my feet as once I was."

"Oh, I am sorry. Can I take your arm?"

"Thank you."

"But I am so glad to see you."

"And I you, my Yann."

Awe quieted me as I remembered the last time I'd seen him. "I thought surely you must die that night of your wounds."

"The well of St. Gilles is always miraculous to heal."

"Certainly I have proof now before my eyes. But surely you should recoup a while longer yet. What tempts you on a journey so far as Blaison?"

"Samonias."

"Samonias?"

"Your curse, Yann."

"Will it not fulfill itself?" I had, in fact, been feeling myself powerless against its blast.

The iron anger in his voice startled me. "This I will not leave to fate."

"Ah. Surely revenge burns you still like the red glow of your scars."

"I hope I am not such an ill child of the Mother that I cannot forgive," he said. "For myself, I forgive. But there is more than myself to revenge now."

His look over my shoulder toward the castle brought the crypt's smell of death back to my nostrils.

I said, "You've heard of Madame, then?"

"Yes."

"Your loss is that of a husband."

"There was a child, too."

"Few knew that. Very few."

"I knew."

"Of course. It was your child."

The Hermit shook his head firmly within the O of his cowl and made me blush for shame as I realized my mistake before he named it. "Not my child. The God's. And that is a loss the world can ill afford in days like these."

"What . . . what will you do?" I struggled to ask before my face was quite cool again.

"I do not know as yet. Have you any ideas, Yann?"

I blushed once more, pleased to be forgiven so easily, to have my opinion asked in such a matter. I told him, haltingly, all the deeds that I had done since I'd last seen him. How I'd worked to keep Gilles from death but had, alas, done nothing for Madame. Had, perhaps, killed her and her daughter while trying to save her son.

The Hermit nodded within his cowl now. "You did well enough. But I think that for such a subtle business as now faces us, a spell like that will not do. Having just been subject to your enchantment their guards—or, rather, his, Sire de Rais', precisely—are up. His wife dead, Amaury off, the obvious vehicles for magic within his circle are now gone. Even Gilles seems closed to me."

"You have tried to send to Gilles?"

"I have. No luck."

"Gilles has suffered deeply from the losses of these past few days. He has not spoken to me since Amaury left." Now that I considered: "He's spoken to no one."

"His soul cannot be reached," the Master assured me. "And I find a great obstacle—greater than usual—in the stones of this castle. I wasn't even sure you were within until I felt you come out into the yard."

A quick look about us at the woods, sensing their power that was the source of ours, gave me the confidence to speak. "Then we must look to nature to help us."

"Exactly as I was thinking."

"We can do nothing until Sire de Rais leaves the cover of his keep."

"It will mean a wait."

"Have you a place to stay while we wait? I hate to think of you out in this damp with your joints still recovering from the shocks of Midsummer."

"I will stay with a family of charcoal burners," the Hermit said. "You know them perhaps?"

"Of course. Their occupation teaches them the ways of the woods well."

"Come and tell me the moment you spy opportunity, Yann."

"I shall indeed." I took his arm more firmly. "But let me see you safely to the charcoal burners' door now."

Returning to the castle later made me think we were fated to a long wait. Indeed, I was certain Samonias must come and go and my prophecy, given under such volatile circumstances, be proved a thing of naught.

Sire de Rais seemed determined to stick to his fireside and his chapel. This was hardly unusual: the weather encouraged it and a man in mourning might be expected to be weighted to his house with loss.

I half hoped the frequency at devotions betrayed some feelings of guilt. But Sire de Rais had always been a strictly pious man. The sense I got was more that he was urging heaven to give him the reward he felt he deserved for having done the right thing by a wicked woman than the flinches of a man who feared judgment.

However the matter, the few spells I attempted to move him seemed only for the good and exercise of my own Craft: they had no effect on him at all.

I also worked a little on Gilles. Stirred by the Hermit's arrival to consider other grief than my own, I reconfirmed my impression that my milk brother had yet to speak a word to anyone. The whole castle shook their heads in sympathy: it's a great shock for a boy to lose his mother at such a tender age. Only I seemed able to count the silence back beyond Madame's death—not all the way back to the infant and the priest, although the haze of those events certainly colored everything. Gilles had fallen deeply—irrevocably, so it seemed—silent the few extra hours before, at the loss of his Amaury.

I worked with basil and pine, woodruff, hawthorn, and the cauldron to fire my milk brother to believe he need not give up on his dreams of knightly deeds. I tried desperately not to let the word "Agincourt" color my thoughts as I proceeded. Let Gilles think his uncle might still live, that feats of arms were a way to regain him.

And then, suddenly one night, in a burst of insight as mistletoe caught fire under my hand, I realized I was pushing things in the wrong direction. That was why the going was so hard. What was needed to reach Sire de Rais was for Gilles to sink deeper, not come out of his grief.

By morning, I could run to my lord and report that his son was much, much worse. So bad, in fact, that there was fear for his life. Not only did Gilles refuse to talk and eat now. He refused to move out of bed.

By afternoon, I was at the charcoal burners' hovel, reporting to my Master that father and son intended to ride forth on the morrow—if the weather held—to revive their spirits with the hunt.

"Monseigneur de Rais says he will have Gilles horsed if he must carry him there himself," I said. "But I do not think he will have to. Gilles seems willing enough—although he still does not speak."

"Ah," the Hermit said. "The whole thing began with Sire de Rais hunting, you will recall. So the world has cycled. Our time has come."

And he set to work winding a laurel wand with vines to make certain the weather could have no choice but to hold.

31

The Noble Rot

—◆—

"But certainly Gilles and his father ride toward the Forest of Brainson," I protested to the Hermit.

The old man led the way with a surety that left me little breath as I tried to keep up. I was weighed down by a wooden grape-pickers hod, empty, but tall enough to peak well over my shoulder at the back. A sound like belling hounds seemed to ring up into my ear from the hod's wide, hollow mouth with every step I took. Certainly, the sound came from behind me, away from the path the Master was pursuing.

He led west toward the small shrine of St. Sulpice. Here, on chalk cliffs above the river, regiments of vines draped their canes from their stakes to the ground with brown, brittling leaves. The day was unseasonably warm; the weather had held.

"Yes." I even turned longingly back to look. "I am certain I hear the hounds there, somewhat behind us and to the south."

"Are you a sorcerer?" The Hermit's voice was as sharp as the billhook he carried.

That brought me around. "Well, yes. I think so. I hope so. I'm learning. Trying to learn." All came out in a stammer.

"Even an apprentice to the Craft should know this much: that he works more in tune with the Balance who walks away from the scene than he who charges toward it like a knight. The sorcerer's power is not the power of the knight, but supersedes and, in some ways, complements it."

After this lecture, which of course I'd known and was ashamed at having to be reminded of, I kept silent. I said nothing until he set me to work in the vineyard. Then again I could not contain my astonishment.

"But these grapes are all rotten!"

I'd known the vintage was over. The cloudy new wine was already appearing on our table and I had considered it an intitiate's duty to participate in the local, ancient festivities celebrating the first pressing. The bathing of little children in the must so their flesh would always have a vigorous pink glow. The singing, dancing, and license tempered only by the fact that so many of the local women were, like their mistress had been—the Mother keep her—big, slow, and awkward dancers, gravid from springtime festivities.

And I'd known the vintners took no care to harvest all this year. Sire de Rais had had word that neither English nor Dutch barges were making their way into Anjou, nor even weighing anchor at Nantes, being all occupied with King Henry's invasion in the north.

"It's not worth anybody's time to press more wine than we on the manor can drink ourselves," the lord had told them. "I will take my share in labor on the roads and digging out the river channel instead, now before the winter rains raise it too high again."

So the grapes had been left in the damp of the past month. Now I saw that mold had grown on them, grown so vigorously that it replaced their skin altogether. The slightest touch sent grey clouds of spore to fumigate the air and the picker's hands and face, overwhelming the nostrils with their sickeningly sweet smell.

"They're all rotten," I protested again.

" 'Tis a noble rot," the Hermit said. Over his grey-dusted beard, his eyes twinkled, as if at a private joke.

The Hermit already had the bottom of his basket covered. Any more doubts or questions would draw energy from the work. I knew this, so I concentrated on picking my share, disgusting as I found the powdery touch of the fruit at first, and its tendency to give much too readily in the hand.

I tried to concentrate on what the Master had in mind so I could send my energy in the same direction. He seemed to relish the small clouds of grey that accompanied our work. He chanted softly under his breath as he moved from vine to vine, and it seemed to me he chanted to the flight of the spores.

"Go!" his deep voice, old as the hills, chanted. "Grow and gather and go—to the man who must die."

Was he calling a fog to come and divert Gilles and his father? Make them lose their way in their own forest not a league from their own beds? That was a possibility.

Then I listened closer to the words of his chant. I heard "noble rot," over and over. That helped me discover the image of a noble house, hanging on the banks of the Loire, a house in the final stages of a rot that seemed to render it useless for anything. And yet, what if the vintner should give the fruit one more pressing? Might it yet produce some last thing of worth?

My training had taught me nothing was better for the land than a rich compost. Decay, death, and rot were the Mother's food, to be prized as much for that as the food she gave us in return was prized for our own bellies. But was there something else here?

Half by accident, I pressed one grape as I picked. The action turned, in fact, more than a little deliberate, as it took some doing. The fruit gave no resistance at first, so unlike the hard defense of a normal grape that gives quickly in a burst of juice.

As I pressed, however, the first real insight came to me. I saw Sire de Rais riding his russet gelding up a shallow incline beneath beech and oaks. This must be Gilles' view of his father, I thought. The old man was wearing his hunting cape of a fine grey napped wool. It flew behind him as he rode: like a cloud of spawning mold. The parallel finally pierced my brain and took hold.

Then I was in the vineyard again, the weak autumn sun slanting into my eyes. And I saw that I had crushed the grape between my two fingers in a cape-swirl of fungus. The once-taut essence of the fruit had been distilled—on the vine, in the sun, by the hand of the God—to a single, thick yellow drop. It was the matter lanced from a boil, promising quick healing. It was a man's vital sap, sweet, sticky, pressed from him in the moment of deepest love, the closest he can come to the Mother—until the instant of his death. And just so much was all that was needed to set new life going in a woman's womb.

I brought my full concentration to the task now, joining the

Hermit's chant when the words came to me, hinging as they did on the image of the "noble rot."

The pressing shed was deserted, not like the bright, garlanded, music-filled place it was at the peak of its usefulness. The vats had been washed out with old wine, then "put to bed" until next year. We roused the place, groggy and grumbling still in the depth of first sleep.

"But the work we have for you is very little," we promised.

To start, the Master set his vine-twisted staff into the vat and dedicated the pressing to our purpose. When he'd doffed the black and stood with the high priest's pure white linen tucked up around his knees, I gave him a hand into the stained cavern made of slatted wood. Our harvest reached only to the middle of his calves. The grey beard bounced on his sunken chest, the scars started vividly in his face, across his twisted hands, and up his bony arms. The power moving him—fueled in part by revenge, but more by a sense of restoring a necessary balance—seemed greater because of its contrast to his own physical frailty.

The Hermit gave only a cursory stomp, to get the magic going. Then I climbed in to replace him, the practical work of conjuring. He left me his staff, to give me balance on the slippery, uneven mass, and to pierce the whole with power.

It was harder going than the usual pressing: globs of grapes clung to each leg each time I lifted it, doubling the weight of my feet and pulling on the hairs of my legs like little pinpricks with each step. And grey fungus dusted the whole.

The glory of the smell spread through my head with the glory of a peacock's fan, heady, and almost too sweet to endure. This blooming spread visions before my eyes.

"I see the thickets and the underbrush," I said.

The Hermit nodded but did not drop the chain of his chant. ". . . Force of the noble rot . . ."

"Grey in their winter loss of leaves. Stags, with the great branching crowns, slip into such places like fingers into gloves. The beaters have circled 'round and are now in place."

"Ah, but the Earth and Her children have ways beyond the ken of men . . . with the force of the noble rot."

"I see Monseigneur de Rais dismount in a swirl of woolly grey and hand the reins to his groom. He and Gilles must proceed on foot up this steep, south-facing hillside. I do not recognize the place, Master. How can they have had time to travel beyond my familiarity?"

"You create the world anew, for yourself, for them, by the power of the noble rot."

And then I could see, overlaying the heaped grey mountainside in my vision, the grape hulls at my ankles—heaped in precisely the same way.

I began to smell it more clearly now, the underpinnings of the grapy press. "I smell." I panted over what felt like iron filings in my lungs. "I smell—truffles."

"Yes. The noble rot."

The noble rot, great clotting fungi. Truffles, likewise rich and musty. And then I remembered why it is that female pigs so eagerly dig for truffles when they are in heat.

Now I saw on the hillside things Sire de Rais was ignoring, his eyes looking only for deer. My squishing steps in the press overlaid those around a shallow pond, the rolled wallow. Here and there appeared a large, cloven print in the place of my more rounded one.

"The nearby oak trunks, moldy with mud rub and bristled with grey-black hair. The signs reach as high as a man's thigh. And the nicks of the tusks in the bark go even higher."

"The power of the noble rot."

Sire de Rais was stalking up the hill, downwind of the deer. I heard echoes of the Stag's voice as I'd heard it when a child, "Help, O child of men!" But I had no need to heed it. The lords of the forest would not require my protection that day.

I could not have done much. The vision of the lord of Rais creeping forward on muffled steps, his arrow nocked, was causing shooting pains through my crippled hand. I had to let go of the Hermit's staff with that hand on account of the pain and balanced badly with the step, slip, step, slip underfoot.

The sucking sound each step made was the sound of coughing through a tile pipe. Contented chuckles, wallowing, grubbing, rooting—then the sudden start.

"Sire de Rais hears something in the grey brush," I reported.

"The power of the noble rot."

And then all the smoky powder of the shriveled grape hulls formed around the grey autumn forest, coalesced and trotted from the thicket with a challenge. Instead of the deer he expected, hoping to counter the evil of twelve years ago when he'd shot at me, Sire de Rais found himself eye to small, flinty, piggy eye with a wild boar.

"Hail, Moccus," the Hermit worshiped. Moccus is the old pig God of the Gauls.

"The boar stops, snorts with surprise, then anger. He begins to trot, the jiggle of all his flesh ridiculous under the raised black bristles of his stubby mane. His ears flap as he trots, like bird flight, a wounded bird, for his ears are tattered and bloody from the many mating battles he's undertaken—and won—at this season of the year."

"The noble rot, O Moccus."

" 'My spear,' Sire de Rais cries, unable to look back to see if he is heard, unable to tear his eyes away from the vision before him. 'My spear.'

"The boar begins to charge now, all feet off the ground at once, suddenly, miraculously graceful and nothing ridiculous at all.

"My lord pulls back the arrow—he is armed with nothing else. The smell of truffles overwhelms him."

"Moccus, Moccus, the smell of the noble rot."

The staff slipped in the pressing vat. The arrow struck a great, hairy shoulder. It would have caused some damage except that, in mating season, boars grow a fleshy shield across their shoulders, sometimes three fingers thick, and even at such range, an iron arrowhead slips off. The staff slipped and I floundered in the vat.

Sire de Rais floundered, too. But what he felt around his hips was not the syrup of moldy grapes. It was mud on the forest floor. And, on the green arc of ferns, the sticky sweet curl of his own blood lanced out of his abdomen by ivory blades longer than a man's hand.

The Master breathed a great sigh and sank onto an empty keg nearby.

"The power of the noble rot. Hail, hail, Moccus."

32

Binding Off

The Hermit of St. Gilles and I set the grey-golden must aside to mature: it would, in time, make a drink of very powerful properties.

We rinsed the evidence out of the press with salt water and old wine, then made our way back to the castle. Pain banded my legs as if I'd walked half a dozen leagues—as indeed I had, under conditions like new-fallen, knee-deep snow.

In spite of the pain, however, I gave the Master back his staff. He needed it and, even with its help, moved slowly and heavily.

Just before the portcullis, we were overtaken by Gilles, riding alone, whipping his horse to a lather, even in the falling cool.

"My father! He's wounded! A boar! In the woods." Gilles gasped his news to whoever would hear it.

That was all my mother needed to hear. In her turn, she whipped the castle into action, boiling water, tearing linen, making the lord's bed, gathering herbs. She took the place as chatelaine she'd long had in fact, only now there was simply no Madame to whom she was nominally answerable.

"Oh, and see to that poor lad," Mother ordered. "He's had a dreadful shock."

The Hermit and I undertook that last task, leading my milk brother before a fire hastily laid and kindled in his room. That was the least we could do, and no one questioned the Master's right to be there.

Gilles did indeed look terrible. He seemed coated in grey-black from head to toe like some rotted grape. The stuff powdered off when I moved to touch him—dried blood. The blood wasn't his own: no wounds were revealed to the Master's inspection. The boar's? Or his father's?

Gilles shook uncontrollably, as if he couldn't leave the movement of the horse even off the saddle.

"Get the lad a blanket," the Hermit directed me. "Get him out of these clothes. Help him into bed."

The Master gave Gilles a sip of the juice we'd just pressed. That seemed to do the most good. His eyes cleared as the liquid passed his lips and he looked into the Master's face with keen recognition. As if he knew exactly what had gone into the pressing.

Some sort of calm was just returning when the captain of what guard was left behind from the hunt came and scratched at the door, demanding admittance.

"There are horsemen at the bridge, my young lord," he said.

Gilles sat up, the quiver returning to this limb and that, his dark eyes wide. "That's my father."

But it was not. "Your grandfather seeks admittance, my lord. He says he comes in peace."

"Let him in." When no one gainsaid him, Gilles spoke louder. "I will see my grandsire."

"I've come." Jean de Craon spoke with difficulty when he was shown into his grandson's room. He was suddenly an old, stooped man. "I've come to make my peace with your father."

He held out his arms from which his cape hung as from a thin clothesline. Gilles went to them.

No one had time to ask "How?" How could the lord of Craon know of the accident so soon? How could he come all the way from Champtocé before the retainers had had time to bring the wounded man back to his own castle? How, if Jean de Craon were not, as my lord had always said, a demon himself?

Before any of this could be asked by anyone, yet more horsemen were in the yard, ruddied now with torchlight, and the lord of Rais returned to his castle at Blaison.

"To die," my mother hissed at me in the old tongue when others couldn't hear.

Behind the litter on which my lord lay moaning, two more of the men carried the boar on a pole, head down between them. Even dead, the sight brought the swirl of grape fungus before my eyes.

"Monseigneur Gilles killed it," the men said. "He heeded his father's call for the spear and then ran it home while the beast was mauling the lord. Certainly young Lord Gilles is to be thanked that his father still lives."

"Although there might have been more mercy in a quicker death." Mother spoke first to me and then turned to the men in their French. "But you brought the beast home instead of letting the hounds at him there in the woods."

"It was Monseigneur Gilles' first kill," the men defended themselves. "I wish you'd seen it, goodwife, and you'd have not believed your women's milk could give such courage. I don't know too many grown men who could have gone into that fray so calmly and purposefully."

"But what am I to do with this carcass?" Mother insisted. "We cannot eat a beast who's killed a man."

The men's tones dropped. "Is the lord really so bad?"

"I don't know how I'm to keep him on earth through a priest's blessing and the night."

At this there were lots of sober crossings of themselves and prayers of "God shield him."

But still the bearers persisted. "Monseigneur Gilles might like a trophy."

Mother lost all patience with this argument for which she had no time and turned to hasten after the stretcher on its way up to the lord's room, dragging me after her.

"Nothing can save a man whose guts have been split like that. No one." She made the old gesture, consigning Sire de Rais to the shadow of the King Stag's antlers.

I left her to her ill-fated work and took up mine with Gilles. But just moments later, she was at my side again.

"He wants to see you."

"Who?"

"His lordship."

"Me? But—but why?"

"I don't know. He won't say. You'll have to come and ask him yourself. But you won't be able to do it at all if you don't leave Gilles and come now."

I cast a glance back to my young friend's face, ashen pale among the rich bolsters, the blue marks on his chin startlingly like bruises. He had just received some very bad news from Sire de Craon that had served to aggravate his shock. Circled as he was by the Hermit, his grandfather, and others, I had not even been able to reach my milk brother in the time since I'd returned. There was nothing I could have done for him, even if I could have imagined what it might be. He needed less company, I thought, not more.

"Yes, come," Mother pressed. "Gilles will be here when you get back. But his lordship—" Her voice trailed off as I followed her down the darkened, drafty hall.

A fire had been lit in the hearth of my lord's room under the age-worn Rais crest of a simple cross set into the stone, faded and hardly distinguishable in this light. Save for a nervous maid come to my mother's relief—and she left gratefully as soon as my mother gave her an errand to do so—the lord was deserted. Folk cluster to the room where there is hope, my mind marked. And the smell of putrefying innards must drive away anyone with a choice.

Weakly, Sire de Rais gestured me to sit in the chair pulled close to his head. I had to move a lap desk with paper and ink to do it, and that, as well as the smell and sight of the lord's mortality, made me hesitate.

Mother gave me a nudge. She checked on her patient without finding anything else she could do for him, while I settled myself. Then she sat in another chair farther off and picked up some sewing. Fabric rewarded her efforts and mended more consistently than flesh.

Or than the spirit's.

"Is the demon here?"

Sire de Rais' voice was thick and raspy. I bent in to hear him. Whatever the cost, a worker of magic must not flinch from the results of his own handiwork.

"Do you mean Sire de Craon, my lord?"

I hoped he didn't know of the Hermit's presence yet. Or that he didn't mean me.

"The demon, yes."

"He is, my lord. Would you like me to fetch him for you?" I was half out of the chair with relief.

"No!" The sudden power of his voice startled me back down. "Yes. I know why he's come."

"He hopes to be reconciled to you, my lord."

"He hovers, like a vulture."

"He did not even know you were wounded, my lord. I think it is God's will that has brought him to you in good time."

Sire de Rais' eyes squinted. At first I thought death closed them, then that they were taking on the beady look of the beast that had gored him. Then I knew he was merely fixing me, seeing through me, with the knowing gaze of the dying man.

"You would tell me of God's will? You who are possessed and crippled by demons?" The eyes squinted yet more fiercely. "Why am I not surprised to feel you were in that monster who gored me? Just in time for Samonias, eh?"

I worked to get to my feet again, though his words made my already worn-out knees unsteady. "I will leave you to God's cure, my lord. My presence only aggrieves you."

"Stay!"

I sagged back behind my lap desk.

"There is no priest in the castle."

"He has been sent for, sir." I looked to my mother for confirmation and she nodded.

"But he will be a while coming and there—there may not be time. You are the only one—in the castle now—who can do this."

I waited patiently, but getting me to stay had taken his strength for the moment. His right hand was all that moved, fumbling weakly among the coverlets at his side. I saw he'd dropped his carved jade rosary—that new aid to devotion—and I handed it to him. He looked at me with gratitude and not a little amazement. But still he hadn't the power to speak. The soft click of dropping beads and the breath of his prayers over swollen lips were the only sounds for some time.

Presently I decided it would not be granted him to speak again and that I should indeed take the part of a priest.

"Monseigneur de Craon has come bearing dreadful news, my lord," I began. "His son Monseigneur Amaury is dead and buried in a mass grave at Agincourt. I think even you would find the old lord changed, sir. And he has no heir left now but his grandsons, Gilles and René. He has no greater hope than to be reconciled with you, my lord."

Then I stopped, for Sire de Rais seemed determined to talk again. He motioned for water and I gave it to him, gently cradling his head in my arms, though I could not keep the image from my mind of that water leaking straight out again through the huge gap in his side along with all that blood and other matter.

"I must write a will, Jean, and you are the only one to write it, with your mother to witness."

"Yes, my lord." I began at once to prepare the quill and ink, glad at last for something to occupy my hands.

"I should have had Père de Boszac write it months ago."

"But he died, my lord."

"Indeed he did."

Sire de Rais' face reflected in just what grim manner the death had come. But he took nothing of my same moral from that event.

"After Marie—died"—I was glad to see the mention of that murder gave him some difficulty, anyway—"I thought it again. But there was no priest. I've sent to Angers to the archbishop for someone and he has had to send to Paris. This Père Victor we have between whiles—well, you know him. Pious enough, I suppose, but he can hardly write his own name. Let him come to shrive me—soon enough, I fancy—but I must have you to write it out."

"I'll write a will for you, my lord."

"Yes, you do fancy yourself a priest, don't you?"

"I feel God has touched me," I said carefully.

"Yes. One has only to look at that hand of yours to see how He's touched you."

His comment made me clumsier than ever. I cursed myself—and my lord—silently, but thanked Père Michel who had not been afraid to give me the gift of letters.

"I don't suppose Latin written with the sinister hand has any less effect than that written with the right?"

He made it a question; his doubt was strong enough to pass on to me. For answer, I gave him only a look. It was such a look that he had to turn away, into the bolsters and his pain for a moment. Under the lid of the lap desk, I forced my left hand to work the symbol of power. Then we were both able to proceed.

The language of Sire de Rais' will presented no challenge for the most part. Only near the end did he dictate something that froze my pen midletter.

" 'And I would that my dear sons, Gilles and René, now left by the will of Almighty God with neither mother nor father to guide their childish steps should be given into the Christian care of my cousin Jean, lord of Tournemine, who shall have complete charge of their education and upbringing until they shall be of age.' "

"Sire de Tournemine, my lord?"

I'd never met the man before, though I thought perhaps I might have heard of him. My mother raised her brows, too, as she met my quick glance. She knew no Tournemine, either.

"Yes, Tournemine has a name for piety, for the foundation of churches and monasteries. For strict penances in himself and in those under him, in pilgrimages . . ."

Either the thought sent my lord into such raptures or his strength failed to complete the list; in any case, he had to submit to silence for a while. When he resumed, it was on a slightly altered track.

"Tournemine will be the best for my boys. For better assurance, you should add, 'Under no circumstances is Monseigneur Jean de Craon to have anything to do with such tender and volatile young souls.' "

Still I hesitated.

"What, boy? Would you refuse a dying man his last request?"

Did you grant my lady her last request? Only that you would stop beating her and love her and her child.

But in the end, I could not refuse. I wrote and signed the paper, helped the lord of Rais to sign and my mother to make her mark.

"Can you send someone to tell Père Vincent to hasten?" I asked my mother. As I sifted the sand over the paper, the lord fell into a coma. "My lord would want that."

"You should go for him yourself," Mother answered. "It seems he got sidetracked here by the case of the Hermit of St. Gilles."

"With the Master?"

"The old man seems to have taken suddenly ill. What did you do, Yann, to wear him out so?"

Mother eyed me keenly, but I didn't stop to answer her. Sire de Rais would want Père Vincent in his final hour. And the Hermit would not. I must go and set the spirit world to rights.

———•———

As it happened, the Master and the lord died within an hour of each other. The Master's was an easy death, once I cleared the priest from him. The Hermit had longed to join his Mother Earth for many years and there was none of the painful ramble that darkened Sire de Rais' last thoughts.

My Master, too, left a will of sorts. He initiated me Master, there on his deathbed, in the ancient but secret manner of the Craft.

"My staff and robe, Yann, all for you," he said. "The horns and mask of the God, the priest's sword, I've buried them by the stones of St. Gilles—you will know the place when you go there."

Otherwise, he breathed his last with the satisfaction of a life well led in the shadow of the King Stag's horns.

"My father's dead?" was Gilles' reaction when they told him.

A sudden life seemed to rise from his grim shock. He picked me out of the faces clustered around him and reached for my hand. I took it.

"My Yann, your curse is fulfilled, just in time for Samonias. Amaury—God rest him—Amaury died a hero and is revenged."

Then I told him the terms of his father's will, that his grandfather should leave Blaison at once and never see him again until he was a man.

At this, Gilles actually laughed out loud. "Oh, Father," he said, wiping tears certainly more of mirth than of sorrow. His grief-struck silence was clearly cured. "You spent your whole life fretting about your status in the hereafter. And what good has it done you? I am the lord of Rais now and this—this Tourlemay did you call him, Yann?"

"Tournemine, Gilles—I mean, my lord."

The light leaped in Gilles' eyes at my term of address. He liked that. "Tourlemay, Tournemine. To hell with Tournemine," he announced, sitting up suddenly in bed. "I am the lord of Rais. If I wish to take Amaury's place in my grandfather's hall, well, then, by God, I shall."

He was right. Sire de Craon was there at Blaison, horses waiting. Tournemine was—well, at Tournemine, one supposed. If not on pilgrimage. More was difficult to say.

"If Tournemine wants these young wards on his hands"—Craon caught sudden life from his grandson, more than he'd had since the courier from Agincourt had arrived—"Which I don't think he will, the needs of life to come weighing too heavily on him. But if he does, he can come to Champtocé looking for them. But you may as well warn him, he'll have to breach her sturdy walls and fight me to get them."

"And me, too."

Gilles was scrambling out of bed and pulling on his hose with the thrill of all the new possibilities his new estate presented.

"I am glad to see my young lord feels better," a valet commented. "Would he like something to eat?"

"Oh, God, yes!" Gilles exclaimed. "I could eat a . . . Where's that hog, man? It seems to me I killed a hog."

"Indeed you did." Craon laughed. "A great, fearsome tusker, son. I've seen him in the yard. I only hope they haven't tossed him to the dogs."

"They wouldn't." Gilles was certain. "They wouldn't dare do that to their lord's first kill. Come, Grandfather."

The two men who ought to have been in mourning clipped one another on the shoulder comradely as if they were of an age instead of grandsire and grandson.

"Come, Grandfather," Gilles repeated. "Let's go roast ourselves a boar."